MACMILLAN STUDIES IN TWENTIETH-CENTURY LITERATURE

Michael Black
D. H. LAWRENCE: THE EARLY FICTION

Carolyn Bliss
PATRICK WHITE'S FICTION

Laurie Clancy
THE NOVELS OF VLADIMIR NABOKOV

Peter J. Conradi
IRIS MURDOCH: THE SAINT AND THE ARTIST

Clare Hanson
SHORT STORIES AND SHORT FICTIONS, 1880–1980

Dominic Hibberd
OWEN THE POET

David Leon Higdon
SHADOWS OF THE PAST IN CONTEMPORARY BRITISH FICTION

Oddvar Holmesland
A CRITICAL INTRODUCTION TO HENRY GREEN'S NOVELS

Holger Klein with John Flower and Eric Homberger (*editors*)
THE SECOND WORLD WAR IN FICTION

Simon Loveday
THE ROMANCES OF JOHN FOWLES

Harold Orel
THE LITERARY ACHIEVEMENT OF REBECCA WEST

Tony Pinkney
WOMEN IN THE POETRY OF T. S. ELIOT

Alan Sandison
GEORGE ORWELL: AFTER 1984

Lars Ole Sauerberg
SECRET AGENTS IN FICTION

Linda M. Shires
BRITISH POETRY OF THE SECOND WORLD WAR

Patrick Swinden
THE ENGLISH NOVEL OF HISTORY AND SOCIETY, 1940–80

Eric Warner (*editor*)
VIRGINIA WOOLF: A CENTENARY PERSPECTIVE

Terry Whalen
PHILIP LARKIN AND ENGLISH POETRY

Anne Wright
LITERATURE OF CRISIS, 1910–22

Further titles in preparation

PATRICK WHITE'S FICTION

The Paradox of Fortunate Failure

Carolyn Bliss

MACMILLAN

First published 1986

Published by
THE MACMILLAN PRESS LTD
Houndmills, Basingstoke, Hampshire RG21 2XS
and London
Companies and representatives
throughout the world

Printed in Hong Kong

British Library Cataloguing in Publication Data
Bliss, Carolyn Jane
Patrick White's fiction: the paradox of
fortunate failure. – (Macmillan studies in
twentieth-century literature)
1. White, Patrick – Criticism and interpretation
I. Title
823   PR9619.3.W5Z/
ISBN 0–333–38869–0

311811

To Jim, who understood how much it meant to me

Contents

Contents

Preface

The 1973 award of the Nobel Prize for literature to the Australian novelist Patrick White focused world attention on a body of fiction which many believe will one day rank with the best produced in the twentieth century. From his birth, White has been as much a citizen of that greater world which honoured him as he is of Australia.

Although descended from generations of large landholders in Australia's Hunter Valley, he was born in London. His Australian parents had taken an extended honeymoon following their marriage in 1910, and their first child, Patrick Victor Martindale, was born to them on 28 May 1912. At the end of that year, they returned to Australia, where a daughter, Suzanne, was born in 1915.

Patrick was first sent to Cranbrook School in Sydney, then, because of severe asthma, to Tudor House in Moss Vale. At thirteen, he was taken back to England to be enrolled at Cheltenham College near Gloucester, where he spent four apparently miserable years. While there, however, he did write the poems which were later collected as *Thirteen Poems*. Returning to Australia in 1929, he went to work as a jackeroo,[1] first near Adaminaby in the Monaro district (roughly the setting of *Happy Valley* and of part of *The Twyborn Affair*), then on an uncle's property near Walgett. While so employed, he began writing fiction, but nothing from this period survives.

In 1932, he again went to England, to read history at Cambridge, but soon changed his emphasis to modern languages. The Cambridge years, in contrast to those at Cheltenham, seem to have been happy ones, full of travel, friends and productive creative efforts. There he wrote the poems which later appeared in the privately printed collection *The Ploughman and Other Poems*. He also wrote plays and sketches for the theatre, some of which were later performed in Australia and London.

Coming down from Cambridge in 1935, White took a bedsitter in Ebury Street, Pimlico, and continued writing plays, fiction and poetry. An Australian painter, Roy de Maistre, broadened his exposure to art and music, and he continued to travel extensively. For a time, he entertained hopes of a career in the theatre, but these were disappointed. With other projects he had more success, publishing a short story, 'The Twitching Colonel', in 1937; a poem, 'The House behind the Barricades', in 1938; and his first novel, *Happy Valley*, in 1939. That same year he took *Happy Valley* to America, finding a publisher for it in Viking Press, and while there began his next book, *The Living and the Dead*, finishing it on a later visit to New York.

With the outbreak of war, he returned to England to serve in the RAF intelligence forces, mainly in the Middle East and Greece. In his autobiographical essay 'The Prodigal Son', White explains that at this time he reassessed his accomplishments to date, found them minimal and 'experienced those first sensations of rootlessness which Alister Kershaw has deplored and explained as the "desire to nuzzle once more at the benevolent teats of the mother country" '.[2] VJ Day found him in Greece, from which he went back to London and thence to 'the mother country' for which he increasingly longed. After a preliminary visit, he decided to resume permanent residence but returned once more to London to settle his affairs. While there, he wrote *The Ham Funeral*, the first of his plays to survive. He also submitted for publication his third novel, *The Aunt's Story*, begun in London after the war and finished *en route* to and in Australia.

Upon moving back to Australia in 1948, White took a house at Castle Hill on the outskirts of Sydney with a Greek friend, Manoly Lascaris, whom he had met during the war and whom he now describes as a man 'of immense moral strength, who became the central mandala in my life's hitherto messy design'.[3] The two raised flowers, vegetables, Schnauzer dogs, and Saanen goats. Disappointed over the Australian reception of his work, he did not publish another novel until *The Tree of Man* in 1955. But *Voss* followed quickly thereafter (in 1957) and since then novels have appeared at fairly regular intervals: *Riders in the Chariot* in 1961, *The Solid Mandala* in 1966, *The Vivisector* in 1970, *The Eye of the Storm* in 1973, *A Fringe of Leaves* in 1976, and *The Twyborn Affair* in 1979. He has also written more plays, numerous short stories and novellas (two collections have appeared), a screenplay and an autobiography.

Disturbed by the infringement of burgeoning Sydney on Castle Hill, White and Lascaris moved in 1963 to Centennial Park, which seemed to offer green space protected from urban encroachment. Subsequently, that protection was threatened by plans to turn Centennial Park into a sports arena, and White became politically active and visible as never before over this and other issues such as Australia's involvement in the Vietnam War, uranium- and sand-mining projects, the possibility of nuclear war, and the rise and fall of the Whitlam Australian Labor Party government. He also drew great attention, much of it unwelcome, when he was awarded the Nobel Prize in 1973. He has used the prize money to establish a fund to honour and assist other Australian writers and has further proved his generosity by establishing scholarships for aboriginal students and donating paintings to the New South Wales Art Gallery.[4]

White's achievements and the world recognition accorded them are hard to reconcile with his continued obscurity among many readers of English-language fiction, particularly in the United States. This book is in part an effort to address this problem by bringing White and his work to the greater attention of scholars of English-language literature as well as the many uninitiated readers whom his fiction would delight, intrigue and deeply move. The book argues that the meaning and inevitability of failure in human experience offer an illuminating avenue of approach to White's fiction and can be seen as informing it thematically, stylistically, structurally and generically. In fact, the possibility that personal failure can promote a paradoxical success within a wider, transpersonal context is seen as a central tenet of White's philosophy of life.

Attention will be centred on the novels, with references made to the short stories and novellas where these are particularly relevant. The plays and poetry will be treated only parenthetically. This choice of emphasis is dictated by the relative quality of White's work in these genres and reflects an evaluation with which he would probably concur.

Except perhaps in the matter of his plays, for White seems irresistibly drawn to the theatre. He once disclaimed further interest in play-writing, because bringing a play to the stage involves 'too many difficulties and warring personalities destructive of one's own'.[5] In the furor following the Adelaide Theatre Guild's 1961 production of his play *The Ham Funeral*, he went so far as to send a letter to the editor of *Nation* declaring, 'One thing at least *The Ham Funeral* has taught me, and that is: never to write another play.'[6] Yet he has since seen six more plays into production, the latest as recently as 1983, and has also written the screenplay for the 1978 film *The Night the Prowler*, based on his short story of the same name. In a 1980 interview, he even hinted at another film script in the offing.[7] Yet his work in the dramatic media is simply not as impressive as his fiction. Nor can his short stories stand up to his novels, as White himself acknowledges. In an interview published in 1969, he says of short stories, 'I don't really like writing them so much. . . . All my effects are cumulative, and one doesn't really have the time to get the effects you want.'[8]

Similarly, his poetry is comparatively constricted in scope. Nor is there very much of it, and the little there is White seeks to disown. In 1935, an edition of 300 numbered copies of his *The Ploughman and Other Poems*, containing thirty-three poems, was privately financed and published by Sydney's Beacon Press; and research has turned up a collection called *Thirteen Poems*, written in 1927–29, but perhaps not 'published' in any real sense at all.[9] White is not anxious to claim either of these volumes.[10] In fact, rumour has it that he wants to recall copies of *The Ploughman and Other Poems* from Australian libraries and has even tried to 'buy' them back with offers to will certain of his papers to the library in exchange for the offending volume. The poems are certainly not bad enough to warrant this treatment, but they should not be taken as representative of his mature effort. White has proved himself as a poet in his fiction, for, as Thelma Herring has said, he is among 'those who have tried to extend the frontiers of the novel in the direction of poetry'.[11] Thus the novels should and will be the focus of interest and evaluation.

Following the Acknowledgements is a List of Abbreviations used in the text and notes. Citations to White's works will be made parenthetically by page number and by the indicated abbreviation, where necessary. The Bibliography begins with a complete, chronological listing of White's published work and indicates the editions which were used in preparing this study.

C.B.

Acknowledgements

Grateful acknowledgement is due to Patrick White and to his publishers and agents for permission to quote copyrighted passages from the following works by Patrick White.

Excerpts from *Happy Valley* (London: Harrap, 1939; New York: Viking Press, 1940), reprinted by permission of Curtis Brown (Aust.) Pty Ltd and Viking Penguin Inc.

Excerpts from *The Living and the Dead* (London: Routledge, 1941; New York: Viking Press, 1941; Toronto: Macmillan, 1941), reprinted by permission of Jonathan Cape Ltd and Viking Penguin Inc.

Excerpts from *The Aunt's Story* (London: Routledge & Kegan Paul, 1948; New York: Viking Press, 1948; Toronto: Macmillan, 1948), reprinted by permission of Jonathan Cape Ltd and Viking Penguin Inc.

Excerpts from *The Tree of Man* (New York: Viking Press, 1955; Toronto: Macmillan, 1955; London: Eyre & Spottiswoode, 1956), reprinted by permission of Viking Penguin Inc. and Curtis Brown (Aust.) Pty Ltd.

Excerpts from *Voss* (London: Eyre & Spottiswoode, 1957; New York: Viking Press, 1957; Toronto: Macmillan, 1957), reprinted by permission of Jonathan Cape Ltd and Viking Penguin Inc.

Excerpts from *Riders in the Chariot* (London: Eyre & Spottiswoode, 1961; New York: Viking Press, 1961), reprinted by permission of Jonathan Cape Ltd and Viking Penguin Inc.

Excerpts from *The Solid Mandala* (London: Eyre & Spottiswoode, 1966; New York: Viking Press, 1966), reprinted by permission of Jonathan Cape Ltd and Viking Penguin Inc.

Excerpts from *The Vivisector* (London: Jonathan Cape, 1970; New York: Viking Press, 1970), reprinted by permission of Jonathan Cape Ltd and Viking Penguin Inc.

xiv *Patrick White's Fiction*

Excerpts from *The Eye of the Storm* (London: Jonathan Cape, 1973; New York: Viking Press, 1974), reprinted by permission of Jonathan Cape Ltd and Viking Penguin Inc.

Excerpts from *A Fringe of Leaves* (London: Jonathan Cape, 1976; New York: Viking Press, 1977), reprinted by permission of Jonathan Cape Ltd and Viking Penguin Inc.

Excerpts from *The Twyborn Affair* (London: Jonathan Cape, 1979; New York: Viking Press, 1979), reprinted by permission of Jonathan Cape Ltd and Viking Penguin Inc.

Excerpts from *Flaws in the Glass: A Self-Portrait* (London: Jonathan Cape, 1981; New York: Viking Press, 1982), reprinted by permission of Jonathan Cape Ltd and Viking Penguin Inc.

I should also like to acknowledge the advice, assistance, encouragement, and critical acumen of Jon Stallworthy and Daniel Schwarz, without whom this book would never have seen publication. I am further indebted to the help of Mary Ann Radzinowicz and Walter Slatoff, and to the stimulating exchange of ideas with a number of Australian scholars and intellectuals, particularly Manning Clark, Alan Lawson and Manfred MacKenzie.

Finally, thanks are owing to Joan Fox of Pymble, Australia, for her help in tracking down necessary research materials and to Dr and Mrs William R. Bliss for their unfailing faith in this project and its author.

List of Abbreviations

AS	*The Aunt's Story* (1948; repr. New York: Avon, 1975).
BO	*The Burnt Ones* (1964; repr. Harmondsworth: Penguin, 1968).
C	*The Cockatoos* (1974; repr. New York: Viking Press, 1975).
ES	*The Eye of the Storm* (1973; repr. New York: Avon, 1975).
FG	*Flaws in the Glass: A Self-Portrait* (New York: Viking Press, 1981)
FL	*A Fringe of Leaves* (1976; repr. New York: Viking Press, 1977).
HV	*Happy Valley* (1939; repr. New York: Viking Press, 1940).
LD	*The Living and the Dead* (New York: Viking Press, 1941).
RC	*Riders in the Chariot* (1961; repr. New York: Avon, 1975).
SM	*The Solid Mandala* (1966; repr. New York: Avon, 1975).
TA	*The Twyborn Affair* (London: Jonathan Cape, 1979).
TM	*The Tree of Man* (1955; repr. New York: Avon, 1975)
V	*Voss* (1957; repr. New York: Avon, 1975).
VS	*The Vivisector* (1970; repr. New York: Avon, 1975).

1 Australia: the Mystique of Failure

In this disturbing country, . . . it is possible more easily to discard the inessential and to attempt the infinite.

(*V*, p. 33)

Until recently, the vast, arid, sparsely settled Australian interior was commonly referred to as the 'Dead Heart'.[1] However, such a label was deemed bad for business by the burgeoning Australian tourist industry. Nowadays, hearty and gregarious Ansett or TAA tour guides fill the long hours of bus rides from Alice Springs to Ayers Rock with cheerful ditties about Australia's 'living heart', the 'bloody good drinkers in the Northern Territory', and 'the rock (clap, clap) called Uluru'. But, unless the desert has been graced with recent rain, the tourist gazing at a heat-parched plain is more likely to subscribe to the notion of a dead heart – beating, if at all, in some macabre and spectral way. It may seem as though the heart of life itself has failed.

Central Australia is shockingly different from the coastal areas where, as Patrick White's Voss put it, most Australians still 'huddle' (*V*, p. 9). The interior is the region of drought so pervasive and prolonged that, when the great drought of the 1890s broke in 1902, outback children were alarmed by the unknown sound of rain falling on iron-roofed homesteads.[2] A Brisbane woman of today tells the story of a college friend, settled in the Northern Territory, whose son did not see rain until his tenth birthday. The Australian interior is also the region of a landscape one had hoped was confined to nightmare: gibber plains so ruthlessly eroded that even the sand is gone, leaving only a paved floor of wind-scoured pebbles; the tortured shapes of the Olgas, formed from the heaped-up scraps of a distant, primeval mountain range; and stark, humped Ayers Rock, a

1

monolith five and a half miles in circumference. The Rock is a kind of monstrous sandstone iceberg reaching 1140 feet above the earth and perhaps as much as 20,000 feet below. Sacred to the Aboriginals, Ayers Rock and the Olgas are sites where myths arose and ancient rituals are still enacted. In the interior, then, both climate and landscape are unsettling in their extremity and their implications. But, most importantly for Australians, the outback is inescapably there, at the centre of the Australian continent and consciousness.

Of course, the first Europeans to see and settle Australia had no idea what awaited them in its interior. They found the coastal regions disquieting enough. As Manning Clark, Australia's premier historian, has said, 'the influence of the spirit of place in the fashioning of Australians . . . begins with that first cry of horror and disappointment of the Dutch seamen'.[3] Two of these Dutchmen, William Jansz in 1606 and Jan Carstensz in 1623, perceived Australia as a place where

> a malign nature, unadorned by the arts of civilization, had nurtured a race of evil-natured and malignant human beings, and had bred in the animal world a similar race of unnatural monsters which had the appearance of being unfinished by their Creator. Here, indeed, was a country where the Creator had not finished his work. Here nature was vast and indifferent to man's hopes and dreams. Here nature was so hostile, so brutish that men in time believed God had cursed both man and the country itself, and hence its barrenness, its sterility, its unsuitability for the arts of civilized human beings, and its suitability as a setting for those uncouth barbarians, the Aborigines.[4]

Civilized European perception facing an intractable land produced one of the 'savage encounter[s]' which Clark sees shaping Australian history.[5] Other collisions were that of the white settlers with the Aborigines they displaced and often slaughtered, and that of the British overseers with the convicts who from 1788 were deported to Australian penal colonies. Clark uses these conflicts to account for much of what he sees in Australia's present political, sociological, and psychological make-up, including the idealization of 'mateship', the insistence on social equality, and the persistence of xenophobia. He also sees that together these experiences encouraged the suspicion that human effort faced inevitable failure:

> The climate and the environment gradually made us accept the values of the Aborigines – become fatalists, acceptors, and skeptics about the fruits of human endeavour. The spirit of the place had contributed to the Australian understanding of failure – to our conviction that no matter how hard a man might try he was bound to fail – that in Australia the spirit of the place makes a man aware of his insignificance, of his impotence in the presence of such a harsh environment. . . . Australians knew from of old that the only glory men know on earth is how they respond to defeat and failure.[6]

For the most part, these are failures imposed upon man by forces outside himself too vast and unwieldy to control. But the philosopher Richard Campbell, analysing the character of religious belief in Australia, shows how the outback may become internalized, thereby lending a peculiarly antipodean quality to man's attempts to address his feeling that the world is, in Heidegger's sense, *unheimlich*: that he is not at home there. 'Perhaps', suggests Campbell, 'we need to ask ourselves . . . why it is that the Outback still figures so forcefully in our imagery, even though we flee from its untameable emptiness into the seeming security of suburbia.' His tentative answer is that the outback is crucial as an image because the Australian 'stand[s] out into emptiness' as a condition of being against which he defines himself, much as the existentialist 'stands out' into nothingness:

> But emptiness is not nothing; it is the uncanny limit of our self-assertion, a beyond, an 'outback' which indwells our existence, curbing any pretensions to absolute knowledge or authority. This deep, inarticulate sense of a limit is the correlative of the recognition of the contingency of our being-in-the-world. Practically, it means that we are driven back into our situation, to grapple with the recalcitrant nature of what is given – [a condition which produces] our so-called materialism and pragmatism. Theologically, it means that the absence of God is not nothing; it is the particular mode of his presence . . . . [Perhaps] a more positive articulation of how we

know ourselves to be contingent beings 'thrown' into a reality
which transcends us and defies our efforts at domestication,
might yet provide a basis for an authentic religious consciousness in this country.[7]

These observations are applicable to the work of Patrick White
in several ways. White seems sometimes to share Campbell's
perception of God as present in His absence, and Campbell's final
sentence would stand as a fair précis of what White's art seeks to
accomplish. Moreover, White uses the landscape of the Australian
interior as a metaphor for the quest towards an understanding of
human limitations and the greater reality which transcends them.
Most centrally in *Voss*, but also in *The Aunt's Story*, *The Tree of
Man* and *A Fringe of Leaves*, landscape can stand for the journey
to discovery and as emblem of the discovery itself. But more to
the immediate purpose is Campbell's observation that the image
of the outback inhabits Australian consciousness primarily because
it suggests a boundary beyond which the self cannot push,
something insuperable and indomitable, something which will
impose failure.

Given, then, that failure is so deeply and ineradicably rooted
in the Australian experience, it is hardly surprising that this
theme should be central both to Australian literature in general
and to the work of Patrick White. Several critics of Australian
writing have recently emphasized this concern in the literature,
pointing, for example, to its preoccupation 'with suffering and
defeat, a preoccupation which arises out of grim experience in an
environment which presses its claims with peculiar intensity'.[8] In
the best Australian literature a tragic sense has been remarked,
at odds with the average Australian reader's 'cheerful acceptance
of the place, blowflies and all'.[9] What *is* perhaps surprising is that
this dark strain in Australian literature should be so tardily
recognized. The Australian critical tradition has largely preferred
to emphasize the sunnier aspects of the Australian scene,[10] and
to endorse the view espoused in A. A. Phillips's influential book
The Australian Tradition, the view that a 'democratic theme', which
stresses inclusivity and egalitarianism, is the cornerstone of
Australian literature.[11]

When the darker underside has surfaced, it has often taken the
form of man's confrontation with the bush, sometimes presented
as a metaphor for his confrontation with the unexplored and

terrifying depths of self.[12] Patrick White is among those Australian writers who have used the outback in this way, as are Douglas Stewart, Randolph Stow, Judith Wright and James McAuley. It must be remembered that the Australian bushland and desert, as well as the life which was led there by the Aborigines, have about them much that is stunningly beautiful, even if that beauty should tend toward Yeats's 'terrible beauty', or to the dimensions of the Romantic sublime. Yet the sense which emerges in so much Australian art and literature, the sense of something sinister, ominous because unknown and unknowable, is undeniably central to the Australian perception of the bush. This is convincingly evidenced in some of Australia's best films, for example, *Walkabout* and *Picnic at Hanging Rock*, and in the work of such painters as William Dobell, Russell Drysdale, Albert Tucker and Robert Dickerson. There does indeed seem to be what Douglas Stewart called a 'horror' there: the horror of a Conradian heart of darkness. It is the horror of that which enforces defeat and thus marks the border of what White has called 'the no-man's-land of human failure' (*VS*, p. 357).

It would appear, then, that Patrick White comes honestly by his concern with the nature and meaning of failure. Indeed, an awareness of Australian art, letters, history and ecology would virtually have forced it into his consciousness. That White is thoroughly acquainted with his Australian heritage and deeply attached to his homeland has been demonstrated by his fiction, his published statements, and most conclusively, his life. Having spent more than half that life outside Australia in Europe, America and the Middle East, he elected to come home after the war and has remained ever since. In his 1958 essay 'The Prodigal Son', he explains why. The essay, written in response to one by the Australian expatriate Alister Kershaw, reveals the depths to which his roots are sunk in Australian soil. It speaks of his persistent 'longing to return to the scenes of childhood, which is, after all, the purest well from which the creative artist draws', and celebrates his Australian home as the source of 'the stimulus of time remembered'.

'The Prodigal Son' suggests that what White most missed in his expatriate days was the Australian landscape, from which he absorbed what Clark called 'the spirit of place'. In his fiction, he shows himself sharply aware of the continuity of that spirit over time and of what today's Australian owes to his heritage, subjects which are treated in *Voss* and *A Fringe of Leaves*. The inheritance is not wholly positive, as he makes plain in the essay's diatribe against Australia's urban culture,

> in which the mind is the least of possessions, in which the rich man is the important man, in which the schoolmaster and the journalist rule what intellectual roost there is, . . . the buttocks of cars grow hourly glassier, food means cake and steak, muscles prevail, and the march of material ugliness does not raise a quiver from the average nerves.[13]

The failure White condemns here is that of a modern, commercial culture to offer anything but its own refuse to fill the void at its centre. It is a theme to which he frequently recurs, but, although he labels what he describes as the 'Great Australian Emptiness', this sort of vacuum is scarcely indigenous nor confined to Australia. It is also not the sort of failure which informs White's vision. The failures on which White focuses are not collective, but individual.

An understanding of the theme of failure in White's fiction begins with the observation that, in his eleven novels to date, major characters experience what seems a necessary, redemptive or facilitating failure. It is a failure which conduces to the character's success in terms of some superseding context, sanctioned by what White has called the 'overreaching grandeur' circumscribing human existence.[14] Whether this grandeur is godly or its values God-given is a question which still provokes lively debate among critics,[15] despite the fact that White strives repeatedly to make himself clear on the subject. For example, in an interview published in 1969 he states boldly,

> Religion. Yes, that's behind all my books. What I am interested in is the relationship between the blundering human being and God. . . . I think there is a Divine Power, a Creator who has an influence on human beings if they are willing to be open to him.[16]

And in a 1970 letter to Peter Beatson he reflects,

> I suppose what I am increasingly trying to do in my books is to give professed unbelievers glimpses of their own unprofessed

factor. I believe most people have a religious factor, but are afraid that by admitting it they will forfeit their right to be considered intellectuals.[17]

In a later interview and in his autobiography, White describes the circumstances under which he was forced to admit his own faith,[18] and in 1979 he is still insisting, 'I have a very strong belief in some supernatural power.'[19] But, while recognizing his belief in this 'supernatural power', one need not and should not confine him within any single religious tradition. White has explained his position:

> I belong to no church, but I have a religious faith; it's an attempt to express that, among other things, that I try to do. . . . In my books I have lifted bits from various religions. . . . Now, as the world becomes more pagan, one has to lead people in the same direction in a different way. . . .[20]

He has also 'lifted bits' from (at least) Hinduism, Aboriginal mythology, and the mystical and occult traditions of both Christianity and Judaism. But it should be clear that, while White's theological position cannot be precisely located, it is within *some* extra-mundane, supra-human context that his characters first fail and subsequently achieve some paradoxical success. For these characters, it is not simply that worldly failure, such as the failure to achieve wealth, power or prestige, is recompensed by otherworldly success in the manner suggested by the Christian Beatitudes. The failures which White inflicts on his characters are moral or spiritual already and are felt by the characters themselves as failures within their own moral/spiritual terms.

Often the crucial failure is the incapacity to love sufficiently or to express that love in positive action. Thus Stan and Amy Parker in *The Tree of Man* are unable to penetrate each other's hearts and are kept at an even greater remove from their children. Voss is repelled (because threatened) by Laura's 'dog-eyed' love (*V*, p. 265), and is only able to accept it, with its prerequisite warmth and weakness, just before his death. Similarly, Arthur Brown of *The Solid Mandala* believes that his love for his twin has been inadequate to subdue the hatred in Waldo and salvage him from death, and *The Vivisector*'s Hurtle Duffield admits that he has been unable to truly love his humpbacked stepsister Rhoda. Elizabeth Hunter of *The Eye of the Storm* fails to love her husband as he deserves and her children as they desperately need. Finally, Ellen Roxburgh of *A Fringe of Leaves* cannot love her husband enough to stay faithful or her convict rescuer enough to reclaim him for civilization. In White's latest novel, *The Twyborn Affair*, Eddie Twyborn's failure may be that he cannot love himself.

A closely related theme in White's fiction is that of the failure to save. Most often this takes the form of the inability or unwillingness to keep from injury or death someone for whom the character feels morally responsible. Himmelfarb of *Riders in the Chariot* is surely the most spectacular example: he fails to become the Messiah–Redeemer his people have awaited. But the other Riders also fail to save: Mary Hare lets her father drown and her pet goat burn, nor can she save Himmelfarb from the fire that consumes his shack; Ruth Godbold cannot rescue her husband from his life of debauchery and dereliction; Alf Dubbo retreats in terror from the scene of Himmelfarb's 'crucifixion', unable to intervene and perhaps prevent the Jew's subsequent death. Arthur Brown fails to save Waldo from a death brought on by his hatred of life, and Hurtle Duffield holds himself to blame for the deaths of Nance and Hero.

Often, as in the case of Arthur Brown, the failure to save is in part attributable to the failure of love, and both are linked to a third sort of failure, the inability to locate, recognize, or perhaps permit the true self. This is a component of Voss's problem, and it is what sends Theodora Goodman of *The Aunt's Story* on her problematic quest. The search for self is also at the heart of Eddie/Eadith Twyborn's ordeal in *The Twyborn Affair*.

But recognition of this class of failures brings the reader up against one of White's most baffling and important paradoxes: that the self must be sought and found only to be relinquished, that the individuality so powerfully expressed by his major characters paradoxically enables them to seek a state of understanding in which selfhood is finally subsumed. In a further permutation of the paradox, the surrender of self which this understanding demands somehow functions to permit the character's fullest realization of the essential self; that is, he becomes most himself when he least seeks to be. In the terms of the related Christian paradox, he finds his life by losing it, or as Emerson put it, 'The man who renounces himself, comes to himself.'[21]

Thus, Voss is most godlike when he abandons his assault on the throne of God and allows himself to be a confused and vulnerable mortal. As Laura understands it, 'When man is truly humbled, when he has learned that he is not God, then he is nearest to becoming so. In the end, he may ascend' (*V*, p. 384). Similarly, Himmelfarb becomes a redemptive agent for Mary, Ruth and Alf when he acknowledges that 'it had not been accorded to him to expiate the sins of the world' (*RC*, p. 459). Hurtle Duffield reaches the pinnacle of his artistic achievement only when he is made the passive instrument of some greater force, and Arthur Brown saves Mrs Poulter's faith only when he must cease trying to save his brother.

But the screw takes still another turn. This paradoxically perfected and surrendered self achieves both states through a process White depicts again and again as 'dissolution' – that is, a process by which the self seems to melt and dissolve, abandoning, as White puts it, the condition of sculpture for that of music and thereby expanding until its limits approach those of the unifying all. This motion is enlarging and acquisitive, permitting the self somehow to appropriate its own uniqueness as it also absorbs the infinite further selves it must become. The process is explicitly described when undergone by Theodora in the final section of *The Aunt's Story*. White says,

> In the peace that . . . spread throughout her body and the speckled shade of surrounding trees, there was no end to the lives of Theodora Goodman. These met and parted, met and parted movingly. They entered into each other. . . . And in the same way that the created lives of Theodora Goodman were interchangeable, the lives into which she had entered, making them momently dependent for love or hate, owing her this portion of their fluctuating personalities, . . . these were the lives of Theodora Goodman, these too.   (pp. 286–7)

Elsewhere in White's fiction, the experience is more often suggested imagistically, as in Le Mesurier's poem which prefigures Voss's death. Here White makes use of the Aboriginal myth of the dispersion of souls after death. Le Mesurier writes,

> Flesh is for hacking, after it has stood the test of time. The poor, frayed flesh. They chase the kangaroo, and when they have cut off his pride and gnawed his charred bones, they

honour him in ochre on a wall. Where is his spirit? They say:
It has gone out, it has gone away, it is everywhere.

O God, my God, I pray that you will take my spirit out of
this my body's remains, and after you have scattered it, grant
that it shall be everywhere, and in the rocks, and in the empty
waterholes, and in true love of all men, and in you, O God,
at last. (*V*, p. 295).

White even envisions such an end for himself: a 'splintering and
coalescing' of all the mornings of his life and of those whose lives
he has watched or shared (*FG*, pp. 256–7).

The experience which Theodora undergoes, Le Mesurier
imagines and White projects is one of accretion and accumulation,
a flowing-out from the centre to circumscribe ever larger circles.
Thus the reverse process, sought by Mary Hare of *Riders* and
initially by Theodora, the process of peeling away layers of the
self to reach a central core, is at best preliminary to the more
exacting task. The same can be said of the stripping undergone
by Ellen Roxburgh in *A Fringe of Leaves*. It may be necessary or
it may seem to be necessary to abandon the excess baggage of
selfhood or to peel off unwanted aspects of the self. But they will
all eventually have to be reclaimed, no matter how grotesque or
shameful, as will everything else.[22] Or perhaps both efforts, both
the peeling-away and the piling-on, are ultimately one. Again,
the Australian continent proves a suggestive metaphor, since
exploration of its interior may be seen both as a progress towards
a central core and as a progressive amassing of new territory.

Finally, what seems to be a series of concentric paradoxes –
the self abandoned, perfected, and dispersed – may be
comprehended in the larger paradox of the Dantesque pattern
which White adopts for his spiritual questers. He subscribes to
the conception of spiritual progress which shapes the *Divine
Comedy*: it is only from the very heart of hell, only after, as it were,
embracing the very flesh and fur of Satan, that the pilgrim can
begin to ascend toward heaven.[23] Thus, in White's fiction, the
via negativa, which may impose a stripping-away or emptying-out
of the self, will be succeeded by a *via affirmativa* which amplifies
the self in the direction of the infinite. Perhaps the best exemplar
of this pattern is Stan Parker in *The Tree of Man*, who vomits out
his God on a Sydney street and later swallows Him in again in
great gulps, since 'It is not natural that emptiness shall prevail . . . '

(p. 431). But the descent to hell must first be endured, and, whether or not it requires the self to be emptied or stripped, it will certainly exact suffering. In White's fiction, the worst of this suffering, the darkest moment of the soul's dark night, tends to be reached when the character most deeply experiences and accedes to his sense of failure.[24]

This last observation suggests the connection which operates in White's work between the theme of necessary or redemptive failure and the larger vision. For White chronicles the drive toward self-discovery and definition in terms of a schema which ultimately absorbs the individual within a self-coherent and homogeneous unity.[25] Or as he puts it (a bit too blatantly) in *The Tree of Man*, it is found that 'One, and no other figure, is the answer to all sums' (p. 508). All separate selves are thus eventually seen as fragments of one great, unified self or consciousness, a vision of existence which adopts a central tenet of Hinduism, Neoplatonism and Transcendentalism. White expresses this perception in his fiction in many ways, among them the continual modulations his characters undergo, so that, for example, all Hurtle Duffield's women are finally recognizable as one woman who is simultaneously mother, sister, wife and daughter. Even more striking is the collapse of male–female distinctions and the positing of an androgynous ideal, motifs which are especially important to *Riders in the Chariot*, *The Solid Mandala*, *The Vivisector* and *The Twyborn Affair*. If all selves are ultimately one, then the single self must fail to separate and complete itself apart from the whole, whether by heroism which can never truly protect, or love which can never be adequate to its task. But, again paradoxically, only those who strive to love, to save, and to be 'themselves', are allowed this failure, which, when judged by its consequences, can be seen as a sort of *felix culpa* or fortunate fall. For failure can open the way to a greatly enlarged understanding and experience of life. Thus we are returned to the efficacy of failure. Its experience both humbles the sufferer and provokes him to further effort. Or as Le Mesurier puts it in *Voss*, 'The mystery of life is not solved by success, which is an end in itself, but in failure, in perpetual struggle, in becoming' (p. 269).

In White's fiction, then, the character's experience of moral or spiritual failure is prerequisite for his understanding of the moral/spiritual universe which White believes obtains. Further, such failure comes increasingly to preoccupy White until it stands at the very centre of his latest work. Having, in *The Vivisector*, concentrated his attention on the problems of the idiosyncratic and personal versus the comprehensive and transpersonal vision, White has turned since then to more painstaking exploration of the process by which the former is found wanting. The novels up to and including *The Vivisector* seem concerned with both the quest and its visionary rewards, but in his last three novels White has confined his attention increasingly to the dark night of the soul and has scarcely gestured to the light beyond. Or, as in the case of Elizabeth Hunter, he has demonstrated his sober recognition that the heart of truth may be penetrated without significantly altering the initiate's mode of existence.

I would hazard a further hypothesis: that White, as a writer of fiercely individual style and vision, is caught in his own philosophical double bind and thus must himself undergo a certain necessary failure. Evidence of this is found in his adoption of an ironic perspective not only on his protagonists (none of whom is ever wholly endorsed and each of whom is occasionally ridiculous), but also on himself as creator of a fictional universe. Like the painter Hurtle Duffield, who sometimes seems to speak with the author's own voice, White appears convinced that his medium will always be inadequate to his message. Although, like Laura in *Voss*, he would 'describe in simple words the immensity of simple knowledge' (p. 236), he often seems to agree with Arthur of *The Solid Mandala* that 'words are not what make you see' (p. 51). Not only do his characters repeatedly voice a disgust with or suspicion of the refractory nature of language, but *in propria persona* White has insisted that he shares their discomfiture. In a 1973 interview he says, 'I am hobbled by words',[26] and in his 'self-portrait', *Flaws in the Glass*, he complains of the difficulty of forcing 'grey, bronchial prose' to 'give visual expression to what I have inside of me' (p. 150).

But this is not the only sort of failure White accuses in himself. Along with his distrust of language goes the deeper and more debilitating distrust of his own ability to penetrate experience and convey its significance. Of course, in the attempt he makes 'to create completely fresh forms out of the rocks and sticks of words',[27] and thereby to 'come close to the core of reality, the structure of reality',[28] he is bound to fall somewhat short. Again and again he comes face to face with the ineffable and can only, in the words of T. S. Eliot, mount 'raid[s] upon the inarticulate'.

In fact, by the time he writes *Flaws in the Glass*, he has come to believe that truth may be 'the property of silence – at any rate the silences filling the space between words', over which he only 'sometimes' has control (p. 42).

To observe that White feels and expresses a kind of contempt for his own artistic enterprise, a contempt grounded in his despair of ever succeeding on the terms he has set himself, is to go some distance towards accounting for certain characteristics of style, tone and point of view which have intrigued or enraged his critics.[29] Chief among these would be his penchant for subjective, conditional and conjectural constructions, his often disconcerting comic sense, his shifting and occasionally unattributable point of view, what is sometimes condemned as an evasive refusal to endorse moral or ethical precepts voiced by the characters, his syllepsis, synaesthesia, and sentence fragments, his frequent use of second-person narration, and his abrupt rejections of the prerogatives of the omniscient narrative stance he has adopted.

Another and related question is that of genre. Apparently seduced by the welter of convincing details in White's novels and his understanding of the springs of human action and emotion, some critics have tacitly assumed that his writing belongs in a realistic–naturalistic tradition and have consequently chided him for unlikely plots or 'impossible' events. (The example most often cited is that of the 'telepathy' between Voss and Laura, but Himmelfarb's 'crucifixion' also causes considerable complaint.[30]) This same critical camp is likely to object that the design of the novels, particularly *Riders in the Chariot* and *The Solid Mandala*, is too patent and that their programmatic quality undercuts any sense of 'felt life' within them.[31]

The alternate move is to decide that the novels are allegories,[32] or, as one critic puts it, 'a kind of wisdom literature seeking to demonstrate' a certain spiritual/ethical system at work in the universe.[33] However, this stance, which sees the characters as abstract concepts or embodied ideas rather than human beings, cannot account for the sympathetic reader response which the novels so often elicit. A middle ground is needed, one which allows the novels both their humanistic impact and their allegorical or symbolic implications.[34]

The premise of this book is that the concept of facilitating failure and related paradoxes can do much to account for some of the distinctive thematic, stylistic, structural and generic features which characterize White's fiction and sometimes confound his critics. Ensuing chapters will first examine the theme of failure as it emerges and develops in the fiction, then consider how this concept may illuminate aspects of White's style and technique, perhaps even his sense of himself and his mission as a writer.

2 The Early Works: Anatomy of Failure

. . . he was in fact empty of all thought, which can be a state of failure, or else of dedication. (*TM*, p. 438)

In White's early fiction, the pattern whereby failure leads to an unlooked-for and very different kind of success is present, but muted or subsidiary to other concerns. The theme is explored and anatomized, but does not take on the importance later accorded it. As his early work reveals the author experimenting in matters of style and technique, it also chronicles his gradual approach to the philosophy of life which would inform his mature fiction. A central feature of this philosophy, the paradox of imperative failure, does not emerge in all its complexity until *Voss*, written some twenty years after the writer's fiction first appeared in print. None the less, the protagonist's experience of significant failure is a feature even of the earliest novel White published.

HAPPY VALLEY

Happy Valley appeared in 1939. It was not the first novel he had written, but copies of three earlier works either have not survived or are not for public consumption.[1]

The novel's plot centres on the adulterous love of Oliver Halliday, a physician with a tubercular wife and two children, for Alys Browne, a convent-educated seamstress and music-teacher who has spent much of her life waiting for something to happen. White suggests that the most exciting event in Alys's life heretofore has been her adolescent decision to make herself more mysterious by changing the spelling of her name from 'Alice'

15

to 'Alys'. Their affair, unpromising at the outset, is further undermined in the reader's eyes by the fact that White parallels it with its own coarse parody: the far less cerebral affair carried on by Vic Moriarty, the schoolmaster's wife, and Clem Hagan, new overseer at the sheep station of the wealthy Furlows.[2] Other characters and relationships abound – so many, in fact, that the reader's attention cannot focus itself into real involvement – but White clearly intends to place these two triangles at the novel's centre. One acts as the distorting mirror of the other, reflecting in the sensuality and melodrama of Vic and Hagan's affair a caricature of certain elements of Oliver and Alys's union. Ultimately, the shoddier relationship intrudes upon and disrupts the other, forcing Oliver and Alys to see their liaison in its terms. As Oliver understands it in the letter he sends Alys after the night the Moriartys die,

> There was all the futility and pain of wilful destruction about that house and two people trying to escape from the inevitable. Talking of the inevitable may sound defeatist perhaps. We might have escaped down that road to some form of personal happiness. But, Alys, I can't, I won't willingly destroy, after facing the meaning of destruction in that house.   (p. 285)

'That house' is the one in which Moriarty kills Vic after discovering her with Hagan and from which he flees to die of a heart attack and be found in the road by Alys and Oliver as they attempt their getaway. This series of catastrophes and coincidences not only leaves Vic and Moriarty dead, but leaves Hagan as good as dead. He extricates himself from suspicion of Vic's murder by submitting to Sidney Furlow's protection, a protection which has aptly been termed psychological cannibalism.[3] However, these same events leave Oliver and Alys reft, but alive.

This is not how we find them. The novel opens in the dead of winter with Dr Halliday officiating at a stillbirth in snowbound Kambala. Of the place, White says, 'There was a general air of hibernation, of life suspended under the snow' (p. 12). The same might be said of Oliver and Alys.

Oliver behaves as though drugged or sleepwalking. His patient is not real to him: 'It was like delivering a cow, he felt. When she moaned it was almost like the lowing of a cow. And that same bewildered stare' (p. 14). His own life seems to be 'Just this coating of the essential sameness with superficial experience'

(p. 18). He tries not to think about it. Alys's mode of life can be gathered from the current status of her vague but longstanding plan to go to California: 'I have nothing to stop me from going to California, except that I cannot make the effort, and after all it is such a long way, and they say the Tasman Sea is rough' (p. 42).

For both Oliver and Alys, apathy seems to stem from their suspicion that their lives are somehow insubstantial and illusory. As he tends to Alys's injured hand, Oliver thinks, 'That Browne girl pitying herself because she had cut her hand was unreal, or he, or Happy Valley, was unreal, removing itself into a world of allegory of which the dominating motif was pain' (p. 77). The unreality here is akin to that of Eliot's 'unreal city': the citizens walk like ghosts through what passes for life; existence is infernal, not to be believed.

But as their love develops, Oliver and Alys make each other reciprocally real; only the world, the not-us, remains dreamlike. Thus Oliver, after he and Alys first make love, thinks,

> I have been asleep. . . . It is like waking. And I must remain awake, or at least conscious, conscious in one person of the whole. The others are asleep, perhaps will never wake. . . . I ought to feel sorry, but there is no regret, which is perhaps a perversion of the moral sense, if finding yourself is a perversion, because this is what I have done.   (p. 161)

To this newly real self, pity for Hilda, his wife, is 'suicide': 'If I start pitying Hilda, that is to kill myself, he felt, the person that Alys has made, that is me . . . ' (p. 194). Similarly, Alys, on the night she and Oliver are to run away, thinks of her previous life as shadow and illusion:

> all this was a dream, she felt, and Hilda Halliday. . . . It is wrong to dream, she said, Oliver is reality. She found herself clenching her hands. I want to live, she said, I have a right to this as much as Hilda Halliday, I shall not be possessed by this half-life, this dream, or is it a dream, or is it a dream, or is Oliver a dream.   (pp. 256–7)

Clearly, for both Oliver and Alys, the 'real' has come to stand for the realized self which love has given them, while the 'unreal' has become synonymous with the world of others. But it is also clear from the tone of Alys's musings that this spectral and repudiated outer world has again begun to intrude its own reality.

White orchestrates this motif of real and unreal, life dreamed or life lived awake, most tellingly in the climactic scene in which Oliver and Alys discover the body of Moriarty while fleeing Happy Valley:

> The light wedged into darkness, split it up into two sectors, with the car spinning down the path of light. Houses, no longer the real structure of houses, were pale beside the road, the paper facades, or masks representative of sleep in a kind of silent allegory. A rabbit crossed the road, lacking in substance, to join the dark. Only the car in fact, you felt, had some reality or purpose. They had given it this with their bodies that sat up straight. . . . She could feel his coat jutting into the half-reality of a dream world and making it almost tangible. This is real now, she said. . . .
>
> He felt her relax . . . and time stretched out blank waiting for an impression that you would make now. It had waited for this. The other shapes were not, that you thought, that you imagined before Alys Browne.
>
> Oliver Halliday, driving his car from Happy Valley to Moorang, swung out to avoid something that he was not sure, on the road, if this. The trees were grey and sharp in the stationary light, the wheel solid, he felt steel, anchored to this the returned thought.
>
> I'll have to go back and look, he said.
>
> Hearing words, she knew they had returned out of another world. He would go and look. She closed her eyes. She did not want to look, not so much at something on the road, as at the sharp outline of trees. Opening the eyes the light stopped short. She could not see along the road, because it ended in that leaden ridge, so very heavy in the headlight, the car clamped down. There was no connexion with motion in the passive body of the car. . . .
>
> Oliver went back. It was Ernest Moriarty lying on the road. He was dead.   (pp. 266–7)

In this passage, 'real' and 'unreal' counterpoint 'self' and 'world'. As the outside world, the world of responsibility to others, presses its claims ever more implacably, the landscape around Alys and

Oliver grows more solid, static and impenetrable, surrounding and circumscribing them. The car, which had seemed a world of their own purposeful and vectored reality, is caught and stopped, mired in the viscous otherness around it. Even the syntax co-operates. Words and sentences flow into each other when Alys and Oliver are in control, but are choppy and brittle when the circumstantial world takes over. From this point on, the reality of others, of 'the world', is not to be gainsaid.

In the terms in which Oliver has come to understand this dichotomy, Hilda has now become as real as Alice. Earlier Oliver had reflected, thinking of Alys, 'I have given myself to you, and you have made me into something superior to myself, but which I must throw away, because of the world I must throw away, because Hilda is the world, poor, sick, and there is no forsaking it' (p. 196). He subsequently submerges this perception under further dreams of a more authentic life with Alys. But the world's poverty and sickness in the shape of Hilda and Moriarty reassert their claim on him.

Finally, then, 'reality' is seen to inhere neither in the revitalized self nor in the unforsaken other, but in both. The fluctuating sense of 'real' in the novel stabilizes as that which conduces to life; life is equated with feeling; and feeling most often is pain. We remember that for Oliver, even when the world was safely confined to allegory, its significance was pain. The epigraph from Mahatma Gandhi sets forth the novel's programme:

> It is impossible to do away with the law of suffering, which is the one indispensable condition of our being. Progress is to be measured by the amount of suffering undergone . . . the purer the suffering, the greater the progress. (p. 7)

There is plenty of suffering for all in Happy Valley; the question is its purity. Part One of the novel, roughly the first third, chronicles one day in the life of Happy Valley's citizens. It begins with a woman in painful and fruitless labour. In the course of the morning, injuries proliferate: Oliver sustains a fall while skiing back from Kambala to Happy Valley, Alys cuts her hand, and Oliver's son Rodney is involved in a fight at school. Other glimpses are provided of the suffering exacted by Hilda's tuberculosis and Moriarty's asthma. Metaphysical pain also abounds. There is the restless dissatisfaction with self and life which becomes bitchiness in Ethel Quong, quiet bitterness in Amy, sentimentality in Vic, and cruelty in Sidney. We see also the easily victimized and the already victimized. It seems finally as though Happy Valley is as Oliver once sees it: 'an embodiment of pain' (p. 119). White depicts the town itself as the aftermath of injury. He describes it as 'an ugly scab somewhere on the body of the earth. . . . Some day it would drop off, leaving a pink, clean place underneath' (p. 29; see also p. 114).

The potential for redemptive suffering is enormous here. But except for Alys and Oliver, the inhabitants of Happy Valley are afflicted with what has been called an 'insufficient . . . capacity for experience'.[4] Rather than using suffering in the way Gandhi intended, they can only burrow deeper into their pain, or find more damaging ways to express it. This latter mode is that of Sidney Furlow, who, out of boredom, fashions her life into a melodramatic fiction and appropriates Hagan in the process. It is also that of Amy Quong, whose anonymous letter to Moriarty alerts him to Vic and Hagan's affair. Finally and most spectacularly, it is the mode of Moriarty himself, who once lashes out at fate when Margaret Quong happens to be in the way, and ultimately tries to strangle deceit and lies in the shape of 'this thing' that 'had been a woman' and his wife (p. 264).

Only Oliver and Alys, then, can undertake the Gandhian project. For Oliver, progress through suffering seems to require not only that he suffer himself, but that he learn to pity other sufferers. Beyond this, he must learn there is finally no difference between those in pain and those who cause it, or, in other words, that victims are also victimizers. Oliver's acquaintance with pain and pity deepens through the novel. Torn between the poles of responsibility to self and to others, loving Alys and Hilda and hating himself, he emerges from the 'anaesthesia of snow' (p. 317) in which we find him. Eventually, the callous equation of his labouring patient with a cow gives way to a pity Oliver extends to the whole world, and which determines him in his decision to stay with Hilda: 'I have learnt this, he felt, that it is pitiable, this Happy Valley, even in its violence that at first you thought deliberately destructive and cruel there is a human core that makes you overflow with pity for it' (p. 213). He finally manages to extend pity even to himself.

Oliver's third lesson, that of the kinship between sufferers and those that make them suffer, is approached more obliquely. At the novel's outset, Oliver watches a circling hawk and reflects,

All its life it would probably know no pain, not like Mrs Chalker writhing about on the bed at Kambala. The hawk was absolved from this, absorbed as an agent into the whole of this frozen landscape, into the mountains that emanated in their silence a dull, frozen pain while remaining exempt from it. There was a kind of universal cleavage between these, the agents, and their objects: the woman at the hotel, forcing the dead child out of her womb, or the township of Happy Valley with its slow festering sore of painfully little intrigue. (pp. 19–20)

Oliver's view here is simplistic and dichotomous. What he must rather understand is that agents and objects can be identical: that he is not simply the physician, reliever of pain, nor only this and the sufferer, but both these and at the same time, like the much later Arthur Brown, a 'getter of pain' (*SM*, p. 288). Oliver speculates on this complex inter-relationship even before he has completely experienced it, and the author clues us to the linkage with his earlier reflection by echoing its language, particularly the words 'cleavage' and 'pain':

There is a mystery of unity about the world, that ignores itself, finding its expression in cleavage and pain, the not-world that demands I shall run away from myself, that I too shall be a creature of cleavage and pain walking with my eyes closed. (*HV*, p. 162)

The implication here may be that separateness and suffering exist because the self ignores or denies its inner unity and its link with all beyond itself. If this is so, then victim and victimizer are ultimately the same, and readers are admitted to a context in which to understand Oliver's final epiphany: 'A flux of moving things, like experience, fused, and Alys Browne, he felt, is part of me for all time, this is not altogether lost, it is still an intimate relationship that no violence can mortify' (p. 317). Agent and object of pain are united here as they never were as lovers.

Alys's progress through suffering parallels Oliver's, but its stations are less clearly marked. She does, however, move from the affected young lady who bluffs her way through life with Schumann and a tea-stained copy of *Anna Karenina*, to the recognition that Oliver has brought her painfully alive.

Both Alys and Oliver, then, have made real progress through

their pain, and this signals a kind of success. We might therefore suspect that in this early White novel, the theme of failure is enacted only peripherally by secondary characters. For it does seem that White has gathered here a collection of those the Australians so accurately call 'no-hopers', and trapped them in a Sartrean hell of each other.

None the less, the theme of failure *is* central, even to this early work, for it is failure which admits Oliver and Alys to their deepened perception and thus conduces to their successful penetration of the meaning and purpose of pain. For both, the facilitating failure is the failure to escape Happy Valley, an experience which, in terms of the novel's theme, represents the failure to elude the dialectic of self and others, personal and social, real and unreal, giver and getter of pain. As White makes clear in *The Aunt's Story*, that 'mystery of unity' to which he later devotes so much attention is not one in which opposites are evaded or reconciled, but rather encompassed and embraced. Antitheses never collapse into some muddy hybrid; they remain themselves, but are held in polar tension, in what White, again in *The Aunt's Story*, calls 'that complementary curse and blessing, a relationship' (p. 200). Apprehending the scheme of things is not a matter of reduction or diminution, but always an act of expansion until more and more is accepted and affirmed. The experience of failure opens this perception to the protagonists.

Alys Browne, who undergoes near the novel's end perhaps the prototypical Whitean moment of illumination, does so in just these terms. She has received Oliver's letter of farewell:

> Alys Browne sat by lamplight holding in her hands a letter that was more than this. It was moving, moving, she could not touch with her hands the circle of light that receded, without circumference, there was no limit to the endless efflorescence of light.   (*HV*, p. 289)

Subsequently, she affirms that, like all experience, Oliver is and will remain with her, 'present and future', 'still alive', 'interminable' (p. 312).

Oliver's similar revelation is phrased in terms of the antinomies he has failed to resolve or ignore – here, as elsewhere, symbolized by Alys and Hilda. He knows,

This is the part of man, to withstand through his relationships the ebb and flow of the seasons, the sullen hostility of rock, the anaesthesia of snow, all those passions that sweep down through negligence or design to consume and desolate, for through Hilda and Alys he can withstand, he is immune from all but the ultimate destruction of the inessential outer shell.   (p. 317)

The implication is that the buffeting of antitheses may not only save but shape man's essential self, a suggestion which receives much further consideration in *The Aunt's Story*.

There is a good deal wrong with *Happy Valley* as a novel. White himself seems ashamed of the book, dismissing it recently as 'best forgotten' (*FG*, p. 75). It is the only one of his novels never to be reissued, and is often omitted from dust-jacket lists of his works. He has acknowledged that it is derivative, 'full of influences' as he says in a 1973 interview, continuing, 'But I didn't consciously imitate other writers. I was very influenced by Joyce in my youth. I think everybody who started writing seriously then was influenced by Joyce a bit. I suppose I was influenced by Lawrence.'[5] Critics have been quick to corroborate both influences, pointing to such Lawrentian moments as the snake-killing episode or to Joycean indebtedness in the clotted stream-of-consciousness passages. The source in Eliot's poetry of the cyclamen symbolism associated with Vic and Hagan's love affair has also been noticed,[6] as has the fact that the prose occasionally finds a Faulknerian rhythm.

Beyond the question of its derivativeness, the novel has other problems. Most noticeable of these is the uncertainty of narrative perspective, which shifts unpredictably from genially Fielding-like first person, through Jamesian central intelligence, garden-variety omniscient, and Joycean interior monologue. White has not yet found either his voice or his vision.

But both are forming, and there are moments when the familiar cadences and metaphysical complexity are in evidence, at least in embryo. The trenchant White wit is also apparent, especially as he uses it to pin down character with a telling detail epigrammatically presented. He says of Mr Furlow, for example, that he 'hadn't a mind, only a mutual understanding between a number of almost dormant instincts' (*HV*, p. 83).

Obviously, *Happy Valley* is apprentice work when measured against White's later achievements. But what is surprising about this novel is how good it is, how much White to the exclusion of other 'influences', how fresh despite derivations, how richly furnished with hints of how the later work will develop.

THE LIVING AND THE DEAD

Although today *The Living and the Dead* (1941) is generally considered an advance on *Happy Valley*, it is not a better novel. For here issues have been reduced to simple antitheses. One is either alive or dead; death is bad, life is good; the interplay of opposites which White was developing in *Happy Valley* has virtually disappeared. Here the protagonist, Elyot Standish, is dead, and the novel's problem is to bring him to life. To accomplish this, it shows him two negative models: his mother, who was once alive but chooses death; and his sister, who comes alive so violently that it kills her.

Throughout the novel, the capacity for life is measured by the ability to love and the courage to sustain an inquiry into the self. To abdicate either responsibility is to allow death to triumph. Elyot's mother undergoes three incarnations in the novel, moving her progressively closer both to physical death and to death as defined in these terms. Each metamorphosis is signalled by a change in her name and a passage in which White notifies us, more or less explicitly, that she has become a different person. First she is Kitty Goose, daughter of a Norwich harness-maker with a social conscience and socialist ideas. Feeling herself excluded from her parents' closed circle of love for each other, she develops pretensions to her father's intellectualism, and self-consciously indulges her own literary leanings. As he did in *Happy Valley*, White catches character in a few telling details. Of Kitty he says, 'At night she lay with her hands above her head, so that her fingers, on waking, would look long, and interesting, and white' (*LD*, p. 16); or again: 'She crammed her head with Swinburnian similes and wove them, on hot, passionate evenings, into verses of her own. Perhaps she was creative. She borrowed a life of Christina Rossetti out of the public library to study symptoms' (p. 19).

Longing to bring forth art out of suffering, Kitty undertakes a sort of parody of the spiritual quest on which White sends so many later characters. She also shows herself the spiritual sister of *Happy Valley*'s Alys Browne. But White is tender with Kitty, as he was with his earlier heroine. There is more depth in both than is suggested by what White calls, in *Happy Valley*, their genteel, 'mauve' exteriors (p. 39). Although Kitty postures, there is a warm, sleepy animal life about her, and she can also sometimes penetrate the speciousness of her own motives.

For example, she is aware that snobbery figures in her decision to marry Willy Standish, whose family is highly placed. At the time, she genuinely loves him, but in becoming his wife she puts much of her genuine self behind her. In this, the first of her metamorphoses, she thinks,

> Now I am Catherine Standish. . . . She began to wear larger, droopy hats, because she felt changed with the changed name. She was conscious of her own impetus entering a room. She was less dumpy, lumpy, anxious, in fact, she was more Catherine Standish than Kitty Goose. This former tenant of her body remained behind in Norwich. . . .　(*LD*, p. 33)

She enters into 'the amusing business of marriage', which her husband finds 'so like an odd and unusually prolonged charade' (p. 34). Quickly the charade begins to tell on her, to sap her sense of the real and living, until she finds it 'sometimes difficult to believe in the substance of things, whether the furniture, or events, . . . the conversation she made with Willy, even their whole relationship' (p. 38). She has soon been reduced to a mere cipher of her former vibrant self, a 'detached shimmer . . . on the surface of facts, of events' (p. 39).

Rebirth is called for, but instead she conceives a child which she at once tries to wedge between herself and the recurring malaise. Through her husband's philandering and a second child, she repeatedly opts not to know, not even to speculate, but deliberately to 'prefer uncertainty' (p. 55).

Her capacity for life increasingly atrophied, Catherine is accompanied through this phase by Aubrey Silk, an exhausted *fin de siècle* phantom whose sole activity is a languid self-indulgence. Once a friend of her husband's, Aubrey squires her after they separate, and, following Willy's death in the First World War, he ritually and at regular intervals asks for her hand. Catherine just as ritually refuses him, because by this time she distrusts any emotion, no matter how pallid, and fears any connection. She prefers to wall herself away in her house, wait for tea, and listen to the cracking of her joints.

At this stage Catherine still has rare moments of uncomfortable self-awareness. In one of these, says White, 'she was faced with her own spuriousness, but that, after all, was a *chef-d'oeuvre*, her one and only, so much more elaborate than a child, so many more years of gestation, endless, endless' (p. 229). In a typically Whitean irony, she seems to be gestating her own death. It is born in the form of the saxophonist Wally Collins, whom even she recognizes as 'her own defeat' (p. 257). As Wally's 'old girl', she takes on her third and further abbreviated identity as Kate. Because Wally fills her emptiness, she assures herself, 'This is recompense enough for a collapse in dignity, for the defection of the interesting Mrs Catherine Standish . . . ' (p. 298).

On the grey sheets of Wally's unmade bed at Godiva Mansions, Kitty/Catherine/Kate succeeds in her attempt to lose what is left of herself (see p. 301), and, through 'destruction self-imposed and chosen', to effect the 'ultimate negation' (p. 306). When the spirit dies, the flesh naturally follows. Thus she undergoes her final reductive metamorphosis: 'depersonalized, anaesthetized. Mrs Standish became *the patient*' (p. 355) who quickly and uninspiringly dies of cancer.

So Mrs Standish gradually drains her reservoir of life until it is emptied. Her daughter Eden, on the other hand, dams up her life force until it bursts through in a destructive cataract. From her infancy, Eden is both perpetrator and victim of 'emotional storms' (p. 63). Named 'in a moment of romantic stress' (ibid.), she seems to suffer from that stress ever after. We see little of Eden as a child or adolescent and hear little of her except an occasional scream of rage and the earnest letter she sends her mother from school. The letter betrays a bottled-up energy desperately seeking an outlet.

Like her mother, Eden undergoes a series of metamorphoses, but, unlike Catherine, she retains through them all a core of identity called 'Eden'. Her first transformation occurs after her schooldays, when, 'In the space of a day, almost in the falling of a velour hat, you became a different person. You forgot the intermediate process, the chrysalis schoolgirl, out of which bursts the white, mysterious moth' (p. 150). In her letter to her mother, she had expressed her longing to be useful, but, once home, apathy supervenes. Then, in one of the series of epiphanic moments in which Eden's life is lived, she hears the singing of a Welsh cripple whom she connects with a bereaved and impoverished woman met during her schooldays. The conjunction has two outcomes: a sense of compassion which 'is oddly physical' (p. 153) and an awakened political conscience, quickly turned toward Marxism.

The self-absorbed, self-pitying Norman Maynard provides her with an opportunity to express that oddly physical compassion, and the pregnancy he leaves her with serves as impetus for her next incarnation. At the house of Mrs Angelotti, abortionist, she is again 'a different person, she was the Mrs Stevens chosen in the bus' (p. 178), but this hastily assumed identity cannot be maintained. Back at home, emptied of the child and with nothing to fill her inner void, she suffers a breakdown.

This point marks the nadir both of selfhood and vitality, a point at which Eden seems a kind of vacuum which must either fill or collapse. Appropriately, Aubrey Silk, a zombie himself, finances her convalescence in the Swiss Alps among other living dead. Here she meets Adelaide Blenkinsop, whose mind, body and being reflect the white nullity of the scenery. This whole section uses the winter landscape as did Lawrence in *Women in Love*:[7] to suggest a seductive, but potentially fatal vacancy, life slowed, blurred, and finally obliterated in the smothering snow. Thus Eden's decision to leave is a triumph, a 'coming alive', out of the 'lethal atmosphere of the Swiss landscape and of Adelaide Blenkinsop's conversation' (*LD*, p. 195). Eden is at last on the road to reclamation of self. Her subsequent refusals of Adelaide's dinner invitations and Elyot's acceptance of them operate as a kind of index to the ascendancy of life in her and the preponderance of death in him.

But Eden at once begins to squander the life she has recovered. As White puts it, 'There was a singular, feverish sense of waste running through Eden Standish's life. As if in her fear of an accusation of withholding, she was determined to give too much' (p. 197). In the grip of her fever she undergoes yet another incarnation through her love for Joe Barnett, a carpenter and nephew of the Standishes' housekeeper Julia Fallon. As Alys and Oliver's love did for them, Joe's love makes Eden real, whole and purposeful. It is Joe who focuses her vague sympathies into a distinct ethical and finally political philosophy, Joe who teaches her that the individual is secondary to some overriding purpose or design. It is also with Joe that she experiences sexual love as a positive force, a healing of the primordial breach. And it is Joe who provokes the outburst of Lawrentian ideology in which the novel's theme is explicitly and unequivocally stated.[8] Eden tells him,

> I believe, Joe, but not in the parties of politics, the exchange of one party for another, which isn't any exchange at all. Oh, I can believe, as sure as I can breathe, feel, in the necessity for change. But it's a change from wrong to right, which is nothing to do with category. I can believe in right as passionately as I have it in me to live. This is what I have to express, with you, with anyone, with everyone who has the same conviction. But passionately, Joe. We were not born to indifference. Indifference denies all the evidence of life. This is what I want to believe, I want to unite those who have the capacity for living, in any circumstance, and make it the one circumstance. I want to oppose them to the destroyers, to the dealers in words, to the diseased, to the most fatally diseased – the indifferent. That can be the only order. Without ideological labels. Labels set a limit at once. And there is no limit to man.　(pp. 270–1)

With these words, Eden defines and opposes the living and the dead.

White clearly means us to see Joe's relationship with Eden as positive and life-giving. At one point, he juxtaposes the love-making of Joe and Eden with that of Elyot and the metallic Muriel to point the difference between vitality and morbidity. While Eden becomes 'a pillar of warmth from which the cold receded' (p. 295), Elyot lies with Muriel 'passive, withdrawn, the whole core remote' (p. 286).

Eden's awareness of the ultimate difference between the living and the dead clearly has White's endorsement. But, when precept becomes practice, Eden allows the dichotomies to blur. By loving Joe, Eden believes she can bring the world to life. For Joe, however, Eden is not real life, but the garden, the earthly paradise which must be forsaken for the sick and needy outside. In this perception he is like Oliver, and, again like Oliver, he is reclaimed by that outside world. Thus he goes off to fight and be killed in the Spanish Civil War. His death prompts in Eden a final incarnation. Left 'blank' by his loss (p. 376), she none the less senses the stirrings of a new self. The imagery, as so often in this novel, is that of procreation: 'Remotely, inside her, something was still perfecting itself. Intent on this process of gestation, she let herself be led' (p. 377). She sees Joe, even in death, as entered upon one more 'state of becoming, of change' (ibid.).

But the self to which she subsequently gives birth is also destined for that ultimate becoming. Though in a different sense from her mother, she too is gestating death. She will also go to Spain to make what Elyot recognizes as the 'protest of self-destruction' (p. 379), to 'infuse into the dying body of the world' her 'more than blood' (p. 334). She will make the categorical mistake of believing that death gives rise to life.

White makes it clear that Eden will not return from Spain, and also that her passionate life could only spill itself in death. Having survived the spiritual death which threatened at her breakdown, Eden has accumulated ever more of life's energy without learning to channel it into what Elyot hopes is 'an intenser form of living' (p. 379). At the novel's end, she is still the child tossing on emotional storms.

Or, more accurately, she is this at the beginning, because it is here the novel opens. Elyot has just seen Eden off for Spain and experienced with her a moment of lowered barriers. He goes home from the train depot, muses about his own life and the lives of his mother and sister, and thereby gives rise to the novel. White uses exactly the same passage to initiate this process and to return us to Elyot's present near the end, framing his novel with an image of life's interpenetration and infinity which the text will teach Elyot to affirm. Sitting alone in the house, Elyot thinks of himself and it as

> two receptacles . . . the one containing the material possessions of those who had lingered in its rooms, the other the aspirations of those he had come in contact with. Even that emotional life he had not experienced himself, but sensed, seemed somehow to have grown explicit. It was as if this emanated from the walls to find interpretation and shelter in his mind. So that the two receptacles were clearly united now. They were like two Chinese boxes, one inside the other, leading to an infinity of other boxes, to an infinity of purpose. Alone, he was yet not

alone, uniting as he did the themes of so many other lives. (pp. 13, 382)

The theme of two of these lives has been failure: the failure to sustain life. One has lost her life through violent eruption, the other by slow erosion. Thus, Elyot's mother's and sister's lives have provided him with two instructive and complementary parables of failure. But Elyot, too, has a whole string of failures to his credit.

Elyot has been aptly called 'a younger Prufrock', in retreat from life.[9] Unlike Eden, he has little vitality, perhaps because his mother thought of him as a possession, a tactic, a bribe and a weapon, but rarely as a person. A crucial incident in his early life and one which may account in part of his emotional atrophy occurs on the night his father and mother separate. After an argument loud and violent enough to wake the boy, his father leaves and his mother comes to seek comfort from her child. In later situations where touch or tenderness is called for, Elyot seems to recoil because reminded of his mother's cloying, suffocating need and his father's desertion. Of a time when his mother asks him to sit on her lap, White writes, 'He did so unwillingly, sat there stiffly, allowed her to stroke his hair. It was too close, too close to the scent of darkness, and the slamming of a door' (p. 76).

As he grows older, Elyot puts ever greater distances between himself and others. He suspects that nothing can be shared, everyone is isolated, each is boxed up in himself. He has not yet understood that boxes can interlock. Emotional paralysis cripples him. When positive action is called for, as when Connie falls out of the mulberry tree, he is unable to produce it. Since he cannot act, others act for him, making his decisions, sending him to Germany and Cambridge. When forced to decide on a career, he adopts 'the intellectual puzzle as a substitute for living' (p. 185), and becomes a scholar. White calls him 'a raker of dust, a rattler of bones' (p. 187). He dwells among the dead, shut away in his room, and shrinks from the life that wafts up from the street below.

Like his mother and sister, Elyot is subjected to a series of relationships, but for most of the novel these do less to alter his essential self than to confirm what is already incipient. The German girl Hildegard uses him to express her love for someone else, while he and Muriel Raphael calculatedly use each other. There is also a third woman, Connie Tiarks, the emotional eiderdown of soft, stifling love. The alternatives of Muriel and Connie – who seem to stand for death by freezing or asphyxiation – are connected in Elyot's mind with the little box that Wally Collins brings to the house, the box Elyot believes is a present from Muriel but which is actually from Connie. The box acts as an image for Elyot both of Muriel's opaque brittleness and the snug enclosure in which Connie would confine him. Beyond this, the box also suggests the 'static, self-contained' nature of a life which attempts to refuse all relationships (p. 265).

The most crucial relationship Elyot refuses is that with his full self. He would deny much of what makes up a whole human being, especially whatever smacks of feeling or illogicality. White explains, 'He had rejected the irrational . . . the possibility of looking inward and finding a dark room' (p. 211).

Elyot has glimpsed another way of life; he has experienced one sphere to oppose to all his sharp-cornered boxes. As a child he finds a place called Ard's Bay:

> It was an almost enclosed, almost circular bay. He spent many hours looking into pools. . . . He took up the smooth stones in his hand, the red and the mauve stones, that shone when you took them out of the water. And standing on the rim of the bay, holding the rounded stones in his hand, everything felt secure and solid, the gentle, enclosed basin of water, the sturdy trees that sprouted from the sides, his own legs planted in the moist sand. At Ard's Bay everything was plain sailing. You looked into water and saw the shape of things.   (p. 104)

But the pebbles he brings from the bay grow dry and dull.[10] He decides the bay must be isolated from quotidian life, and it is not until the novel circles back on itself that the bay again becomes accessible to his experience. By this time, the moment of his farewell to Eden, Elyot too has turned back to recover something of the lost self. As he touches Eden, he can once more touch the bay (p. 381). The compartmentalizing boxes of his life have begun to round and interlock.

This moment stands as the culmination of the first phase in Elyot's awakening to life. Unlike his mother and sister, he does not undergo a series of incarnations; it takes him the whole novel to get himself properly born. The process perhaps begins when he meets Eden's Joe and senses the couple's full, fleshly reality as against his own attentuated and cerebral substance. It continues in the intimations of mystery he cannot quite expunge from his life and in the discovery that Muriel has not sent him the box. One box, at least has been escaped: 'It was like discarding an illusion. . . . It was like recovering part of yourself' (p. 315). Milestones on the road to life now start to accumulate.

His awareness expands. He perceives that his mother is in essence dead and has been for some time. He has a dream in which his eyes become a mirror that reflects his own sterility (p. 323). At one point, he feels anticipation, and the next morning recalls a conversation with a Spaniard. It was, he thinks,

> As if the Spaniard were presenting the choice of the two ways, of the living or the dead. You wanted instinctively to close the eyes. . . . Because the alternative, to recognize the pulse beyond the membrane, the sick heartbeat, or the gangrenous growth, this was too much, even at the risk of sacrificing awareness, and the other moments, the drunken, disorderly passions of existence, that created but at the same time consumed.
>
> This morning it was as clear as glass, if the choice no less bewildering. To recognize the sickness and accept the ecstasy. (p. 326)

Later that morning, when Joe comes to announce his departure for Spain, Elyot struggles to accept the emotions newly aroused in him: 'the sickness and the ecstasy at once' (p. 328). Like Oliver Halliday, he is emerging from anaesthesia to an awareness of life's full emotional spectrum.

Although the reader may well complain that all this comes about too quickly and with unconvincing ease, White apparently intends that Elyot's recognition of his own failures and those of his mother and sister should have brought him a long way toward life. But it is not yet far enough. For all this progress still leaves him bidding Eden goodbye at the station – still leaves him, that is, at the novel's beginning. He must undergo another crucial failure.

Walking home from the station he catches sight of a drunk on the kerb. He has already begun to reinstate the distance, the 'remoteness' between himself and others, even Eden. In other words, he is starting to die again. The drunk lurches off the kerb; Elyot sees that the man will be hit by a bus and knows he must act. But he remains immobile and the drunk is struck. Immediately, he feels that 'He had failed', but is unable to 'seize on the significance of this' (p. 6). Back in the empty house, Elyot finds that the face of the drunk on the pavement persists, having 'asked for admission' (p. 13). The whole of his ensuing reverie, which constitutes the entire novel, may be viewed as Elyot's attempt to understand the meaning of his failure and to admit the stranger.

In this effort he succeeds, and the experience brings him fully alive. White describes it as a birth and a waking, but, as he did in *Happy Valley*, he also uses the imagery of expansion towards infinity. In these final passages, boxes have dissolved into enlarging spheres. It is worth noting that Elyot's expansion entails an accumulation of selves and an acknowledgement of relationship, processes which will be central to *The Aunt's Story*:

> He had sat how long, since the station, in the empty house? A queasy drunk still sidled uneasily along the carpet's edge. You accepted him now. It got to being part of yourself, said Joe, like Eden's disappearing glove, like the face that crumbled under rouge, like Onkel Rudi's gramophone, as if you can keep it parcelled out, because it's right here, Elyot, sure as ever there's right and wrong. Or not so particularly confined, it flowed, it overflowed, a gritty protest of the walls that opened out, rain that passed across the mouth, the wheeze of mortar falling, and of powdered brick. All this had served its purpose, you felt. (*LD*, p. 382)

He leaves the house and boards a bus, deliberately associating himself now with the vehicle and those aboard it which he had earlier shunned:

> A bus received Elyot Standish. It was any bus. He was bound nowhere in particular. There were no reservations of time or place, no longer even the tyranny of a personal routine. It was enough to feel a darkness, a distance unfurling. There was no end to this in the bus, trundling down its dark tunnel, in which the faces smiled gravely out of sleep, the mouths almost spoke. If only to touch these almost sentient faces into life, to reach

with your hand, to listen to the voices, like the voices of people
who wake and find they have come to the end of a journey,
saying: Then we are here, we have slept, but we have really
got here at last.

He yawned. He felt like someone who had been asleep and
had only just woken.   (p. 383)

In the imagery of enlargement, acquisition, unification, extension,
and awakening, the author depicts Elyot opening himself to life.
As was also true for Oliver Halliday, a crucial failure and his
understanding of it have supplied the key to far greater success:
the affirmation and assumption of life's full dimensions.

One critic says gently that *The Living and the Dead* is 'very much
of its period'. [11] Elyot's name, the continued use of Joycean interior
monologue, and the fact that the title seems to derive either from
Eliot or Joyce may be adduced in support of this claim. [12] There
is also White's frequent use of two Woolfian images: the well-
known one of the envelope of personality and the less familiar
'vast nest of Chinese boxes' from 'Kew Gardens'. Finally, there
is the awareness, albeit shallow, [13] of period politics and ideological
conflicts – Communism and the Spanish Civil War – which figure
to such an extent in no other White novel.

But, clearly, D. H. Lawrence is the major influence here.
The novel demonstrates that White shares with Lawrence an
appreciation of the irrational and instinctual, and an acute
awareness that, through retreat to sterile intellectualism, full life
is obviated and betrayed. Elyot Standish cowering in his cocoon
of a room, rummaging the intellectual past for protection against
the present, exemplifies Lawrence's insular intellectual, and
headstrong Eden might have been on her way to becoming a
Gudrun had she not met her equally Lawrentian lover Joe. Joe
teaches her Lawrence's lesson about the importance of living
passionately and acknowledging the needs of the body and heart,
as well as those of the mind. White's ideological affinities with
Lawrence are nowhere so plain and pervasive as in this novel.

Technically, *The Living and the Dead* is an advance over *Happy
Valley*. Point of view is handled with more assurance. The narrator
shifts his attention among the three major characters, usually
allowing the perspective of one to dominate in any given chapter,
but he also subtly alters the balance so that Catherine's viewpoint

predominates in the early pages, Eden's in the middle of the novel, and Elyot's at the end. With characterization he is not so deft. Catherine emerges as the novel's most compelling character, an effect clearly unintended. And Eden's characterization is insufficient for the importance of the role White wants to assign her. But the novel's most serious fault is that a dichotomous view of experience has replaced the dialectic which was developing in *Happy Valley*. What we find here White had described in a poem: 'Life that is made too bright by the shadow of Death' ('Lines Written after an Encounter with Death in a Country Lane', *Ploughman*). The greys are gone from *The Living and the Dead*.

The technical failures of this novel, like the different failures of *Happy Valley*, do not reflect the deliberate assumption of limits which White will later impose on himself, but rather the missteps of apprenticeship. Perhaps White's own assessment of the novel is the best summary statement on it. In an interview he says, 'It's fatal to hurry into a book; the book I like least, *The Living and the Dead*, I had to hurry because of the war.'[14] With his next novel, he apparently had all the time he needed.

THE AUNT'S STORY

In *The Aunt's Story* (1948), White finds his mature voice. Influences have been absorbed to the point where they are no longer discernible as such. For example, what had still, in *The Living and the Dead*, amounted to an awkward and mannered handling of interior monologue has been replaced in *The Aunt's Story* by a free and fluid passage between external and internal 'realities', the worlds before and behind the perceiving eye, with equal value and veracity granted to both. In this, style mirrors the larger vision, and it is this correspondence of part to whole which impresses us as a marked improvement upon *The Living and the Dead*. Nor is our attention diluted by a number of characters, some of whom cannot bear the thematic weight White wants them to shoulder. Instead, he centres the reader's attention wholly on one character, Theodora Goodman, with the result that she comes alive as no White character before her.

Moreover, White here takes up for the first time what will become a subject of consuming interest: the person who has and recognizes a hypertrophied capacity to know and experience. Oliver Halliday and Elyot Standish were steps toward Theodora

Goodman, and they were forced to learn hard lessons. But they were not the conscious, deliberate questers of the lineage that begins with Theodora and continues through Stan Parker, Voss and Laura, the four Riders, Hurtle Duffield and Elizabeth Hunter. (Arthur Brown, Ellen Roxburgh and Eddie Twyborn present more vexing problems, which will be taken up later.) Except for rare moments when Elyot dimly senses a 'mystery of juxtaposition' about the world (*LD*, p. 211), these early protagonists are not plagued as the visionaries are by the sense of something veiled but evocative, some ultimate reality 'beyond the bone' (*AS*, p. 57). Though Oliver and Elyot are finally forced to know, they do not, like Theodora, seek to know. Theodora Goodman, in other words, is White's first Faust.

As this central subject comes to the fore, the theme of failure is also treated in a new and more integral way. In the earlier novels, failure acted as an impetus. Oliver's failure to evade life's dialectic permitted him eventually to acknowledge that dialectic and its importance, while Elyot's failure to save the drunk prompted the long reverie from which he woke to life. But *The Aunt's Story* failure is not merely facilitating; it is imperative. Theodora's failure structures her entire experience. And, as hers is the prototypical Whitean quest, so too is her failure paradigmatic for later White characters. It is the failure to destroy herself.

Virtually every critic of *The Aunt's Story* quotes the passage near the end of Part One in which Theodora longs to annihilate 'the great monster Self' and to achieve 'that desirable state . . . which resembles, one would imagine, nothing more than air or water' (p. 127). The usual procedure is to see White as endorsing this project and then to trace Theodora's destruction of self to her end, in a small-town madhouse somewhere in the midwestern United States.[15] This interpretative strategy is tempting, if only because a number of characters in other works seem to undertake analogous tasks. For example, in White's first published story, 'The Twitching Colonel' (1937), the Colonel decides, 'I shall strip myself, the onion-folds of prejudice, till standing naked though conscious I see myself complete or else consumed like the Hindu conjuror who is translated into space' (p. 606). Similarly, Mary Hare in *Riders in the Chariot* imagines, 'Eventually I shall discover what is at the centre, if enough of me is peeled away' (p. 58). And, in *Voss*, Brendan Boyle of Jildra insists that his own quest, 'to explore the depths of one's own repulsive nature, is more than irresistible – it is necessary. . . . To peel down to the last layer. . . . There is always another, and yet another, of more exquisite sublety' (p. 165).

In Brendan Boyle's case, however, two things should make us question White's sanction of this and similar programmes. First, Boyle likens his obsession with his own sordid self to Voss's compulsion to reach ever 'deeper layers, of irresistible disaster' (p. 165). But White's intent in this novel is radically to revise the goal of Voss's quest such that it becomes humility and 'human status' (p. 390), rather than the apotheosis and apocalypse he originally seeks. If Boyle's quest parallels Voss's, then its value is doubtful. Secondly, Boyle and his life at Jildra have been presented as a demonic parody of Sanderson and his idyllic existence at Rhine Towers, where the exploring party first pauses for rest and supplies. If Rhine Towers is a kind of heaven, Jildra is hell, and we would not expect White to subscribe to the devil's definition of the nature of spiritual inquiry. Thus White's position in regard to the peeling-away, stripping, or destruction of the self is at best problematical. There are obvious dangers in extrapolating from one novel to another, particularly from a later to an earlier one, but even within *The Aunt's Story* White provides ample evidence that Theodora's hopes of destroying the 'great monster Self' will not and should be realized.

In the first of the novel's three sections, Theodora suffers a series of deaths, or diminutions of self, most of them suicides. The novel begins with one such death; its startling opening sentence is, 'But old Mrs Goodman did die at last' (*AS*, p. 3). Theodora's mother's death is also her own, since it saps her sense of identity. But this event occurs when Theodora is middle-aged. Chronologically, her first death takes place when she shoots the little hawk.

Previously she has identified herself with the hawk, but in a way which stresses and exults in the predatory side of all natures, including her own:

Once the hawk flew down, straight and sure, out of the skeleton forest. He was a little hawk, with a reddish-golden eye, that looked at her as he stood on the sheep's carcass, and coldly tore through the dead wool. The little hawk tore and paused, tore and paused. Soon he would tear through the wool and the maggots and reach the offal in the belly of the sheep.

Theodora looked at the hawk. She could not judge his act, because her eye had contracted, it was reddish-gold, and her curved face cut the wind. Death, said Father, lasts for a long time. Like the bones of the sheep that would lie, and dry, and whiten, and clatter under horses. But the act of the hawk, which she watched, hawk-like, was a moment of shrill beauty that rose above the endlessness of bones. The red eye spoke of worlds that were brief and fierce.   (pp. 26–7)

Watching the hawk, Theodora celebrates the beauty of brevity and ferocity, the beauty which inheres in life's energy even when violently expressed. This is a side of themselves which most would prefer to ignore, but Theodora is no ordinary child. Moreover, her environment has schooled her in the interdependence of life and death, an interdependence which *The Living and the Dead* had seemed to deny.

The farm where she grows up is a serene and fruitful place, whose garden has sprawled into luxuriance, and where her childhood is enacted as an 'epoch of roselight' (*AS*, p. 15). But the garden is on the south side of the house. On the north is its complement: the pines, which express in their ceaseless 'motion' a 'brooding and vague discontent', and beyond them the dead 'abstractions of trees with their roots in Ethiopia' (p. 14).

The Goodmans' predecessors on the farm had given it the fanciful name 'Meroë', because its setting among volcanic hills evoked the Ethiopian Meroë, 'a dead place' of 'suffocating cinder breath' (pp. 16–17). By Theodora's time, 'The hills round ... had conspired with the name, to darken, or to split deeper open their black rock, or to frown with a fiercer, Ethiopian intensity' (p. 13). This imagery suggests hell or death, but, as Northrop Frye points out, Ethiopia is one of the Classical locales of a paradisal Golden Age.[16] Johnson's *Rasselas* also sets the earthly paradise in Abyssinia, another name for Ethiopia.[17] Here, then as elsewhere in White's work, we find that imagery can assume either or both of what Frye has called demonic and apocalyptic modes.[18] Imagery reinforces vision: life and death, joy and sorrow, heaven and hell, are inextricable from each other and ultimately subsumed by the larger scheme. The dichotomous view of *The Living and the Dead* has given way again to the dialectics of *Happy Valley*.

As Theodora discovers, there are days when 'the roselight

hardened and blackened' (*AS*, p. 21). Through her childhood, she sees the double realities, life and death, inseparably juxtaposed. For the White of this and later novels, death is life's precursor and prerequisite. As Mary Hare comes to understand in *Riders in the Chariot*, 'disintegration was the only permanent, perhaps the only desirable state' (p. 464). It is a mark of Theodora's status as apprentice illuminate that she knows this and cannot 'subtract' the grub at the heart of the rose 'from the sum total of the garden' (*AS*, p. 15).

If Theodora understands this much, even as a child, it is perhaps more credible that she seems to understand the significance of her action in shooting the little hawk. Describing the event, White says, 'She took aim, and it was like aiming at her own red eye' (p. 66). Later she reflects, 'I was wrong . . . but I shall continue to destroy myself, right down to the last of my several lives' (ibid.). Since the hawk seems to stand for a ferocious will to live, its killing fittingly initiates a larger suicidal project.

When Theodora shoots the hawk, she is with Frank Parrott, who had earlier missed it. Although it is doubtful that Theodora ever could have returned the affection of this phlegmatic man, the shooting-incident puts an end to the tentative interest Frank has been developing in her. He subsequently marries Theodora's sister Fanny, becoming 'the father of her complacency' (p. 260), as well as her children. Later in Theodora's life, a similar incident ends her relationship with Huntly Clarkson, a more likely suitor. Kind, affluent, cultured and alone, Clarkson is intrigued by the challenge of Theodora's elusiveness. But for Theodora he is less a challenge than a threat. She associates him with 'the rich sinuous sensations of silk and sables' (p. 102), and, while these are seductive, they also menace her with suffocation. She is afraid of what Huntly wants to give, and must therefore kill his love in her as she did the hawk's predatory energy.

The suicides are accomplished in much the same way. While attending an agricultural show with Clarkson and some friends, she watches the men try their luck at a shooting-gallery, with little success. Then Theodora picks up the rifle:

They watched the clay ducks shatter each time Theodora fired, and it was as if each time a secret life was shattered, of which they had not been aware, and probably never would have,

> but they resented the possibility removed. It was something
> mysterious, shameful, and grotesque. (p. 118)

Again, Theodora has destroyed part of herself. To ensure that
the reader will recognize the parallel with the earlier incident,
White has her immediately recall 'the swift moment of the hawk,
when her eye had not quivered' (ibid.).

She commits still another suicide soon after. With her sister
married and her father dead, it has fallen to her to take care of
their aging mother, a cantankerous and cruel woman of whom
White says, 'It was the great tragedy of Mrs Goodman's life that
she had never done a murder. Her husband had escaped into the
ground, and Theodora into silences' (p. 93). When Theodora
confronts Mrs Goodman with her viciousness, the mother turns
the accusation back on her daughter, making Theodora suspect
a 'core of evil' in herself (p. 119). Perhaps in an attempt both to
confirm and eradicate that core, Theodora thinks of stabbing her
mother. She does not, because of a dim sense that 'this . . . does
not cut the knot' (p. 121), but she accepts the guilt for the act
none the less, believing 'it is the same thing, blood is only an
accompaniment' (ibid.). White adds, 'So neither Mrs Goodman
nor Huntly Clarkson had survived in more than shape' (p. 122).
She has excised both from her life, and with them vital pieces of
herself.

In fact, of the several deaths Theodora endures in Part One,
only one is not self-inflicted. This is the death of her father,
whose unfinished Odyssean quest she inherits.[19] After his death,
Theodora is left 'thin as grey light, as if she had just died. She
would not wake the others. It was still too terrible to tell, too
private an experience. As if she were to go into the room and
say: Mother, I am dead, I am dead' (p. 80). Thus this death,
too, even though unsought, is felt as a diminution of self.

Counterpointing the series of deaths in Part One are a number
of incidents in which Theodora's life is deepened and intensified.
These moments are brought about by contact with other initiates,
people who recognize her as one of their own. First of these is the
old prospecting friend of her father's, the Man who was Given
his Dinner. He prophesies that she will see deeply and be broken,
but perhaps survive. Later there is the Greek cellist Moraïtis,
who acknowledges that they are 'compatriots in the country of
the bones', where things are bare and stripped, and 'It is easier

to see' (pp. 106–7). Theodora listens to Moraïtis in concert, and by the agency of music achieves a kind of meta-sexual union with him, whose issue is her spiritual child Lou, daughter of her sister Fanny.

It is from Lou that Theodora subsequently takes her meagre and second-hand identity: 'this thing a spinster which, at best, becomes that institution an aunt' (p. 4). But apparently even this is too full an identity. The project of self-destruction is ruthlessly pursued, and at the end of Part One we find her denying Lou in hopes of vacating herself. Freed by her mother's death, she has reached that place described by Olive Schreiner in *The Story of an African Farm*, from which White takes the epigraph for Part One: 'that solitary land of the individual experience, in which no fellow footfall is ever heard'. But this is not the end of her journey.

Theodora may have emptied her present, but she is still clogged with her past. In Part Two of the novel, '*Jardin Exotique*', she attempts to discard this too by imaginatively projecting herself into the lives of others and reconstituting her past out of bits of their memories.[20] A strikingly apt description of what happens in this section can be found in the writings of Carl Jung:[21]

> The psychological rule says that when an inner situation is not made conscious, it happens outside, as fate. That is to say, when the individual remains undivided and does not become conscious of his inner contradictions, the world must perforce act out the conflict and be torn in opposite halves.[22]

Theodora thus enacts her own conflicts and contradictions through the agency of others. Only in Part Three of the novel does she learn to accept the fact that she herself is 'torn in two' (*AS*, p. 280).

Part Two is set in the French Hôtel du Midi where Theodora rests after aimlessly wandering through Europe. Here, as in Part One, the 'opposite halves' of reality and the dialectic into which they enter are reflected in her environment. The hotel's *jardin exotique*, which is 'static, rigid, the equation of a garden' (p. 138), and the sea, which suggests the 'continuity of being' (p. 179), take on the respective implications of the dead abstractions of trees and the rose garden at Meroë. They function as repositories for the imagery of death and life, both forcing themselves upon the consciousness.

Within a context which insists on dialectic and doubleness, Theodora is finally unable to pursue her quest for the ultimate unification of emptiness. Instead of expunging her past, she begins to incorporate it. Through her relationship with Katina she learns to express in positive action the love she had felt for Lou, but she also learns that nothing can shield the beloved from the hard lessons of experience, whether taught by natural disaster or by human duplicity. In her relationship with Mrs Rapollo, Theodora learns to feel the pity she could never give to her mother. White makes the linkage by associating with both women the imagery of mineral encrustation. The resolution which Sokolnikov facilitates is less clear. He may help her to mediate between reality and illusion, or to see, as Holstius later tells her, that these are finally interchangeable. Sokolnikov also instigates the nautilus theft, an incident which provides Theodora with further proof that perfection is 'breakable' (p. 232) and that it is impossible 'to hold' (p. 211).

As these others help Theodora accept rather than expel her past,[23] she does the same for them. Mrs Rapallo confesses to Theodora that her lovely daughter Gloria, the Principessa of the brilliant marriage, is wholly imaginary. More importantly, Theodora helps Sokilnikov expiate his guilt over the desertion of his dying sister. Becoming his sister Ludmilla, Theodora relives with him the night during the Russian Revolution of 1917 when Ludmilla was shot.

This re-enactment of Sokolnikov's past also gives Theodora, as Ludmilla, still another chance to die. But this time, she protests her death. White says, 'Her life was moving around her. She heard a burst of pigeons released from the silver bellies of the trees beside the lake. She bit her mouth for the loveliness of many heavy, breaking summers' (p. 209). She is subsequently able to tell Sokolnikov that death is as simple, clear, and empty as a bottle which they then agree to discard (p. 210). The suggestion is that both have begun to renounce self-destruction.

From the standpoint of Theodora's failure to destroy herself, her most crucial relationship at the Hôtel du Midi is that with Lieselotte, for Lieselotte enacts her own suicidal project. She tells Theodora, 'We have destroyed so much, but we have not destroyed enough. We must destroy everything, everything, even ourselves' (p. 167). Her relationships with others are as malignant as that with self, particularly her sado-masochistic affair with

Wetherby, the poet *manqué*. In view of Lieselotte's destructiveness, it is appropriate that the fire which razes the Hôtel du Midi should not only consume Lieselotte, but be started by her, in a moment of fury when she hurls an oil lamp at Wetherby.

When the fire breaks out, Lieselotte appeals in panic to Theodora. But Theodora cannot shake off a strange sort of lethargy in which she admires the beauty of Lieselotte's terror, yet cannot help her. What she does instead is to recover the garnet ring left her by her mother. White says, 'It was rather an ugly little ring, but part of the flesh' (p. 249). In accepting the garnet, she may also have accepted her mother as part of herself,[24] but the affirmation further functions to repudiate Lieselotte, the death wish.

Because Lieselotte incarnates all that is suicidal in Theodora, she must be denied and abandoned. In the purgative fire she ignites, all that is fever-ridden or necrotic in the Hôtel du Midi (that is, in Theodora) is incinerated. The living – Sokolnikov and Katina – are preserved, in part, White suggests, by the instrumentality of Theodora's now active affection. Outside the still blazing hotel, she feels herself released and contemplates her homecoming.

The epigraph for Part Two of the novel is from Henry Miller and speaks of the 'great fragmentation of maturity', a 'split[ting] into myriad fragments'. This Theodora has endured in the mistaken assumption that she could thereby dispose of her identity. But in the final words of this section Theodora tells Katina, 'We must join the others. Listen. They are calling us' (p. 254). She is beginning to hear the call of her many selves, the call to join or reunite the fragments. That call is answered in Part Three.

The Hôtel du Midi, then, is a kind of midpoint in Theodora's pilgrimage toward self-recovery, less a hell than a purgatory. Part Three functions to reintegrate her and to bring her home. This section is called 'Holstius', after the imaginary mentor who completes Theodora's rehabilitation. White has indicated that he took this name from the German word *Holz*, in English 'wood',[25] and he does give to Holstius the 'ingrained humility', purity and sturdiness he associates with wood (p. 281). But I suspect that the name's suggestion of 'wholeness' also appealed to White, for this is his gift to Theodora.

As Part Three opens, we find Theodora travelling by train

through midwestern America, on her way back to Australia. In one finely wrought passage, she perceives the landscape as a symphony:

> Sometimes against the full golden theme of corn and the whiter pizzicato of the telephone wires there was a counterpoint of houses. Theodora Goodman sat. The other side of the incessant train she could read the music off. There were the single notes of houses, that gathered into gravely structural phrases. There was a smooth passage of ponds and trees. There was a big brass barn. All the square faces of the wooden houses, as they came, overflowed with solemnity, that was a solemnity of living, a passage of days. Where children played with tins, or a girl waited at a window, or calves lolloped in long grass, it was a frill of flutes twisted round a higher theme, to grace, but only grace, the solemnity of living and of days. There were now the two coiled themes. There was the flowing corn song, and the deliberate accompaniment of houses, which did not impede, however structural, because it was part of the same integrity of purpose and of being.   (p. 261)

The harmony of landscape, in which antitheses blend without muting each other, hints of the nature of reality as Holstius will later present it. But Theodora is not yet ready to hear it. Instead, she senses her own discordance and blames the cacophony on her still strident self.

In one last and misguided attempt to subdue that stridency, she leaves the train at some anonymous siding and begins to divest herself of all remnants of identity. She tears up her train and steamship tickets, and, when the mountain road she has randomly chosen brings her to the Johnson cabin, she gives a false name. In the Johnson boy, Zack, she recognizes another spiritual child of her own, like Lou and Katina, but she refuses the attachment which seems offered. Finally she discards even her hat with its emblematic black gauze rose.

Leaving the Johnsons' she walks on up the mountain and comes to a deserted shack. The shack is reminiscent of the madman's cabin near Meroë, and the whole setting recalls the people and places of her childhood. Like Meroë, the house which seems immediately her own is set amidst disintegrating hills, and is flanked on one side by louring pine trees and on the other by deciduous growth. The hallucinatory Holstius also recapitulates her past by combining aspects of all the men who have been important to her: like her father, he is associated with trees (pp. 16 and 19); he reminds her of the Man who was Given his Dinner (p. 279); and, much as Moraïtis once did, Holstius will play upon 'her own instrument some final, if also fatal, music' (p. 284).

In this setting of the restored past, Theodora can begin to accept what the entire novel has been demonstrating: that 'true permanence' consists of a flux between irreducible and abiding antitheses, 'a state of multiplication and division' or 'the eternal complement of skeleton and spawn' (pp. 286–7). No longer, as was true in *The Living and the Dead*, can one antithesis eradicate another. With Holstius's help, she can also see that her condition is analogous. Observing that she is 'torn in two', Holstius tells her, 'I expect you to accept the two irreconcilable halves', and explains,

> You cannot reconcile joy and sorrow. . . . Or flesh and marble, or illusion and reality, or life and death. For this reason, Theodora Goodman, you must accept. And you have already found that one constantly deludes the other into taking fresh shapes, so that there is sometimes little to choose between the reality of illusion and the illusion of reality. Each of your several lives is evidence of this. (p. 280)

The challenge, then, is not to nullify the self, but to acknowledge the proliferation of selves and the conflicts and contradictions they entail.

When Theodora absorbs this knowledge, her moment of illumination is described, as it was for Oliver and Elyot, in terms of accumulation and expansion. But, in Theodora's case, what she acquires is explicitly the profusion of selves she had tried to deny. White says of Theodora at this moment,

> In the peace that Holstius spread throughout her body and the speckled shade of surrounding trees, there was no end to the lives of Theodora Goodman. These met and parted, met and parted, movingly. They entered into each other, so that the impulse for music in Katina Pavlou's hands, and the steamy exasperation of Sokolnikov, and Mrs Rapallo's baroque and narcotized despair were the same and understandable. And in

the same way that the created lives of Theodora Goodman
were interchangeable, the lives into which she had entered,
making them momently dependent for love or hate, owing her
this portion of their fluctuating personalities, whether George
or Julia Goodman, only apparently decreased, or Huntly
Clarkson, or Moraïtis, or Lou, or Zack, these were the lives of
Theodora Goodman, these too.   (pp. 286–7)

Accepting her multiple selves, she has enlarged to become what
one writer calls 'encyclopaedic'.[26]

At this point Holstius disappears, reincorporated as one of
these many selves. Soon the concerned, well-meaning Johnsons
arrive with a doctor who will oversee Theodora's admission to a
local mental institution. As this section's epigraph from Olive
Schreiner suggests, that pitch of reality to which Theodora has
attained looks to the normal world like madness. Holstius has
warned her of this, and Theodora accepts it. More importantly,
she accepts the restoration of her hat which the Johnsons return
to her. The novel ends with these enigmatic words:

> So Theodora Goodman took her hat and put it on her head,
> as it was suggested she should do. Her face was long and yellow
> under the great black hat. The hat sat straight, but the doubtful
> rose trembled and glittered, leading a life of its own.   (p. 290)

Several key points are made or implied by these sentences. First,
the rose seems to stand for Theodora, who has been trying to
lead a life of her own since the novel's first page, that is, since
her mother's death. Each of her crucial moves – away from
Sydney when her mother dies, away from the Hôtel du Midi
after the fire, off the train in America, and out of the Johnsons'
house – has been inspired by a search for freedom, especially the
freedom of self-annihilation. It is a typically Whitean irony that
she should attain the greatest degree of freedom, the freedom
conferred not by self-annihilation but by full being, at the moment
when she is about to be most closely confined. A second suggestion
is made by the juxtaposition of yellow and black, rose and black,
for these are the antithetical colours associated with Meroë and
its intimations of life and death, process and stasis. Particularly
in the black rose, White yokes but does not resolve the antitheses,
thereby culminating a pervasive pattern of imagery in a way
which abets the novel's vision. But most important for the present

purposes is the passage's implication that in putting on the hat Theodora has resumed her now enormously intricate identity. She has not only failed to destroy herself, but has finally stopped trying.

Yet the novel does not award Theodora an unambiguous triumph. Although her vastly expanded emotional–mental–spiritual being may survive and even flourish in the madhouse cell Holstius predicts for her, the reader cannot help but pity her this fate and regret the fact that she is to be walled away from those many others she has finally learned to touch. We are uncertain how to respond to her confinement, and our uncertainty derives from a new evasiveness on White's part. Clearly Elyot Standish's awakening to life was to be applauded, and the ultimate significance of Alys and Oliver's love was made equally clear. But in *The Aunt's Story* White leaves such final determinations to the reader, a tactic he will use increasingly and even more disturbingly in later fiction.

It should also be noticed that the many lives of Theodora Goodman are both masculine and feminine. In fact, long before she attains the comprehensiveness which supersedes sexual distinctions, White establishes her essential androgyny. As a child she enjoys traditionally masculine pursuits, and some of her parents' friends think she 'should have been a boy' (p. 25). As an adult she develops a slight moustache, and is sometimes called a bloke in skirts. In one of her dreams she appears as a man calling himself 'Epaphroditos', or 'beloved of Aphrodite' (pp. 199–200). Theodora can thus be seen as among the first in a series of Whitean hermaphrodites, a series which at least one critic would begin even earlier with the masculinely named Sidney Furlow and Vic Moriarty of *Happy Valley*.[27] In *The Aunt's Story*, White uses the imagery of androgyny in the traditional way, described by Joseph Campbell as a means of recalling a prelapsarian unity and of entering a realm in which all dualities are encompassed.[28] It is a concept to which he will frequently recur, continuing to remark and celebrate the depth and subtlety of character which 'comes from the masculine principle in . . . women, the feminine in . . . men' (*FG*, p. 155).

When asked to name his favourites among his novels, White always mentions *The Aunt's Story*.[29] In an interview published in 1969, he suggests that his preference is a way of compensating for what he feels has been the book's neglect.[30] But there are surely other reasons the novel means so much to him. One may be that it was written during the time he was deciding to repatriate,[31] and experiments with symbolic uses of the Australian landscape which are further developed in *The Tree of Man* and *Voss*. He also uses the novel to address questions he must have been asking himself about the importance of recovering one's past and of establishing a sense of home.

Still other reasons for the book's importance to him are suggested by an autobiographical sketch published in the centenary issue of the *Bulletin* (January 1980) and later expanded into his 'self-portrait', *Flaws in the Glass*. In both he tells the story of the 'Mad Woman', in the 'great hat she always wore', who scavenged for food in the Whites' garbage bins. One night the boy came across her in the garden, stealing not food, but handfuls of guelder roses. One of the servants was called and wrestled with her. Later that same night, the child was taken to the theatre. White remembers,

> all around me in the plush tiers of the theatre families were offering one another chocolates and smiles and enjoying the predicaments and final apotheosis of a waif-heroine into the wife of a millionaire. For the first time I was a skeleton at the Australian feast. I could not have told about it, and went out of my way to present the normalcy and smiles expected of me, while drawn back into the dusk, and storm of shattered guelder roses, enveloping the Mad Woman and myself.[32]

Theodora differs in many respects from the down and out alcoholic White describes here, and, as he goes on to say in *Flaws in the Glass*, she is more directly based on his godmother, Gertrude Morrice (pp. 24–5). None the less, the incident may be the Jamesian germ of *The Aunt's Story*. Thin and sallow Theodora is also a skeleton at the Australian feast and the first of many that White will treat tenderly. Moreover, what she seeks is less sustenance than something akin to guelder roses.

Finally, *The Aunt's Story* is important because it marks White's coming of age as an artist. The novel is built upon the idea of a necessary failure, the failure to empty or evade the self, a failure which opens the way toward wholeness. White will use this and related patterns again and again in subsequent fiction. In fact in his very next novel, *The Tree of Man* (1955), the theme finds its first explicit statement.

THE TREE OF MAN

Seven years passed between what White felt to be the disappointing reception of *The Aunt's Story* and the publication of *The Tree of Man* (1955). During this period, there were times, White confesses, when he considered ceasing to write altogether.[33] But, as he explains in his 1958 essay 'The Prodigal Son', what he saw as the vacuity and mediocrity of modern Australian life suddenly overwhelmed him and he began to plan another novel. He says of it,

> Because the void I had to fill was so immense, I wanted to try to suggest in this book every possible aspect of life, through the lives of an ordinary man and woman. But at the same time I wanted to discover the extraordinary behind the ordinary, the mystery and poetry . . . .[34]

In an interview given fifteen years later, he clarifies what he meant by 'mystery' and the 'extraordinary behind the ordinary', indicating that *The Tree of Man* reflects a recovered religious faith:

> If I say I had no religious tendencies between adolescence and *The Tree of Man*, it's because I was sufficiently vain and egotistical to feel one can ignore certain realities. (I think the turning point came during a season of unending rain at Castle Hill when I fell flat on my back one day in the mud and started cursing a God I had convinced myself didn't exist. My personal scheme of things till then at once seemed too foolish to continue holding.)[35]

In *The Tree of Man*, then, a novel which was originally to be titled 'A Life Sentence on Earth', White sets out to convey what he calls 'a splendour, a transcendence, which is . . . above human realities'.[36] But the realities Theodora Goodman had to understand were also superhuman, at least in the sense that they were transpersonal. It is thus appropriate that the natural world which was her mentor should become Stan Parker's prophet.

Like most Whitean protagonists, Stan has a quest. What he seeks is permanence, a stable place for himself in a solid and intelligible world. This quest is sanctioned by what White terms the delusive 'gospel of the stationary' (p. 96) – that is, a belief in the unchanging and imperishable as terrestrial possibilities. To approach the truth, Stan must rather accept what White calls, in a revision of Wordsworth, 'intimations of mortality' (p. 71). Nature's message to Stan, therefore, is that all hopes of permanence on the human plane are illusory, that reality, as it was for Theodora Goodman, is transience and mutability.

Nature illustrates these truths with storm, flood, fire and drought. One storm reduces Stan to a 'thing of gristle', groping for secure footing in a reeling world (p. 48). A later storm reinforces his sense of insignificance and teaches the proper response to its recognition:

> He was firm and strong, husband, father and owner of cattle. . . . But as the storm increased, his flesh had doubts, and he began to experience humility. The lightning, which could have struck open basalt, had, it seemed, the power to open souls. . . . In his new humility weakness and acceptance had become virtues. . . . The darkness was full of wonder. (pp. 159–60)

Elsewhere in the novel, a flood begins in days of rain during which Stan's sense of personal, responsible existence is 'sluiced out of him' (p. 75). Rowing across the flooded lands around Wullunya on a largely futile rescue mission, Stan watches as the 'fragments of the still, safe lives that are lived in houses flowed past'. He sees that 'in the dissolved world of flowing water, under the drifting trees, it was obvious that solidity is not' (p. 77). From his environment, then, Stan learns to humble himself and to accept ceaseless flux as the only permanence.

But, as was also the case in *The Aunt's Story*, transience is not nature's single or even most imperative message. If particulate life passes, its larger ground does not. What White seeks to convey is akin to the theme of Spenser's Mutabilitie Cantos: the very constancy of change circumscribes and stabilizes it. Life as a whole is an on-going process of disintegration and renewal; as death follows life, life also follows death; the fire-blackened acres around Glastonbury are soon sprouting a tender green; time, as White says early in the novel, both shapes and dissolves (*TM*, p. 15). For this lesson, Stan's teachers are the trees.

His story and the novel begin and end with trees. When he first arrives in the virgin bushland he will settle, two trees form the gate which admits him. He makes his first mark on the wilderness by scarring a tree with his axe, and later fells many. Yet, even after his death, the trees remain. As Stan's young grandson walks among them, White says that the child 'could not believe in death', and, as he thinks of the 'poem of life' he will write, he is described as 'Putting out shoots of green thought.[37] So that, in the end, there was no end' (p. 511). Like the trees, the boy will grow, blossom, and propagate. According to the Housman poem from which the novel's title is drawn, 'The tree of man was never quiet', and its saplings are bent double by the gale of time (p. 398). But man, for whom the tree stands as metaphor, will survive to reproduce himself, to ensure that there is no end.

The trees have a further point to make: that of the beauty and nobility of the natural in all its forms. Thus Stan first sees his stringybarks 'rising above the involved scrub with the simplicity of true grandeur' (p. 7). Much later he takes his son Ray into the bush and attempts to show him 'the great simplicities', 'the essentials of tree and shrub' (p. 234), and to communicate the awe these arouse in him.

Ultimately, of course, Stan discovers that such simplicities are not only beautiful but also holy. In this process, too, the trees assist, for, as Stan thinks at one point, 'Each leaf or scroll of bark was heavy in its implications' (p. 363). In comprehending the Hopkins-like inscape through which nature indicates God, Stan's understanding exceeds Theodora's. For, while the realities both learn to accept are similar, they are apprehended within different contexts. Theodora must become herself the whole which contains the two irreconcilable halves. But Stan perceives that antitheses are counterpoised within a divine unity; it is made 'clear that One, and no other figure, is the answer to all sums' (p. 508). As an illuminate, Stan sees that the struggle of life is also its joy and that the profane partakes of the sacred to such an extent that God can be found in a gob of spittle (p. 506).[38] In bringing Stan to this knowledge, the natural world has been priest and prophet, ministering by means of what is once called the 'communion of soul and scene' (p. 420). Finally, Stan realizes, even nature's 'acts of terror did begin to illuminate the opposite goodness and serenity of the many faces of God' (p. 263). Those many faces have been reified in landscape.

In a letter to Marjorie Barnard, author of the first full-length study of White's work ever published,[39] he congratulated her on her acumen in treating *The Tree of Man*:

> Your phrase 'the vanity of writing has passed away' is a magnificent and telling one. Nor has any other critic, however sympathetic, put his finger so firmly on the point of *The Tree of Man* as you have in your: 'Each man's life is a mystery between himself and God.'[40]

The natural world and its catastrophes serve to initiate man into this mystery,[41] and Stan is clearly successful in heeding the message nature would promulgate. In the realm of human relationships, however, he suffers a series of failures. The theme of illuminating failure is not so structurally integral to this novel as it was to *The Aunt's Story*, yet this facet of Stan's experience does contribute to his final penetration of the mystery. In fact, in Stan and Amy Parker, White gives us two studies in failure: the one illuminating and the other obscuring.

Stan's first significant experience of failure occurs in the Wullunya floods. Riding the floodwaters in a boat with other rescuers, Stan is the only one to spot the body of an old and bearded man caught in a tree.[42] However, he does not alert the others and they row on. Soon after, the rescue boat picks up a woman who tells them,

> I thought youse were never coming. . . . I been waitin and waitin. Dad is gone in a little gimcrack bit of a boat the kids made one summer. I said, 'You're mad, you'll never do no such thing.' But he'd seen a ram stuck in a tree.   (p. 78)

The woman's peculiar closing remark becomes important later when the incident recurs to Stan and he connects the man with the ram. It happens at the season of his life when he approaches emotional extinction and spiritual despair, the time of Amy's sordid liaison with the proverbial travelling salesman. Stan and

Amy have entered the 'years of drought' and Stan understandably remembers the flood. In one of those coincidences, which White uses with as much effect as Dickens, the memory comes on the very night after Amy first goes to bed with Leo. Stan has recently met the grandson of the man in the tree, and he tells Amy,

> I saw his grandfather. . . . He was an old man with a beard hanging upside down in a tree. And we rowed past. Nobody else saw him. He was almost certainly dead. I would'uv liked to think it was a ram. I persuaded myself perhaps, while there was still time to tell. But we rowed. And soon it was too late.   (p. 326)

Although Stan's words foreground the issue of guilt with which both must deal, Amy tries to justify Stan's act and to implicate others in it (strategies she adopts for dealing with her own failings). For Stan, however, 'his guilt remained, and because of this he was humble' (p. 327).

Stan recalls the man in the tree again, after his suspicions of Amy's infidelity have been confirmed and he has gone on a suicidal binge in Sydney. White describes him in a pub:

> Stan Parker looked round at the place seeing that it was now pretty full, and writhing, yet he was alone with his thoughts, could look at a wall, if he chose, between the heads of eels. So that the water, which was flowing where the grass had been, rowed past, and he could have caught at the old ram by the horn. But it was now too late. This is the key to me, Amy, he said, I cannot see things in time. . . .
>
> After this he began to go outside . . . it seemed so necessary to locate a degradation. . . . There was a paper sky, quite flat, and white and Godless. He spat at the absent God then, mumbling till it ran down his chin. He spat and farted, because he was full to bursting; he pissed in the street until he was empty, quite empty. Then the paper sky was tearing, he saw. He was tearing the last sacredness, before he fell down amongst some empty crates, mercifully reduced to his body for a time.   (p. 345)

This is the nadir of Stan's *via negativa*, the moment when he is darkest and most empty. (Notice, however, that mercy penetrates even the depths of hell.) The reader is alerted to the importance of Stan's failure to respond to the man in the tree, because the incident is recalled at this crucial juncture. But White has also supplied other indications of the way the experience functions for Stan.

In addition to the obvious Christian allusion to a man's death by hanging in a tree, implications also arise from Stan's recurrent tendency to see or want to see the man as a ram. It is as though he prefers to believe that the man was not human, not an Isaac, but rather the substitute sacrifice, the ram in the thicket, which God accepted from Abraham in Isaac's place. The ram, of course, also suggests Christ, the Lamb who *was* sacrificed for man's redemption. These implications, dimly but deeply felt, intensify Stan's guilt, which acts, in turn, to humiliate and humble him, to pitch him deeper into despair, and so to accelerate the process by which he will be reclaimed. It is in this way, as White later observes, that a 'state of failure' can become one of 'dedication' (p. 438).

When Stan's emptiness does fill again, when God rushes back into him, White describes the experience in terms which make direct reference to the vomiting-out of God and more oblique reference to the old man in the flood. Stan, now an old man himself, has been out hunting, has tripped and fallen on his gun, and has nearly shot himself:

> 'Oh God, oh God', said Stan Parker.
> He was suspended.
> Then his agreeable life, which had been empty for many years, began to fill. It is not natural that emptiness shall prevail, it will fill eventually, whether with water, or children, or dust, or spirit. So the old man sat gulping in. His mouth was dry and caked, that had also vomited out his life that night, he remembered, in the street.   (p. 431)

Allusions to an old man who gulps in rising water identify that man in the flood as an agent of Stan's redemption.

Stan's failures with his family also humble him. His failure with Amy is as much her fault at his, for what she perceives as his refusal of intimacy Stan understands as his claim to the respect due to personal 'mysteries' (p. 155). For whatever reasons, however, he will not let her possess him, and this frustration accounts in part for her turning to Leo. White describes her adultery in terms which will be echoed when Stan spits out his God, thus linking the acts and equating their import. With Leo, Amy reflects, 'It was as if she had spat into the face of her husband, or still further, into the mystery of her husband's God, that she saw by glimpses but could not reach deeper to' (p. 322). For Stan, atonement is possible; he gulps God in again. In Amy's case, no such forgiveness will be found. She has entered on her own destruction.

With Amy, Stan fails by being inaccessible; with his children, by simply being absent. From their birth Amy absorbs their attention; Stan feels, and is, superfluous. Buttressed by her children, Amy is stronger than he and jealously guards her advantage. Service in the First World War further separates Stan from the children, and when he returns he prefers to abdicate responsibility. He makes one bungled attempt to communicate with his son Ray and then resigns himself to impotence and silence. Thus, when Ray is later involved in the scandal surrounding a fixed horse race, Stan is helpless. Later still, when Ray is murdered, Stan confronts Amy with the extent of their failure as parents and probes the mystery behind it. In this crucial encounter (pp. 474–5), Stan sees and even makes Amy acknowledge the mystery of necessary failure. Because it forces us to the edge of the incomprehensible, 'Inadequacy', as Stan reflects, 'can be, in a sense, a prize' (p. 442). Although he cannot understand this, Stan accepts it. Amy can do neither.

Near the end of the novel Amy is described as 'Lost at times in the jungle of her past failures' (p. 443). While Stan's failures have made a clearing in his life and let him look out from it, hers have enclosed her. While his vision has clarified, hers has been obscured. Perhaps this is because, in Whitean terms, Amy has sinned more grievously than Stan. While his love has been inadequate, hers has overpowered. He may have failed to touch, but she has tried to strangle.

Amy's vision remains resolutely material throughout the novel. Owning and holding are the limits of her understanding, and she bitterly resents losing possession of people or things. She is repeatedly associated with the imagery of grasping, confining, engulfing and devouring. Of the boy she and Stan find in the Wullunya floods, Amy thinks, 'She would imprison the child in her house by force of love' (p. 102); and, of her own son Ray,

'She could not love him enough, not even by slow, devouring kisses. Sometimes her moist eyes longed almost to have him safe inside her again' (p. 120). She has the same hopes for her husband: 'Amy Parker had grown greedy for love. She had not succeeded in eating her husband, though she had often promised herself in moments of indulgence that she would achieve this at some future date' (p. 133). But she never does. With increasing conviction and anger, she knows he will always be 'closed to her' (p. 158). She therefore turns to others, trying to appropriate their lives and experience as she might their goods. She imagines herself as the society beauty Madeleine, and, while Stan is away during the war, she lives vicariously in the lives of passing strangers from whom she encourages confidences.

As if to point up the futility of this approach to relationships, White contrasts it with the one instance in which Amy does not try to own another person. About her grandson he says, 'Amy Parker had not attempted to possess this remote child, with the consequence that he had come closer than her own' (p. 406).

With the exception of her grandson, those she cannot grasp she cannot love. Loss of control erodes her love for Ray and even for her husband. Several times she suspects this, entertaining and dismissing the suspicion that she is unworthy of Stan and has never loved him as he deserves. She refuses to face this failing in herself, but the reader sees the truth in her sporadic self-accusations.

Amy fails in other ways as well. As she had loved Ray too much, she loves her daughter Thelma too little. Both the cruelty Ray uses to escape others and the prim self-absorption in which Thelma wraps her 'thin' soul (p. 137) may be attributable to their mother's early treatment of them. Amy also fails Mrs O'Dowd and Doll Quigley in their respective crises. Lest we miss the point, White tells us plainly near the end of the novel that Amy is 'superficial and sensual' (p. 496), and 'a weak woman, who had failed in everything in life' (p. 494).[43] But her failures, unlike Stan's, are debilitating, reductive and irredeemable. She who would imprison others finds herself left to serve out her life sentence while her husband is emancipated. White describes her terror at the moment of Stan's death:

> They clung together for a minute on the broken concrete path, their two souls wrestling together. She would have dragged him back if she could, to share her further sentence,

which she could not contemplate for that moment, except in terms of solitary confinement. So she was holding him with all the strength of her body and her will. But he was escaping from her.   (p. 508)

In the end, she fails to hold him, as she had always failed to love him.

Stan's failures do not confine him. Because he has acquiesced to them, they help to extricate him from the immediate and mortal and admit him to a greater understanding. His approach to the Whitean moment of enlargement is marked by a series of circle images which place Stan at their centre and prepare the reader for the final revelation. In the early part of the novel and of Stan's life, the energy of these circles is centripetal. Stan feels himself securely at the centre, the hub of a world of his own creating. Everything refers itself to him. In his own eyes and Amy's he seems the 'core of reality' (p. 141; see also pp. 115 and 117). But, as both Stan and the novel develop, he sees that he has not imposed the design; rather, it has incorporated him. Hints of his revised status in the universe are offered fairly early in the novel by the storm which forces him from its centre to shelter on its periphery (pp. 159–60). Other events, natural and manmade, further dislodge him from his position of control in his own life and the lives of his family. By the time he returns from the war, in fact, Stan 'no longer believe[s] anything can be effected by human intervention' (p. 223).

The revelation he achieves at the end of his life reinstates him at the heart of a great pattern, but that 'triumphal scheme' is no longer of his making (p. 505). Stan finds himself at the pivot of a great cosmic wheel of concentric apposition whose force is emphatically centrifugal. Movement is toward the final, comprehensive circle, and Stan's understanding enlarges with the circles:

Out there at the back, the grass, you could hardly call it a lawn, had formed a circle in the shrubs and trees which the old woman had not so much planted as stuck in during her lifetime. There was little of design in the garden originally, though one had formed out of the wilderness. It was perfectly obvious that the man was seated at the heart of it, and from this heart the trees radiated, with grave movements of life, and

beyond them the sweep of a vegetable garden, which had gone
to weed during the months of the man's illness, presented the
austere skeletons of cabbages and the wands of onion seed. All
was circumference to the centre, and beyond that the worlds
of other circles, whether crescent of purple villas or the bare
patches of earth, on which rabbits sat and observed some
abstract spectacle for minutes on end, in a paddock not yet
built upon. The last circle but one was the cold and golden
bowl of winter, enclosing all that was visible and material, and
at which the man would blink from time to time, out of his
watery eyes, unequal to the effort of realizing he was the centre
of it.   (pp. 504–5)

If the penultimate circle encloses 'all that [is] visible and material',
the ultimate circle must be God Himself. But God is also at the
centre, in Stan's very being. These circles enclose all antitheses.
Both life and death – living trees and cabbage skeletons – are
embraced. Stan is subsequently permitted to see God in a gob of
his spittle, joy in the struggle of the ants, and his failures in their
true, redeeming light: 'Even the most obscure, the most sickening
incidents of his life were clear. In that light' (p. 507). Failure, in
fact, has helped to shed the light which finally illuminates.

In some respects, *The Tree of Man* is itself an illuminating failure.
White points to the novel's major weakness in 'The Prodigal Son',
when he tells us that he wanted to 'suggest in this book every
possible aspect of life' and 'at the same time . . . discover the
extraordinary behind the ordinary'.[44] It is simply too much for
one novel to handle. Thus *The Tree of Man* is not the tight,
intricately wrought and patterned work that *The Aunt's Story* is.
If *The Aunt's Story* is a kind of fine and closely woven reticule,
The Tree of Man is more of a sumptuous but somewhat haphazard
patchwork quilt. It leaves the reader feeling, as one writer put
it, that '*The Tree of Man* must be praised for the gallantry of the
attempt rather than for the sureness of its achievement.'[45]

When it was first released, critics differed markedly in their
assessment of the novel. At one extreme was A. D. Hope's
annoyance at White's 'irritating and persistent omniscience' and
his notorious dismissal of the prose as 'pretentious and illiterate
verbal sludge'.[46] At the other was what has been characterized

as the 'eulogistic abandon' of reviewers for the *New York Times Book Review, New York Herald Tribune, New York Post* and *Chicago Sunday Tribune*.[47] By now, however, the critical storm that blew up over *The Tree of Man* has subsided, and debate over the novel's merits has given way to a more important recognition: that it drew worldwide attention as had no previous work of Australian literature.[48]

In other words, White now had the international ear; he was recognized in his own land and abroad as a writer of major importance. In the course of writing four novels, his vision had matured with his voice, and among the things he saw with increasing clarity was the role of failure in opening the way to a paradoxical kind of success. As his view of reality grew increasingly dialectical, so too did his view of such success: constituted by admission to the dialectic of enlarged understanding and acceptance of limits. While in Elyot Standish and Stan Parker he had explored the consequences of a failure to act or to interact, in Oliver Halliday and Theodora Goodman he confronted the more crucial failure to evade or deny the self and the nature of its being in the world. In Theodora, he had studied the failure to destroy the self by distancing and attrition; in his next novel he would treat the failure to destroy that self by deification.

3 The Major Phase: the Mystery of Failure

The mystery of life is not solved by success, which is an end in itself, but in failure, in perpetual struggle, in becoming. (V, p. 269)

Although the division of works into categories or periods is risky with any author, especially a living one, I think it safe to say that the four novels White published from 1957 to 1970 constitute a major phase. Within these works, the Whitean concern with the quest towards apprehension of a greater reality finds its fullest treatment. Moreover, the novels represent a major phase in regard to the author's conscious, careful, and increasingly complex exploration of the theme of failure.

The concept of the necessary, illuminating and redemptive failure is indispensable to an understanding of *Voss* (1957), the story of a man who abjures all human emotion and connection to attempt apotheosis of self in the image of a deity whose nature he disastrously misapprehends. The novel demonstrates that success for Voss would be suicide of the most profound and perverse variety: by expunging the human in himself he would also destroy the divine. Thus failure is quite clearly the condition on which Voss's reclamation depends, for it is the precondition for a right understanding of his God. Laura Trevelyan, whom White has recently identified as Voss's 'anima',[1] must undergo a similar experience of failure. As befits her role as mirror image of Voss, however, Laura's failure is the obverse of his: while his monstrous pride must fail him, Laura must fail in exercising her no less suspect humility. White shows that, for both, the success which salvation represents is predicated on 'failure' as judged in shortsighted human terms.[2]

The theme is less explicitly stated in the author's subsequent three novels, but it is no less central. The reader of *Riders in the Chariot* (1961) becomes convinced that Himmelfarb not only will but must fail 'to expiate the sins of the world' (p. 459), and that Dubbo, Mary Hare and Ruth Godbold must fail to preserve the life he would give in the effort. In *The Solid Mandala* (1966) and *The Vivisector* (1970), Arthur and Hurtle repeatedly accuse themselves of the failure sufficiently to love their siblings, and White gives increasing weight to their inadequacy. For them, as for the Riders, Voss and Laura, awareness and admission of failure open the way to a kind of success they could not have foreseen.

Of course, the theme of failure does not disappear from White's work after 1970. But in his most recent novels it modulates into a different key. It is in the novels of this major phase that the concept is most clearly formulated and its permutations most exhaustively explored.

VOSS

An understanding of *Voss* and of the function of failure in the novel must be built upon the identification of two key thematic and structural principles. The first of these is that Voss and Laura are doubles or counterparts, mirror images of each other. In a letter to Voss accepting his proposal of marriage, Laura recognizes this relationship, asking 'can two such faulty beings endure to face each other, almost as in a looking-glass?' (p. 183). Voss and Laura reflect each other's arrogance and isolation: their presumed self-sufficiency, reliance on the intellect, distrust of emotion, and active aversion to its physical expression.

The novel begins with Voss's visit to the house of Mr Bonner, chief sponsor of the expedition Voss will undertake. The Bonners are at church, but Laura, who has recently decided that the concept of God cannot sustain rational inquiry, has stayed home pleading a headache. When Voss and Laura meet, White encourages our perception of the affinity between them by paralleling Laura's priggishness and Voss's distaste for the flesh, Laura's smug self-reliance and Voss's belief that others are unnecessary. Even their positions in the room are used to reinforce our sense that they reflect each other: for their stilted conversation they sit 'in almost identical positions, on simple chairs, on either side of the generous window' (p. 10).

Nowhere is this mirroring more apparent than in their views on God. Voss is appalled to discover that Laura has abandoned her faith, but his horror springs from his conviction that 'Atheists are atheists usually for mean reasons. . . . The meanest of them is that they themselves are so lacking in magnificence they cannot conceive the idea of a Divine Power' (p. 86). For Voss, in other words, the denial of God is the denial of self, and it is in this sense that, as he shortly insists, '*Atheismus* is self-murder' (p. 87). Actually, Voss endorses no deity but himself. The Moravian Brother Müller speaks for White when he tells Voss, 'you have a contempt for God, because He is not in your own image' (p.47).

In his remark to Laura, Voss has made a statement of much greater profundity than he knows. His experience will teach him that atheism is indeed self-murder in that the divine is immanent and manifest in all men. Thus to reject God *is* to destroy a part of oneself. At the moment he speaks, however, his words function chiefly to alert Laura to the monstrous nature of his pride and the danger to which it subjects him:

> It was clear. She saw him standing in the glare of his own brilliant desert. Of course, He was Himself indestructible.
> And she did then begin to pity him. She no longer pitied herself. . . . Love seemed to return to her with humility. Her weakness was delectable.   (p. 87)

As readers, we do right to doubt that such a complete reversal can be accomplished in an instant. Love and humility are not so quickly recovered, and, in fact, Laura will spend the rest of the novel in the effort. What *is* credible is that, from this moment, Laura begins to mirror Voss from an adjusted angle. From now on, his flaws, especially those she shares with him, will come into ever sharper and more painful focus. Perceived in this way, Voss does become, as Laura claims, her own desert (p. 85). Through involvement with him, she enlists herself as one of the 'few stubborn ones [who] blunder on, painfully, out of the luxuriant world of their pretensions into the desert of mortification and reward' (p. 72).

Like the later Arthur and Waldo Brown, then, Voss and Laura

can usefully be understood as a severed whole, halves of a single self which longs to be reconciled and reintegrated.[3] Part of the task which the novel sets these two is to come to terms with those aspects of each other which they have ignored or repudiated in themselves. Voss must acknowledge impulses which he thinks of as feminine and identifies with Laura – impulses toward gentleness, self-effacement, and the giving and receiving of love. Similarly, Laura must deal with the Voss in herself: the pride which survives her profession of humility, and her abhorrence of the flesh. Both Voss and Laura, that is, must be brought out of their insulated, incomplete selves and made whole, in part through the union with each other.

The question of whether or not this union occurs, and, if so, to what effect, is complicated both by the fact of Voss's death and by its timing in the novel. Again as in the case of the later Arthur and Waldo, one half of the divided self vanishes, leaving readers to debate the wholeness of the survivor. The disappearance also leaves that survivor to carry on alone.

Voss does not close with something analogous to the brief, reassuring coda of *The Tree of Man*, in which Stan Parker's grandson is offered as proof that life renews itself. Rather, for the first time we are shown a Whitean visionary forced to live with and live out the vision. White left Oliver Halliday of *Happy Valley* at the moment when he most fully understood the meaning of his love for Alys and his choice to stay with Hilda. Similarly, *The Living and the Dead* ends with Elyot Standish undertaking to transform himself into one of the 'living'. Oliver's and Elyot's subsequent lives will be different, we assume, but we do not see them living those lives. Nor do we see Theodora Goodman in the madhouse. Finally, Stan Parker, first exemplar of a pattern which will become increasingly attractive to White, dies at the moment when his lifelong inquiry is capped by revelation. The same is true of Voss, although the nature of his final understanding is not spelled out as is Stan Parker's. But White gives (or inflicts upon) Laura twenty years to reflect on the ordeal she and Voss undergo. It is she, if anyone, who must show us the shape of a life informed by the knowledge Voss died with. In another novel, White tells us that illumination is finally synonymous with blinding (*RC*, p. 27), but Laura's illuminated eyes stay open.

It is through Laura, then, that Voss's life and death are

interpreted, an observation which brings us to a second structuring principle White uses in *Voss*: the novel begins and ends with Laura.[4] In her life, Voss's experience is not only paralleled and reflected, but mediated to us. Laura becomes Voss translated, Voss made intelligible and, most of all, accessible.

Thus White puts Laura to some crucial thematic purposes. He also makes use of her to secure reader sympathy for Voss and involvement with him, no easy task in that Voss is among the least sympathetic protagonists in the White corpus. Coldly aloof, often cruel and sometimes sadistic, Voss seems to combine Clem Hagan's conceit, Elyot Standish's impassiveness and self-absorption, and Ray Parker's perversity. White has repeatedly insisted that, while his final conception of Voss derives in part from historical explorers of Australia, particularly Eyre and Leichhardt,[5] the 'real Voss' was 'a creature of [my wartime experiences in] the Egyptian desert, conceived by the perverse side of my nature at a time when all our lives were dominated by that greater German megalomaniac' (*FG*, p. 104). The allusion to Hitler suggests the difficulties White faced in inducing readers to have anything to do with Voss.

These difficulties are largely overcome through Laura, who gives us a less strident rendition of Voss. While Laura shares many of Voss's proclivities, she indulges them as she lives her life, on a comparatively reduced scale. For example, Laura's fastidious distaste for physical affection is mildly amusing, but we are shocked when Voss shoots a dog because others suspect him of loving her. Laura provides us with an avenue by which we can approach Voss, so that, as one critic puts it, her involvement with and concern for him become 'the strongest argument in his favour'.[6]

But Laura's is only one point of view on Voss. White's perspective on him is ironic to an extent unprecedented in his earlier fiction, and the irony arises from his use of multiple viewpoints to counterbalance and correct each other. Like Virginia Woolf, that is, White often builds character by piling layer upon layer of sometimes contradictory perspectives supplied by the narrator, the character himself, and others around him. A single act or emotion of Voss's, for instance, may be complacently approved by him and at the same time call forth Laura's tender pity and the narrator's scorn or amusement.

In the scenes involving Voss and Laura, White often lets her do the ironic undercutting, but elsewhere Laura is subjected to a similar operation. White's introduction of Laura is designed to reveal her as at once unique and ordinary, both the proud rebel against the 'fuzz of faith' and 'the expert mistress of trivialities' in the social sphere (*V*, pp. 7–8). At the first meeting of Voss and Laura, we are invited to view both of them with a curious mixture of fascination, uneasiness, admiration and mirth. It is precisely the mixture with which they view each other.

By the close of the first two chapters, White has established reader ambivalence toward both characters, but especially toward Voss. Nowhere in White's earlier work does the reader find himself so unsettled about the proper response to major characters. The reader response White seeks here is more complex, more deeply ambivalent, than he demanded previously, because he wants the reader to recognize that these characters must fail to attain the inhuman perfection which both feel is within their grasp. Had they continued as they began, Voss would risk deification and Laura sainthood.[7]

Voss's goal, and one which becomes ludicrous as soon as it is formulated, is to usurp the throne of heaven. Precisely what this means is never clear, least of all to Voss himself. Some of his aims are Faustian, others Promethean. At times he seems to wish simply to be as God in the eyes of his men; at others he contemplates sacrificing them as well as himself to achieve apotheosis in some vaguely apprehended other sphere. What *is* clear is that Voss's purposes require him to renounce all gentler emotions, avoid all human relationships, and utterly repudiate the comforts of the flesh. This side of life he condemns as weakness, identifies with the feminine in general and Laura in particular, and rejects as inappropriate to incipient deity. Thus when we meet Voss he is already fragmented, having denied so much of his full self. As Laura knows, man's nature partakes of both the human and the divine. If he is to reclaim his wholeness, he must do justice to the godlike in himself by embracing the human, or that which Laura represents and encourages. It is this crucial failure, this surrender of Voss to the whole self, which the novel traces.

In *The Poetry of Experience*, Robert Langbaum describes 'a new kind of allegory in which [other characters] represent conflicting

aspects of the hero's self with the hero's problem to reconcile his
internal conflict through self-development'. Langbaum describes
this allegory as

> a monodrama – to the extent that only one character is
> unequivocally actual, with the incidents and the other
> characters existing as occasions for his self-expression and self-
> development, as a means of objectifying an essentially internal
> action.[8]

From one point of view, of course, *Voss* is not such a 'monodrama',
since Laura is as 'unequivocally actual' in the novel as is Voss.
Viewed in another way, however, Laura and Voss can be seen
as parts of one composite self, and in this case Langbaum's
hypothesized 'new allegory' offers a useful framework of approach
to the roles of lesser figures.[9] These tend to pair and to present
Voss and Laura (as well as the reader) with exemplars of certain
dichotomies which set the novel's terms of debate. This function
is most obviously performed by Sanderson and Boyle.

These two preside over the novel's patently paradisal and
infernal demesnes. Approaching Sanderson's settlement at Rhine
Towers, through a 'gentle, healing landscape', Voss reflects that
here a 'world of gods' has become accessible to men (p. 122).
Sanderson, caretaker of this Eden, is described as 'tend[ing] his
flocks and herds like any other Christian' and 'wash[ing] his
servants' feet in many thoughtful and imperceptible ways' (p.
124). In this kingdom of light, Voss is mightily tempted by the
prevailing climate of love and serenity. However, Voss not only
resists, but vows to punish himself (and incidentally his party)
for his momentary vacillation, mistaking a deep attraction to the
good and the beautiful for a surrender to voluptuousness.

At Brendan Boyle's settlement, Jildra, the temptations are of
a very different nature. Jildra itself is a kind of demonic parody
of Rhine Towers. Where Sanderson loved and respected learning,
Boyle has torn the boards from a copy of Homer to prop a table
leg, and uses the pages of other books to mop up spills. Where
the description of Rhine Towers made it a heaven on earth, at
Jildra the imagery of hell predominates. Under a 'blood red' sky,
Voss's party approaches a place where smoke, dust, filth and the
'vapours of night' render everything 'confused' and chaotic (p.
164). Where the life of Sanderson reached outward, Boyle is
obsessed by what is clearly a perverse plumbing of the reaches of

self: 'to explore the depths of one's own repulsive nature' (p.165). Boyle at once recognizes the kinship between Voss's obsession and his own and that both lead toward 'irresistible disaster' (p. 165).

Thus Sanderson and Boyle stand, as it were, at opposite ends of the continuum along which human life is possible. Under the influence of Rhine Towers, Voss's determination to remain a self-contained monolith erodes, at least to the extent that he writes the cold, stiff, and supercilious letter to Laura inviting her to share his life. Significantly, it is Laura's reply, accepting his proposal, which rescues him from Jildra, thus releasing Voss from a kind of evil enchantment to lead his party on their literal and allegorical journey. Neither Rhine Towers nor Jildra can finally hold him, for to reach either heaven or hell he must first navigate his personal purgatory.

Other dichotomies are embodied in other character pairings. One of these, composed of Frank Le Mesurier and Harry Robarts, is like Laura in constituting aspects of the unadmitted self. In Le Mesurier, we watch the workings of the ruthless intellect, in nothing more ruthless than against itself. It is trenchant and cynical, uninformed by the belief in any purpose, human or divine. White says of Le Mesurier, Voss 'knew this young man as he knew his own blacker thoughts' (p. 33), and he later adds that Voss had 'sensed, early in their association, that the young man was possessed of a gristly will, or daemon, not unlike his own' (p. 247). In Le Mesurier, Voss recognizes what he himself would be, were he stripped of his sense of destiny.

Of course, without Voss's obsession to obscure his vision, Le Mesurier can often see farther and deeper than his leader, and the path his understanding takes prefigures that of Voss. He responds, as Voss would only like to do, to the goodness of life at Rhine Towers. He helps Mrs Sanderson care for the children, and later he begins writing poetry. Unfortunately, his state of grace is temporary, for Voss's will is stronger than his and compels the younger man to follow him. None the less, his subordinate's experience at Rhine Towers offers the explorer an unsettling glimpse into the possibility of a life of peace and plentitude in which 'the days began to explain' (p. 139).

Le Mesurier's later poetry proves even more disturbing to Voss in that it shows him himself. In the journal which he appropriates while Le Mesurier is ill and helpless, Voss finds prose poems which trace Le Mesurier's fall from arrogance and predict a

similar course for Voss. After describing his leader as one whom
'fevers turned . . . from Man into God', Le Mesurier writes,

> Humility is my brigalow, that I must remember: here I shall
> find a thin shade in which to sit. As I grow weaker, so I shall
> become strong. . . . Only goodness is fed. . . .
> Now that I am nothing, I am, and love is the simplest of
> all tongues.
> Then I am not God, but Man. . . .
> O God, my God, I pray that you will take my spirit out of
> this my body's remains, and after you have scattered it, grant
> that it shall be everywhere, and in the rocks, and in the empty
> waterholes, and in true love of all men, and in you, O God,
> at last.   (pp. 294–5)

Le Mesurier's prayer recalls and petitions for an ecstasy he
had earlier experienced. Like that of other Whitean initiates, it
is precipitated by the sense of self dissolved but simultaneously
expanding. Riding through a rainstorm, Le Mesurier finds himself

> immersed in the mystery of it, he was dissolved, he was running
> into crannies, and sucked into the mouths of the earth, and
> disputed, and distributed, but again and again, for some
> purpose, was made one by the strength of a will not his
> own.   (p. 248)

This moment marks the apogee of Le Mesurier's awareness and
perhaps predicts a similar awareness for Voss once he is similarly
humbled. But, like the serene days at Rhine Towers, the moment
is transient. The spectre of Voss intrudes upon the vision and
destroys it (p. 249). This is appropriate in that Voss at this point
must still deny what the vision reveals. Moreover, he cannot yet
accept the function of failure in bringing one to such perception.
  It is Frank who articulates the role of failure when he tells him,
'The mystery of life is not solved by success, which is an end in
itself, but in failure, in perpetual struggle, in becoming' (p. 269).
His words recall the stress in Goethe's *Faust* upon the redemptive
power of unwearied striving and aspiration, for the emphasis here
is on process: failure provokes further struggle, which tends towards becoming. In the world of White's fiction, failure is both
humbling and enabling to the man of spiritual hungers. It repre-

sents not a closure, but an opening: a goad to further efforts which themselves can never succeed, but which permit the quester the only progress possible to him. In this passage Le Mesurier voices one of the central tenets on which the moral universe obtaining in the novel and in all White's work is founded.

But all this prescience and acuity on Le Mesurier's part leaves the reader doubly troubled by the conundrum of his suicide. The novel suggests that Le Mesurier slits his throat because Voss has resigned his claim to omniscience and omnipotence, but Le Mesurier had long foreseen this abdication and should not have despaired when it came. Three solutions to this riddle might be offered. On the thematic level, Le Mesurier may represent a man who has reached the core of self, who has discarded every protection, dream and delusion, without being able to initiate the complementary movement of accretion and expansion. The mystic moment he experienced in the storm would thus be irrecoverable, and he would be bereft of the resources to do what Voss finally demands of him: to wring out hope for himself. Alternatively, the moment in the storm may represent a culmination beyond which Le Mesurier would neither hope nor wish to go. Subsequently, he might seek death as a release from a life so inadequate to his vision. Either of these explanations has psychological validity and thematic resonances. But a structural imperative may also dictate that Le Mesurier disappear at this point in the novel. For, as Voss approaches his own death, he must incorporate the several selves which previously have been encountered in the expedition members. Thus Le Mesurier as separate self must vanish. To this end Voss is also deprived of Harry Robarts.

In the beginning, Le Mesurier cannot resist baiting the slow and simple Harry. In fact, Le Mesurier's treatment of Harry recalls Voss's contempt for his own body. This is fitting, because, if Le Mesurier in one sense mirrors Voss's soul, Harry can be seen as a projection of his flesh, particularly that part of him which, doglike, longs to serve and be caressed. Very early in the novel, Voss thinks of Harry as a 'dumb animal' (p. 39), but at the same time is disturbed by inklings of a strength of innocence (p. 30). Harry possesses the paradoxical invulnerability of those who make themselves vulnerable, a quality which also troubles Voss in Judd and Palfreyman and which he comes to identify sometimes with the canine, more often with the feminine.[10] Since

Harry reflects the animal in Voss, it is appropriate that he be drawn to Judd, who sometimes seems half animal himself; and, since Harry also embodies those qualities Voss labels feminine, it is fitting that Harry's decaying corpse should become for Voss a 'green woman' (p. 386). The effectiveness of this image is increased when we recall that Laura has been persistently associated with the colour green. In a final modulation of this motif, the Aborigines joke about the corpses of the two white men, suggesting that the dried, masculine remains of Le Mesurier and the swollen, feminine body of Harry may mate and breed maggots together (p. 386). In terms of their symbolic functions, they have in fact mated in Voss and bred a tentative rapprochement of two aspects of his warring self.

While Harry and Le Mesurier are, as White once explicitly states, 'emanations of the one man' (p. 357), another pair, that of Judd and Palfreyman, are not so much pieces of Voss himself as objectifications of a spiritual conflict within him. Together, they illustrate the 'paradox of man in Christ and Christ in man' (p. 340) which Palfreyman's plainly sacrificial death brings home to the party. It should be stressed at once that neither Palfreyman nor Judd is a traditional 'Christ figure', or that, if either is so viewed, he is as many-sided and equivocal in this role as is Faulkner's Joe Christmas. Still, both are avatars of the enigma and challenge which the nature of Christ poses for Voss. The novel's imagery and plot repeatedly associate these two with aspects of Christ and with each other.

Judd, the emancipist convict who has been 'tempered in hell, and . . . survived' (p. 134), is presented in imagery which evokes Christ crucified and resurrected. White says of him,

> He was . . . a union of strength and delicacy, like some gnarled trees that have been tortured and twisted by time and weather. . . . the injustice and contempt that he had experienced during a certain period sealed him up. Risen from the tomb of that dead life, he could not yet bring himself to recognize it as a miracle . . . .   (p. 131)

Later, it is Judd who reminds the party that Christmas is approaching, and requests that it be celebrated. He is twice explicitly linked to the blood of the lamb (pp. 145–6 and 195), and his 'Christlike humility', even before those who cause his suffering, is extolled by Palfreyman and despised by Voss (p. 148).

Critical discussions of Judd, when they do not propose him as a Judas, often emphasize his role as 'natural man' or 'man-animal'.[11] From this point of view, he is the graceless man who, though good, is unfit to endure the transfiguring ordeal which Voss will undergo, and so abandons the expedition and turns back. One passage cited in support of this analysis describes Judd, after witnessing Palfreyman's death, deciding to abandon the expedition. Judd has been searching for stray stock and finds them along the banks of a nearly dry river bed:

> The man–animal joined them and sat for a while upon the scorching bank. It was possibly this communion with the beasts that did finally rouse his bemused human intellect, for in their company, he sensed the threat of the knife, never far distant from the animal throat.
>
> 'I will not! I will not!' he cried at last, shaking his emaciated body.
>
> Since his own fat paddocks, not the deserts of mysticism, nor the transfiguration of Christ, are the fate of common man, he was yearning for the big breasts of his wife, that would smell of fresh-baked bread even after she had taken off her shift. (p. 343)

At this point Judd does allow the animal in him ascendancy. But Judd here becomes the 'man-animal' or 'common man' not because this is all he is, but because this is all he need be now. The Passion Play which he and Palfreyman have enacted for Voss's benefit has climaxed in Palfreyman's death, and, from this point on in the novel, Voss will need to understand the Christ in himself and in all men without the instructive parable of Palfreyman and Judd. Thus Judd departs, as he believes it is 'intended' he should do (p. 344). But, as befits one who has already died and risen, he is the expedition's sole survivor. His later confusion of Palfreyman's death, which he saw, with Voss's, which he didn't, conflates the novel's avatars of Christ. It also corroborates Laura's belief that man may become most Godlike when he feels himself least so, a condition both Voss and Palfreyman reached just before their deaths. As she puts it, 'When man is truly humbled, when he has learned that he is not God, then he is nearest to becoming so. In the end, he may ascend' (p. 384).

If part of Judd's function is to represent Christ resurrected, it
falls to Palfreyman to actualize the Christ of doubt, suffering and
death, the Christ of Gethsemane and Golgotha.[12] A scientist,
Palfreyman has built a bridge between his work and faith, but
the frail structure is often in danger of collapse. Voss, who cannot
tolerate faith in anything or anyone except himself, delights in
taunting Palfreyman into doubting his own acts of charity and
compassion. Voss also probes until he discovers Palfreyman's
debilitating secret: his inability to return the love of a hunchbacked
sister and to relieve her agnostic despair. Voss accuses Palfreyman
of escaping his sister and his guilt by fleeing to Australia, but
Palfreyman is clearly attempting to redeem that sin when he
obeys Voss's order to confront a party of Aboriginals. His
willingness to give his life for Voss takes on added significance in
that the sister whom he would love and save is so like his leader:
wilful, perverse, self-punishing, and anxious to make others in
her image. Above all, she, like Voss, is in love with 'the Gothic
splendours of death' (p. 262). As will later be the case for Hurtle
Duffield and the hunchbacked Rhoda of *The Vivisector*, Miss
Palfreyman's hump acts as a kind of objective correlative for
Voss's skewed moral and emotional nature. Thus Palfreyman's
self-sacrifice reflects his desire to save both these deformed and
suffering beings.

As Palfreyman approaches the blacks, the watching party of
white men 'All remembered the face of Christ that they had seen
at some point in their lives, either in churches or in visions, before
retreating from what they had not understood, the paradox of
man in Christ and Christ in man' (*V*, p. 340). Dying with a spear
wound in his side, Palfreyman believes he has failed, as Christ
once feared He had. But his failure is a typically Whitean one,
for he has succeeded in resurrecting what Voss contemptuously
calls the 'Christ-picture' (p. 343) for others of the party, and
eventually for Voss himself.

Palfreyman and Judd thus provide another spectrum along
which Voss's spiritual self can be explored and finally recovered.
Like Le Mesurier and Harry, they are ultimately discarded
because incorporated by Voss in the whole self he reclaims before
his death. One further pair of white men on the expedition
remain, and what they embody must also be accepted. These
two, Angus and Turner, seem present in part to prove that
pettiness and mediocrity exist at both ends of the social scale and

to provide for each other the uncomfortable experience of self-recognition. Beyond this, however, by representing all the sordidness and silliness Voss has sought to escape, they show that such escape is impossible. Thus, in his last dream-vision of Laura, Voss imagines himself as scrofulous and carbuncular as Turner (p. 381), and in the Aboriginal village he finds himself as much the helpless animal as Angus.

A final pair of characters is composed of the expedition's Aboriginal guides, Dugald and Jackie, but these two are linked more by their shared race than by shared thematic function. In other words, they do not stand at opposing poles of a continuum of choice or possibility. Dugald's role is largely oracular. While with the party, he delivers occasional pronouncements of astounding penetration. But like Judd, Dugald turns back, preferring the simple and seasonal life of his people to the white man's relentless obsession. In fact, if there is an exemplar of the purely natural man in the novel, it is certainly Dugald rather than Judd. Beyond this, however, he has little to do. Jackie's role, on the other hand, is crucial, less because he wields the knife which kills Voss than because he suggests a kind of Jungian shadow which Voss would deny, and which therefore destroys him. This interpretation is supported by the fact that Voss gives the boy the knife which Jackie turns against him. Even more suggestive is the circumstance that, after Voss's death, Jackie is possessed by his spirit to the point that he must recapitulate his life. While his people look to him as a prophet, Jackie wanders confused, haunted, in search of what he cannot find.

Thus Voss remains a part of Jackie as the boy and the other expedition members were of Voss. Early in the novel White provides us with an image of how the expedition will come to function. Voss is discoursing on musical composition with the music-master Topp. He tells him, 'I would set myself the task of creating a composition by which the various instruments would represent the moral characteristics of human beings in conflict with one another' (p. 40). The exploring party subsequently becomes, in several senses, Voss's instrument.

In critical treatments of *Voss*, much has been made of the way White has used desert climate and scenery to reflect the equally vast and forbidding terrain of Voss's soul.[13] Like the Marabar Caves of E. M. Forster's *A Passage to India*, White's Australian outback seems a landscape of incontrovertible power, but one which also reflects and responds to the state of the soul that is brought to it. The novel's allegorical landscape remains one of its most stunning achievements, but it is important to recognize that Voss moves also in an allegorical human landscape where characters offer the choices he must make to reclaim his renounced humanity. Of course, Le Mesurier, Palfreyman, Judd and the others also function as characters in their own right and elicit reader response to their predicaments as human beings as well as to their status as symbolic vehicles. Yet, their most important role is still defined by their impact upon Voss. Through their agency, and more particularly through that of Laura, with whom he communicates first by letter and then by dream and vision,[14] Voss is led to resume the 'human status' in which, paradoxically, he most closely approximates the godhood he once sought (p. 390).

Voss's pilgrimage moves largely by fits and starts. Whenever he allows pre-eminence to his sense of Laura, what she is and what she requires of him, he is likely to make some progress, but such moments are often followed by reaction. Terrified that love will weaken him, Voss tries to retrench after every assault on his isolation. In one of the oxymoronic inversions which White uses frequently in the novel, Voss often finds himself *tempted* to love or selflessness, and resists such temptation mightily (pp. 205, 214, 287).

Eventually, however, he does succumb, embracing in Laura that side of himself which she both nurtures and enacts. Early in the novel, when she realized the dimensions of his pride, she had begun to recover love and humility (p. 87). Voss's spiritual growth finally traces a similar pattern. When he can love Laura, he can also extend that love to others, and can humbly admit to his remaining party that he is but a weak and frightened mortal. Relinquishing even his will, he becomes the 'man who was not God' (p. 377), the man who can only trust to God:

> He himself, he realized, had always been most abominably frightened, even at the height of his divine power, a frail god upon a rickety throne. . . .
> Now, at least, reduced to the bones of manhood, he could admit to all this, and listen to his teeth rattling in the darkness.
> '*O Jesus*,' he cried, '*rette mich nur! Du lieber!*'
> Of this too, mortally frightened, of the arms, or sticks, reaching down from the eternal tree, and tears of blood, and candlewax. Of the great legend becoming truth.   (p. 387)

The spiritual distance Voss has covered between his 'rickety throne' and the twig hut in which he dies is measured by a final series of dreams or visions of Laura in which sexual and religious imagery increasingly interweave to suggest Voss's acceptance of his human state: its mortality, its fleshy pains and pleasures, and its Christlike capacity for love and compassion. In the last of these visions, Voss and Laura celebrate a Eucharist which solemnizes Voss's resumption of the flesh. At the same time, its mingled orders of imagery force reader awareness that, for White, the sacred and profane are of the same order of existence, and the flesh itself is holy. Voss sees himself and Laura riding together:

> Once, upon the banks of a transparent river, the waters of which were not needed to quench thirst, so persuasive was the air which flowed into and over their bodies, they dismounted to pick the lilies[15] that were growing there. They were the prayers, she said, which she had let fall during the outward journey to his coronation, and which, on the cancellation of that ceremony, had sprung up as food to tide them over the long journey back in search of human status. She advised him to sample these nourishing blooms. So they stood there, munching awhile. The lilies tasted floury, but wholesome. Moreover, he suspected that the juices present in the stalks would enable them to be rendered down easily into a gelatinous, sustaining soup. But of greater importance were his own words of love that he was able at last to put into her mouth. So great was her faith, she received these white wafers without surprise. (p. 390)

Voss has failed to achieve 'coronation', but, in the manner suggested by Le Mesurier, his very failure has prompted the more imperative quest for recovered 'human status'. The divine sanction of this second quest is suggested by the Eucharist which marks its inception, significantly with Voss acting as communicating priest. Here imagery enforces vision. In repudiating the body, Voss had starved the spirit. Now, he both offers the Host and himself takes and eats. In his failed apotheosis, then, Voss has become not only most human, but most like the God he sought to unseat.

Describing Voss's death, White concentrates on Jackie, the executioner, and is silent about Voss's thoughts or feelings. In other words, his reconciling vision of Laura is as close as Voss comes to the experiences of Stan Parker, Theodora Goodman or Frank Le Mesurier, in which the periphery of self expands to coincide with infinity. This reticence on White's part forces us to turn, as he intends we should, to Laura for an understanding of the full significance of Voss's life and death. It is Laura who is granted a moment which prefigures and parallels Le Mesurier's dissolving in the storm (p. 237), and Laura whose life is asked to reflect the vision she and Voss have shared.

Like Voss, Laura is incomplete; she has developed her intellectual life to the exclusion of the emotional and sexual. Also like Voss, she must acknowledge and accept neglected aspects of the self and is assisted in this effort by having these aspects projected as paired characters with whom she deals. But, where Voss had to contend with several such couples, Laura has only Rose and Belle.

Rose Portion, the Bonner maid, embodies all the unsavoury aspects of the flesh. Her heavy, stolid, stupid presence oppresses Laura from the book's memorable opening lines:

> 'There is a man here, miss, asking for your uncle', said Rose. And stood breathing. (p. 5)

Like the later Rhoda Courtney, Rose is deformed, offensive to the aesthetic sense, and often described in animal imagery. But, again like Rhoda, who is herself both rodent and rose, she becomes a vehicle through which Laura can experience and express a compassionate love. It is also through Rose that Laura comes to terms with her own sexuality.

As Voss was, Laura has been wary of the demands which sexual love would make on her. Says the narrator, 'Persistent touch was terrifying to her' (p. 120), and both she and Voss tend to shrink from physical contact. But in the course of Rose's pregnancy and the birth of her bastard daughter Mercy, Laura overcomes the revulsion her maid's bovine body arouses in her to the extent that the body and its burden become her own. Describing Mercy's birth, White employs a careful ambiguity of pronominal reference to stress Laura's sense that she, too, has been delivered. The scene also emphasizes the continuity of this new life with all other, and the child's symbolic role as saving grace:

It is moving, we are moving, we are saved, Laura Trevelyan would have cried, if all sound had not continued frozen inside her throat. The supreme agony of joy was twisted, twisting, twisting.

Then the dawn was shrieking with jubilation. For it had begun to live. The cocks were shrilling. Doves began to soothe. Sleepers wrapped their dreams closer about them, and participated in great events. The red light was flowing out along the veins of the morning.

Laura Trevelyan bit the inside of her cheek, as the child came away from her body.   (p. 228)

Laura adopts Mercy as the 'visible token of the love with which she was filled' (p. 234). This is in part the love of Voss, the sexual side of which she faces in the pregnancy of Rose and birth of Mercy. But it is also the love she learned to offer Rose and the love of God which manifests itself in mercy. Thus the child is indispensable, especially in any Christian-based scheme of salvation. Laura's humility, in which she is sometimes as smugly complacent as is Voss in his pride,[16] therefore must fail her when she demands of it the strength to sacrifice Mercy. This is her crucial failure, a failure which complements Voss's. Both must fail to evade God's mercy.

White conveys all this subtly but insistently in the scene in which Laura decides to give up the child for Voss's sake. This occurs near the height of the fever which she suffers while Voss is imprisoned and murdered, and which seems to admit her to immediate knowledge of events overtaking him. In apparent delirium, Laura proposes 'making some big sacrifice, . . . something of a personal nature that will convince a wavering mind. If it is only human sacrifice that will convince man that he is not God' (p. 369). Her aunt Mrs Bonner, who also loves Mercy, is quite rightly appalled by Laura's plan to send the child away, and fails to act on it. Later Laura realizes that her 'will wavered' in the matter of Mercy's banishment, and she pleads that her failure be judged 'in the light of intentions' (p. 393).

White, who would have this wavering of will seen as a positive sign, clearly intends us to recognize the arrogant wrongheadedness of Laura's assumptions and to view her failure as facilitating further emotional and spiritual growth. On the allegorical level, it denies the efficacy of human sacrifice, stressing instead the need to realize one's humanity, and leaves Mercy still within her grasp. But, lest we be misled by Laura's oracular intensity when she orders that Mercy be surrendered, White has the smell of rotting pears accompany the scene.

These pears, a gift from Mr Bonner inadvertently left in the sickroom, have earlier been associated with Laura's cousin Belle Bonner. This is 'Belle the golden, who would smell of ripe pears' (p. 353) and who, at Laura's suggestion, carries pear blossoms in her wedding. In fact, Belle is associated with all that is ripe, blooming, fruitful and life-giving. Like Rose she is an animal, but animal in her enjoyment of life and its sensual pleasures. She seems to embody life's fullness and joy as Rose did its privation and pain. Animal exuberance, however, is only one side of Belle. Love, concern, compassion and candour are also highly developed in her.

Laura has suppressed or denied the Belle in herself, as she has the Rose, and her sacrifice of Mercy would have been a further affront to that loving and nurturing side of herself, as the stench of rotting pears implies. Belle's warmth and her forthright, often physical, expression of her feelings must become part of Laura's experience as did Rose's suffering. Laura, that is, must respond to what invites in the life of the flesh as well as to what repels. Around the time of Belle's wedding, when her cousin's influence is at its strongest, Laura does take a step in this direction. For the first time she writes Voss a letter confessing her need for him and envisaging herself and Voss as man and wife, not merely partners in some uplifting moral project. Where earlier she had lectured, now she openly longs for him. At last, she has given vent to that part of herself which Belle embodies. However, as the battle for the humble acceptance of suffering must be constantly rewaged, so must the campaign for joy. Laura is still far from winning it – so far that, after the ordeal of her illness and Voss's death, it remains the major challenge of her life.

At the moment Voss is decapitated in his 'pocket of purgatory' (p. 390), Laura's purgatorial fever breaks. In her protracted pain, she has come to see that suffering is an inescapable condition of the full experience of one's being. At the height of her fever, she understands that even Christ had to suffer in order to realize the second of the three-stage process He opened to men: 'Of God into man. Man. And man returning into God' (pp. 383—4). This phase of Laura's assumption of her total self concludes with her echo of Christ's words on the cross – 'It is over' (p. 392) – uttered when her fever breaks and Voss is executed. Near the end of the novel, she speculates that 'Perhaps true knowledge only comes of death by torture in the country of the mind' (p. 443). Laura and Voss have now suffered that death.

But Laura is not at once resurrected. Rather, she seems to remain at least emotionally dead for the six years which pass before the novel resumes her story. During this time Belle is physically distanced from her and what she represents seems equally inaccessible. When we next see Laura, she is a teacher at a girls' school and has been invited to a reception for the explorer Colenel Hebden, who has just returned from a futile search for the remains of Voss and his party. In the years that have elapsed since Voss's death, Laura has withdrawn into almost monastic seclusion, becoming what both the narrator and Mrs Bonner liken to a 'nun' (p. 401). 'Completely detached' (p. 407), Laura chooses to look at and love the world from a safe distance. But under Colonel Hebden's interrogation she is tortured back to life. The scene, which takes place in a plaited-twig summerhouse, is clearly meant to recall the scene of Voss's decapitation in a native hut. At one point, in fact, Laura accuses the Colonel of similar designs: 'You would cut my head off, if letting my blood run would do you any good' (p. 410). The encounter with Miss Trevelyan sends Colonel Hebden back into the desert to renew his search for Voss. The effect of the meeting on Laura must be judged from the novel's last chapter.

This final chapter, which is set twenty years after the reception, has several crucial functions. First, it allows Laura, the inheritor of Voss's experience, to offer a final summation of its meaning. In so doing, she stresses the Whitean theme of necessary failure, insisting, 'I am convinced that Voss had in him a little of Christ, like other men. If he was composed of evil along with the good, he struggled with that evil. And failed' (p. 441). The reader is by now aware of how imperative that failure was in rendering Voss fully human and thus most true to the Christ in himself.

A second function of the final chapter is to identify Laura's heirs, those whose struggle will be to shape significant experience: Mercy, the musician Topp, and the painter Pringle, whom Laura charges with 'express[ing] what we others have experienced by

living' (p. 443). Like Stan Parker's grandson or Theodora
Goodman's spiritual children, these are the perpetuators, those
who will attempt to explore and articulate the mysteries.

Finally, the last chapter gives us a parting view of Laura and
a chance to gauge how far back into life she has ventured. On
this matter, White is unclear. Laura's re-established contact with
and obvious affection for Belle seem to argue in her favour. Even
more convincing are her determination to stay at Belle's party
and White's description of her as the 'headmistress', offering her
pupils wisdom, strength and love:

> individuals, of great longing but little daring, suspecting that
> the knowledge and strength of the headmistress might be
> accessible to them, began to approach by degrees. Even
> her beauty was translated for them into terms they could
> understand. As the night poured in through the windows and
> the open doors, her eyes were overflowing with a love that
> might have appeared supernatural, if it had not been for the
> evidence of her earthly body: the slightly chapped skin of her
> neck, and the small hole in the finger of one glove, which, in
> her distraction and haste, she had forgotten to mend.   (p. 442)

Here Laura reminds us of Belle as White described her at the
prenuptial ball: almost a goddess and yet a scruffy, careless beast.
In other words, she seems a whole woman, possessed of both body
and soul. None the less, the reader cannot help but be disturbed
by the sententiousness of Laura's remarks and the fact that White
leaves her at the novel's end rummaging for lozenges. The
difficulties lessen, however, when we recall that Laura was not
spared the ironic perspective which was trained on Voss, a
perspective which serves so often in this novel to remind us that
ridiculousness and pomposity are themselves aspects of the full
humanity which Voss and Laura acknowledge. Laura may be
the bearer of grace to Voss,[17] but the state of grace is not one she
inhabits uninterruptedly. If this seems imprecise and unsettled,
White probably intended that effect. Like Laura, we readers are
left with some integrative work to do. We enlist ourselves
with those other inheritors who have been troubled enough by
experience to explore it. And, as was also true in Laura's case,
our failure to find satisfactory closure proves instructive, allowing
meaning to proliferate and interpretation to continue.

In writing this novel White has said he reached toward 'the textures of music, the sensuousness of paint, to convey . . . what Delacroix and Blake might have seen, what Mahler and Liszt might have heard'. 'Above all,' he continues, 'I was determined to prove that the Australian novel is not necessarily the dreary, dun-coloured offspring of journalistic realism.'[18] One assessment of how well he succeeded in making language sound and shimmer was offered by the poet Ted Hughes, who concluded, 'In this prose, Patrick White is the most exciting poet Australia has yet produced.'[19]

In light of Hughes's remarks, it is fitting that Judith Wright, herself a fine Australian poet, should have written lines which would admirably stand as an epigraph to *Voss*:

> Wounded we cross the desert's emptiness
> and must be false to what would make us whole.
> For only change and distance shape for us
> some new tremendous symbol for the soul.[20]

Both 'The Harp and the King', from which these lines are drawn, and the novel take the unconquerable Australian interior as a metaphor for the finally unfathomable self. Thus the ironic light in which Voss's enterprise appears is shed not only by the narrative perspective, but also by the lowering presence of the Australian landscape and the sobering record of assaults upon it. White uses his quintessentially Australian setting, a landscape which he later describes as 'indifferen[t]... to human limitations' (*FG* p. 29), to underscore the necessity of Voss's failure. In addition, because the novel parallels Voss's literal/allegoric trek and Laura's more methaphorical journey, that same Australian emptiness is seen to stand sardonically behind the complacency of Sydney society, and to insist on a similar acknowledgement of failure in the social sphere.

The lines from Judith Wright also suit the novel in their emphasis on process: over time, change and distance, man must be false to his wholeness, for only the failure to find it keeps him searching. This is precisely the import of Le Mesurier's claim that 'The mystery of life is not solved by success, . . . but in failure . . . ' (*V*, p. 269). Le Mesurier's words imply, as well, that such failure can resolve itself into a paradoxical but profound success.

RIDERS IN THE CHARIOT

The four protagonists of *Riders in the Chariot* (1961) are also false to what would make them whole, because wholeness must come from each other, and their successful conjunction can be reached only through each Rider's experience and acceptance of failure. The entire novel is required for this process.

The quaternity archetype, as we know from Jung, is used by the self as a vehicle conducing to psychic integration and coherence.[21] It is not surprising, then, that a number of critics have advanced the opinion that the four Riders represent faculties which in combination would produce a complete human being or society. Mordecai Himmelfarb seems associated with intellect, Mary Hare with instinct, Ruth Godbold with emotion, and Alf Dubbo with imagination. The Riders have been taken as more or less allegorized representations of the four Jungian faculties of the mind, Blake's four Zoas, the four elements, and four segments of Australian society.[22] Since they finally take their places as the four Living Creatures in Dubbo's painting of Ezekiel's chariot, they might also be viewed as the four archetypal human beings of Kabbalistic tradition.[23] But determination of precisely what each stands for is less important that the recognition that they are, ultimately, one, in their sense of election, dedication to a sometimes dimly conceived mission, experience of the vision of the chariot, and acknowledgement of each other. That their 'fellowship', as Mary says, may 'confirm rather than expound a mystery' makes that relationship all the more imperative (p. 27).

The mystery confirmed here is, in part, that of failure. Shortly before his death, Himmelfarb decides that

> the mystery of failure might be pierced only by those of extreme simplicity of soul, or else by one who was about to doff the outgrown garment of the body. He was weak enough, certainly, by now, to make the attempt which demands the ultimate in strength. (p. 490)

Brought to an extremity of body, soul, or both, each of the four Riders is weak enough, if only momentarily, to penetrate this mystery.

Himmelfarb's failure is much like that of Voss. While Voss had to fail to be God, Himmelfarb must fail to be Christ, or the

Expected One of Judaism. But in Himmelfarb's case this is a task which demands that he disappoint others as well as himself.

In choosing the name Mordecai for Himmelfarb, White may have intended an allusion to the Mordecai of George Eliot's *Daniel Deronda*, for Himmelfarb shares with the Eliot character a commitment to Jewish faith, culture and history, and a deep sense of mission and destiny. Even in Himmelfarb's infancy, his mother had detected signs of his election and had sought a rabbi's confirmation. Himmelfarb himself, though for a time suspending his faith (he never wholly rejects it), comes increasingly to affirm his Messianic role and his duty to his people. His belief in his mission is reinforced by the enigmatic predictions of the dyer Israel and by the simple but bottomless faith of his wife Reha that he is the one to whom 'much will be made clear' (p. 157). In time, Himmelfarb starts to demand of himself what others do, until he believes, as he solemnly tells Mary, 'It was I . . . upon whom others were depending to redeem their sins' (p. 170). Obviously, he must be disabused of this notion, and White subjects him no less than three times to the failure to function as Saviour–Redeemer. Each time the incidents are couched in imagery which recalls Christ's Passion and thus contrasts Himmelfarb's experience with that of a true Saviour.

Himmelfarb first fails to save his wife from capture and subsequent death at the hands of the Nazis. On his way home from the German university where he teaches, on a night when for him, as for Christ in the Garden, 'comfort is not to be found', he suddenly takes panicked flight (p. 162). He seeks reassurance from his Gentile friends the Stauffers, unaware that on this very night the Germans are rounding up Jews, among them his wife. After this incident, which he sees as a betrayal of his wife and people, he hides in the Stauffers' country retreat, but he is as if 'dead' (p. 173), and his little room alternately seems a tomb or an egg from which he may be reborn (p. 183). In other words, resurrection is possible, but, when Himmelfarb does return to life, it is only to die again.

After another night reminiscent of Gethsemane, a solitary night of doubt and fear while bombs drop around his retreat, Himmelfarb emerges to undergo his second ordeal. Accepting 'some unspecified duty' (p. 183) which demands he fuse his suffering to that of the 'mass soul' of his people (p. 189), he surrenders himself to authorities. He and a trainload of other

Jews are sent to an extermination camp from which Himmelfarb escapes during an inmates' revolt. His torn hands and the barbs that pierce his forehead as he flees the death camp, the fence on which he briefly hangs, the women who dress his wounds, and the news of the outer world he receives on the third day all suggest that the 'miracle' of his survival is to be seen in terms of Christ's death and resurrection (pp. 203–5). But it must be emphasized that this comparison, like the earlier one, is made for the sake of contrast. The 'miracle' of Himmelfarb's preservation is not that of atonement for sins.

Himmelfarb, however, has not yet acknowledged the difference. On his way to Jerusalem, he is still insisting, 'It is I who must make amends' (p. 207), and he chooses Australia as his final destination because it seems to promise the suffering he seeks.

Once in Australia, Himmelfarb, who now believes that 'The intellect has failed us' (p. 219), begins penitentially to abase that faculty by taking a mindless assembly-line job in the Brighta Bicycle Lamp Factory. The factory is located in the Sydney suburb of Barranugli ('bare-and-ugly' or 'barren-ugly'), but he lives in another suburb, called Sarsaparilla.

It is worth remarking here the first appearance in White's fiction of this setting, probably based on the Sydney suburb of Castle Hill as it was during the years he lived there, from his return to Australia after the Second World War until 1963, when he moved into Sydney. White comes to use Sarsaparilla somewhat as Faulkner uses Yoknapatawpha County, but with less consistency and far fewer recurring characters. The refuge of self-satisfied suburbanites, it houses what White most deplores in modern urban life, particularly its complacency, hypocrisy, herd instincts, and love of plastics. But in this novel Sarsaparilla must share these honours with the more pretentious suburb of Paradise East, where, says White, 'humidity and conformity remained around 93' (p. 421). The author also castigates Sydney itself, which is once described with a loathing reaching surrealistic intensity:

> The train was easing through the city which knives had sliced open to serve up with all the juices running – red, and green and purple. All the syrups of the sundaes oozing into the streets to sweeten. The neon syrup coloured the pools of vomit and the sailors' piss. By that light, the eyes of the younger gabardine men were a blinding, blinder blue, when not actually

burnt out. The blue-haired grannies had purpled from the roots of their hair down to the ankles of their pants, not from shame, but neon, as their breasts chafed to escape from shammy-leather back to youth, or else roundly asserted themselves, like chamberpots in concrete. . . . There were the kiddies, too. The kiddies would continue to suck at their slabs of neon, until they had learnt to tell the time, until it was time to mouth other sweets. . . .

As the darkness spat sparks, and asphalt sinews ran with salt sweat, the fuddled trams would be tunnelling farther into the furry air, over the bottletops, through the smell of squashed pennies, and not omitting from time to time to tear an arm out of its screeching socket. (pp. 430–1)

In urban Australia, then, the would-be Christ has found a hell to harrow.

Presiding over hell are the satanic Mrs Flack and Mrs Jolley. These women, whom White repeatedly describes in terms taken from demonology and witchcraft, engineer the mock crucifixion which gives Himmelfarb his third and final chance to play the Messianic role. Mesdames Flack and Jolley, like most of Sarsaparilla, are outraged and threatened by Himmelfarb's foreignness, his Jewishness, his maddening humility, and most of all his unthinkable friendship with the washerwoman Mrs Godbold. During Easter week, it is a simple matter for Mrs Flack to incite the brutish Blue, already drunk on beer and his luck at the lottery, to lead his mates in playing a little joke on Himmelfarb, who, after all, is one of those who 'crucified Our Saviour' (p. 437).

The collusion of Flack and Jolley against Himmelfarb, while hardly unmotivated, is perhaps undermotivated when matched with its consequences: Himmelfarb dies as a result of the prank Mrs Flack instigates.[24] But White uses Mrs Flack and Mrs Jolley to make a twofold point: first that evil at any level, however seemingly innocuous and impotent, can quickly get out of control; and, secondly, that, as Mary tells Mrs Jolley, 'All bad things have a family resemblance . . . ' (p. 326). Readers are not asked to equate the mock crucifixion with the Holocaust and other monstrosities,[25] but are invited to see the family resemblance. White's own remarks on the subject offer perhaps the best rebuttal to objections that the crucifixion is melodramatic, unlikely, or unmotivated. In an autobiographical statement prepared for the

Nobel Foundation, he said of this scene, it 'outraged the blokes and the bluestockings alike. Naturally, "it couldn't happen here", – except that it does, in all quarters, in many infinitely humiliating ways, as I, a foreigner in my own country, learned from personal experience'.[26]

As the week of Passion and Passover moves toward its climax on Good Friday, White intensifies the conjunction of Christian and Jewish imagery which has surrounded Himmelfarb and which will culminate in his deathbed dream. We first see a Seder meal which is also a Last Supper. The shank bone of a lamb given him by Mrs Godbold duplicates that already set out by Himmelfarb. But this Last Supper must be celebrated without disciples, and, as a Jew, Himmelfarb regrets the absence of other faithful on a night which should be shared. Accordingly, he goes to the home of Harry Rosetree (once Haim Rosenbaum), the immigrant Jew who Christianized himself and family and now manages the bicycle-lamp factory. Himmelfarb wants to rejoice in a sense of Jewish community on Seder night. But, of course, the Rosetrees' whole life has denied that community in an attempt to escape the demands made on the Chosen Ones. They can only reject him, although Rosetree contributes to the accumulating crucifixion imagery by remarking that Himmelfarb looks 'pretty well flogged' (p. 424). The rejection leaves him for the third time as alone as was Christ at Gethsemane.

As the events of the following day unfold, Christ's triumphal entry into Jerusalem finds its distant and dislocated echo in the circus and funeral processions which collide under the windows of the factory.[27] The incident is also proleptic. A circus clown pantomimes a public hanging, which is followed shortly by Himmelfarb's crucifixion. And in the stalled and entangled funeral procession, the watching widow comes to terms with 'the depth, and duration, and truth of grief', which Himmelfarb's death will teach the other Riders (p. 445).

The Jew's incomplete and inadequate Passion is like the clown's pantomime: both are farce with tragic implications. In one of the clearest statements of a principle which informs much of his work, White insists, 'there is almost no tragedy which cannot be given a red nose' (p. 449). Life, White has said repeatedly, is 'tragi-farce'.[28] Himmelfarb can and indeed must be simultaneously Christ and clown, mythic hero and muddled human being. It is to this curious double stance of the Riders (and all Whitean protagonists) that White refers when telling interviewers, 'As visionaries [the Riders] are not treated ironically. But as human beings, in the details of their daily lives, it is impossible to avoid irony.'[29] As Robert M. Adams has observed of Don Quixote, Himmelfarb is at once the buffoon and a 'type of the divine'.[30] To be wholly one or the other would be to cheat one's humanity. And for Himmelfarb, as for Voss, it is full humanity which enables man's closest approach to divinity.

White emphasizes this paradox by allowing the crucifixion scene and its aftermath to strain towards but stop just short of allegory. As Himmelfarb is hoisted onto the mutilated jacaranda tree, his hands, temples and side are pierced or gashed, the crowd mocks and spits at him, and an earthquake widens a crack in Mary Hare's crumbling mansion. Although these events take place on Maundy Thursday, Himmelfarb survives the ordeal, to die shortly after midnight, thus allowing Ruth Godbold to observe, 'Mr Himmelfarb, too, has died on the Friday' (p. 491). Other characters take or trade off parts in the Passion Play. Ruth becomes Mary, the mother of Jesus, Mary Hare the second Mary, Harry Rosetree perhaps a Judas (fittingly, he later hangs himself), but also the Pilate who absolves himself of all responsibility. The half-caste Aboriginal artist, Alf Dubbo, seems a Pilate in his repeated washing of his hands after he fails to rescue Himmelfarb. But later he is Peter denying knowledge of the Jew. All these characters, however, are also and unremittingly themselves, as is Himmelfarb, whose final martyrdom at first seems as futile as the others. After he is lowered from the tree, White says of him, 'Very quietly Himmelfarb left the factory in which it had not been accorded to him to expiate the sins of the world' (p. 459). At this moment, he concedes his failure.

However, in one of White's familiar ironic reversals, it is precisely his failure to become Christ, coupled with his recognition and acceptance of that failure, which renders him most Christlike and most potent in that capacity for the other Riders. For Alf Dubbo, Himmelfarb brings Christ to life. White describes the Aboriginal when, too terrified to act, he watches Himmelfarb upon the tree:

> All that he had ever suffered, all that he had failed to understand, rose to the surface in Dubbo. . . . As he watched, the colour flowed through the veins of the cold, childhood

Christ, at last the nails entered wherever it was acknowledged
they should. . . . So he understood the concept of the blood,
which was sometimes . . . the clear crimson of redemption. He
was blinded now. Choking now. Physically feebler for the
revelation that knowledge would never cut the cords which
bound the Saviour to the tree. Not that it was asked. Nothing
was asked. So he began also to understand acceptance. . . .

And love in its many kinds began to trouble him as he
looked.   (pp. 453–4)

The Jew has resurrected Christ for Dubbo and will have an
analogous impact on the lives of the other two Riders.

Himmelfarb's failure is his inability to redeem. That this failure
is itself redemptive is clear from his visions both on the jacaranda
tree and as he later dies. At the height of his ordeal, he had
prayed for a sign and 'was conscious of a stillness and clarity,
which was the stillness and clarity of pure water, at the centre of
which his God was reflected' (p. 454). Later, in Mrs Godbold's
shed, he attains the Whitean vision of inclusion. As Alf's did, his
vision embraces many kinds of love, Jewish and Christian, *eros*
and *agape*:

He was swallowed up by the whiteness. He was received as
seldom. . . . Again, he was the Man Kadmon, descending from
the Tree of Light to take the Bride. Trembling with white,
holding the cup in her chapped hands, she advanced to stand
beneath the *chuppah*. So they were brought together in the smell
of all primordial velvets. This, explained the cousins and aunts,
is at last the Shekinah whom you have carried all these years
under your left breast. As he received her, she bent and kissed
the wound in his hand. Then they were truly one. They did
not break the cup, as the wedding guests expected, but took
and drank, again and again.   (pp. 472–3)

Obviously this passage contributes to the thematically central
modulation between Jewish and Christian ceremony and symbology. It also provides an image of the androgyne, 'the symbol', as
Emerson put it, 'of the finished soul',[31] and a being whom White
often uses to represent wholeness. Its appearance here and its
association with Himmelfarb suggest that his fragmented self has
been healed. Beyond this, the conjunction of the Man Kadmon

and the Shekinah is of crucial importance in creating the sense of comprehensiveness White wants to convey. Adam Kadmon is the Kabbalah's archetypal or celestial man, the Logos or form-giver, sometimes identified with Christ. In Himmelfarb's vision, he is brought into fruitful embrace with the Shekinah, who shows forth the presence of God in the world, divinity manifest in creation.[32] In other words, creator and created unite here in a marriage which also evokes the apocalyptic marriage of the Lamb, as well as that of primordial Adam with Eve, who was formed from his body. The image of the marriage thus links Himmelfarb to a host of archetypes. His being has achieved inconceivable perimeters.

As was also true for Theodora Goodman, Stan Parker, and Voss, Himmelfarb's failure has opened the way to success. The remaining three Riders – Mary Hare, Ruth Godbold, and Alf Dubbo – must fail and find their vision in terms set by Himmelfarb's experience. In all three cases, the climactic failure is the inability to save the Jew. But, like him, each also suffers a series of preliminary failures.

As a blotched and brindled child, Mary Hare can only outrage the acute aesthetic sense of her father. For Norbert Hare, truth is beauty, a precept he puts into architectural practice in the fanciful home he names 'Xanadu'. Because Mary is unlovely, he can neither love nor acknowledge her. Her mother, on the other hand, is less offended than bored by the awkward fledgling she has hatched. White says, 'Mrs Hare had soon taken refuge from Mary in a rational kindness, with which she continued to deal her a series of savage blows during what passed for childhood' (p. 24). Understandably, Mary finds it increasingly hard to love people and instead turns to birds, animals, even plants. In fact, she makes a virtual religion of nature, performing her rites in the overgrown grounds around Xanadu.

Through Himmelfarb her love for human beings is rekindled. When she first meets him, they celebrate a kind of marriage under the canopy provided by the branches of a plum tree. In the course of their relationship, he draws her into deepening involvement in the human predicament, until she makes the willing sacrifice implicit in her surname (pp. 103–4). Himmelfarb identifies her as one of the generation's hidden *zaddikim*, the holy ones who teach, heal, and interpret. But if Mary becomes a *zaddik*, it is only through Himmelfarb's agency. At the time she meets him,

she is relearning a quite different set of skills: those required for
cruelty and evil.

It is tempting to see Mary's life at Xanadu as an Edenic one,
invaded by the serpent in the form of Mrs Jolley. Evidence for
this interpretation is Mrs Jolley's linkage with the serpent through
her killing of a snake which Mary has understood more in
Lawrentian terms, as one of the 'Lords of Life', than in its
traditional Christian role as Satan's deputy. Moreover, it is
certainly Mary's torment at the hands of Mrs Jolley which drives
her to retaliate with taunts and deceit. But evil does not arrive
with Mrs Jolley; it is no stranger, either to Mary or to Xanadu.

At a crucial moment of Mary's childhood, the revulsion she
aroused in her father had prompted his awful verdict, 'Ugly as
a foetus. Ripped out too soon' (p. 62). Ironically, his description
seems to place her among the 'unborn', whom he had earlier
acknowledged as the only souls to be 'whole' and 'pure' (p. 40).
Unborn innocence and integrity are restored to Mary near the
end of the novel when Dubbo paints her in his *Deposition* as 'curled,
like a ring-tail possum, in a dreamtime womb of transparent skin'
(p. 501). But in the meantime Mary must endure fragmentation
and must perpetrate as well as suffer evil. She begins on the very
day that her father pronounces his judgement on her, and soon
after, drowns in the cistern.

White leaves deliberately vague the nature and extent of
Mary's responsibility for her father's death. What matters is less
Mary's actual guilt than her belief in it, a belief Mrs Jolley uses
to intimidate and manipulate her. Similarly, Mary accepts
responsibility for the death of her pet goat. A too-possessive love
for the creature had driven her to secure it at night in a shed,
and, when the shed catches fire, the goat burns to death.

Significantly, in both cases Mary has failed to save a life. The
third failure occurs when she plunges into Himmelfarb's burning
shack only to find him already gone. This failure, however, is
analogous to the others only in its outcome, since here action has
replaced the inaction or inadequate action of the earlier instances.
Through her growing concern for Himmelfarb, Mary has come
to recognize in him that 'lovingkindness which might redeem'
(p. 331). In the self-sacrifice of her rescue attempt, she has allowed
a human 'lovingkindness' to triumph over her instinctive, animal
terror. As a result and almost as a reward, she is subsequently
'translated' into more human terms: 'Her animal body became
the least part of her, as breathing thought turned to being'

(p. 475). At the same time, however, that uniquely animal nature achieves its fullest expression. Like Himmelfarb, that is, she becomes most herself when she least seeks to be. By transcending the self, she expands it until it permeates the world around her. Hers is another of those typically Whitean moments in which the self is diffused and distributed. White describes her as she leaves the Godbold hut after Himmelfarb's death:

> In the friable white light, she too was crumbling, . . . no longer held in check by the many purposes which direct animal, or human life. . . . Her instinct suggested . . . that she was being dispersed, but that in so experiencing, she was entering the final ecstasy. . . . she had become all-pervasive: scent, sound, the steely dew, the blue glare of white light off rocks. She was all but identified.   (pp. 482–3)

Early in the novel Mary had decided, 'Eventually I shall discover what is at the centre if enough of me is peeled away' (p. 58). This enterprise is akin to that of *Voss's* Brendan Boyle and just as spurious, a judgement White suggests by describing it as the product of Mary's unusually lucid reasoning. Like many of his protagonists, White distrusts reason and knows its limitations. The mystical union attained by his initiates will not yield to rational analysis or explanation. Moreover, reason, like the project of shedding layers of the self, is analytic and reductive.[33] The movement Mary and other illuminati must make is in the opposite direction: outward from the self and towards inclusiveness. For Mary Hare, who disappears from the novel after experiencing dispersal, this enlargement seems to come because she at last expresses love for another human being and yet accepts the human limits of that love, especially its impotence to save.

Ruth Godbold also bears the guilt for several lives she has not saved.[34] But, while Mary's failures first spring from inability to love, Ruth fails because of overabundant love: a determination to care and nurture which White once describes as 'relentless' (p. 71). The maiden name White gives her, Joyner, suggests her lifelong project. But love will not always make the centre hold, and when things fall apart, Ruth accuses herself. Thus she takes the blame for the death of her brother, although White's recounting of the haymaking accident absolves her of any real responsibility (p. 264).

At the earlier death of her mother, Ruth had assumed the care of her siblings, and this role, like her brother's body, proves a burden she is loath to surrender. When her father remarries, however, Ruth emigrates from her home in England to Australia, both to avoid replacement by a stepmother and to punish herself for what she tells her suitor Tom Godbold was 'too much' love for her father (p. 288). As her husband, Tom learns to understand the concept of 'too much' love. Eventually, his wife's meek, self-effacing and implacably forgiving love, supported by a faith which grows in her like a gestating child, drives him to greater and greater excesses of cruelty and debauchery. The effect on him is very like that of Hickey's wife on him in O'Neill's *The Iceman Cometh*.[35] Her forbearance and belief in him keep his unworthiness before him and hound him into bars and brothels. Even here, Ruth pursues Tom like an unshakable Fury, until she proves to him he is not 'strong enough to suffer the full force of his wife's love' (p. 315). He disappears and dies some years later in poverty.

Ruth Godbold is undeniably good and a force for good in the novel. Hers, in fact, is the most unalloyed good the novel offers, and a former employer, Mrs Chalmers-Robinson, goes so far as to claim that Ruth is a saint. But to be wholly the saint would be inhuman, and even goodness can be a disease, as White shows in the case of Miss Docker of the play and short story *A Cheery Soul*.[36] Thus Ruth's nature must undergo revision.

In her relationship with Himmelfarb, her overweening and obsessive love is tempered, so that what begins as charity develops into friendship. Similarly, in her brief encounter with Alf at Mrs Khalil's brothel, her love finds a different dimension of expression, becoming like the Aboriginal's paintings, her 'work of art' (p. 313). Her relationship with the third Rider, Mary Hare, is also such that she is suffered to give, but not permitted to possess. Through her association with the other Riders, then, Ruth learns more about love, its limits and its proper sphere, as Mary learns more about her instincts, Himmelfarb about his intellect, and Alf about his art.

Although Ruth, too, must fail to save Himmelfarb, she is 'exalted' by her attempt (p. 471) and subsequently becomes the novel's locus of values. In its final pages she is made an emblem of a spiritual and fleshly fecundity which strives to repopulate the world with goodness. At one point she thinks of her six daughters and of how she had shot her six arrows at the face of darkness, and halted it. And wherever her arrows struck, she saw other arrows breed. And out of those arrows, others still would split off, from the straight white shafts.

So her arrows would continue to be aimed at the forms of darkness, and she herself was, in fact, the infinite quiver. (p. 539)

Thus Ruth finds the most effective expression of the militant love which is her nature, after the failure of that love to save or subdue its objects. In the familiar manner, her essential self is most potently realized only after its fundamental impotence is exposed and admitted. For Ruth, as for the others, the process by which the self is abandoned and recovered is capped by a perception of the inherent unity of all things, whether aspects of the physical world or constructs of the mind and heart. This understanding is explicit in the assurance Ruth gives Mr Rosetree that Judaism and Christianity are 'the same'. Explaining why she has given Himmelfarb a Christian burial, she tells Rosetree, 'Men are the same before they are born. They are the same at birth, perhaps you will agree. It is only the coat they are told to put on that makes them all that different' (p. 490).

Significantly, Mrs Godbold's use of the metaphor of religion as a coat recalls Himmelfarb's youthful musing that religion was 'like a winter overcoat' (p. 111). Ruth and Himmelfarb also share, without communicating it, an awareness expressed in merged Neoplatonic and Kabbalistic imagery: that all creation encapsulates sparks of the divine fire and that all things are 'fragments of the one light' (p. 267). Such echoes, especially since they link the most and least articulate, most and least intellectual sides of the quadrant, reinforce our impression that the Riders themselves ultimately fuse. This fusion is solemnized and celebrated in the work of the fourth Rider, Alf Dubbo.

Early in his career as a painter, Alf imagines how he may eventually translate into art his conception of the Chariot in 'forms partly transcendental, partly evolved from his struggle with daily becoming, and experience of suffering' (p. 377). For White, these are the sources of all significant experience: struggle and suffering illuminated by glimpses of the 'transcendental' forms which structure them. In this novel, as in *Voss*, the emphasis is on failure as an impetus in this struggle of becoming. As Konrad

Stauffer speculates to Himmelfarb, 'I wonder whether the pure aren't those who have tried, but not succeeded. . . . atonement is possible perhaps only where there has been failure' (pp. 179–80).

Like the other Riders, Alf has already failed before Himmelfarb gives him the chance to fail finally and crucially. Most damning of his failures in his own eyes is what he condemns as infidelity to his creative self. The prostitute Hannah introduces him to a Humphrey Mortimer, an art-connoisseur, who coaxes Alf into showing him his work. Subsequently, Dubbo feels queasy and frightened: 'As if, in a moment of exuberant vanity, he had betrayed some mystery, of which he was the humblest and most recent initiate' (p. 397). For Alf, his work has been his 'proof of an Absolute' and 'act of faith' (p. 379). When Hannah later sells some of his paintings to Mortimer, Alf feels that his impiety has been fittingly punished. He destroys the remaining paintings and disappears, only later attempting to expiate his guilt through further artistic efforts.

Alf's second important failing is his refusal to accept the Christ offered him by the Reverend Calderon and Mrs Pask, a white clergyman and his sister who adopt Alf as part of their 'Great Experiment' in civilizing the natives. Mrs Pask encourages the boy's artistic talent but is shocked at the results, while Mr Calderon preaches brotherly love and practices homosexual seduction. They and other whites Alf meets reduce Christ to a bloodless and baffling conundrum. After leaving Hannah's place Alf thinks,

> he would fail, as he had always failed before, to reconcile the Gospels' truths with what he had experienced. Where he could accept God because of the spirit that would work in him at times, the duplicity of the white man prevented him considering Christ, except as an ambitious abstraction, or realistically, as a man.   (p. 407)

Himmelfarb's suffering restores flesh and blood to Dubbo's abstract Christ. But, just as importantly, his guilt over the failure to save Himmelfarb or even to testify to his experience prods him into bearing witness in the most powerful works he has ever produced, the *Deposition* and the *Chariot*. In painting them, he is not giving form to any personal conception, but is acting as the instrument of a superhuman force. He seems to work with some unseen 'assistance' (p. 499), in accord with revelation (p. 504). He is 'driven . . . to give expression to the love he had witnessed, and which, inwardly, he had always known must exist' (p. 500). Thus Alf, like the other Riders, enacts a version of the Christian paradox in which one finds his life by losing it: he is most the artist when least deliberately so, most able to express his love after its absolute paralysis in the moment of Himmelfarb's need.

As Alf locates and evinces his fundamental self in his final paintings, the other Riders appear in those works in forms suggestive of their own essential natures. In his *Deposition*, he paints Ruth Godbold as the 'immemorial woman' whose breasts are 'running with . . . milk' (ibid.). Mary Hare is drawn in one of the 'trustful attitudes of many oblivious animals', and 'illuminated by the light of instinct inside the transparent weft of whirling, procreative wind' (p. 501). In other words, Ruth is revealed as the Magna Mater, Mary as the archetypal child, whose unborn innocence derives from her instinctual, natural being. Himmelfarb, the Christ of the *Deposition*, appears as both God and man, as Laura Trevelyan knew all men were. In the *Chariot* painting, where Dubbo completes the quartet, he depicts his own head as a 'whirling spectrum' (p. 505), source of the agitation which has issued in the colours of his art.

Dubbo paints much of his *Deposition* in a 'panegyric blue' (p. 479), which prefigures the indigo Hurtle Duffield will seek in *The Vivisector*. As in *Voss* the colour green was associated both with growth and decomposition, in *Riders in the Chariot*, the colour blue takes on what Northrop Frye would call apocalyptic and demonic modes. In its apocalyptic manifestations it appears not only in Dubbo's paintings, but on the hands of the ugly little dyer whom Himmelfarb learns to accept as a part of himself, and in Himmelfarb's very name, which literally translated from the German means 'heaven colour'. In its demonic cast, blue is associated with Mrs Jolley, who has blue eyes and arrives wearing blue. More strikingly, it is the only name given to the ringleader of the gang that hoists Himmelfarb onto the tree. White uses these modulations as an imagistic means of underscoring the awareness to which his visionaries are admitted, the knowledge that good and evil are both encompassed in one comprehensive scheme, so that, as Alf comes to see, 'Everything, finally, was a source of wonder, not to say love' (p. 503).

It should be emphasized, however, that, while White insists

that we acknowledge evil, see it as within the grand framework, and attempt to understand it, he does not condone it, especially as practised by Mrs Flack, Mrs Jolley and their ilk. Rather like Judas, these women are viewed as necessary to the scheme of things but none the less deserving of damnation. In fact, rarely in a White novel do evildoers suffer such retribution as do these harpies. The ladies are allowed to discover each other's dark secrets: Blue is Mrs Flack's illegitimate son and both women are implicated in their husbands' deaths. But, unlike the Riders, they are incapable of admitting their crimes or using them to positive purposes. Thus they are left together, living in a hell constituted by each other. Their fate is especially fitting in a novel which makes so much use of Judaism, since it exemplifies the Jewish belief that evil thoughts, motives and actions take on actual existence, as evil angels or 'the objectification of malevolence'.[37] Flack and Jolley become each other's evil angels; in each, the other's malice is mirrored and glares back at her.

In its closing pages, the novel moves rapidly from the hell of Flack and Jolley to the obscure 'purgatory' of Mrs Chalmers-Robinson and her fashionable friends (p. 536), and then to the heavenly demesne where Ruth Godbold is 'enshrined' (p. 528). As readers we see that a proper hierarchy has been restored; order is reinstated. Fittingly, White ends the novel with Ruth, the sole survivor among the quaternity and the one whose life, like Laura's, can best reflect her vision. Surprisingly, however, he sets her final affirmations amidst the prefabricated homes which have risen on the site of Xanadu.

The new settlement seems to be a typical Whitean suburb, sustained by what he elsewhere calls a 'mystical union with banality' (p. 420). But Mrs Godbold sees it differently. Although moved by her memories of Xanadu, she is ready to comfort and cherish the new residents. While such a sentiment is true to Ruth's nature, the reader wonders how she can condone and even celebrate the supplanting of magnificent Xanadu by a jerry-built suburb. To approach this problem, we must return to the concept of the chariot, both as vision and as work of art.

His painting of the chariot is Dubbo's articulation of the vision all four have shared. Mary has inherited the vision from her father, who in one anomalous moment of closeness with his daughter shows her the chariot in a sunset with its 'great swinging trace-chains of . . . light' (p. 27). Himmelfarb finds the chariot first in ancient books of mysticism, Dubbo in another artist's painting, and Ruth seems to come to it through music. But, for all, the vision recurs and assumes personal dimensions and implications.

Mary receives her visions in epileptic-like fits, and their emotional ambience often matches her own. Thus, on the night before Mrs Jolley arrives at Xanadu, the vision comes to her in a premonitory 'aura of terror' (p. 41). Himmelfarb sees the chariot 'streaming with implications' (p. 149). It is both the terrible Throne of God and the merciful agent of atonement and redemption. At one point, he tells Mary that the hidden *zaddikim* may themselves be the Chariot of God (p. 171). Alf has approached the concept through a French painting of Apollo's chariot, but enriched it with the addition, from Ezekiel (1:4–28), of the four Living Creatures. Most important to Alf in the chariot is its movement, its flowing with light and fire. In his final version, however, he makes the discovery that motion is only another form of permanence (p. 504), an insight which has also occurred to Mary. For Ruth, as we might expect, the chariot is propelled by 'wings of love and charity' (p. 540).

The chariot as symbol in the novel has obvious biblical, classical and mythological roots. White seems to have added to this symbolic complex aspects of Jewish *Merkabah* ('heavenly chariot') tradition, which inquires into the nature of God. Also relevant may be the Kabbalistic belief that the four figures in the chariot represent the four possible archetypes on which all human life is based.[38] Further, White may have intended reference to the use of the chariot in Jewish symbology as a vehicle by means of which Divine Plenty descends to the created world and the plenty of our world arises – a kind of crossroads at which the sacred and secular meet.[39] Thematic resonances in the novel could be identified for all these associations.[40]

But what is perhaps the most significant about the chariot is that its concept provides an ideal order, reified in Dubbo's painting, within which the Riders unite as they cannot in life. During their lives, all four come together only once: when Dubbo hides outside the Godbold shack, sees the dying Himmelfarb cared for by Mary and Ruth, and watches his *Deposition* take shape before him. In the case of this painting and his *Chariot*, life seems to serve the purposes of art or at least to be perfected and interpreted through art. But we must reconcile this sense with the fact that these paintings are casually auctioned off after Dubbo's death and then utterly vanish.

An analogous fate is in store for Xanadu, the novel's other work of art.[41] What begins as Norbert Hare's pledge of allegiance to pleasure and beauty is in ruins even as the novel begins and is finally razed to make way for suburban sprawl. As Norbert Hare conceived and built it, Xanadu was a 'materialization of beauty' (p. 21). Yet it is somehow menaced, almost from the moment of completion, by the encroaching scrub. Like the dream vision of Coleridge's poem from which it takes its name, Xanadu is a mere mental construct, designedly otherworldly and removed from life. Its fate demonstrates that the fullness of life, particularly its demand for growth, process, and change, is not to be denied, even by art. Art, as in the case of Dubbo's *Chariot* and *Deposition*, may organize, emblematize and interpret experience, but it must not be allowed to supersede it. What we have in White is not the emphasis of Shakespeare's sonnets on art as preserving significant experience from the flux of time, but the Keatsian recognition that this immunity may exact a terrible price. In White's work, even art is subjected to the discipline of failure; even art must come face to face with its own limitations. Thus Xanadu crumbles and Alf Dubbo's paintings disappear.

What does not fail in the novel is life, life seen as a cyclic process of growth and decay in which, as Mary Hare comes to recognize, 'disintegration was the only permanent, perhaps the only desirable state', and truth is not some intellectual abstraction but 'a stillness and a light' (p. 464). In such a world, as Else Godbold knows, 'goodness must return, like grass' (p. 516). Thus the novel leaves us with Mrs Godbold's goodness, but stresses its procreative nature. Among Ruth's final visions is that of goodness and light breeding exponentially, and her ultimate affirmation is for the life, however squalid, that pulses in the growing suburb. At the novel's end, Mrs Godbold is among those who 'wore the crown' not least because her 'feet were still planted firmly on the earth' (p. 524). Herself a kind of organic growth, she encourages such growth everywhere she finds it. The novel's last words are, 'she continued to live' (p. 542).

Thus, the book ends by celebrating more than it questions or condemns. Even the virulent satire directed against urban life in general and its Rosetrees, Flacks, and Jolleys in particular is tempered by Mrs Godbold's final awareness that life in any form is precious. The dichotomous division of visionary elect from ordinary mortals which had obtained earlier in the novel begins to be healed through the agency of Ruth's reconciling vision. She thus becomes like Laura in *Voss*, a vehicle through which the experience of the novel is mediated and interpreted. Again like Laura, she survives the redemptive failure to demonstrate in her on-going life the meaning of redemption.

THE SOLID MANDALA

The nature of redemption is also at the heart of White's next novel, *The Solid Mandala* (1966). Here, too, the theme is enacted by a quaternity of characters, all of whom are sometimes seen as aspects of a single self. Moreover, in the new novel as in *Riders in the Chariot*, the Judaeo–Christian tradition supplies many of the allusions and the unifying myth. But here the similarities cease. Among the more obvious differences is the fact that, in *The Solid Mandala*, narrative attention is not distributed among the four major characters, but is focused on two: the twin Brown brothers, who are themselves halves of a severed whole. In fact, as White has recently indicated, they may be halves of the author's own self (*FG*, p. 146).

There are also other differences between *Riders* and *The Solid Mandala*. In the earlier work, three of the four main characters die while one survives. With the addition of this plot device, the quaternity is resolved into unity in two ways: through its emblematic presentation in Dubbo's *Chariot*, and in the person of Ruth Godbold, Magna Mater of all goodness, in whose memory the Riders are sustained. In *The Solid Mandala*, the reverse occurs. One dies, while three live. Here, then, a quaternity becomes a trinity, or, in other words, a pattern associated with the earthly and real modulates into a paradigm of the divine and ideal. Viewed in another way, the division and dissension of the twins can be seen to be resolved in the final triad.[42] In either case, important implications for our understanding of the novel arise, implications to which I shall return.

Finally, there are important differences in the way *The Solid Mandala* handles the theme of failure. True to the familiar Whitean scheme, both Arthur and Waldo Brown fail significantly, but Waldo's failure is different in character from that of any previous protagonist, and Arthur's is different in consequence.

In part, these differences can be attributed to White's work in other genres. Between the release of *Riders in the Chariot* in 1961 and *The Solid Mandala* in 1966, he had published his *Four Plays* (1965), three of them written in the early sixties, and his first collection of short stories, *The Burnt Ones* (1964). These excursions into other forms allowed him to experiment, particularly in the handling of character. Among his experiments was the extended treatment of characters like Mrs Flack and Mrs Jolley: unlovely and unloving, spiteful, life-denying people, people who are 'burnt ones' in the sense that some vital capacity in them has been seared away or irreparably maimed. White lends support to this interpretation of the collection's title when he remarks, in *Flaws in the Glass*, that the 'Burnt Ones' is the name given to a formation of 'glowering volcanic fragments' on the Greek island of Santorini (p. 188). Like the formation, the characters in these stories are in some crucial way extinct. Most often, the lost faculty is the ability to love.[43] For example, 'Dead Roses', a study in sterility, concerns a woman who seeks and finds a state of 'impregnable negation' (*BO*, p. 62). The heroine of this story, Anthea Mortlock, is, as her name suggests, locked in death. In a variation on this theme, White uses Miss Docker of 'A Cheery Soul' to demonstrate that the acts of love without love behind them can render even goodness a deformity. Sometimes, the burnt one suffers most acutely himself, as is true for the title character of 'Clay' and Charles Polkinghorn of 'The Letters'.[44] In other instances, such as that of Philippides in 'A Glass of Tea', the mutilated person inflicts his own pain on others.

In other words, with rare exceptions such as Daise Morrow of 'Down at the Dump', the protagonists of the short stories are not people for whom failure can act as a stimulus to further discovery of self; rather, they are those for whom failure, the failure to love and ultimately to live, *is* the fullest expression of self. They are thus irretrievably damned. The same tends to be true of characters in the plays, although all four plays have at least one saving or salvageable figure. The clearest examples are the Young Man in *The Ham Funeral*, Pippy in *The Season at Sarsaparilla*, the Reverend Wakeman in *A Cheery Soul*, and the Goat Woman in *Night on Bald Mountain*. The rest of the casts, however, are composed of such people as the Sarsaparilla suburbanites, obsessed with maintaining spotless linoleum, or the destructive and self-despising Swords of *Night on Bald Mountain*, whose sudden renascence in the final act is, at best, hard to credit. These characters, and many like them in the shorter fiction, offered White new scope for exploration of a type he had tended to satirize, condemn, and dismiss.

Waldo Brown is the first such character to take centre stage in a novel. In him we watch the development of what Arthur only belatedly sees is 'the hatred Waldo . . . had always directed, at all living things' (*SM*, p. 288). As readers, however, we have identified this hate in Waldo long before Arthur can, since throughout the novel's second section, White forces us to see the world and the novel's events through Waldo's eyes.

Waldo's section is one of four into which the novel is divided. This is a happy organizational choice, since in its adoption of a four-part structure the book reflects the Jungian mandala, which is its organizing metaphor and to which the novel's title alludes. Jung saw this geometric figure, often a squared circle or a circle quadrisected by a cross, as a pattern generated by the psyche in its attempt to integrate itself and to find wholeness. At one point, Arthur is browsing through an encyclopedia, stumbles across a definition of the mandala, and haltingly reads it out: 'The Mandala is a symbol of totality. It is believed to be the "dwelling of the god". Its protective circle is a pattern of order super – imposed on – psychic – chaos . . . ' (p. 232). This highly Jungian formulation may have been adopted from Jung's essay 'Mandalas', and at any rate refers to concepts explicated at length in *AION, The Archetypes and the Collective Unconscious, Psychology and Religion* and *Psychology and Alchemy*.[45] The mandala's four-part structure derives from the conjunction of opposites which are juxtaposed and held in dialectic tension but are not annihilated.[46] It is thus that imaginative order is brought to bear on chaos. The novel reflects this schema by juxtaposing the very different 'Waldo' and 'Arthur' sections and enclosing these within shorter sections in which the brothers' constricted world is contrasted with a larger one on which they finally impinge.[47]

For the most part, the two exterior sections are given from the point of view which that external world imposes. The opening section, 'In the Bus', consists of nervous small talk which Mrs Poulter makes while riding the bus with her new friend Mrs Dun. We approach the Brown brothers as these women do, at the distance of gossip and by way of a quick glimpse from a bus window. Even the excruciatingly painful and personal events of the final section come to us filtered through the responses of others: the horror and nausea of the police sergeant and his young assistant, the terror of Mrs Dun, the ribaldry of the drunks in the alley, and the unfeeling officiousness of the librarians. At this point the world of events, whether of bodies piled up for TV newscasts or of Arthur's 'murdered' brother, intrudes itself even between Arthur and his beloved Dulcie. He is forced to watch and yearn for her outside her window, very much as Alf Dubbo watched and yearned outside the window of the Godbold shed. In both the outer sections, the reader, too, is kept at a certain remove.

But for the two interior sections, those named after Waldo and Arthur, White adopts an almost uninterrupted use of indirect discourse, revealing the novel's events first as Waldo sees them, then as Arthur does. This technique is not new to White. From his earliest fiction he had employed indirect discourse, in which the narrator's voice speaks in the phrases and cadences which would be used by the character, thereby disclosing feelings, values and reactions appropriate to that character. Clearly, this is one of White's favourite methods for maintaining an ironic perspective on character and one of the sharpest weapons in his satiric and comedic arsenal. From *The Tree of Man* on, he increasingly chooses this mediated method for the rendering of interior monologue, the method preferred by Virginia Woolf, in place of the Joycean tapping of stream of consciousness which figured prominently in his earlier works. In his middle and later fiction, in fact, the unmarked shift from authorially endorsed narrative to Woolfian indirect discourse sometimes causes confusion over whose point of view is in force.[48]

In *The Solid Mandala*, however, the use of indirect discourse seems primarily strategic. For in no other way could the reader be brought to understand Waldo enough to credit Arthur's love for him and to acknowledge what he represents. Only by seeing through his own eyes and those of his always loving brother can the reader approach Waldo at all, for the very essence of his being is to repel others.[49]

Waldo, who 'was born with his innards twisted' (p. 26), comes to be emblematized in the novel by the marble Arthur thinks of as Waldo's mandala: the one with the knot at the centre which Waldo will never untie (pp. 266–7). Tense, rigid, involuted, and self-enclosed, Waldo tells himself he is preserving the integrity of his literary genius from contamination by human contact. He wants to 'Write', but thinks that

To submit himself to the ephemeral, the superficial relationships, might damage the crystal core holding itself in reserve for some imminent moment of higher idealism. Just as he had avoided fleshly love – while understanding its algebra, of course – the better to convey eventually its essence. (p. 176)

Waldo's actual incapacity either for imaginative work or for real love is tellingly exposed when he contemplates marriage to Dulcie Feinstein. White says,

> As he walked along the roadside, thoughtfully decapitating the weeds, Waldo went over the ways in which he would benefit by marriage with Dulcie. . . . Undoubtedly he would benefit by having a home of his own. A bed to himself . . . . But it was his work, his real work, which would benefit most. . . . One of the first things he intended to do was to buy a filing cabinet to install in his study. (p. 143)

Waldo thinks of married love in terms of a bed to himself and of creativity in terms of a filing cabinet.

Love will not pierce Waldo's shield of fastidious disgust, intellectual pretensions, and general superciliousness. Not even Arthur's love can release him, though Waldo is forced to recognize Arthur as 'part of his own parcel of flesh' and therefore inescapable (p. 69). For Waldo this relationship breeds only frustration. As the bright and promising lad saddled with a brother who appears to be 'a shingle short', Waldo thinks of Arthur as a handicap analogous to their father's club foot (p. 41). Arthur embarrasses Waldo, particularly in his open demonstrations of affection. Even more disturbing is his intuitive irrationalism, his ability to 'drag . . . Waldo back repeatedly behind the line where knowledge didn't protect' (p. 40). Waldo needs to express himself in words in order to verify and validate his existence (p. 76), but, as Arthur reminds him, 'Words are not what make you see' or be (p. 51).[50] None the less, Arthur uses words to better effect than his brother. While Waldo's anaemic and derivative prose fragment *Teiresias a Youngish Man* stagnates in a dress box, Arthur dashes off the clumsy but terrifying poem which celebrates mankind's common pain and drives Waldo to jealous fury. Arthur's life is thus a perpetual repudiation and revision of Waldo's, so much so that, when Waldo thinks of encountering his own doubts, he imagines facing Arthur (p. 100).

Waldo's steadily growing hatred of his brother expresses itself in a series of rejections: the rejection of things, pursuits or people Arthur loves; the rejection of the proffered mandala; and finally the rejection of Arthur himself, which occurs in the library where Waldo works. Coming across Arthur reading the 'Grand Inquisitor' section of *The Brothers Karamazov*, Waldo is appalled by Arthur's understanding of the novel's implications. Arthur tells Waldo that the book has taught him something about their renegade-Baptist father, who embraced rationalism, repudiated God, and burned his copy of *The Brothers Karamazov*. Arthur explains,

> That is why our father was afraid. It wasn't so much because of the blood, however awful, pouring out where the nails went in. He was afraid to worship some thing. Or body. Which is what I take it this Dostoevski is partly going on about. (p. 192).

Waldo, who has also relied on his own will in a godless world, is so threatened by Arthur's suggestion and so worried lest their fraternal relationship be recognized by his library colleagues that he orders his brother out of the reading-room, addressing him as 'sir' and thereby 'Indicating that he, Arthur, his brother, his flesh, his breath, was a total stranger' (p. 279). For Waldo, everyone, not least himself, must ultimately be a stranger.

Waldo's problem is not that he lacks all emotions and impulses, but rather that these are malformed or misdirected. For example, in the general euphoria which greets the end of the Second World War, Waldo feels the urge to make some kind of contact, but he responds by buying a large, plastic doll which he gives to Mrs Poulter. Understandably the gift disturbs and even frightens her. Though Arthur subsequently finds her dressing the doll, she never speaks of it to Waldo and does not make it the basis for a friendship. If the doll is as close as Waldo can come to giving her the child she longs for, it is fitting that he should father something rubbery and lifeless. His gesture of friendship to Mrs Poulter's labourer husband is similarly inappropriate. Couched as an offer to lend books (thereby moulding the other's inchoate mind), it is sure to be repulsed. Bill Poulter treats Waldo's overture as though it had been an 'indecent proposition' (p. 137).

Waldo cannot even feel affection for a pet. While Arthur romps with their dogs Runt and Scruffy, seemingly half animal himself,

Waldo undertakes the care of a dog as a moral exercise in self-abasement: 'To atone for dishonesty in other men . . . – he had thought it out, oh, seriously – he would mortify himself through love for this innocent, though in every other way repulsive creature, his dog' (p. 173). White insists repeatedly that Waldo is incapable of love, whether for dog, brother, parent, friend or lover. He is equally unable to love himself.

Clearly, it is self-hatred Waldo vents in his hatred of Arthur, for Arthur is part of himself. It is also self-hatred which is communicated in the scene where Waldo preens himself before the mirror in his mother's ball gown. His transvestism is denial not only of his own identity, but also that of his whole family, both the nonconformist Brown side and his mother's aristocratic Quantrells. It marks his attempt not to integrate the past, as Dulcie had suggested, but to conquer it, to become 'Memory herself' who authorizes its existence: 'because . . . memory is . . . licensed to improve on life' (p. 184). Starting from a 'marrow of memory' to rebuild himself from the inside out, Waldo when arrayed in his mother's gown imagines 'All great occasions streamed up the Gothick stair to kiss the rings of Memory, which she held out stiff, and watched the sycophantic lips cut open, teeth knocking on cabuchons and carved ice' (p. 185). The element of voluptuous self-punishment is plain in this passage, since Waldo himself has been among those pressing sycophantic lips to 'Memory's skin' (p. 187). For years he had probed his mother's memory for bits of her Quantrell past. Now, as Memory herself, he enjoys the spectacle of his own grovelling after another's history. Self-punishment is also the underlying, if unacknowledged, motive for his later attempt on the life of his twin.

The specific impetus for the murder attempt is Arthur's poem, which, like their mother's gown, is a mirror held up to Waldo. Arthur writes,

my heart is bleeding for the Viviseckshunist
Cordelia is bleeding for her father's life
all Marys in the end bleed
but do not complane because they know
the cannot have it any other way   (p. 204)

The sense of connection and community, as well as the simple feeling in Arthur's awkward poem, brings forcibly home to Waldo his own sterility and anomie. He burns his bits of prose and poetry, his life's work, and afterwards feels his lack of substance. Determined to be free even of Arthur, he tries to kill him. But Arthur is his only connection to life, the only viable part of him. Thus it is Waldo who dies in the effort. Unlike the protagonists of other White novels, Waldo fails finally and absolutely. His inability to love his brother is a failure of the very force which keeps him alive.

The 'Waldo' section is told largely as a series of flashbacks stimulated by incidents which occur while the elderly brothers take their daily constitutional. This walk, which occupies nearly two thirds of the book, takes place probably only a few days or weeks before the murder attempt, with which the 'Waldo' section culminates. White accomplishes two things by organizing Waldo's section in this manner. First, he gives us a sense of the stagnation of Waldo's life: so much time, so much talk, and so little motion. Waldo lodges himself in the imagination, endlessly plodding but never progressing. Secondly, because chronology is utterly disrupted, we sense the incoherence and anarchy which Waldo's nihilism has wrought. Whatever force he does exert seems to explode in all directions, leaving him precisely where he was. Narrative method here effects a kind of mimesis of the inner being. In fact, the entire 'Waldo' section constitutes the psychic chaos to which Arthur in his section at once starts to apply his ordering, mandalic imagination.

Where the 'Waldo' section was disjointed, its events standing isolated and discrete, 'Arthur' is cohesively chronological. Even in the case of the occasional brief flashback, the relationship of events to time and to each other is preserved. The tendency of the 'Arthur' section to organize and synthesize the material of the preceding section is evident from its opening lines:

> In the beginning there was the sea of sleep of such blue in which they lay together with iced cakes and the fragments of glass nesting in each other's arms the furry waves of sleep nuzzling at them like animals.
> Dreaming and dozing.
> The voices of passengers after Cape Town promised icebergs to the south, two-thirds submerged . . . .
> Then suddenly he noticed for the first time without strain, it seemed, the red-gold disc of the sun. He was so happy, he

ran to reach, to climb on the rails, reaching up. His hands seemed to flutter his breath mewing with the willing effort.

Voices screaming lifted him back, and he noticed he had been scratched by ladies.

'You must never never climb on the rails at sea!' said Mother. 'You might fall over, and then you would be lost forever.'

He looked at her and said, 'Yes. I might. Forever.'

Feeling the cold circles eddying out and away from him. (p. 209)

This incident occurs on the ship which carries Anne Quantrell, her unsuitable husband, and their young twin sons from England to a new start in Australia. In its imagery and allusions the passage has already begun the section's work of enclosing scattered bits of the 'Waldo' section and establishing those patterns which will order 'Arthur'. The colour blue and the imagery of ice and shattered glass recall Waldo, particularly Waldo posing in his mother's ice-blue dress, while the mention of furry, nuzzling sleep reminds us that Waldo has often thought of Arthur as a soft, burrowing animal. In addition we have the first mention of the 'red-gold disc of the sun', which, like all other circles and spheres, becomes a kind of talisman for Arthur and a proof that mandalas exist on all scales: from his tiny, but also talismanic, marbles to the great world and beyond. Moreover, the passage establishes the image of an orange disc over icebergs, an image which becomes emblematic of Arthur's attempt to penetrate and relate the heights and the depths of human experience and also suggests the living mind at work on the ice of memory. Finally, the closing lines place Arthur at the heart of a mandala (here a series of concentric circles), in the position which Stan Parker of *The Tree of Man* finally attained and which Arthur will occupy repeatedly in this novel.

As we discover a few pages later, Arthur's mental icebergs shatter, but not into the sharp, stinging splinters which slit flesh in Waldo's vision. Rather they break 'into glass balls which he gathered in his protected hands' (*SM*,p. 212). Already, then, Arthur is making mandalas: bringing coherence to what Waldo deranged.

On the level of the novel's action, Arthur continues the project, amending the perverted gestures which Waldo makes toward others, reviving Waldo's morbid relationships as healthy and loving interchanges. With Dulcie, for example, Arthur gives genuine love in the place of what even Waldo can see was an 'exercise' and 'imitation' (p. 50). Arthur's love concerns itself only with Dulcie, while Waldo concentrates on himself. Similarly, where Waldo's gift of the doll to Mrs Poulter has the effect of mocking her desire for children, Arthur simply offers himself, becoming for her 'this child too tender to be born' (p. 307).

Appropriately, those moments in 'Waldo' when Arthur seems most stupid, clumsy, insensitive or incomprehensible are revealed in Arthur's account to be times when his love achieved its subtlest expression. For instance, the bizarre 'cow tragedy' which Arthur enacts for his bewildered family is explained as a manoeuvre designed to distract them from their awful self-absorption and to induce them to share something, if only agony. In another incident, after Waldo is struck by a car, Arthur sits at his hospital bedside blubbering. He seems terrified that he will be left to make arrangements after Waldo's death. This behaviour, which seems incredibly callous when reported in 'Waldo' is shown in Arthur's telling to spring from his attempt to impress upon his brother his abiding need for him. 'Love', Arthur realizes, 'is more acceptable to some when twisted out of its true shape' (p. 273).

Within this pattern of action and emotion revised and redeemed, Waldo's sordid episode of transvestism is transformed in Arthur's experience into the joyous recognition that men and women are not 'all that different' (p. 218). In his desultory but somehow directed reading, Arthur comes across an arresting passage: 'As the shadow continually follows the body of one who walks in the sun, so our hermaphroditic Adam, though he appears in the form of a male, nevertheless always carries about with him Eve, or his wife, hidden in his body' (p. 275).[51] We recall that the same idea, in closely parallel language, was expressed in Himmelfarb's deathbed dream. White describes Arthur's reaction:

He warmed to that repeatedly after he had recovered from the shock. And if one wife, why not two? Or three? He could not have chosen between them. He could not sacrifice his first, his fruitful darling, whose mourning even streamed with a white light. Nor the burnt flower-pots, the russet apples of his second. Or did the message in the book refer, rather, to his third, his veiled bride?   (Ibid.)

The first 'wife', of course, is Dulcie; the second is Mrs Poulter.[52] That the third or 'veiled bride' is Waldo is suggested a few pages later when White echoes the 'hermaphroditic Adam' passage in his description of Arthur leaving the library: 'He walked across the hall, steady enough, and out the main entrance, his shadow following him in the sun, as he carried away inside him – his brother' (p. 279).

The implication is that Arthur, like the hermaphrodite, could embrace within his single life and being these conflicting opposites, that he could bring quaternity and sexual duality into the controlled but dynamic juxtaposition which the mandala symbolizes. Arthur nearly does this, if only once and only briefly, in the mandala dance he performs for Mrs Poulter. In this ritual celebration of his fullness, he dances the essences of the four beings who shape his life. First there is himself, whose life is 'always prayerful' despite his atheist parents' denial of the gods. Next is Dulcie Feinstein, who has recovered her faith in Judaism through her love for Len Saporta and for Arthur, and who thus offers Arthur a 'three-cornered relationship' suggestive both of the Christian trinity and the triangular components of the Star of David. Third is Mrs Poulter, for whom Arthur becomes 'the child she had never carried' (pp. 259–60). But when he dances his brother, the fourth and final element, Arthur finds himself hampered by 'words and ideas skewered to paper'. He realizes, 'He couldn't dance his brother out of him, not fully', nor can he save him (p. 260).

Thus in the mandala's centre, the 'dwelling of the god', Arthur must dance what can save: Christ's Passion which can be the passion of 'all their lives' (ibid). Here Arthur acknowledges the redemptive power of Christ's suffering and love. It is a similar love and willingness to suffer which Arthur offers the quaternity.

Arthur's four marbles, the microcosmic spheres which are his 'solid mandalas' (p. 247), are destined for the four members of the quaternity. Dulcie and Mrs Poulter accept theirs. The marble with the red and green whorls, 'in which the double spiral knit and unknit so reasonably' (p. 274), is his own and suggests the most felicitous structure his interaction with his brother might take. But their relationship never assumes this comfortable configuration. Waldo refuses the gift of his mandala, the one with the knot at its heart. On the night after Waldo's death, a disconsolate Arthur loses the marble in a filthy back alley, a circumstance which suggests Waldo's irretrievable loss. Thus Arthur's mandala remains an image of unrealized hope.

Waldo, then, is never saved by Arthur's love. Even Arthur knows his love has been inadequate to this huge task. Shortly before Waldo tries to murder him, Arthur tells his brother, 'Love . . . is what I fail in worst' (p. 200). As early as their confrontation in the library, Arthur saw that 'he could never give out from his own soul enough of that love which was there to give. So his brother remained cold and dry' (p. 278). All his gestures of love, comfort and service, whether holding his brother in his arms or cleaning up after an attack of diarrhoea, leave Waldo unresponsive or humiliated. Finally Arthur decides that he is to blame for Waldo's death. Calling himself 'the getter of pain' (p. 288), Arthur accuses himself of Waldo's murder.

The failure of love to be strong enough or true enough to save is a familiar vehicle for the theme of failure in White's fiction. We have already encountered it in Stan Parker, Mary Hare, Ruth Godbold and Alf Dubbo. But something different is at work here, for, while these other characters were able to use their failures to lead them towards a vastly expanded and synthetic understanding, Arthur's understanding seems to contract, his vision to collapse as a result of his failure. For a time he tries only to lose himself in dirt and darkness. Finally he returns to Mrs Poulter, but appears in her kitchen confused and pathetic. From there he is docilely led away to an asylum.

The madhouse, it will be recalled, was also Theodora Goodman's fate, but her confinement was preceded by a moment of illumination in which she apprehended the essential coherence of all lives and all experience. For Arthur there is now no such moment; he has never again danced out of the fullness he felt on the day he made the mandala for Mrs Poulter. Comprehensiveness, like comprehension, is denied him. The loss of Waldo's marble makes the point most forcibly: Waldo is not absorbed, but amputated. This reverses the typical Whitean pattern in which, as Theodora saw, even the darker and life-denying impulses are incorporated into the schema. Rather than including within himself what Waldo stands for, Arthur has been purged of Waldo.

So the consequences of Arthur's failure are in this way very different from those we have grown to expect. In another way, however, they are familiar. For Arthur, without Waldo, does come to be more purely himself. Just as Alf Dubbo achieved his fullest expression of himself as artist after his failure to bear witness for Himmelfarb, Arthur, after failing to overcome Waldo's hatred, is most effectively the 'instrument' Dulcie had named him (p. 272).

His instrumentality had begun much earlier for Dulcie and her family. With the 'enlightened' Mr Feinstein, Arthur functions to return him to his faith before his death, reminding him that faith can act as a mandala, imposing significant pattern on experience. With Dulcie, Arthur's role is less to show her the mandala than to celebrate the fact that she has found it and 'would be made round' in her marriage to Len (p. 245). After Waldo's death, Arthur sees her surrounded by her adoring family on a Sabbath Eve, overflowing with the holy love of which she is a vessel. At this moment he knows that Dulcie has no further need of him. Accordingly he returns to Mrs Poulter, who, despite his gift of the mandala, has remained incomplete.

In the final section of the novel, called 'Mrs Poulter and the Zeitgeist',[53] we learn that Mrs Poulter's love, whether for little pigs, her stillborn daughter, or her strong, young husband, has always been frustrated or shamed. The pigs are strung up to be bled, the sisters took away her little girl, and her husband recoiled from her too eager affection. In defence, Mrs Poulter has distracted herself with the suffering safely boxed up in her TV set and doled out in palatable dabs. Her faith has also provided a refuge, but one to which she resorts without real conviction.

When she discovers Waldo's body, gnawed by the starving dogs, evil and suffering are suddenly made real for her. Her conception of God cannot survive this Armageddon. White says, 'He released His hands from the nails. And fell down, in a thwack of canvas, a cloud of dust' (p. 299). The use of the words 'canvas' and 'dust' suggests that this Christ was a mere stage prop, a lifeless image too flimsy to withstand the pressure of real experience.

Almost immediately after this, Arthur arrives. White alerts the reader to his effect on Mrs Poulter with a pun: 'When he got there she turned round' (p. 305). Like Dulcie, that is, Mrs Poulter can be made whole, and Arthur will be the instrument of her completion. As Alf Dubbo took from Himmelfarb's ordeal the likeness of a flesh and blood Christ in whom he could believe, Mrs Poulter sets Arthur in the place of the pasteboard god who came crashing down. Through her love and belief in him, Mrs Poulter is brought to embrace her 'joy and duty' in the love of all men everywhere (p. 307), and, when Arthur is taken away, he leaves her with an 'actual sphere of life' (p. 312). Mrs Poulter, too, has been 'made round'.

As a young child in England, Arthur is taken to a performance of *Götterdämmerung* and wonders, 'Who and where were the gods?' White says, 'He could not have told, but knew, in his flooded depths' (p. 211). As it turns out, those very depths *are* 'the dwelling of the god' and Arthur himself is the solid heart of the mandala 'ritually' encircled by Mrs Poulter's protective arms in an emblematic moment near the novel's end (p. 307). In this closing section, he functions as Christ-bearer for Mrs Poulter, while at the same time suiting the *Zeitgeist* by remaining a mere mortal in whom one can rationally believe. In a world of dead and dying gods, he is the 'man-child' given 'as token of everlasting life' (p. 307).[54]

To underscore Arthur's assumption of this role, White makes other allusions to Christian belief and practice. In the library confrontation over 'The Grand Inquisitor', he had already presented Arthur as a Christ persecuted by the inquisitorial Waldo.[55] Subsequently, he sets Waldo's death on a Thursday and Arthur's reappearance at Mrs Poulter's on the Saturday. Thus Arthur is absent for the traditional three days, although the timetable of the Passion has been slightly skewed. Much more striking in its reference is the detail that, when Mrs Poulter rises from Arthur's side, the police sergeant is 'reminded of a boyhood smell of cold, almost deserted churches, and old people rising transparent and hopeful, chafing the blood back into their flesh after the sacrament' (p. 309).

These words recall the lines from Dostoyevsky which stand as one of the novel's four epigraphs. Dostoyevsky is evoked not only here and in the several references to *The Brothers Karamazov*, but in the very character of Arthur who, while owing something to Alyosha, owes more to *The Idiot's* Prince Myshkin. In his notebooks for *The Idiot*, Dostoyevsky wrote of Myshkin, 'The chief thing is that they all need him.'[56] Like Arthur, that is, Myshkin is a man whose simplicity is often misunderstood and sometimes manipulated, but he is also an instrument through whom others may come to increased consciousness. Dostoyevsky's and White's heroes also share states of affliction which accord them heightened vision and admit them sometimes to a perception of a unity, balance and beauty about existence. Finally, however, both Myshkin and Arthur are overwhelmed by their experiences and end in institutions. In some sense, they are sacrificed for others, and in this, as in other ways, both evoke Christ.

Jung has said that Christ is inadequate as an archetype of the integrated self, since He utterly excludes the shadow.[57] Similarly, although the trinity may symbolize the process of Jungian individuation, it must become quaternity, usually by inclusion of the dark or shadow self, before it stands as archetype of the wholeness possible to earthly experience and sought through the conjunction of opposites.[58] In Jungian terms, this novel may be viewed as moving from the conflicting duality of Arthur–Waldo to the resolved unity of the trinitarian Arthur–Dulcie–Mrs Poulter. Alternatively, it may be seen as producing that trinity by lopping off one side of a mandalic quaternity composed of all four major characters. In both cases the otherworldly and ideal ultimately predominate, and in neither case does the novel enact Arthur's mandala. Rather, like the Christ whose Passion he danced at the centre of his mandala, Arthur's human wholeness is sacrificed for that of others. He becomes, as Mrs Poulter declares, less a full human being than a 'saint' (p. 310). At the same time, however, Arthur's sainthood is achieved in an emphatically postlapsarian world. Like Adam, he endures the fall into pain and ambiguity. It is therefore fitting that, when Mrs Poulter's Christ comes crashing down from the stage of her own self-dramatization, he should rise as the idiot Arthur.

In a world unfriendly to other gods, Arthur thus houses the god within. In this sense he encloses and comprehends the 'other world' spoken of in two of the novel's epigraphs: Paul Eluard's 'There is another world, but it is in this one', and Meister Eckhart's 'It is not outside, it is inside: wholly within.' In this act of comprehension and enclosure Arthur's experience mirrors that of other Whitean protagonists, but it must still be insisted that his final vision is fundamentally different. Having at one point seen the whole, he has lost sight of it by the end. But, in doing so, he has opened the vista to others.

Like Waldo, Arthur is a character whose type has appeared earlier in the White corpus but never before as a protagonist. His fictional antecedents reach back through Harry Robarts of *Voss* and Doll and Bub Quigley of *The Tree of Man* to a much less developed prototype in Chuffy Chambers of *Happy Valley*. These are divine fools: the afflicted or despised who are granted some insight for which those with greater faculties must strive far harder. In their case the vision is unearned; it is rather the gift of grace. The typical Whitean protagonist undergoes a tortuous progress toward understanding which the fool is spared. Thus, in treating such a character, White's problem is not, as it was with the others, to trace the developing vision, but rather its impact on others. Arthur, as White plainly states, comes to the novel's other characters with an 'annunciation' (p. 65). Interest thus shifts to their response and to ours as readers.

This alteration in narrative design is accompanied by an altered narrative perspective. Because Arthur is born to his visionary status, he is subjected to very little of the irony White usually trains on his protagonists. Waldo, on the other hand, is treated with a satire more biting and a contempt more unmitigated than any previous protagonist has undergone. It is as though the two selves which White distinguished in each of the Riders – the fully endorsed visionary and the ironically viewed human being – are here split into two characters.

Thus *The Solid Mandala* marks several departures for White, but these departures took him in directions he continues to approve. With *The Aunt's Story* and *The Twyborn Affair*, White names this novel as one of his favourites. About it he has said, 'it's a very personal kind of book, I suppose, and comes closest to what I've wanted'.[59] Perhaps he means by this remark that, in creating a character who is the bearer of grace and vision to others, he has brought Arthur closest to accomplishing what he as an artist has hoped to do.

In naming these three works as his favourites, he may also mean to stress their similarities. All have protagonists whom the world considers at least eccentric if not outright mad (although this could be said of other White novels as well), and all end disquietingly. They are full of what White calls 'ambivalence and unease' (*FG*, p. 146). All three pose problems of tone which leave the reader uncertain as to how the author means him to take the protagonist's fate. And, finally, all problematize the theme of necessary or redemptive failure, extrapolating from White's usual treatment to explore equivocal aspects of the pattern and to suggest that the author–artist himself may fail to fully comprehend its workings. As is clear from his next novel, this is not the only failure White accuses in the artist.

THE VIVISECTOR

The artist's role and its inherent ambiguities become the focus of *The Vivisector* (1970), a work in which White turns his probing and profoundly ironic vision squarely on his own enterprise. As Manfred Mackenzie said of *The Solid Mandala*, this is a novel which 'penitentially' exposes the artist to himself and explores the intricate relationship of art to life.[60]

It is not surprising that White, like Joyce Cary, should have chosen a painter as the subject of his *Künstlerroman*.[61] In a 1958 essay, White admits to being 'something of a frustrated painter and a composer *manqué*',[62] and, in an interview published eleven years later, he remarks on the importance to his work of painters and painting, concluding that his friend the painter Roy de Maistre 'taught me to write by teaching me to look at paintings and get beneath the surface'.[63] He says nearly the same thing in a 1973 interview and again in his 'self-portrait', *Flaws in the Glass*. In this work, whose title and subtitle both allude to portraiture, he goes on to describe his attempts to achieve in prose some of the effects possible in painting, such as that of an explosive burst of colour.[64]

Indeed, the flamboyance of visual art, especially its capacity to shock, to achieve an immediate, unified and overwhelming impact, accounts in part for White's attraction to painting and is the most pronounced effect he attributes to Hurtle Duffield's work. Sometimes the shock is compounded of horror and recoil, sometimes of wonder and amazement; sometimes it is simply that of recognition. Thus Boo Davenport, a childhood acquaintance of Hurtle's and later the wealthy, twice-widowed patron of his work, groans in guilty pity before Hurtle's study of his hunchbacked adoptive sister, Rhoda. And Hero Pavloussi, the wife of a Greek shipping-tycoon whom Boo procures as Hurtle's mistress, is driven to a suicide attempt by Hurtle's painting of a woman in the act of self-destruction. In both cases, the work has jarred the woman into admitting something in herself she would rather have suppressed.

Nor are such illuminations confined to the beholders of the paintings; they sometimes extend to their creator. The novel's most striking example of this occurs when the prostitute Nance Lightfoot visits Hurtle in the bush shack to which he has retreated, and finds him lovingly at work on a self-portrait. In a moment which recalls *The Picture of Dorian Gray*, Hurtle is forced to confront his 'devilish, furtive, ingrown' self-portrait in the light of Nance's understanding of its meaning and inspiration (*VS*, p. 242). Overwhelmed by self-disgust, Hurtle smears it with his own excrement, in an attempt to obliterate the too-true mirror and to repudiate what it shows him of his solipsism.

Frequently the shock produced by a Duffield work is also orgasmic. White makes this linkage at one point by describing the sounds Boo Davenport emits before a *Pythoness at Tripod* as reminding Hurtle of Nance's moans when she reached orgasm. By stressing these aspects of the paintings' impact and describing them in the language of violence and violation, White underscores connections he makes repeatedly through incident, imagery and Hurtle's own reflections: complex connections among art, sex, procreation, and the giving and getting of pain.

The novel's controlling metaphor is indicated in its title: art as vivisection, the dissection of living beings for the purposes of analysing how they function. Nor is this metaphor allowed to remain at the suggestive level. Through the involvement, dilettantish as it is, of Hurtle's adoptive mother Alfreda Courtney in the anti-vivisection campaign, we are brought uncomfortably close to some horrifying images and are forced to realize the agony which vivisection inflicts. Hurtle's very name (a misspelling of the family name Hertel imposed on him, as was Tristram Shandy's, through an error during christening) and his nickname 'Hurt' suggest that he will be an instrument of violence and torture.

In the case of Hurtle's specimens, or victims, the agony is unmitigated by the fact that no actual blood is drawn. Nearly all the women with whom Hurtle is involved – Alfreda, Rhoda, Nance, Boo, Hero – accuse him at some point of laying them open in his search for artistic truth. Nance expresses most vividly, if also most crudely, both the nature of Hurtle's operation and its effect on those who undergo it. She tells him,

> with an artist you're never free he's makun use of yer in the name of the Holy Mother of Truth. He thinks. The Truth! . . . When the only brand of truth 'e recognizes is 'is own it is inside 'im 'e reckons and as 'e digs inter poor fucker *You* 'e hopes you'll help 'im let it out. . . . By turnun yer into a shambles. . . . Out of the shambles 'e paints what 'e calls 'is bloody work of art! (*VS*, p. 242).

Hurtle's method as he vivisects his subjects is akin to the scientist's: he ignores their status as integral living beings with a right to that integrity, in order to discover what supports it. Thus Hurtle always seeks to 'dissect on his drawing board down to the core, the nerves of matter' (p. 215). And, if, like Nance and Hero, the subject does not survive the surgery, at least the work of art remains as testimony to the truth disclosed.

The imagery of physical violence modulates into that of violent sexuality and the pain of childbirth, where White finds further analogues for art-making. The connection with childbirth is made, for example, when Hurtle tells the grocer Cutbush that art is 'dragged out of you, in torment and anguish, by a pair of forceps' (p. 254). Adopting a metaphor which White has used to describe his own creative process, that of prolonged labour and difficult delivery, Hurtle here suggests that giving birth to art means undergoing a kind of vivisection.[65] Similarly, love-making can be a violation akin to vivisection. In this novel, the love-making is not only carnal but carnivorous, described in the language of swallowing, gulping and devouring.

The relationship between creativity and sexuality which obtains in *The Vivisector* has been viewed as Lawrentian, but, as one critic remarks, the sexual analogies figure less as metaphysic than conceit.[66] Thus Hurtle's art can originate in masturbatory impulses of annoyance and frustration, in the deliberate onanism of self-absorption, or in his more loving intercourse with others. Examples of the latter interchange range from the conversation with the homosexual grocer which bears fruit in *Lantana Lovers* to his near rape by Hero and seduction by the young musician Kathy Volkov, each of these spawning a series of paintings.

By whatever means they are generated, Hurtle's paintings are his children, his heirs, his hedge against death. In this pattern of imagery, White pursues the connections between art and procreation, while at the same time seeming to favour flesh and blood over canvas progeny. Like Yeats at 'close on forty-nine' with 'nothing but a book',[67] Hurtle finds that his paintings are all he can oppose to the fecundity of others. As an old man unexpectedly meeting his sister Lena, whom he had put behind him when he left the Duffield shack for the Courtneys' Sunningdale, Hurtle hears of her four children, thirteen grandchildren, and expected great-grandchild. Mentally he starts a frantic count of his paintings, desperate to produce some evidence that he, too, 'had multiplied, if not through his loins; he was no frivolous masturbator tossing his seed onto wasteland' (p. 495). It is only at the very end of his life that he realizes the lust and lovelessness in which most of his work was bred.

Until near his death, Hurtle is a man for whom art is the sole *raison d'être*. His god is his own creativity, and he believes that the artist within must be cherished and served at whatever cost to the rest of himself or to his models. In critical discussions of this novel, the metaphor of the artist as vivisector has been linked to Joyce's *Stephen Hero*[68] and George Bernard Shaw's *Man and Superman*,[69] while the wider conception of the artist as a man of extraordinary powers and privileged status is more often found to be rooted in Romanticism and particularly Romantic Prometheanism.[70] One of the novel's epigraphs, taken from Rimbaud's *Theórie du voyant*, sums up Hurtle's conception of himself, a view both Romantic and Promethean: 'He becomes beyond all others the great Invalid, the great Criminal, the great Accursed One – and the Supreme Knower. For he reaches the unknown' (*VS*, p. 7). As one critic cautions, however, this is Hurtle's view, not White's,[71] and, while White clearly believes that the artist can assault the unknown, he does not endorse the strategies of Hurtle's campaign.

Not only are Hurtle's methods frequently cruel: they are fundamentally misguided. For, in valuing art over life, Hurtle is not merely distinguishing between the two. Rather than contenting himself with opposing life *to* art, in the manner of the aesthetes, he opposes life *with* art. In other words, whenever life threatens truly to engage him, whenever experience begins to demand real response, Hurtle achieves a distance and detachment by transforming the experience into art. It is as though he shoves a painting between himself and life, a painting which not only blocks his view of the offensive or insistent experience, but allows him to control it by shaping it to his own vision. He admits years later to Rhoda that a ghastly childhood painting depicting the suicide of his tutor Mr Shewcroft was done in an attempt 'to find some formal order behind a moment of chaos and unreason. Otherwise it would have been too horrible and terrifying' (pp. 503–4). As Rhoda understands it, 'The horrors are less horrible if you've created them yourself' (p. 503).

Sometimes his work is a substitution of art for life. Thus he leaps out of Nance's bed to devote his energies, sexual and otherwise, to his 'Marriage of Light', a work which ostensibly celebrates what he precipitately leaves to paint it. For him, as for Jocelyn in Hardy's *The Well-Beloved*, the loved one becomes the 'formal vessel' of artistic vision, the momentary avatar of the ideal (*VS*, p. 198).[72]

More often, Hurtle's art reflects a full-scale withdrawal from life, all the more effective because unconscious. His usual practice is to do a series of paintings, for example the rock series or the several studies of *Pythoness at Tripod*, which moves from the relatively naturalistic toward the increasingly abstract. In this way too, he retreats from life. Of course, White is not implying an aesthetic judgement in favour of figurative techniques over those of abstraction, or traditional mimesis over symbolism. Such a preference would hardly accord with his work in novels such as *The Aunt's Story*, *Voss* and *The Twyborn Affair*. Hurtle's manner is not at fault, but rather the purposes to which he puts it, for he uses abstraction as another means of neutralizing the painful and personal. What was a crippled sister is reduced to a series of vaguely evocative shapes.

Hurtle's typical procedure for deflecting life's demands finds it clearest examplar in an incident from his adolescence, beginning on the rainy afternoon in London when he, Rhoda and 'Maman' (as Alfreda Courtney asks her adopted son to call her) come upon a shop window which displays the replica of a vivisected dog. This is not direct experience – the little dog is stuffed, not real – but it is art at its most horrifically graphic, and, like the others, Hurtle is severely traumatized. Later he and Rhoda sit over their hotel dinners (Maman is too distraught to eat) and he lashes his sister with a cruel remark. White writes of Hurtle,

> His own behaviour on top of other things hurt and horrified him to such an extent he took up the pencil the waiter had forgotten and began drawing in the margin of the menu, as he always did when a situation became unbearable, practically as though playing with himself. (p. 132)

Shortly after, Rhoda catches sight of his sketch; he has drawn the tortured dog and defends his act by saying, 'I was trying to work something out' (p. 132). Hurtle is trying to 'work something out' here as one might work out a splinter or alleviate sexual tension. It is a way of easing pain by objectifying it, or, in another of the novel's metaphors, by giving birth to it: in any case, working it out of the self.

Even when Hurtle is not actually reifying life in art, he is trying to force it into his own configurations. Because he sees a 'great discrepancy between aesthetic truth and sleazy reality' (p. 188) and emphatically prefers the former, he is wont to impose form on amorphous experience and then to affirm the superior ontological status of his version. With Nance, for example, he quickly reaches the point where 'he could only believe in his vision of her, which already . . . he had translated into concrete forms' (p. 184).

The aesthetic truth which he decides Hero Pavloussi will incarnate demands that she be his 'spiritual bride' (p. 313), the 'pure soul' (p. 319) who will renew him. When he discovers that she is not his soulmate, but a woman whose sexual appetite is appeased only by the 'ultimate in depravity' (p. 343), Hurtle laments that 'nothing develops as conceived: the pure soul, for example; the innocent child, already deformed, or putrefying, in the womb' (p. 342).

Since artistic creation has been imaged in the novel as childbirth, it is appropriate that teratology, abortion or miscarriage should supply the imagery when the human 'work of art' refuses the form her creator would impose on her (p. 309). Such imagery is later used to describe Hurtle's loss of Kathy Volkov, who was also to be his work of art. But here the metaphor is even more effective, since Kathy is envisaged from the first as his daughter. As Hero was to be his spiritual bride, Kathy is 'his spiritual child of infinite possibilities' (p. 411). When she, too, seduces him, with practised efficiency, Hurtle imagines her 'digging into his maternal, his creative entrails' to abort herself (p. 453). True to habit, he seeks relief in art and has soon manufactured a canvas Kathy to replace the real.

Similarly, Hurtle imaginatively recasts himself and gives that self-image priority. He repeatedly counters accusations of cruelty with the claim that he is an artist, as if this status either gives him the right to commit atrocities or absolves his acts from being so construed. In fact, his construct of himself as artist is the only self he finds 'convincing' (p. 204). Just as he erects his paintings as a shield between himself and others, he uses his role as artist to evade moral accountability.

Nowhere is this clearer than in Hurtle's responses to Rhoda

on the night these adoptive siblings meet after years of separation. Quite by accident, Hurtle comes upon his dwarfed and hunchbacked sister dragging a cart of horse meat through the streets to feed stray cats. He coaxes her home with him, but she sees there an early *Pythoness* painting, a work inspired by the incident years before in which Hurtle opened her bedroom door to find her naked and sponging herself beside a bidet. Of the moment when brother and sister stand before the painting, White says,

> His own horror at their finding themselves in the present situation couldn't prevent him from experiencing a twinge of appreciation for his forgotten achievement: the thin, transparent arm; the sponge as organic as the human claw clutching it; the delicate but indestructible architecture of the tripod-bidet, beside which the rosy figure was stood up for eternity.
> This aesthetic orgasm lasted what seemed only a long second before the moral sponge was squeezed: its icy judgment was trickling in actual sweat down his petrified ribs. . . .
> 'I can't help it,' he apologized, 'if I turned out to be an artist.' (p. 434)

In an interview, White explained Hurtle's position in this and similar situations: 'Duffield, though an artist, experiences moments of guilt as a human being.'[73] The basis of that guilt is suggested in White's 'self-portrait', *Flaws in the Glass*, where the author reflects that 'truth', such truth as the artist relentlessly seeks, 'can be the worst destroyer of all' (p. 70). Later in that work he laments, 'My pursuit of that razor-blade truth has made me a slasher' (p. 155). Artistic truth must somehow be made compatible with humanism. Hurtle's problem, like that of many Whitean protagonists, is to bring together these and related antinomies within some framework flexible and commodious enough to contain them. Hurtle's initial tendency, however, is to polarize.

As Hurtle sees it, he was the product of a 'dirty deal' between Sunningdale and Cox Street, and these two locales mirror his essential dichotomy. The son of a Cox Street 'bottle-o' and a washerwoman, he is dearly bought by the Courtneys of Sunningdale, who have no child except the misshapen Rhoda. Clearly the arrangement is in the boy's best interests, a fact of which his mother is well aware. Yet Hurtle carries with him to his new home not only a sense of betrayal, but also an indelible identity. Although he comes to love his foster father and is legally adopted by him, he remains a Duffield as well, and proudly affixes this name to his paintings. The double names provide a neat device by which White can suggest his divided identity. 'Courtney' designates Hurtle's social self, the one to whom others appeal in the name of moral principle; 'Duffield' is the artist who will not succumb to importunity. White uses the same device to suggest analogous fractures in other characters; examples are the little Aboriginal girl Alice/Soso, and most spectacularly Boo/ Olivia/Hollingrake/Lopez/Davenport, who marries yet again and so acquires still another name which isn't even mentioned in the novel. Even Rhoda, although she answers to a single name, is alternately seen as rose and rodent.

The Cox Street/Sunningdale antithesis is echoed in that of Flint Street and Chubb Lane, the two streets onto which Hurtle's house opens. While Flint Street is one of decaying but determined gentility, the Lane with its 'mingled smell of poor washing, sump oil, rotting vegetables, goatish male bodies, and soggy female armpits' suggests life at its most rudimentary (p. 260). The sense White promotes here of juxtaposed opposites recalls the view from Theodora Goodman's house in *The Aunt's Story* and suggests again the reconciliation project Hurtle faces.

Among the further antinomies he must seek to encompass in his life and art are those of beauty and ugliness and God as the author of both. In his dunny, itself both a shabby outhouse and a 'shrine of light' (*VS*, p. 301), Hurtle scribbles an inscription he is unable to finish:

> God the Vivisector
> God the Artist
> God   (p. 301)

For Hurtle, God is both creator and destroyer, kind and cruel. He is both the God who seems a 'formal necessity' in a serene and harmonious landscape (p. 379) and the God he imagines in one painting as a black satrap drowning a metaphorical sackful of cats. Hurtle leaves the inscription on the privy wall unfinished because he cannot find the mediating term between these polarized extremes. White himself admits a similar dilemma when he describes one of the continuing themes of his work as the problem of 'how to accept a supernatural force, which on the one hand blesses and on the other destroys'.[74]

The antitheses which afflict Hurtle and his world ultimately reduce to that between chaos and order: the world as experienced in all its unsettling flux, and the world as revised, stabilized and controlled through art. This dichotomy is emblematized in the novel by the imagery associated on the one hand with fragmented light, often refracted by shattered glass, and on the other with light organized in the prismatic hues reflected from a chandelier.[75]

As a child, Hurtle gazes in delight at a chandelier in the Courtneys' house. Here light is splayed into a 'broken rainbow' (p. 25) and the boy holds 'his face almost flat, for the light to trickle and collect on it' (p. 31). A subsequent series of paintings in which something is showered from above (blood, semen, excrement, and finally light) recalls Hurtle's moment under the chandelier and reinforces its importance. The chandelier breaks white light into colours but holds them in relation. It thus represents a kind of intermediary between an ideal unity and the sharp, multifaceted shards of experience, imaged in the broken glass. Because it offers a way of bringing antitheses into dynamic relation, the light shed by the chandelier registers itself as a model upon which much of Hurtle's later work is based.

Hurtle also sometimes glimpses other reconciling mechanisms. On their expiatory pilgrimage to the island of Perialos, Hero is overcome with disgust at the worldliness of the nuns, the desecration of the hermit's chapel, and the mound of human excrement which is all she finds at the altar.[76] She tells her lover that everything is *Dreck*, using the German word for filth. But Hurtle has perceived the resignation and redemptive beauty of a little golden hen pecking around them, who 'flashed her wings: not in flight; she remained consecrated to this earth even while scurrying through illuminated dust' (p. 384). In other words, though he cannot communicate his insight to Hero, he understands that *Dreck* can be 'illuminated', even if it cannot and should not be transcended, and that beauty coexists with dirt and ugliness.

For Hurtle, then, the hen becomes a mediating agent, joining other mediators which might be used to formulate an encompassing vision. Among these are Rhoda and Boo, two characters who stand to him as mirrors.

Boo, of course, is far less important than Rhoda, either to Hurtle or to the novel. None the less she mirrors his essentially voyeuristic attitude to life. Nance once accuses him of 'being a kind of perv – perving on people – even on bloody rocks' (p. 218), and Boo is later described as a '*voyeuse*', watching Hurtle 'gently stroking paint to life' (p. 297). Again like him, she tries to turn life into art, in her case by sculpting relationships. The most telling example of this tendency is her procurement of Hero as his mistress, in an attempt, as she says, to 'bring . . . together the two halves of a friendship – into a[n aesthetically satisfying] whole' (p. 307). Although the heiress of a sugar fortune, Boo was a bitter draught for the three husbands she survives. In their number, they parallel Hurtle's three mistresses, of whom he loses two to death and one to distance. Although we learn the fate of only the first husband, White suggests that Boo kills them all by refusing to understand and share their pain, or, as Shakespeare put it, to see 'feelingly'. In this she is also like Hurtle, who sees without feeling and ignores his lovers' humanity while remaking them to fit his vision.

Hurtle never seems to recognize himself in Boo, but Rhoda is a more inescapable mirror. When the Courtneys tell him that this stunted creature is his sister, he denies the relationship and continues to do so for most of his adulthood. But in later life their kinship is forced upon his consciousness and conscience. Near the end of his life, says White, he can finally 'recognize . . . himself in the glass she was holding up to him' (p. 589).

Rhoda acts as his glass because her misshapen body externalizes, almost allegorizes, his affliction. Hurtle has allowed the artist in himself to swell like Rhoda's hump, or like the cancer which forms a characteristic motif in his painting.[77] White makes the connection explicit, having Rhoda tell her brother, 'Almost everybody carries a hump, not always visible, and not always of the same shape' (p. 457).

Part of her function in the novel is to show Hurtle the shape of his. Informing him that he sees the truth 'too large, and too hectic' (p. 458), she confronts him with the spuriousness of his pursuit of it. In her nihilism and isolation, she also alerts him to the dangers of his solipsism. You believe, she says, only in 'Your painting. And yourself. But those, too, are "gods" which could fail you' (p. 504).

Rhoda is also herself his hump, the 'growth' he must learn to carry (p. 502). The novel frequently associates her with Hurtle's suppressed conscience, and her misshapen form mirrors for him the world's anarchy, ugliness and pain. Alone among his women she withstands his revisionary imagination. 'Born vivisected', she will not be again (p. 434). Instead she demands to be accepted, even loved.

On some level Hurtle is aware that 'Rhoda, the reality, . . . was what he had been given to love' (p. 496). But his love for Rhoda would signal a move toward love and acceptance of his full, flawed self, and thereby a turning toward the whole of life which he has abbreviated to pursue his art. Hurtle once comes to this realization, admitting, 'If he hadn't been able to love Rhoda, he couldn't love his own parti-coloured soul' (p. 333). Except perhaps at the moment of his death, however, when he recognizes Rhoda as the mystic 'Rose' (p. 603), he fails to love her truly. Shortly before the stroke which ends his life, Hurtle acknowledges this crucial failure:

> To be honest: he had failed to love Rhoda. Pity is another matter: his 'Pythoness at Tripod' had expressed a brilliant, objective pity for an injured, cryptic soul and a body only malice could have created. But pity is half-hearted love. (p. 600)

With Hurtle Duffield, then, we are back in the mainstream of the Whitean theme of failure. His failure wholeheartedly to love the sister who is also himself and his related failure to engage himself wholeheartedly in life lead Hurtle toward a context of understanding and acceptance within which this wholeheartedness is possible.[78] As did Laura, Voss and the four Riders, he eventually inhabits such a context, and, within it, becomes most fully himself. But again like these earlier protagonists, Hurtle discovers that enlightenment cannot be compelled. In fact, until his stroke he makes little progress toward it. The novel's structure presents his experience as a series of cyclic deaths and rebirths,[79] which do not spiral toward the vision, but rather leave him each time essentially where he began. Eventually, even Hurtle knows he has remained inchoate. In one of his later drawings he depicts himself as a foetus (p. 505), and at a retrospective exhibition of his paintings, held well after his first stroke, he tells Boo, 'I'm just beginning. I'm only learning' (p. 572).[80]

Hurtle undergoes six such cycles, each associated with a woman lost or escaped and each ending with a symbolic death or disappearance which issues into rebirth. Several transitions are overseen by one of the novel's series of androgynous figures, beginning with the art-dealer Caldicott and moving through the homosexual grocer Cutbush, the widowed printer Mothersole, and the art student Don Lethbridge. Kathy Volkov is also sometimes seen as an androgyne, and it is she, as psychopomp, who presides over Hurtle's ultimate transition through admission to the vision and to death.

The role of these androgynous figures is complex. Here they do not seem themselves to embody the possibility of self-completion, as did the hermophrodite in *The Solid Mandala*. Rather, they offer completion through interaction. They guide Hurtle out of himself, toward a recognition that he depends on life, even in its most unappetizing forms, to seed his imagination.

When Hurtle abandons autogenesis for 'intercourse' with these hermaphrodites, the encounter is often fruitful. Because of Caldicott's guilty love for him, Hurtle 'give[s] birth' to an image which generates a series of paintings (p. 214). Later, he and Cutbush together conceive the bitter *Lantana Lovers under Moonfire*, in a collaboration Cutbush insists be recognized as consummation leading to birth (p. 548). Similarly, after his conversation with Mothersole, he feels himself 'born again by grace of Mothersole's warm, middle-class womb' (p. 396), and at the same time himself impregnated with a seed which will germinate as his spiritual child, Kathy Volkov. Finally, Don Lethbridge, who cares for him after his first stroke, is the 'neophyte prostitute' (p. 543) who helps him to 'mount' the platform he has built and so produce his final, most important paintings (p. 552).

Of course, Don's function is further complicated by his becoming Hurtle's 'disciple' (p. 543), and himself a Christ figure as well. He washes Hurtle's feet; he is a carpenter's son; and, when Hurtle confuses him with Sid Cupples of the Courtney sheep station, the names he calls him – Cuppaidge or Cup Lethbridge – suggest the cup of Communion. Then, too, Don assists Kathy in the role of psychopomp. As his surname implies, he is a bridge over the River Lethe, a bridge from life to death. But he, like the other androgynes, is also the lover with whom art is begotten.

Perhaps White chooses to locate this procreative function in the ambiguous, uncertain sexuality of the androgynes, because Hurtle is unable to use clear-cut female sexuality for procreative purposes. He is too busy denying its demands, distancing himself through flight or art. This pattern obtains in each of his six cyclic deaths and rebirths.

He first loses 'Mumma' when the Courtneys adopt him and he begins a new life as their child. At the Courtneys, Mumma's place is taken by Alfreda, or 'Maman', who at once opens a campaign of seduction by which she believes she can secure the boy for ever. Her first move is to thrust his head amongst the gowns hanging in her closet, producing in him a sensation of 'delicious suffocation' (p. 86). Later, she makes a more blatantly sexual appeal by calling him into her bed to share chocolate. Later still, it is Alfreda's attempt to make love to him which drives him out of the house and into the war. This escape is the occasion of his second rebirth. The house seems to him 'a quilted egg, or womb' (p. 160), and, when he announces his departure, he feels 'he has broken the caul' (p. 163).

His next rebirth comes through the agency of Cutbush, to whom he confesses his guilt over Nance's suicide, a guilt which has deadened the artist in him. Though Nance is lost, life and art are regained. Hurtle recalls his encounter with Cutbush as 'another occasion when he had risen from the dead' (p. 396).

In his next cycle Boo reappears, but tantalizes and denies him as she had when they were adolescents. In this phase the real loss is that of Hero, who leaves him, her love disappointed, and subsequently dies from cancer. When her husband writes Hurtle a letter blaming him for her death, he is plunged again into guilt and creative impotence. Mothersole delivers him from these and into yet another 'rebirth' (p. 396).

In his subsequent and penultimate incarnation, Kathy is found, loved and lost, and rebirth comes by means of a stroke. Again White makes the point through imagery. Groping his way back to life and to work after the stroke, Hurtle's is a 'new, incalculable self' (p. 540), a renascent spirit with a 'mind more hesitant because too green and tender, shooting in all directions from the old cut-back wood' (p. 545). Hurtle is launched on his last life.

If there is a woman loved and lost in this final phase, it is his sister Rhoda. (His biological sister Lena also reappears and is rejected just before his first stroke.) Hurtle lays full claim to his Rose only at his death. But in doing so he may be making an appeal to all the discarded women in his life, since ultimately all can be seen as one. White orchestrates the reader's awareness of this identification in two ways. First, all are associated with sexuality. Even 'Mumma' is remembered chiefly in connection with a squeaking bed, and Rhoda is once visualized as his wife (p. 595) and his partner in the creation of Kathy (p. 487). The implication is that all are potentially fecund and life-giving, and that Hurtle's rejection of any reflects a rejection of life. Secondly, each woman is linked with all the others through associated imagery, recurring physical traits, echoed cadences of speech or even phrases, and connections made in Hurtle's memory. For example, when Kathy first appears, her long hair recalls Nance, and its golden colour reminds us that Boo always took on a golden cast for Hurtle. Later, the rhythm and grammar of her speech evoke Nance again (p. 425), and another linkage with Boo is made when an early painting of Kathy draws on Hurtle's recent experience with Boo at a party. Kathy calls Hero to mind in her aggressive sexuality and apparent need to devour her lover. Then, when Kathy brings Hurtle a cat, we remember that Hero's husband drowned a sackful of cats and that Hurtle painted this act as a metaphor for God's casual destruction of men. The cat also connects Kathy with Rhoda, whom Hurtle finds feeding stray cats. Rhoda is further linked with Kathy in that both seem childlike to Hurtle (p. 450). Finally, Kathy re-enacts the incident of Maman and the chocolate (p. 424).

White works similar permutations with all the novel's major female characters. Their synthesis is confirmed in the drawing Hurtle does 'in which all the women he had ever loved were joined by umbilical cords to the navel of the same enormous child' (p. 505) – that is, himself. But the 'love' he has felt for them is problematical at best. Alone or severally, they seem to embody the threat of love, which he decides quite early 'must be resisted', because it is 'overwhelming, like religion' (p. 173). Perhaps this is why, in the drawing, only the woman with the severed cord seems to be 'charging the great, tumorous, sprawling child with infernal or miraculous life' (p. 505). Only by disconnecting himself can he counteract the threat and maintain his diseased existence.

Not long after this drawing is done, Hurtle falls from his Promethean heights. A stroke prostrates him, ironically at the feet of the despised Cutbush, and only minutes after his cruel dismissal of his sister Lena has made him suspect that he lacks a soul. It is the soul he must now seek. Earlier he had found all gods but self impossible to approach or comprehend. But, while sprawled before the Cutbush grocery store, he sees the colour of the sky as an 'extra indigo', which he seizes on as a clue to 'the last and first secret' (p. 537). Subsequently he finds himself, to his amazement, 'looking for a god – a *God* – in every heap of rusty tins amongst the wormeaten furniture out the window in the dunny of brown blowflies and unfinished inscriptions' (p. 549). In other words, he seeks God, the ultimate ordering principle, in the world of *Dreck* and uncertainty, the world he had once opposed to the divine order of art. Art is now made to serve the search. In his paintings Hurtle embarks on a 'wretched trembling act of faith' (p. 552) through which he hopes to recover the blessed indigo.

Hurtle has always relied on his own will. But, when he begins the series of works which a sceptical public will call the 'God paintings' (p. 575), he finds himself 'forced to surrender his will' (p. 553), until, instead of painting, he is 'being painted with, and through, and on' (p. 600). His surrender is like that of Alf Dubbo or Voss. 'Stroked by God', he responds like a willing lover (p. 599). Their conjunction will bring forth his best artistic fruit.

In the first of the final three paintings White describes for us, Hurtle must confess himself and be shriven. White says, 'Before he could contemplate his vision of indigo, he had to paint out the death which had stroked him', 'all that he had experienced under the dead pressure of despair' (p. 552). In this painting he acknowledges the dark night of the soul, and begins to move toward the plentitude of light. Unlike Arthur's loss of Waldo, the painting does not purge him of darkness, but rather forces its recognition. It remains as a testament.

In his next painting, he continues to reclaim his full self. Don names the work *The Whole of Life* (p. 593), and within it Hurtle expresses the encompassing vision which has been granted to so many Whitean illuminati. It is appropriate that in Hurtle's case, he should be acquiring experience, life itself, even experiences he never had. He strives here for a vision which 'would convey the whole' (p. 590).

This painting is a paean raised to life in all its fragmentation and to flesh in its ephemerality, both of which he now affirms. *The Vivisector* has been called the most scatological of White's works, and is appropriately so because its protagonist's mode of perception focuses on life's filth and refuse, a fact which accounts in part for his recoil from life into art.[81] Now, however, the vision opened to him and to us reveals what the artist Willie Pringle saw, at the end of *Voss:* that even 'The blowfly on its bed of offal is but a variation of the rainbow. Common forms are continually

breaking into brilliant shapes' (p. 443). Nor can the common
and the brilliant, or, for that matter, any of the novel's other
antitheses, be disentangled. The little hen on Perialos moves in
a medium of both dust and illumination, and glorious visions can
descend outside the dunny. Hurtle shares this perception with
other Whitean initiates and voices it in a passage hymning the
joys and distresses of the flesh in terms which still retain the
artist's organizing perspective on them.[82] He celebrates

> yellow light licking as voluptuously as tongues; green shade
> dribbled like saliva on nakedness; all the stickinesses: honey,
> sap, semen, sweat melting into sweat; the velvets of roseflesh
> threatened by teeth; exhausted, ugly, human furniture, bulging
> with an accumulation of experience acquired in years or by a
> stroke of lightning.   (p. 589)

In this perception, art and life are melded.

Having accepted multiplicity, Hurtle is ready to attempt to
find unity. Mixing 'the never-yet-attainable blue', he starts to paint
the blessed indigo (p. 602). Even at this culminating
moment, however, hairs from his brush cling to the painting,
keeping it humanly imperfect. Hurtle may reach toward God,
but never to Him. Appropriately, then, it is in trying to repair
these blemishes that Hurtle is stroked again and tumbles backward
to his death.[83]

The last words of Hurtle and of the novel are, 'Too tired too
endless obvi indi-ggodd' (p. 603), a kind of cipher encoding at
least the words 'endlessness', 'sob', 'obvious', 'vindicate', 'indicate'
and 'God'.[84] These words also equate God with the 'otherwise
unnameable I-N-D-I-G-O' (p. 602), suggesting that the dunny
inscription was not unfinished after all: God is the final unity in
which all such antitheses as artist/vivisector or creator/destroyer
are subsumed. Beyond these implications, however, the vision
remains inaccessible and ineffable, much more so than in the case
of Stan Parker or Mordecai Himmelfarb. Like the stroke which
completes Lily Briscoe's painting in Virginia Woolf's *To the
Lighthouse*, Hurtle's confrontation with the Indigod carries with
it a sense of decisive finality, but both novels leave us to determine
the precise significance of these highly charged acts. Thus Hurtle's
illumination is less specific in its import than were those of earlier
protagonists. None the less, his vision is like theirs in being
attained after the awareness and acknowledgement of failure and

after a surrender of self by means of which the self achieves its most profound expression.

Frequently in this novel, White seems deliberately self-referential, a fact which encourages the reader's equation of Hurtle with the author. For example, he refers to a jackeroo at the sheep station who, like White in his jackeroo days, wants to be a novelist (p. 106). In another instance, Hurtle's stepfather speaks of having some of Leichhardt's letters (p. 155), and we recall that the character of Voss drew on Leichhardt. Again, the conversation of those attending the Duffield Retrospective sounds like a compendium of remarks made by critics, detractors and avid but uniformed enthusiasts of White's own writing. Clearly the reader is not justified in attributing all Hurtle's thoughts, feelings and opinions to the author. White is deeply critical of Hurtle's conception of the artist as amoral creator/destroyer and uses the novel to depose him as god of his own artistic universe and to make him instead the humble instrument of a greater God. Nevertheless, the author's self-references allow us to speculate that White's censure of Hurtle is sometimes self-directed.

Indeed, *The Vivisector* is White's most direct confrontation of the ambiguous morality of art as it draws from and influences life. Although the novel ends by affirming the artistic enterprise, it does not shirk awareness of the odious or misguided ends to which the artist's search for 'truth' is sometimes put. Like earlier works, *The Vivisector* refuses to endorse the project of peeling away, cutting down to the core, or laying bare the inner workings. Here, such activity is explicitly vivisection: cruel and usually lethal. The movement White urges is toward synthesis and expansion, not analysis and reduction. Thus the approach to art which Hurtle takes for most of the novel must be repudiated and revised. The kind of art finally endorsed is that which derives from love, humility and moral engagement.

In the familiar pattern to which White has returned after *The Solid Mandala*, the experience of failure is an important step in reaching this awareness. Hurtle's understanding of his failure to love and his analogous failure to live ultimately opens the way to his enlightened perspective. At one point in the novel, White speaks of 'that state of half-cocked reality, neither life not art, which is perhaps the no-man's-land of human failure' (p. 357). Apart from life and art, this territory none the less communicates with both and provides Hurtle Duffield with a vantage point from which both may be observed and apprehended.

In the four novels from *Voss* to *The Vivisector*, then, failure is prerequisite to vision. In all four works, failure acts to humble the initiate before the enormity of the unknowable, while at the same time provoking further efforts to approach it. Ultimately, failure forces the surrender of the self, but, paradoxically, the relinquished self is often perfected by the otherness into which it is dissolved. These major tenets of the theme of failure can be found in every novel of this period. Arthur Brown of *The Solid Mandala* represents a departure from the pattern, but only because he is not rewarded with the comprehensive vision accorded most of White's illuminati. Rather, he bestows on others the possibility of wholeness he relinquishes.

These novels are, of course, much more than allegories of redemptive failure. Such a view would deny White's awareness of complexity. Since allegory tends toward the simplistic and reductive, the one-to-one equation of character and concept, its extreme form would be abhorrent to White's sensibility. The novels of this period, in fact, grow increasingly uncertain and complex, especially when contrasted with *The Living and the Dead* or *The Tree of Man*. In those that follow, however, uncertainty approaches the status of aesthetic principle.

4 The Later Works: the State of Failure

Her every attempt at love had been a failure. Perhaps she was fated never to enter the lives of others except vicariously. To enter, or to be entered: that surely was the question in most lives. (TA, p. 374)

Shortly after the 1979 release of White's novel *The Twyborn Affair*, his friend and fellow novelist Elizabeth Harrower called him to discuss the book. She reports that he accepted her assessment of its outlook as 'bleak' and added that he didn't see how anyone these days could feel otherwise.[1] Although the novel is not, in fact, unrelievedly dark, its predominantly sombre hues do point the direction White's work took in the seventies. We have only to compare Eudoxia/Eddie/Eadith's grisly and equivocal death to Hurtle Duffield's demise in a glory of panegyric blue to measure the distance White has come in that decade. Undoubtedly his view was influenced by the tenor of the times as reflected politically and economically: Australia's participation in the Vietnam War, threats to his beloved Centennial Park, plans for uranium-mining in the interior and for destructive sand-mining on Fraser Island, and most importantly the sack of the Whitlam Labor government in 1975.[2] Under these influences, White seems to have altered his perceptions of the nature of visionary experience, the prospect of communicating it, and the likelihood that what is culled from it may be sustained in life.

In the three novels which followed *The Vivisector* – *The Eye of the Storm* (1973), *A Fringe of Leaves* (1976) and *The Twyborn Affair* (1979) – White grew increasingly wary of articulating transcendental experience, to the extent that in *The Twyborn Affair* he scarcely even alludes to it. Elizabeth Hunter's heightened awareness in the eye of the storm is firmly in the tradition of Stan Parker's moment in the garden and Himmelfarb's vision from the jacaranda tree, and what she learns there is akin to the discoveries opened to Laura Trevelyan in fever and Hurtle Duffield in disability. But the emphasis in this later novel is upon the moment's fragility, transience and gratuitousness. Its peace and beauty are quickly destroyed by the storm always boiling on its periphery. The understanding Elizabeth gains in the storm remains to gall, but not always to guide and comfort, her. Unlike Laura Trevelyan, she is not so much profoundly changed by her experience, as made aware that she should have been.

In *A Fringe of Leaves* there is no strict analogue to Elizabeth Hunter's experience when the eye of the storm is trained upon her, although I shall argue that Ellen's moment of beatitude in Pilcher's makeshift chapel comes the closest. But more revealing in terms of White's changing direction is that the knowledge she comes to is so different from that bestowed on Elizabeth Hunter. While Elizabeth, like Stan Parker, experienced a oneness with nature, a sense of community and continuity in which the self radiated outward infinitely, Ellen is made to acknowledge a darkness at the core of self and her shared responsibility for the world's vast evil. In a sense, her task is the obverse or complement of that imposed on Voss, hero of White's other 'historical' novel. Where Voss had to acknowledge human weakness, vulnerability and love, and to surrender the awesome instrument of will, the docile and passive Ellen must dredge from within herself a will which has never been wielded. With it she discovers her strength, tenacity, rapaciousness and cruelty. These qualities come to enlarge and refine the definition of that 'human status' which was Voss's ultimate, if unlooked for, goal, and Ellen's dark epiphanies serve as gloss on Laura's conclusion that all men are composed of both good and evil.

In *The Twyborn Affair* both project and goal are obscure. Battered by ambivalence toward his sexual identity and his past, the novel's hero/heroine longs not to expand or integrate his sense of self so much as to amputate that part of it which keeps him constantly unsettled. The fact that he dies because a part of him *is* amputated (his hand is blown off by an exploding bomb) suggests that here, as elsewhere, White refuses to endorse the vivisectionist's approach to self-analysis and understanding. But it is unclear what the novel does endorse. Part of the reader's confusion on this matter arises from the fact that Eddie/Eadith's yearnings to locate the noumenal behind the phenomenal, yearnings typical of Whitean protagonists, are rarely mentioned, never explored, and only ambiguously rewarded in a few brief moments of communion with the Australian landscape. Significantly, this communion serves not to enlarge his possibilities, as it did for Voss, but to restrict them.

Thus, in the novels since *The Vivisector* we have both a constriction and a darkening of authorial vision. The possibility of redemptive otherness remains, even in *The Twyborn Affair*, but its intimations grow increasingly equivocal. Worse still, this otherness may seem itself as menacing as the 'Judge-Pantocrator' who appears in Twyborn's last, surrealistic vision. In consequence, the White of these works peers more closely into that dark glass which dulls our vision now, while looking less and less toward the light beyond. The narrative tends to anchor itself in everyday reality, leaving otherworldly implications to the reader.

Within these recentred concerns, the theme of failure serves the author in a new, but no less crucial manner. Where, before, failure opened the way to transcendence of the human condition, the emphasis now falls on failure as the inescapable context of that condition. The otherness which enfolded Stan Parker can still reach out, as it does to gather Elizabeth Hunter at the moment of her death. But more often it acts as the standard by which human life is measured and found wanting. Thus Elizabeth tortures herself with the memory of the irrecoverable moment of calm in the storm, and the legend 'GOD IS LOVE' in Pilcher's chapel sets Ellen Roxburgh to reliving her own betrayals of love and to musing on love's inadequacy.

Failure, then, is increasingly defined as inadequacy and seen as a state to which man is condemned, a feature of his 'life sentence on earth', as White had once thought of calling *The Tree of Man*. Failure retains a relevance to redemptive potential, itself an ever-more-tenuous possibility in the novels, if only that the greater a character's perception and spiritual capacity, the more deeply he will acknowledge his failure. Moreoever, failure may still transform itself into success, as it does in the case of Elizabeth and, less obviously, Ellen. But in these later novels the recognition of failure is often a consequence of revelation, rather than its precondition. Whereas Hurtle Duffield could not even seek the Indigod before understanding his transgressions against life in the name of art, Elizabeth Hunter's encounter with the ineffable makes her aware of her unworthiness. Thus White has perhaps come to see failure at both the beginning and end of spiritual aspiration.

THE EYE OF THE STORM

Just as Hurtle Duffield erected art as a screen between himself and life, Elizabeth Hunter shields herself behind her role as *grande dame*, gracious hostess, and legendary beauty. Beneath this mask, she is calculating, self-obsessed and frequently cruel. Love to her has always meant possession, both of things and people. For most of her life, she is much as her daughter describes her: 'sensual, mendacious, materialistic [and] superficial (p. 527).

Elizabeth is a character type White has treated before, but without the sympathy and understanding she here receives. Her precursors in the *oeuvre* go back as far as Catherine Standish of *The Living and the Dead* and continue through Theodora Goodman's mother in *The Aunt's Story*, Madeleine and perhaps Amy of *The Tree of Man*,[3] and most recognizably Alfreda Courtney of *The Vivisector*. The bitch-goddess Mag Bosanquet of White's 1978 play, *Big Toys*, is also related, although even more corrupt. Beyond these models, White's conception of Elizabeth may owe something to D. H. Lawrence's strong-willed and devouring women.[4] But Elizabeth also has a dimension most of these others lack: a longing to understand and experience what White calls the 'sublimity'[5] of which she always had an inkling.

In part, this 'sublimity' consists in a sheer intensity of living,[6] an intensity Elizabeth first senses as a child when she imagines the flight of her friend's older sister with a Russian lover. Kate Nutley has told the then Elizabeth Salkeld that her sister Lilian was found murdered. 'But', says White,

> Elizabeth Salkeld could not cry for Kate's sister Lilian galloping wildly towards her death on the great Asiatic river. By comparison, their own shallow life, their stagnant days, were

becoming unbearable. Elizabeth Salkeld could have slapped her friend for not hearing the thud of hooves, or seeing the magnificence of Lilian's full gallop. (*ES*, p. 24)

A similar sense of life at full gallop, even if rushing toward pain and death, is part of Elizabeth's experience in the storm. But a more important component of the 'sublimity' she seeks is the reception of a mitigating love.

She merits little love from anyone. To her good and gentle husband Alfred she has been occasionally unfaithful and always unreachable – always, that is, until his slow death by cancer reduces him to childlike dependence on her. From this position of power and control, she comes close enough to regret the pain she caused by taking herself and their children off to a house in Sydney while he remained on their country property, Kudjeri. As Alfred approaches death, the pair are permitted a 'sere honeymoon of the hopeful spirit' (p. 179) which reaches a 'climax of trustfulness' (p. 184). But this brief closeness with her husband fails to undo a lifetime of indifference and neglect. As Elizabeth herself nears death in the novel's present, she is forced to the realization that she never loved him as he deserved and wanted.

She also substitutes control for love in the case of her two children, and, consequently, both grow up incapable of loving. As a child, Dorothy had longed for a 'person in whom beauty was united with kindliness' (p. 327). Not finding that in her elegant but distant mother, she shyly offers her love to a series of maids,[7] then withdraws it altogether. But neglect is not Elizabeth's most reprehensible sin against her daughter. Into her seventies, she is sexually competitive with Dorothy, even when the prize is a man she doesn't want, such as the insipid Edvard Pehl. Worse still, she engineers Dorothy's unsatisfactory marriage to enhance the family's prestige. In later life, Elizabeth remembers a moment of 'spiritual gooseflesh' experienced on the realization that she was 'prostituting' Dorothy to the French prince who humiliated and abandoned her (p. 62).

Her son Basil, who succeeds spectacularly as an actor, is also unable to maintain a real-life love relationship. He has two unsuccessful marriages and a daughter only nominally his. As an adult he bitterly remembers being a sort of trophy for which Alfred and Elizabeth contended, his father out of love and his

mother from a need for power. As part of her experience in the
storm, Elizabeth is forced to recognize the damage she did Basil.
She recalls

> poor little Basil sucking first at one unresponsive teat and then
> the other the breasts which will not fill. . . . Instead of milk,
> 'my baby' (surely the most tragic expression?) must have drawn
> off the pus from everything begrudged withheld to fester inside
> the breast he was cruelly offered.   (p. 380)

Elizabeth Hunter fails utterly at love: love for her husband
and children, and even for two casual lovers she takes and
dismisses. One of these she uses in a gesture of defiance toward
death. She seduces the family lawyer when he brings a will for
her signature. The other helps her indulge an animal lust at odds
with her civilized veneer.

As the novel progresses, the reader comes to understand that
Elizabeth's nature *is* like an animal's: rudimentary, predatory,
desperate to live. Increasing age and feebleness allow this bestiality
to surface, revealing itself beneath the still potent mask of her
fabled beauty. The image White provides for this composite
creature is that of Odilon Redon's skiapod,[8] a voracious being,
part woman, part fish, in whom Elizabeth finds her 'spiritual
semblance' (p. 181). In dreams, she sees the skiapod attracting
prey with its alluring light and swallowing victims much larger
than itself (pp. 362–3). Clearly these activities are metaphorical
equivalents for many of her own. But even the skiapod is to be
forgiven, because a quester: 'in search of something it would
probably never find' (p. 363). The suggestion is that Elizabeth's
failures at love will not preclude her seeking the moment of
sublimity.

However, these failures do not function in the familiar Whitean
manner to prepare her for that moment. It is only in the storm,
and not before, that Elizabeth admits her inadequacies. The
moment at the storm's eye is therefore not apocalypse, still less
apotheosis, but a paradigm: a precious jewel of a moment,
crystallized out of her life, which glows ever after as a pledge of
what is possible within a state of grace. The experience alters her
life at its deepest core but does little to disturb its surface
configurations. To others she remains cold, demanding,
ingeniously cruel, and increasingly irascible. In an interview,
White offers this succinct explanation: 'She remained a bitch

because there was that side of her nature, too, but she did have, I think, more insights after the storm.'[9]

Her experience in the storm has a ritualistic quality which recalls Stan's epiphany at the heart of his mandalic garden or Arthur Brown's mandala dance for Mrs Poulter, But in Elizabeth's case the moment is more elaborately prepared, this preparation clearly meant to evoke the rituals of confession and absolution, communion and baptism, with Elizabeth alternately taking the roles of penitent and priest. In this way a supernatural sanction is accorded to the whole experience without having to call directly on the God Elizabeth would just as soon dispense with.

The storm comes on a day when Elizabeth is alone on Brumby Island. The suggestively named Warmings, who had invited her, Dorothy and the marine ecologist Edvard Pehl to their vacation cottage on the island, have left to join a sick child on the mainland. Dorothy departs in a jealous rage over Elizabeth's seductive manner with Pehl, and Edvard escapes because warned of the storm. Thus, like most candidates for ritual initiation, Elizabeth is isolated from her fellows. On this most important day of her life, she takes a morning walk, musing on what strikes her as the 'mystery of her strength, her elect life', and confessing her faults, if only to herself (p. 373). She begins to feel unworthy and consequently humbled. Coming upon some foresters at work, she tastes a chip from a recently felled tree which becomes a 'transmuted wafer' (p. 375). In her presence, White says, 'the men were as reverent as a cloister of nuns' (ibid.).

That evening she anoints herself and dresses in the white she favours but which also suggests the innocence of one about to be initiated. When the storm strikes, she runs outside, hoping to find Pehl, and is first grazed in the temple by a wind-driven piece of wood, then drenched by rain. Taking refuge in the bunker where the wine is stored, she listens to the storm raging and increasingly accepts responsibility for her cruelty to husband, children and lovers. Imagery and incident thus combine to suggest confession and absolution. She has taken communion, begun with the wafer in the woods and completed with the wine in the bunker, and has been baptized by rainwater, blood, and the rising sea.

Other elements of her experience recall analogous moments in earlier novels. She senses her being as convincing and inclusive, yet impersonal. Like Theodora Goodman, she feels herself composed of all the lives she has touched. Equally familiar is her sense of herself as pivot to creation's circle. Emerging into the sudden hush of the storm's eye,

> she was no longer a body, least of all a woman: the myth of her womanhood had been exploded by the storm. She was instead a being, or more likely a flaw at the centre of this jewel of light: the jewel itself blinding and tremulous at the same time, existed, flaw and all, only by grace .... (p. 381)

Seabirds float at rest around her, and by this point she is sufficiently shriven to minister to these, her fellow worshippers. The sea provides her with a loaf of sodden bread and she presides at another Eucharistic ceremony, feeding the seven black swans who approach her. In rendering the scene, White stresses the kinship of woman and swans, and affirms their union in grace.[10]

Elizabeth would have chosen to remain for ever in this 'lustrous state of perfect beatitude' (ibid). But to do so would be to succumb to the black swans' temptation to a *Liebestod*,[11] and she has rather been 'saved up' (p. 384) for 'further trial' (p. 381). Thus, the body of a gull, impaled upon a broken tree branch, recalls her to her sense of self and an awareness that life exacts suffering. She concludes that she 'had not experienced enough of living' and retreats to her bunker (p. 382). The storm has renewed its howling.

In Elizabeth's sense of a dissolving self which expands from the heart of a mandalic 'jewel of light', we recognize the typical configuration of the Whitean vision. Yet the emphasis here is on the vision's fleetingness. All too soon the eye is no longer upon her; she is decentred, peripheral. Nor can the joy and peace of the vision be recalled at will. Rather the memory serves most often as a mirror within whose compass the rest of her life is reflected for judgement. Only by measuring her life against the terms set by the vision can she hope to re-enter the eye.

Elizabeth weathers the storm at the age of seventy. Sixteen years later, in the novel's present, she lies felled by a stroke, attended by three shifts of nurses and a housekeeper-cook, awaiting the deathbed visit of her children. From the novel's opening pages, she acknowledges her yearning to return to the moment in the storm. However, it is not to be recaptured until she again surrenders her still formidable will, and accepts the death which the seven black swans have prepared for her. White presents this second consummate moment of her life in language and incident resonant with echoes of the first.

Like the vision in the storm's eye, death exacts from her an admission of failure and assumption of responsibility, a kind of recapitulation of the catechism which the storm had taught. To these is added the affirmation of 'a faith in love and joy' (p. 486), celebrated in the dance performed by Lotte Lippmann. Lotte, an ex-cabaret dancer, is a German Jew, guilt-ridden over her escape from the gas ovens, who has become Mrs Hunter's housekeeper–cook and a grateful disciple. The dance and the relationship it ratifies between the two women provide the sense of communion which was earlier supplied by the bark 'wafer' and the woodsmen. Where, before, Elizabeth had adorned herself in virginal white, for this occasion she is decked out by her bored and spiteful nurse Flora in stained brocade and a ghastly mask of green and silver make-up. Still the sense of ritual preparation is similar. The memory of a cow dying in a drought of Elizabeth Salkeld's youth recalls both to her and to the reader the 'skewered' gull on Brumby Island (p. 382). Additional allusions to wind, waves, light, the sound of roaring and the sensation of galloping further evoke the moment in the storm and, beyond that, Lilian Nutley's fatal flight with her lover. There is even a hint of the sacrificial and cleansing blood which ran from ELizabeth's temple in Flora's 'lovely blessed BLOOD' whose flow announces that she is not, as she had feared, pregnant by Sir Basil (p. 490). The stage is now fully set for the swans' return.

The swans come for Elizabeth a few minutes later as, still dressed in her garish costume, she strains on the commode to 'relieve' herself both of faeces and the dross of flesh (p. 489). It is typical of White to supply such a grotesque, ironic context for an epiphanic moment. We recall that Hurtle Duffield's synoptic inscription was written on the dunny wall; and the unfortunate Rosenbaum of *Riders in the Chariot* was informed of his election to greet the Saviour while standing by a privy in the stench of urine. White's intention in these instances is to underscore his belief that even vision is rooted in life. Like James Joyce, that is, he remembers that the aspiring spirit and creative imagination are housed in a body which must regularly visit the dunny. Or, as the novel itself puts it, 'souls have an anus they are never allowed to forget it' (p. 176).[12] The visionary is not excused from life's undignified contingencies.

Not that the ironic context blunts the intensity or efficacy of the transcendent experience. Despite its grotesque setting, Elizabeth's final vision recovers her first.

> To move the feet by some miraculous dispensation to feel sand benign and soft between the toes the importance of the decision makes the going heavy at first the same wind stirring the balconies of cloud as blows between the ribs it would explain the howling of what must be the soul not for fear that it will blow away in any case it will but in anticipation of its first experience of precious water as it filters in through the cracks the cavities of the body blue pyramidal waves with swans waiting by appointment each a suppressed black explosion the crimson beaks savaging only those born to a different legend to end in legend is what frightens most people more than cold water climbing mercifully towards the overrated but necessary heart a fleshy fist to love and fight with not to survive except as a kindness or gift of a jewel.
>
> The seven swans are perhaps massed after all to destroy a human will once the equal of their own weapons its thwack as crimson painful its wings as violently abrasive don't oh DON'T my dark birds of light let us rather – enfold.
>
> Till I am no longer filling the void with mock substance; myself is this endlessness. (p. 492)

Again we have the familiar and prototypical elements: the surrender of will, the immersion in creation, and an infinite outward flowing of the dissolved and expanded self. Yet something has been added.

White's insistent emphasis in this passage on sensation – the feel of soft sand, the shock of cold water, the thwack of the swans' beaks, and the abrasive beating of their wings – calls attention to the central aspect of Elizabeth Hunter's moral and emotional growth since the storm. For Elizabeth, nearly blind in her final days, has at last learned to see, not with her eyes, but *feelingly*. This allusion to the capacity developed by Gloucester in *King Lear* (iv.vi) is part of an elaborate network of references to and reflections upon the play which begin on its very first page.

The novel opens at dawn. Mrs Hunter, fretful and restless, complains to her night nurse Mary de Santis, 'Oh dear, will it never be morning?' Mary answers, 'It is, . . . can't you – can't you *feel* it?' (*ES*, p. 11). She has started to reply, 'Can't you see it?', but remembers in time that her patient is almost blind, and also makes an unconscious allusion to the faculty Elizabeth will develop. By the novel's end, Elizabeth can feel; she can perceive through sensation and emotion, as most perceive through sight. It is this capacity which allows her to apprehend the nuances of Lotte's final dance and to apply the insights of emotion to the events of her own life.

More direct references to the themes, concerns, and *dramatis personae* of *Lear* come with the entrance of Basil, the famous actor who has played what he himself judges to be a 'bloody superficial' Lear (p. 314), but is obsessed with undertaking the role again. Clearly, however, it is Elizabeth, not Basil, who takes the part of the old King here. The roles of Goneril and Regan go to Basil and Dorothy, who plot to maximize their inheritance by dismissing Elizabeth's retinue of nurses and servants and removing her to the less expensive surroundings of Thorogood Village for the elderly.[13] Obviously, too, it is Elizabeth who has the heath scene,[14] discovering herself in the storm as 'the thing itself. Unaccommodated man' and a 'bare, forked animal' (*Lear*, III.iv). Poor Basil's closest approach to such a scene and its revelations occurs at Kudjeri to which he and Dorothy retreat in hopes of calming their consciences and reclaiming their childhoods. But Basil's moment at the dam where he romped as a boy, a moment in which he approaches a synthesis of art and life, ends abruptly and humiliatingly when he cuts his foot on a piece of rubbish (*ES*, pp. 441–2). As always, Basil is upstaged by his mother.

If this piece suggests no ready Cordelia, it may be because her role is shared; at various points in the novel, nurses Mary and Flora, husband Alfred, solicitor Wyburd, and even housekeeper Lotte take on aspects of Cordelia's attributes and functions. Alternatively, Cordelia may be absent because White's conception of human nature would not permit a character of such unmitigated goodness.[15] A final possibility is that Elizabeth Hunter must be her own Cordelia and must herself 'redeem . . . [her] nature from the general curse' (*Lear*, IV.vi), by penetrating, understanding and forgiving it.

This she can do, albeit fitfully and sometimes grudgingly, by applying the insights gained in the eye of the storm. Thus the emphasis in this novel, as not in the earlier works, is upon the vision embedded in life, sometimes as an irritant, sometimes as a nucleus around which something precious may accrue. Like the moments of intense experience in Virginia Woolf, it is 'globed', whole and permanent, in a world of process, flux and fragments.

Moreover, just as the experience in the storm is embedded in Elizabeth Hunter's life, her very being is both literally and figuratively embedded in the lives around her and serves for them an analogous function. In several senses, she is the eye of the novel's storm. Critics have suggested that she holds this position in the narrative structure, or, in other words, that the novel's action and passions rage around the still centre of the room where she lies bedridden.[16] But encounters with Elizabeth Hunter rarely produce the tranquillity which she experienced at the storm's heart. Rather, and far more importantly, she is the eye of the novel's storm in that, under her influence, others may come to see themselves as truly as she did on Brumby Island. To those who are strong and courageous enough she offers the chance she was given: the chance to recognize and realize one's nature.

At the same time, the efforts of her satellites to come to terms with themselves, or their resistance to the project, further comment on Elizabeth's own quest, since, like *Voss*, this novel is a monodrama. Each of the other principals mirrors some salient aspect of Elizabeth's character. In Mary de Santis, for example, we see her spiritual yearnings, while Flora Manhood reflects her sensuality and her selfish withholding of love. The third nurse, Badgery, has Elizabeth's greed for food and material goods. In Dorothy, we see that tendency turned on people, for, like her mother, Dorothy would devour others.[17] Basil has inherited Elizabeth's talent for acting instead of living life. Finally, in the housekeeper Lotte we identify the darker side of Elizabeth, a desire to atone which sometimes reaches the proportions of a death wish. Perhaps because she recognizes what she shares with each, Elizabeth can bring them face to face with themselves.

Her children, however, shun the encounter. In fact, their avoidance of their mother becomes emblematic of their self-deception. Although Basil has returned from England and Dorothy from France ostensibly to visit her, they see her as little as possible and manage to absent themselves from both her deathbed and her funeral. Part of this avoidance stems from guilt over the plan they are hatching to have her put away, but it is also a response to the fact that they feel threatened in her presence. Dorothy, for example, thinks of her mother as a 'jewelled scabbard in which a sword was hidden' (*ES*, p. 68).

Dorothy's difficulty is that she has several 'selves' but is comfortable in none of them (p. 44). As white puts it, 'Dorothy Hunter's misfortune was to feel at her most French in Australia, her most Australian in France' (p. 46). Besides being on the one hand the gawky daughter of the dazzling Elizabeth Hunter, and on the other the Princesse de Lascabanes, estranged wife of a French prince, she also imagines herself as Sanseverina, heroine of her favourite novel, Stendhal's *Charterhouse of Parma*.[18] But in more sober moments, she is bitterly aware that her mother, not she, recalls the fabulous Duchess. Although Dorothy tells herself, 'I have never managed to escape being this thing Myself' (*ES*, p. 47), her real problem is that she has never managed to find it.

Part of the predicament for her as well as Basil derives from a failure to come to terms with the past. An uneasy relationship with her father has soured since his death into a kind of incestuous desire for a father figure, a role in which she casts first her husband, then later the family solicitor Arnold Wyburd, and finally even Basil. Her resentment and jealousy of her mother preclude any resolution in that direction, so she is left with 'a lopsided existence' (p. 337). Briefly she hopes that alliance with her feared and admired brother may right the balance. But her pilgrimage with Basil to Kudjeri, a journey which is to be one of recovery and reconciliation, reaches its logical if horrifying climax in incest, and Dorothy again recoils.

During her stay with the Macrory family, who occupy Kudjeri, Dorothy does take some steps toward finding herself. With Rory, the husband, she must deny and repress a sexual attraction, but with his wife Anne and their daughters she starts to develop relationships real enough to validate her existence. She thinks, 'If she could have remained enclosed by this circle of love and trust, she might have accepted herself by living up to their opinion of her' (p. 457). But the circle is broken by Dorothy's discovery that the Macrorys have loved not herself, but her likeness to her mother. On the night of the incest, Dorothy dons her mother's characteristic white and courts the disaster of identification.

After the incest and the discovery that Elizabeth has died on the same night, the past becomes too horrible and overwhelming to confront. After wounding both herself and Basil by denying their relationship, she congratulates herself on having reached 'impersonality', a sort of negative identity (p. 525). But this is not the Whitean impersonality of conjunction and expansion, nor is it granted. Dorothy's mutilated self stays with her. The novel's last glimpse of her shows that she writhes under the sense of ineradicable stain (p. 527).

Basil's problems mirror his sister's and he similarly fails to solve them. Like her, he has too many selves; he is a compound of his roles. Moreover, like his mother he has substituted art for life and acting for interacting to the point where he can rarely tell the difference.

Again like Dorothy, Basil is alienated from his past; but, while she strives to close the rift by locating a father, Basil seeks a mother to ease his sense of exile by giving him rebirth. From a dream recounted early in the novel in which Basil sees himself as the 'Primordial Baby' (p. 130), to his last dream, in which he is reborn only to be dismembered, White stresses Basil's obsession with renascence. The visit he and Dorothy make to Kudjeri is suggestively described as 'allowing the past to suck them back through this choked intestine recorded on maps as the Parramatta Road' (p. 416). But a return to the womb has obvious sexual implications, and Basil's yearning for regeneration shades easily into his Oedipal desires for Elizabeth. Like Dorothy, he projects such inadmissible urges; thus his relationships all smack of incest.

As his sister finds surrogate fathers, Basil finds a mother substitute in Mitty Jacka. The identification of Mitty and Elizabeth is made almost too patent by the fact that when he meets Mitty she is wearing a ring exactly like the one he had given his mother. She also admits to stealing it 'from someone who didn't appreciate what they had' (pp. 215–16). She appropriates Basil from Elizabeth in the same way.

Mitty is a playwright of sorts and holds out to Basil the tantalizing prospect of an improvised work in which his role will be himself. As Mitty puts it in a note to herself, 'an actor tends to ignore the part which fits him best *his life* Lear the old unplayable is in the end a safer bet than the unplayed I' (p. 222). This would seem to be precisely the challenge Basil should accept, but throughout the novel he likens his undertaking of this role to suicide. The project is also made questionable by its dependence upon money extorted from the dying Elizabeth and by the likeness of Mitty's surname to 'jackal'. The implication seems to be that to play Mitty's version of the 'unplayed I' is to step behind 'that grey screen, or backcloth, he had seen in his boyhood as standing between himself and nothing' (p. 219). The image comes from a childhood experience of being frightened by shadows on a screen set up to keep off draughts, but the screen has functioned in his adult life as a shield between himself and the terrifying shapes taken by reality. No Captain Ahab, Basil is not brave or strong enough to breach the blankness. To do so would be to invite destruction.

The apparent acceptance of Mitty's invitation to suicide accounts in part for his final dream, in which he is torn apart by Mitty with the help of all the other women in his life. In this dream, Basil undergoes a parodic reversal of the Whitean visionary moment. Instead of sensing the self dissolved and rushing outward toward others, Basil is dismembered when others rush in on him (p. 532). The suggestion that he may actually desire such a stripping of self is reinforced by his allusions, within the dream sequence and elsewhere, to Lear's line in the storm, 'Come, unbutton here' (*Lear*, iii.iv), and to the King's final, 'Pray you, undo this button' (v.iii). Like Lear, Basil seems to want to be released from a repugnant self. Moreover, because Basil has resisted seeing his mother as Lear and playing Cordelia to her King, the role of Cordelia is excised from the play as he dreams it. There is no force here to mitigate the 'general curse'.

Basil, then, cannot get himself reborn. Even at Kudjeri he can only travesty the past, not regenerate it. In a nostalgic moment in the family garage, he puts on one of his father's old boots only to have it adhere to him like a deformity. But his ultimate defilement of the past is the incest with his sister, which takes place in the bed where both were conceived. In this act, Basil and Dorothy attempt to eradicate their parents by replacing them and at the same time perhaps to re-conceive themselves.[19] They may also be responding with cynical and vengeful acquiescence to the awareness that for the Macrorys they *are* Alfred and Elizabeth Hunter. Finally, each is probably aroused by the parent perceived in the other, and moved to make this final, perverse attempt at self-completion through union. But, whatever its motives, the act fails to work its expected alchemy. Afterwards Dorothy rises from their bed to open the window on the winter night:

> 'You've got to admit it's beautiful.' It was her brother looking over her shoulder at the landscape at 'Kudjeri'.
> 'Oh God, yes, we know that', she had to agree; 'beautiful – but sterile'.
> 'That's what it isn't, in other circumstances.'
> 'Other circumstances aren't ours.' (p. 471)

Their circumstances are sterility and isolation; they are a part neither of the land, nor of each other.

As this passage suggests, and as Basil's final dream and Dorothy's thoughts corroborate, brother and sister do achieve some self-awareness, especially the awareness of failure. But in their case White varies his familiar theme, for their admission of failure acts to cripple rather than encourage self-realization. Ultimately, Basil and Dorothy quail before the challenge of the storm's eye. Their failures are not facilitating but absolute; their quests end in a *cul-de-sac*. But others of Elizabeth's retinue, most notably her cook and two of her nurses, or 'sisters',[20] succeed in approaching their essential selves under her provoking eye.

Sister Flora Manhood, as her name too plainly suggests, begins the novel as a collision of contradictions. Young and healthy, she is in the flower of her womanhood and sexuality, aspects of her being which she celebrates with her lover, Col Pardoe. Elizabeth has decreed that she is destined for Col, and at times even Flora admits that he completes her. In dreams she is clamoured over by countless children, all with his features. But the part of her nature suggested by her surname makes her wary and resentful of the loss of independence which marriage and childbearing would entail. Thus, sometimes she feels Col's love like a gun levelled at her and imagines life with him as a series of 'snotty noses, nappies, and a man's weight to increase your body's exhaustion' (p. 79).

In misguided attempts to appease both sides of herself, Flora toys with the idea of a Lesbian relation with her albino cousin Snow, then decides to conceive a child by Sir Basil and to raise it herself without his knowledge. Either project would evade the destiny that Elizabeth has seen for her; either would deny the self. As if to make this point, Elizabeth keeps Col before her, giving her a pink sapphire to wear in token of their betrothal. Feeling that she has betrayed him with Basil, Flora resists accepting Col as her future husband until, on the night of Elizabeth's death, she sees menstrual blood and knows she isn't pregnant. The moment is presented as both reprieve and renewal, a kind of baptism into recovered possibilities. This, coupled with the love she allows herself to feel for Mrs Hunter as she lays out the body, works within her warring self the necessary rapprochement.

Flora reflects that, for her, Mrs Hunter had 'stood for . . . Life, perhaps. She whipped you on' (p. 505). Now Flora declares allegiance to that life. Refusing an appeal from Snow, she goes to Col. A final dream clarifies Elizabeth's role in this process. In the dream, Mrs Hunter

> is knocking on wood with her sapphire the pink it is yours isn't it the coffin Nurse is where one sows one's last seed I can see it germinating inside you like a lot of little skinned rabbits oh Mrs Hunter how can you be so *unkind* (giggle) always hated obstets but your own flesh is different my children are human we hope Mrs Hunter if the blessed sapphire works.   (p. 513)

Elizabeth has sowed the seeds in Flora's nature which will germinate as love for Colin and their children.

The allegiances of Lotte Lippman are very different from Flora's but are also explored with the help of Elizabeth Hunter. A Jew who escaped the Nazi holocaust, Lotte cannot forgive herself her survival. Although, unlike Himmelfarb, she does not delude herself that she may have a Messianic mission, Lotte shares with him the compulsion to carry 'a cross of proportions no Christian could conceive' (p. 486).

Lotta seeks the atonement of death, and Elizabeth helps her to find it. Together, on the night Elizabeth dies, they celebrate the mysteries of life and death, mysteries akin to those of the storm's eye and in which both women are adept. After the death of her protector, Lotte opens her veins. As it stains the bathwater, her blood is described as 'a flush of roses, of increasing crimson' which 'she was offering to those others pressed always more suffocatingly close around her' (p. 543). As she had told Mary de Santis when the sister inquired where she would go after the house was sold, Mrs Lippmann will 'be with friends' (p. 542) – not only Elizabeth, but the many she has left behind in Germany. She too, then, enjoys a moment in which the self is dissolved, dispersed and embraced, even though the embrace finally stifles.

The movement of her vision is both centrifugal and centripetal: outward in the flowing blood, inward in the press of others. This fact perhaps marks the status of her vision as midway between Basil's abortion and Elizabeth's achievement. This would be appropriate in that, while death enfolds her as it did her mistress, she has sought, rather than accepted, it. Instead of surrendering her will, she has exercised it. None the less, her death is an offering of roses which Mrs Hunter helped her to cultivate.

The mention of roses in this, the novel's penultimate scene, links it to the final passages in which Mary de Santis walks at dawn in the Hunter rose garden and chooses a rose for her new patient, Irene Fletcher.[21] The moment returns us to the novel's beginning, also at dawn, with Mary devotedly ministering to Elizabeth. Thus Mary, light and service encircle the novel, and in these White invests the ultimate significance of Elizabeth's experience.

Under Elizabeth's dimming eye, Mary, like Flora and Lotte, has come to see herself more truly and wholly, but in this case the self so revealed is infinitely more profound. Whereas Lotte found herself a devotee of death, Mary confirms her vocation as a 'votary of life' (p. 144). She is so not in the sense of Flora, who will propagate life, but in the sense that she will serve and celebrate it as a force opposing apathy, pain and evil. In this spirit she accepts her next assignment with Irene Fletcher, a crippled girl 'so warped', as her mother tells Mary, 'she is only convinced by what is evil' (p. 541). Mary will begin convincing Irene of good by bringing her the quintessential 'first and last rose' from her former patient's garden (p. 544).

Having undertaken what is imaged as a new novitiate, Mary is granted her own moment of ecstasy, with which the novel closes. As several critics have noticed, its elements are those of Elizabeth's eye of the storm: light, moisture, violence, motion, the feeding of birds, and a deep sense of joy.[22]

> She poured the remainder of the seed into the dish on the upper terrace. The birds already clutching the terracotta rim, scattered as she blundered amongst them, then wheeled back, clashing, curving, descending and ascending, shaking the tassels of light or seed suspended from the dish. She could feel claws snatching for a hold in her hair.
>
> She ducked, to escape from this prism of dew and light, this tumult of wings and her own unmanageable joy. Once she raised an arm to brush aside a blue wedge of pigeon's feathers. The light she could not ward off: it was by now too solid, too possessive; herself possessed.
>
> Shortly after she went inside the house. In the hall she bowed her head, amazed and not a little frightened by what she saw in Elizabeth Hunter's looking glass.   (Ibid.)

White's use of the image of the looking-glass implies that Mary has assumed Elizabeth's power with her knowledge. It is she who offers Mrs Hunter immortality.

Mary begins the novel already the 'archpriestess' (p. 19) to Elizabeth's divinity and custodian of the mystery which Mrs Hunter embodies:

> that this ruin of an over-indulged and beautiful youth . . . was also a soul about to leave the body it had worn, and already able to emancipate itself so completely from human emotions, it became at times as redemptive as water, as clear as morning light.   (p. 13)

Mary reveres Elizabeth because she can put off 'human emotions', but those emotions are precisely what Mary must explore. The nurse's preference of night over day and the spiritual over the fleshly are symptomatic of her denial of aspects of self, particularly sexual desire and the need for close human relationships.

The little we learn of Mary's past suggests that her fear of sexuality is bound up with ambivalent feelings toward her father, whom she both adored and pitied, and from whose loving relationship with her mother she felt gently but firmly excluded. Her association of Basil with her father complicates the desire he arouses in her and makes her feel more than ever defiled by it. Yet she still fantasizes making love with Basil and later goes to him, ostensibly to plead against his and Dorothy's plans for their mother, but actually to bask in his physical presence. Even at Mrs Hunter's funeral, Mary appears dressed in a hat she hoped might please the absent Basil.

From these occasions, Mary emerges feeling unclean and in need of absolution. But experiencing these feelings is apparently necessary to her spiritual and emotional growth, just as 'her opulent breasts, a surprise in an otherwise austere figure' (p. 13), are undeniably part of her. She warns herself against her attraction to Basil; but the awareness of her sensuality alters her perspective, enlarging her capacity for response. Even Elizabeth becomes for her less purely the 'holy relic to which your faith bowed down in worship'. Instead, she sees her as 'distressingly human' (p. 414).

White does not show us the process completing itself, but by the end of the novel it has. Sexual desire has erupted, burned and consumed itself as have those other appetites of the 'personal life' she will gladly renounce for her new patient (p. 541). Thus she ends the novel more whole and integrated than she began it, having experienced aspects of herself she had earlier repressed. All aspects of self, fleshly and spiritual, are preserved in that wholeness. White insists that her spirit 'continued throbbing, flickering, inside her [still] clumsy body' (p. 544). As it had for Elizabeth Hunter, her vision remains vulnerable to life.

Early in the novel, Mary understands love as service and expects such service to exhaust her resources and reduce her to the purity of nothingness. But Elizabeth gives her a seal with a phoenix carved into it, suggesting that Mary must rather be repeatedly renewed, to serve again and again. This is the essence of the 'love as she had come to understand it' which she carries to Irene with the perfect but perishable rose (p. 544). Love, like vision, must be sought perpetually, and service to Elizabeth has shown her this, as it has shown her herself. An initial failure to accept her true self, like the analogous failures of Flora and Lotte, is redeemed through the agency of Mrs. Hunter's vision. Thus Elizabeth's most precious legacy, as the novel's last line suggests, is to reveal Mary to herself 'in Elizabeth Hunter's looking glass' (p. 544).

Shortly after completing *The Eye of the Storm*, Patrick White wrote to Ingmar Björksten expressing his belief that in this novel he had 'come closer to giving the final answer'.[23] This enigmatic remark may reflect his awareness that by implanting the vision in life where it might act as irritant and constant challenge, he had come closer than before to conveying his sense of how the transcendent and mundane must interact.

Elizabeth is no Arthur Brown; she does not sacrifice herself for others. But she does function as a kind of spiritual gadfly, driving others toward greater consciousness. Even staid old Arnold Wyburd is brought to acknowledge his life's one moment of 'poetry' in Elizabeth Hunter's bed (p. 534). Significantly, her own experience in the storm works on her in like manner. It holds out the promise of poetry while exposing vast stretches of her life as the flattest prose.

All lives, White seems to say, must be largely prosaic. Even after the storm, Elizabeth remains a querulous and often cruel old woman, haunted by the memory of unaccountable election. Similarly, Mary de Santis's striving spirit stays trapped in her graceless body. Yet the hope of poetry is always at hand. The vision thus becomes that which validates the past, motivates the present, and inhabits the future, a condition which renders time in the novel as an eternal now upon which visionary experience perpetually reflects. White reinforces our sense of this with his narrative technique, keeping Elizabeth's approaching death and her memory of the storm's eye squarely in the novel's present, while ranging forward in anticipation and prolepsis, backward in memory, from this still but charged double centre.

Because of its existence outside time, the vision which is both goad and goal is not to be securely possessed. Human lives are time-bound. The eye turns away, and the storm breaks again. Thus the condition of even the fullest, most deeply lived lives becomes failure, the failure to sustain the vision. But it is the kind of failure which, as in previous novels, can motivate further and finally rewarding search.

White published *The Eye of the Storm* in 1973, and later that same year received the Nobel Prize for literature. The Nobel citation commended him for his

> ever deeper restlessness and seeking urge, an onslaught against vital problems that have never ceased to engage him, and a wrestling with the language in order to extract all its power and all its nuances, to the verge of the unattainable. (*ES*, flyleaf)

It is significant that the Royal Swedish Academy should have admired in White what he admired in Elizabeth Hunter: the quester who perseveres 'to the verge of the unattainable', in full knowledge both of inevitable failure and of the worth of the attempt.

A FRINGE OF LEAVES

In 1974 White published *The Cockatoos*, his second collection of short fiction. Although half these stories and novellas had been printed earlier, the collection as a whole seems a sort of preparatory exercise for his next novel, *A Fringe of Leaves*, which would appear in 1976. Like the novel, these tales are concerned with the darkness within.

In 'A Woman's Hand', for example, Evelyn and Harold, a couple involved in a long, dull and complacent marriage, rediscover the homosexual drives they once felt toward another pair, drives they repress by manipulating these others into a marriage of their own. In this clumsy and destructive liaison, Clem and Nesta, the unfortunate alter egos, suffer the rage which has simmered between Evelyn and Harold. In 'Sicilian Vespers', a vacationing woman whose husband is incapacitated by a toothache drifts into brief adultery with a fellow tourist, but uses this sordid episode to shield herself from awareness of her deep religious yearnings. Later, of course, she must also refuse to acknowledge the lust which her lover aroused in her. Counterpointing these stories in which the invitation to navigate one's own depths is refused are those in which revelation is imposed on the protagonist. In 'The Full Belly'[24] a boy discovers how physical need erodes spiritual strength and moral resolve, and in 'Five-Twenty' a woman is made aware that her love has vitiated and victimized its objects.

Two stories suggest a transit of internal darknesses. In 'The Night the Prowler', a story White liked well enough to revise as a screenplay in 1976, a girl who vents the anger and violence within her is ultimately brought to affirm life as the antithesis of nothingness and a process of 'perpetual becoming' (*C*, p. 168). In the collection's title piece, a young boy is the beneficiary of a search through what is here imaged as the dark and cobwebby cupboard of self. In this story, as in *The Eye of the Storm* and throughout this collection, birds come to symbolize the possibilities of life lived fully and keenly.[25] To respond to these possibilities can be dangerous, even fatal, as the story's events attest, but the project is none the less endorsed as an opting for life over death. Still, it must be noted that this story ends more ambiguously than does 'The Night the Prowler'. The fact that the story closes on the boy's birthday suggests new beginnings. But we leave him in the midst of sober reflection that the guilt he feels over killing an aged and infirm cockatoo cannot be locked up like the cupboard where he secrets its crest.

A similar ambiguity pervades the final scene of *A Fringe of Leaves*.[26] It is disconcerting to find a woman such as Ellen Roxburgh, a woman whose very survival testifies to her enormous strength, meekly accepting the fate of her sex in the shape of the merchant Jevons. Only by evaluating the experiences which have brought her to this point can we decide whether her acceptance of Jevons represents a triumph or capitulation.

The story of Ellen Roxburgh's misadventures after her 1836 shipwerck off the Queensland coast – her capture and enslavement by Aboriginals and her rescue by an escaped convict – was inspired by the life of Mrs Eliza Fraser, who was shipwrecked in the same place, month and year as White's heroine and underwent many of the same trials – some documented, some apocryphal.[27] But Ellen is 'based' on Eliza Fraser in much the same way that Voss was 'based' on Leichhardt and the other explorers of Australia. White's book is not a historical novel; the journeys Ellen makes are as much metaphysical as physical; and the focus here, as always, is upon the former.

As if to emphasize this point, White insists on the novel's artifice, as he has not since *Happy Valley*. Like Thackeray playing puppet-master in *Vanity Fair*, he constructs a 'prologue' to be performed by 'minor actors' who hint at the significance of what will follow (*FL*, p. 24). This prologue is 'spoken' by Mr and Mrs Merivale and their friend Miss Scrimshaw, who have just paid a courtesy call on Mr and Mrs Austin Roxburgh as they await departure for England from Sydney harbour. The sibylline Miss Scrimshaw pronounces her judgement that 'Mrs Roxburgh could feel life has cheated her out of some ultimate in experience. For which she would be prepared to suffer, if need be' (p. 21). She also remarks portentously that 'Every woman has secret depths with which even she, perhaps, is unacquainted, and which sooner or later must be troubled' (p. 20). Equally impobably, Mr Merivale wonders aloud 'how Mrs Roxburgh would react to suffering if faced with it' (p. 24). Then White ushers his minor actors off stage and turns our attention to his heroine. As Voss prophesied that Le Mesurier would cut his throat, Miss Scrimshaw and the Merivales predict a fate for Ellen which the novel enacts. The plot and its essential fictionality thus firmly established, reader interest shifts from events to their implications.

The prologue further suggests that, like the nineteenth-century authors with whom he claims affinity, White is writing a moral fable.[28] The twentieth-century touch is that, after so declaring himself, he refuses to point those moral lessons, leaving the reader to piece together the import of Ellen's experiences. In this project the reader must follow Ellen's lead, for the author sets her a similar task of integration and interpretation.

From the days of her Cornish girlhood as Ellen Gluyas, she has suspected unexplored depths in herself. The love and hate she bears toward her father and the shameful excitement she feels at his touch are among the things that will not bear examination. Her own intimations are others. At one point, oppressed by a 'presentiment of an evil she would have to face sooner or later', she walks the several miles from her farm to St Hya's Well to immerse herself in its icy, black and supposedly purgative waters (p. 110). This, it has been observed, is the first of a series of baptisms Ellen undergoes in the novel,[29] but it does not succeed in cleansing her. Afterwards, she hopes 'she had exorcised the threat by immersion in the pool', whereas in reality she has only numbed her inner darkness (p. 111). It first begins to thaw in the steamy Australian heat of Van Diemen's Land and Queensland.

Following her parents' deaths, she marries Austin Roxburgh, the sickly gentleman who had come as a lodger to their farm. Austin chooses her because the frustrated artist in him hopes to render this malleable country lass into his one convincing 'work of art' (p. 61). Telling himself, 'There were remedies for chapped hands and indifferent grammar', he and his mother begin to apply them (ibid.). But what they produce is a hothouse plant less equipped to deal with the real world or her own emotions than was the rough-skinned farm girl. When, for example, Ellen responds with unfeigned ardour to Austin's lovemaking, her experiment in honest self-expression is quickly discouraged. White says, she 'discovered on her husband's face an expression of having tasted something bitter, or of looking too deep. So she replaced the mask which evidently she was expected to wear . . . ' (p. 76). As this passage suggests, the refining to which the Roxburghs subject her splits her identity, and throughout the novel White calls her by one or the other of her two names – Gluyas or Roxburgh – to signal which self is in ascendancy. Yet beyond these there is still another and deeper self. It is this ultimate self she must come to know.

Her introduction begins with the visit she and her husband make to Garnet Roxburgh, Austin's reprobate brother who has fled to Van Diemen's Land (now Tasmania) to escape prosecution for forgery. Ellen is both attracted and repelled by her brother-in-law, recognizing in him cruelty and coarseness, but also vitality. At this time, Van Diemen's Land was a penal colony, and the sight of chained men, who are perhaps no more 'miscreant' (p. 89) than Garnet or even herself, disturbs her almost as much as her mixed emotions toward her husband's brother. In the beginning, however, all this is suppressed, tamped down behind a façade of cool civility which provokes Garnet more than would outright flirtation.

Eventually, Ellen's unrecognized self must surface. In a Lawrentian moment, while horseback riding, she allows her unruly emotions their head. A subsequent fall from the horse leaves her seemingly at Garnet's mercy, but even as she succumbs to him she admits her shared guilt. She knows that Garnet is 'less her seducer than the instrument she had chosen for measuring the depths she was tempted to explore' (p. 117).

Predictably, Ellen recoils from this tentative essay in exploration, heaping recriminations on herself and tenderly ministering to her husband in his renewed illness. Retreating from the scene of her crime, she takes Austin from Van Diemen's Land to Sydney to await passage home to England. In the journal which Austin's mother had taught her to keep, she consoles herself with the reflection that 'whatever bad I find in myself is of no account beside the positive evil I discover in others' (p. 138). Clearly Ellen has much to learn.

So has her husband. To Austin, who has lived his whole life secondhand and for whom even death is 'something of a literary conceit' (p. 35), his precious copy of the Elzevir Virgil becomes the very proof of his valid existence. It is the sole possession he preserves from the shipwreck, even risking his life to retrieve it from his upended cabin, and afterwards cuddling and coddling it like a child. Austin's obsession with Virgil suggests his work as the literary subtext of his novel, serving it as, for example, the *Odyssey* serves *The Aunt's Story*, as Dostoyevsky's novels serve *The Solid Mandala*, or as *Lear* does *The Eye of the Storm*. Testing this proposition, we find that, although Virgil's presence does not permeate *A Fringe of Leaves* as Shakespeare's does *The Eye of the Storm*, his work provides a relevant contrasting framework. What Austin calls 'the light which prevails' in the *Eclogues* comments ironically on the far from idyllic interlude with nature which Ellen is about to undergo (*FL*, p. 35).[30] An even more ironic perspective is brought to bear on Ellen's coming enterprise by Virgil's 'black streak', as revealed in the passage which Austin quotes to her and then patronizingly translates. Austin's version reads, 'Happy is he . . . who has unveiled the cause of things, and who can ignore inexorable fate and the roar of insatiate Hell' (p. 34). Virgil's point, of course, is that there is no such man, while White's redaction adds the twist that to unveil the cause is also and necessarily to open one's ears to the roars of Hell. It is a sound with which Ellen grows all too familiar.

Although for most of his life Austin's 'perceptive apparatus . . . has been clogged with waste knowledge and moral inhibitions' (p. 146), he is granted a breakthrough before his death. In many ways, his growth in understanding predicts and synopsizes Ellen's more protracted progress. First he undergoes the stripping of pretensions, an experience which foreshadows Ellen's divestiture by the blacks, and which for both marks the putting-off of comforting but constricting conventions. Ellen's next step is to temper with pity the revulsion she feels toward a diseased Aboriginal child given into her care. Austin prefigures this, too, by overcoming his squeamishness and treating the inflamed sea boil of the steward Spurgeon. Guilty over his habitual retreat to the safety of abstractions, Austin tries to atone with a poultice and comes to love Spurgeon and his boil for giving him the chance for real human contact. Later he is again brought to 'equal terms with reality' (p. 228) by delivering his wife of a stillborn child. The incident points to the several confrontations with death which Ellen is to face.

Continuing this proleptic pattern, the dream Austin has after Spurgeon's death prepares us for Ellen's later Eucharistic sacrament. In the dream, as in the subsequent event, the always implicit connection between Communion and cannibalism is made explicit, as is the affinity of hungers of all kinds. White says,

As one who had hungered all his life after friendships which eluded him, Austin Roxburgh did luxuriate on losing a solitary allegiance. It stimulated his actual hunger until now dormant, and he fell to thinking how the steward, had he not been such an unappetizing morsel, might have contributed appreciably to an exhausted larder. At once Mr Roxburgh's self-disgust knew no bounds. He was glad that night had fallen and that everyone around him was sleeping. Yet his thoughts were only cut to a traditional pattern, as Captan Purdew must have recognized who now came stepping between the heads of the sleepers to bend and whisper, *This is the body of Spurgeon which I have reserved for thee, take eat, and give thanks for a boil which was spiritual matter* . . . Austin Roxburgh was not only ravenous for the living flesh, but found himself anxiously licking the corners of his mouth to prevent any overflow of precious blood. (p. 231; italics White's)

One of several communions which, like the baptisms, form a series in the novel, this dream renders Ellen's later gnawing of a human thigh bone both more admissible and more comprehensible. Here, too, Austin prefigures her, as he also does in the manner of his death. Always a passive man whose life has been lived vicariously, he astounds himself by taking action when their party is threatened by hostile blacks. Although he is killed while trying to assist the wounded captain, his surprising courage sets the pattern for Ellen's subsequent discovery that beneath her own passivity and acquiescence is enough strength of will to survive.

In tracing her development, as in many other ways, *A Fringe of Leaves* proves the obverse of *Voss*. While Voss is all will, Ellen is will-less, and each must discover the complementary faculty. Throughout the novel, Ellen is more acted upon than acting. Yet she locates in herself a determination which upholds survival as *summum bonum*.[31] Ellen is also Voss's counterpart in that, while Voss must recognize the human good in himself, Ellen must acknowledge her equally human capacity for cruelty and evil. Before she can reconstitute a whole, authentic self, she must virtually complete Brendan Boyle's project in *Voss*: to peel down to the final layer of the self's perversity and darkness. From this core, she must rebuild herself anew.

Ellen does not reach this point until long after she is stripped by the Aboriginal women. At that moment, she seeks to re-cover herself by twisting strands of convolvulus vines about her waist, thus clothing herself in a 'fringe of leaves' (*FL*, p. 245). The phrase of course supplies the novel's title, but does double duty by echoing several earlier descriptions of Ellen's lovely and unusual shawl.[32] The leaf-patterned shawl, whose tones vary 'from sombre ash, through the living green which leaves flaunt in the wind', is trimmed with a 'heavy woollen fringe' (p. 28). By attaching the same key words and colours to the shawl and the convolvulus girdle, White makes the point that important aspects of Ellen's situation remain constant whether she is chatting over tea in her mother-in-law's Cheltenham drawing-room or playing pack animal for her adoptive tribe. In either case, a complex, socially sanctioned network of rules and expectations is in place. The suggestion, a frequent one in the novel, is that no fundamental difference exists in society as it manifests itself in Cheltenham, Hobart, Moreton Bay, or the wilds of Aboriginal Queensland.

In her semi-savage state, Ellen makes a gesture to remembered propriety by securing her wedding-ring amongst the runners of her makeshift skirt. Eventually, when she crawls from the forest onto the fields of the Oakeses' farm, she will have lost both vines and ring and will confront her rescuers 'naked as a newborn child' (p. 330). At this point she will be ready for rebirth. But, as is usually true for White's heroes and heroines, the project of transcending the past to begin anew must be approached through increasing awareness of entanglement in both a personal and collective past. In Ellen's case, these are the bonds of shared culpability. As she finally tells Captain Lovell at Moreton Bay, 'No one is to blame, and everybody, for whatever happens' (p. 363).

She begins to explore this complicity by discovering how like her captors she can be. Beaten, starved and prodded by the Aboriginals, she quickly learns the survival value of ferocity and cunning, and is soon squabbling with the camp dogs over scraps. As Mrs Roxburgh, she had felt a tepid pity for all brutalized or suffering creatures. Now she routs terrified opossums from trees and hurls them to the ground to be clubbed to death by the blacks. Moreover, she develops a resilience and a resignation which would shock cultivated sensibilities. Even before her capture, she had decided that 'death promised to become an everyday occurrence in which tuberose sentiments and even sincere grief might sound superfluous' (p. 225). Through her days of slavery, the phenomenon of death grows commonplace enough to be recognized as part of life. The distance she has come is revealed when she happens upon the burned and half-eaten body of another survivor from the *Bristol Maid* shipwreck. Although temporarily transfixed with horror, Ellen can almost at once cavort with a couple of black children sent to fetch her and can feel 'so extraordinarily content she wished it could have lasted forever, the two black little bodies united in the sun with her own blackened skin-and-bones' (p. 257). In this passage, white skin charred by sun or fire is seen to be the same as black, and death is seen as contributory to life.

In another metamorphosis in the direction of the simple and instinctual, the repressed lust which Garnet Roxburgh had aroused in her is reignited by the beautiful bodies of the Aboriginal men. Although bodily hungers drive Ellen toward the bestial, her reward is to experience a nearly spiritual 'ecstasy' from physical sensation (p. 266). White insists here as elsewhere that the spiritual and material are not dichotomous, but yoked as they are in the oxymoronic description of Spurgeon's boil as 'spiritual matter' (p. 231; see also p. 262).[33] Just as black and white, Cheltenham and Queensland, civilized and savage are the same, so at last are flesh and spirit.[34]

Ellen's initiation into this awareness culminates when she partakes of a cannibalistic communion which feeds both the flesh and the spirit.[35] After this act, which she recognizes as simultaneously a 'sacrament' and an outrage to 'Christian morality' (p. 272), she reflects that 'she could not have explained how tasting flesh from a human thigh-bone in the stillness of a forest morning had nourished not only her animal body but some darker need of the hungry spirit' (p. 274).

Her need is to penetrate her own 'heart of darkness', to realize her bestial self. However, in a typically Whitean paradox, her most monstrous transgression against human decency also marks an apogee of spiritual awareness. In fact, the height reached in the one experience seems directly proportionate to the depth sounded in the other. Not that this dimly perceived relationship absolves Ellen of guilt or responsibility: it rather intensifies these as well as her sense of affinity with the savages who have shown her the savagery in herself.

Following her cannibalism, Ellen feels 'she might have come to terms with darkness' (p. 274). But this is not wholly true. She has expressed herself at her most brutish, but she has not yet explored the underside of her more human emotions, nor her complicity in the civilized forms of atrocity. The suggestively named Jack Chance offers her the opportunity to pursue her quest to the centre of self.

Jack Chance, escaped convict and survivor of several vicious floggings at the 'triangle', is only too aware of the true parameters of human nature. When Ellen begs him to help her return to Moreton Bay, the penal colony from which he fled, she coaxes,

'They can't refuse you a pardon – Jack – if you bring me to them. It would be unjust and unnatural.' His terse reply is, 'Men is unnatural and unjust' (p. 281). Ellen, whose education is still incomplete, assures Jack that she can be trusted to secure him clemency. Only briefly does her conscience remind her that she was not always worthy of her husband's trust (p. 291).

Jack's rescue of Ellen is imaged as a kind of wedding. As the two run, their hands are 'welded together'; and it seems 'ordained' that they will be 'Always joined' (p. 288). White's use of such allusions foregrounds the issues of fidelity and love by suggesting that Ellen now owes to Jack what she once owed Austin. But true love and faithfulness elude the pair. Instead of loving they use each other as instruments of expiation. Through Ellen, Jack expresses gratitude to the woman who assisted his escape and tries to atone for the jealous rage in which he murdered his girlfriend Mab. On her part, Ellen hopes that love for Jack can redeem past failures: her 'inadequate affection' for her husband (p. 112), her lust for Garnet, even what she condemns as her betrayal of the cabin boy who adored and died for her.

Finally, though, her love neither convinces nor redeems. Shortly before she and Jack reach civilization they share a halcyon moment of union, splashing about in a forest pond. But Ellen's 'restlessness' drives her to climb an inviting tree (p. 317). The incident is presented as symbolic action expressing Ellen's need to escape Jack and reassert her independence by regaining superior social status. Although Jack climbs after her, she will not permit him to reach her level. Fittingly, it is from this tree that she sights the Oakeses' barn and knows that the 'civilized' world is again within reach. After this, it comes as no surprise that she begins to fear others' censure of her liaison with Jack. Social categories are reinstated and her lover has become again 'the convict'. Nor is it surprising that, on the edge of the Oakeses' field, Jack turns and runs in terror, both from the retribution he dreads and from the woman who has forfeited his trust.

At one point in their relationship, Ellen had hoped for access, through Jack, to 'layers of experience deeper still' than any she had plumbed (p. 300). This hope is realized in several ways. In part, her experience deepens through imaginative participation in Jack's murder of Mab for her infidelity, his subsequent flight to a life of scavenging in sewers, and his discovery of the dead, untended songbirds in his cottage. Knowing herself as faithless as

Mab and as capable of violence, debasement and neglect as Jack, she is brought face to face with the 'wobbling moral self' on whom Jack must depend for his pardon (p. 328). But, just as importantly, her relationship with the convict forces her to acknowledge her failure to give the love which might have saved, to her father, husband or lovers.[36]

With this knowledge she touches the very depths of the soul's darkness, and on it she must base a reborn self.[37] Obsessed with her guilt, she cannot begin at once. She declares herself Jack's murderess and thinks of her future life as a sentence she must serve for her crimes. Back in Moreton Bay, she pleads for Jack's pardon, but is no longer sure that justice will prevail. She seeks further humiliation and a deeper sense of shared wrongdoing by putting herself in the way of parties of male and female convicts being herded to their work. She is grateful when one of the men spits in her face and more grateful for her brief communication with the woman who might have helped Jack to escape. Finally, when young Kate Lovell, daughter of the Moreton Bay Commandant who gives her shelter, kills and mutilates a chick, Ellen accuses herself of bringing evil into an idyllic childhood world.

As the pattern of Ellen's increasing bestiality culminated in cannibalism, so this movement toward assuming culpability reaches its climax when she hears the screams of a prisoner being flogged. In her horror that Jack's fate is being visited on others and her deeper horror at her impotence to stop it, Ellen, too, begins a frenzied screaming which answers the convict's. At this point she wholly identifies herself both with the victim and the victimizer. Like the much earlier Oliver Halliday, she has assumed the full dimensions of her humanity, recognizing herself as both giver and getter of pain.

Only one lesson remains for Ellen, but a necessary one if she is to overcome the moral paralysis into which guilt has plunged her, and use what she already knows. This lesson she learns in Pilcher's rude chapel. Pilcher, second mate of the *Bristol Maid*, is the voyage's only other survivor. Having stayed alive by cunning and cruelty, Pilcher returns to civilization determined to do penance and builds a small, unconsecrated chapel. Coming upon it unexpectedly, Ellen finds little there except a Communion table bearing an empty bird's nest and, above the altar, the scribbled legend, 'GOD IS LOVE.' In this setting, Ellen weeps as she relives 'the betrayal of her earthly loves' (p. 390). Here the novel comes its closest to granting her the kind of vision vouchsafed to Elizabeth Hunter in the storm's eye. White says,

> she could not have seen more clearly, down to the cracks on the wooden bench, the bird-droppings on the rudimentary altar. She did not attempt to interpret a peace of mind which had descended on her . . . but let the silence enclose her like a beatitude. (pp. 390–1)

The sense of gratuitous serenity and heightened vision is familiar from similar moments in White's fiction. But to understand what Ellen sees so clearly, we must recall an incident to which she alludes in this scene: her experience on Christmas Day in the church near Garnet Roxburgh's estate. During the services, Ellen had found herself unaccountably troubled by the words emblazoned above the church's central arch: 'HOLY HOLY HOLY LORD GOD OF HOSTS' (pp. 107–8). Subsequently, these words recur in her memory accompanied by suggestions of power, brutality and ruthlessness. This, she begins to see, is the slogan of the cruel and conquering God, the God of the Roxburghs, the God who provides the model for so much of man's *imitatio dei*. Part of what she sees in Pilcher's chapel, then, is that her God is not 'the Roxburgh's LORD GOD OF HOSTS who continued charging in apparent triumph, trampling the words she was contemplating' (p. 390). Her allegiance is to the God of Love celebrated in Pilcher's clumsy script.[38] Beyond this, however, she examines her own insufficient love in the light of a loving God and sees it pale before its holy source and counterpart. As did Elizabeth Hunter, she discovers that failure, particularly love's failure, is enjoined by the human condition. Only the black swans can enfold without reservation; only God is truly love. Yet man, in his ineffectual way, must keep trying. As the novel's epigraph from Louis Aragon says bluntly, 'Love is your last chance. There is really nothing else on earth to keep you here' (p. 5).

This awareness frees Ellen to resume her life, without, however, diminishing her guilt or assuaging self-knowledge with reassuring maxims. The past and what it has revealed in her are not annulled; as Ellen in her Gluyas voice once ruefully admits to Jack, 'I dun't believe a person is ever really cured of what they was born with' (pp. 331–2). Thus Ellen's new beginning is less a rebirth than a resurrection; she bears her past with her as she enters on another life.

White stresses this point by describing Mr Jevons, her probable future husband, in terms which recall the other significant men in her life. Like Austin he wears a ring, and, like Garnet, he is fleshy but firmly built. He is large and dark like Jack and even reminds her of Commandant Lovell (p. 395). However, unlike most of these others, he shows kindness, a quality her experience has taught her to prize.

The modest Jevons also suits Ellen's revised expectations, which have been tempered by extremity. When Miss Scrimshaw waxes hyperbolic about her desire to soar like an eagle above the mundane, Ellen soberly reflects that she, on the other hand, is 'ineluctably earthbound':

> 'I was slashed and gashed too often', she tried to explain. 'Oh no, the crags are not for me!' She might have been left at a loss had not the words of her humbler friend Mrs Oakes found their way into her mouth. 'A woman, as I see, is more like moss or lichen that takes to some tree or rock as she takes to her husband.'   (p. 402)

Far from sounding White's condemnation of women's liberation or announcing his heroine's adoption of the Victorian role of 'angel in the house', this passage rather embodies Ellen's understanding of the task her life has set her: to love as well as she can while never well enough. She thus turns back to life as we leave her, a movement White further emphasizes by dressing her for the closing scene in a gown of garnet-coloured silk.

Throughout the novel, White has used the word 'garnet', whether as name, jewel, or colour, as a centre for image clusters evocative of vitality. This force is to be understood as less Bergsonian than Lawrentian, an intensity which can be fearful or ferocious, but which is not to be suppressed. White's use of garnets in this novel can best be compared to his use of birds in *The Cockatoos* or *The Eye of the Storm*; in both cases the image suggests energy and potency.[39]

If garnets are understood to carry these implications, then Ellen's adultery with Garnet Roxburgh is an effort to make contact with a life force lacking in her own husband and marriage. Within this same symbolic pattern, her timidity before the encounter is suggested by the fact that she gives her garnet earrings to the convict girl who is her brother-in-law's servant and mistress. After her adventure, she retreats again to a position of wariness, marked by her willing surrender to the greedy Pilcher of a garnet ring he demands. She is all the more anxious to buy him off with the ring since, like Conrad's Gentleman Brown with Lord Jim, he arouses in her a guilty sense of confederacy. When Pilcher admires the garnets, Ellen confesses, 'I've never truthfully felt they were mine' (p. 222). It is as though she lays no claim to the fiery life force.

After her return to civilization, Ellen is for a time too numbed by guilt and shock to undertake life's challenges. Thus, when a charitable lady donates a gown of garnet silk, Ellen puts in on but hastily removes it, disturbed to find herself 'smouldering and glowing inside the panels of her dress' (p. 349). Similarly when Pilcher returns the stolen ring, she is unprepared to receive it and tosses it away. Her donning of the garnet dress for tea with Mr Jevons is therefore a mark of her readiness to resume life, and perhaps to propagate it. White adds this latter implication by placing her beside the fecund Mrs Lovell and showing us the scene from Jevons's perspective: 'He could not give over contemplating the smouldering figure in garnet silk beside the pregnant mother in her nest of drowsy roly-poly children, a breathing statuary contained within the same ellipse of light' (pp. 404–5). In the past, Ellen has miscarried one child, had a second stillborn, and lost a third in infancy. Even the cabin boy, whom she briefly loves, becomes for her another lost child. As was true with her men, so with her children; she could not seem to love enough to save. But White's suggestion here is that the love she finds with Jevons will sustain a child. Moreover, his use of the image of the mother in her *nest* of children recalls the empty nest on the altar of Pilcher's chapel and suggests both that love can fill it and that such an offering is acceptable in God's sight.

The novel ends with these implications and with the curious incident of the tea-spilling. Mr Jevons is fetching Mrs Roxburgh's tea when he stumbles and spills a cup into her lap. In his embarrassment, he reverts to abashed childhood, and Ellen resorts to her Cornish dialect to comfort him. Perhaps White included this petty mishap in part to show us Ellen successfully mothering Jevons as opposed to her unsuccessful mothering of Austin, Jack, and her children. The incident also brings the couple closer than would hours of polite conversation, thereby reinforcing the reader's sense that they will soon be closer still. Beyond this, it may not be too far-fetched to suggest that, from behind the 'widening' tea stain, Ellen approaches as near as this novel allows her to the Whitean visionary moment in which the self spreads outward to encompass and embrace existence (p. 404).[40]

To speculate this way, however, is to notice how far White has retreated from explicit treatment of such states. In fact, ever since he specified the nature and meaning of Stan Parker's vision in the garden, he has rendered analogous scenes more equivocally. By *The Eye of the Storm*, we have not even Hurtle Duffield's moment of incoherent illumination, but rather an experience, perfectly credible in a naturalistic context, to which the participant gives mystical import. Like her daughter Dorothy, the reader may be sceptical of Elizabeth's moment in the storm's eye, attributing her memories of peace and joy to delirium instead of revelation. Taking the next logical step, *A Fringe of Leaves* remains even more firmly anchored in the conventions of traditional realism, appropriating some of this aura from its basis in historical fact. White therefore gives us Ellen's moment in the chapel and the spreading tea stain, but leaves the implications largely to the reader. In this novel, the author elects to stay as 'ineluctably earthbound' as his heroine.

The reasons for his choice are probably several. First, White has become progressively less sanguine about language's capacity to function on such frontiers. Viewed chronologically, his work reveals a growing tendency to allude rather than articulate. The choice may also be bound up in what he saw as the novel's purpose and described in *Flaws in the Glass*. Speaking of the adulation which greeted *Voss*, White said,

> Half those professing to admire *Voss* did so because they saw no connection between themselves and the Nineteenth Century society portrayed in the novel. As child-adults, many Australians . . . shy away from the deep end of the unconscious. So they cannot accept much of what I have written about the century in which we are living. . . . (If there is less gush about that other so-called 'historical' novel *A Fringe of Leaves* it is perhaps because they sense in its images and narrative the reasons why we have become what we are today.) (p. 104).

White's remarks suggest that the novel's aim was to convince readers of a continuity between past and present. Such a project would be facilitated if credibility were not strained with 'visions', or the principal characters presented as elect and therefore apart from ordinary mortals.

What 'reasons' does the novel suggest for 'why we have become what we are today'? Chief among them is the failure of most people to accept, as Ellen finally does, their capacity for cruelty and their complicity in societal evil. The novel's vision of the human condition is a dark one, but it also insists that only by piercing the darkness can we start toward the light. Only by accepting a share of responsibility for what is wrong can we begin to right it. The stance White takes here toward failure matches the novel's wider moral vision. Ellen's failures are in part inevitable, for human love will never measure up to its own demands or its transcendental archetype. But we are granted some possibilities, specifically a 'loving-kindness which inspires trust' (p. 367), and we are left to suppose that Ellen will yet learn to exercise it.

THE TWYBORN AFFAIR

The issue in White's next and latest novel is also the failure of love, but here the problem is complicated by the protagonist's primary failure to love him/herself. Like the book with its three-part, discontinuous structure, the protagonist, who bears a different name in each section, feels himself fragmented and disjointed.[41] His obsessive desire is to achieve a recognizable shape, to become convincing to himself.

In part the anguish of Eudoxia Vatatzes/Eddie Twyborn/Eadith Trist stems from gender confusion. Eddie, who once describes himself as a 'pseudo-man-cum-crypto-woman' (p. 298), is neither simply a transvestite nor a homosexual, but rather a fluctuating transsexual who is comfortable as neither male nor female. At no time is Eddie's sexual identity more than precariously achieved; it is always unstable and threatened.

Eddie's search for a sexual self is confounded by a related but less conscious quest – the quest for his[42] past. Apparently the genesis of Eddie's sexual ambivalence is classically Freudian: his upbringing by a mannish and possessive mother, herself unsettled sexually, and a deeply loved but umdemonstrative father who frightened and awed his son.[43] Feeling himself a freak, Eddie flees these parents and the Australia of his childhood, which put such a premium on health and normality. He believes he is setting out in search of self, but his flight actually enforces a devastating self-alienation. Only by incorporating his rejected past can he hope to begin reassembling the scattered 'jig-saw' of his being (p. 146).

Eddie rarely glimpses the inexorable continuity of past, present and future. The novel's very structure reflects his hopes that the self can be reborn, uncontaminated by the past. Each of its three sections is separated by years and presents Eddie in a new guise, unrelated to his earlier self. Yet through every section the past pursues Eddie until, finally, he turns to face it.

The first event the novel chronicles is just such an invasion by the past. Joanie Golson, a rich and bored Australian, absorbing European culture with her apathetic husband, discovers on one of her idle drives a charming little villa and its two intriguing tenants. The year is 1914 and the setting is St Mayeul, in France, to which Angelos Vatatzes, who believes himself descended from Byzantine emperors,[44] has retreated with his 'hetaira' Eudoxia. Joanie has had a fling or two at Lesbianism with Eddie's mother Eadie in Sydney and is quickly infatuated with the mysterious Eudoxia. Consequently, she's delighted when the accident of the girl's sprained ankle allows her to offer assistance and thereby earn an invitation to the villa. Eudoxia is terrified by the threat this incursion poses to her identity and her relationship with Angelos. Yet, at the same time, she is subtly drawn to Joanie, not sexually, but through their shared past.

That past is itself a threat. In her journal, Eudoxia admits her fear of opening her history to Angelos (p. 28). But she also sometimes sees the past's potential. Having committed herself to further meetings by writing to thank Joanie for her aid on the day of the accident, she wonders, again in her journal, 'Was this why I wrote the letter to Joanie Golson? to enlist her sympathy, her help? Can you escape into the past? Perhaps you can begin again that way. If you can escape at all' (p. 80). As it did for Ellen Roxburgh, acceptance of the past holds out the possibility of renewal and rediscovered coherence. But, when Eudoxia escapes, she flees from rather than to the past. Moreover, she takes her aging lover with her, although their liaison has imposed a sometimes galling confinement.

Angelos, the failed and disenfranchised, survivor of the Smyrna catastrophe and embittered heir of Byzantine emperors, is constantly confronting his Eudoxia with the complementary spectres of her own perversity and the saintliness of his departed wife. Although she often admits to wanting Angelos and always to needing him, Eudoxia none the less rebels against the man to whom, she tells herself, she is 'committed by fate and orgasm – never love' (p. 36). In the mirror of his eyes, Angelos has shown her what her own glass won't, a self 'consecutive, complete' (p. 27). Yet she cannot own this self because Angelos has authored it. Again in her journal, she remarks, 'he has created the aesthetic version of me – so different, far more different than he could ever understand. For all his languages he could never understand the one I speak' (p. 77).

She makes fitful and feeble resolves to get free of him. There is even one half-hearted attempt at suicide, but the gesture fails apparently because there is not enough self to destroy. Reflecting on the incident, Eudoxia writes, 'nothing of me is mine, not even the body I was given to inhabit, nor the disguises chosen for it – A. decides on these, seldom without my agreement. The real E. has not yet been discovered, and perhaps never will be' (p. 79). Despite this recognition, it is on a journey not of self-discovery but of self-evasion that she hurries with Angelos near the close of Part One.

Only after the escape does the reader learn precisely what she is fleeing – that is, Joanie's recognition of her as Eddie Twyborn. In retrospect, we realize that the section was liberally strewn with hints of Eudoxia's maleness. We remember that her feet are large, her chest flat, her knees bony. We have learned that she is Australian and a Twyborn. There are also suggestive journal entries such as the one in which Eudoxia refers to herself as 'him or her' (p. 23). Still, it is a moment worthy of O. Henry when the dying Angelos tells his companion, 'I have had from you, dear boy, the only happiness I've ever known' (p. 126). The shock to the reader is unparalleled in White's fiction, but it is no mere technical flourish.[45] Rather, it functions to show readers how we, like Joanie and even Eudoxia, have been seduced by the surface and ignored the depths, how we, like they, prefer to shape our perceptions in accord with expectations and not to examine too closely what might prove awkward, equivocal or perverse.

Part One closes not with this illumination but with Joanie's letter to Eadie Twyborn, describing her feelings for Eudoxia and certain inklings as to who she really is. A striking feature of this novel is that all three parts begin and end at a remove from

Eddie's consciousness. Part One begins with Joanie's crush and ends with her distraught attempt to convey that experience to Eadie. Part Two opens with two paragraphs on Eddie (who is described but not named), then shifts to the impression he is making on two young girls aboard ship. The part closes with Eadie's letter of condolence to Marcia Lushington over the loss of a son she conceived by Eddie. Part Three is introduced from the perspective of the old-maidish Bellasis sisters, who conjecture about the goings-on across the street, where the exotic Mrs Trist has set up shop. In the closing pages of Part Three and the novel, we are returned to the consciousness of Eadie, awaiting a visit from the son/daughter who has just died a block from her hotel room.

The effect of these ventures behind other eyes, all trained on the protagonist, is akin to that of the shock with which we realize that Eudoxia Vatatzes *is* Eddie Twyborn. In each instance the reader is made aware of the difference and disjunction between appearance and reality, and of the way the perceiving mind shapes and colours perceptions. For example, Eadie's letter to Marcia voices her pain at her own bereavement, the loss occasioned by Eddie's disappearance. Thus her letter reveals to the reader, as Eddie could not, that she, too, has suffered. But at the same time the letter betrays her myopic refusal to recognize what Eddie is and why he fled. In this way, White deepens the reader's understanding of both Eddie and his mother and shows us how they have misread each other. By focusing on others' perceptions, the technique also underscores Eddie's programme in the novel: his attempts to manipulate those perceptions into a coherent whole he can himself accept.

The project of constructing a convincing self demands engagement with the past. In particular, Eddie must face and perhaps revise his feelings for a mother who sometimes drowned him in love and at other times ignored him. Even more problematical are his feelings toward a father who will not recall the few moments of intimacy shared with his son, moments so precious to the boy that they recur repeatedly in dreams. In Part One, the only step Eddie takes towards recovery of the past is to recognize that Eudoxia's love for Angelos was largely due to Eddie's displaced and rejected love for Judge Edward Twyborn. In Part Two he confronts his past far more deliberately, but not more successfully.

Part Two begins on board a ship sailing for Australia. It is 1920 and Lieutenant Eddie Twyborn, having earned the DSO in battle during the First World War, is returning to his homeland, thereby embarking on a campaign of self-recovery and self-validation. To win it, he must conquer personal and cultural history, coming to terms with himself as a Twyborn and an Australian. He hopes for victory. Says White, 'He liked to think . . . that he would emerge at last from the bombardment, not only of a past war, but the past' (p. 133).

Early skirmishes, however, prove disastrous. He allows his mother to take possession of himself and his belongings (she summarily dismisses his plan to stay in a hotel), but cannot be more than passive before her 'landslide of emotion' (p. 148). Grimly, he acknowledges that he and Eadie mirror each other. So alike are they, in fact, that he thinks of her as 'himself in disguise' (p. 151). But, precisely for this reason, he cannot return her love. To love her would be to love himself, a challenge he cannot yet meet. Instead, he makes a tentative gesture to his father. For his father, however, Eddie becomes 'the defendant', and judgement is quickly passed: 'In the shaft of light the Judge's concern glistened like bone: that his son whom he loved – he did, didn't he? should have perverted justice by his disappearance' (p. 156). Clearly the judge is not equipped to deal with Eddie or his appeals. Thus his son remains 'bogged down in memory' (p. 158). A particularly precious memory is that of the night in a country inn, a night of closeness with the judge which occurred when he had taken the boy to the sitting of a circuit court (p. 158). In refusing to corroborate the memory, Justice Twyborn condemns Eddie to a past which is neither revived nor exorcized. Rather, it remains to fester with the sense of lost possibilities.

In the imagery of lost battles and guilty felons, White makes the point that Eddie's foray into the personal past has failed. Assuring himself that such failure is inevitable, he turns from his parents to a less unsettling aspect of his heritage, the Australian land. Accordingly, he advances the surprising plan of going to work as a jackeroo in the Monaro as a 'way perhaps of getting to know a country I've never belonged to' (p. 161).

At once Eddie suspects that his motives are less to seek his Australian roots than to have an excuse for 'escaping from himself into a landscape' (p. 161). Yet he tells himself, 'the landscape would respond' and so it does (ibid.), offering him its subtleties and quiet beauties as well as a sense of acceptance and serenity he has felt nowhere else.[46] At one point, Eddie speculates that, for those whom self-searching has failed, salvation may lie in natural phenomena. However, unlike Stan Parker, Eddie will approach neither God nor self through nature. The freedom and wholeness he sometimes feels in the natural world are not revelations but respites, brief solaces before the quest must be renewed. Even Eddie is aware of this imperative. Once, while alone in the mountains, he reflects,

> He could not remember ever having felt happier. At the same time he wondered whether he could really exist without the sources of unhappiness. Half-dozing, half-waking to the tune of his horse's regular cropping, and in his half-sleep what sounded like a pricking of early frost or needling by stars, he knew that his body and his mind craved the everlasting torments. (p. 272)

Here, even nature is 'pricking' and 'needling' him to resume the painful task of self-discovery.

The passage further suggests that, like many Whitean protagonists, Eddie must define himself in and through the struggle. Failure is inevitable for all these questers, but Eddie's plight is worsened by the fact that he is struggling in the wrong direction. For, during his months on the Monaro, Eddie does not so much suspend the quest as lose his way. Attention which should be devoted to Eadie and Edward Twyborn is displaced instead onto figures who merely evoke his parents, his employers Greg and Marcia Lushington.

Greg Lushington is associated with his father through the two men's youthful friendship. But Greg differs from the austere judge in being warmer, more approachable, more likely to embrace the 'son *manqué*' that Eddie rapidly becomes (p. 231). The attraction deepens when Eddie discovers that, like himself, his employer hides unsuspected depths. Greg is a poet, who astonishes the young man by being more concerned with the rightness of words than the soundness of sheep. Yet, despite the promise in their relationship, Greg, too, is bound to disappoint. He leaves on a long and unannounced journey, causing Eddie to suspect in his 'adoptive father' the coldness of his so-called 'natural' parent (p. 238).

His relationship with Marcia also sours. Despite his admiration and respect for Greg, Eddie allows himself to be enmeshed in an affair with her. He knows that his motive is in part that of 'self-vindication' (p. 217), to prove himself capable of sex with a woman. Of his deeper motives Eddie is only vaguely suspicious, but White stresses that through her he seeks his mother's womb. Marcia has earlier been linked to Eadie Twyborn through their shared need to consume those near them, and the identification is made explicit after Marcia and Eddie first make love:

> He was won over by a voice wooing him back into childhood, the pervasive warmth of a no longer sexual, but protective body, cajoling him into morning embraces in a bed disarrayed by a male, reviving memories of toast, chilblains, rising bread, scented plums, cats curled on sheets of mountain violets, hibiscus trumpets furling into stickly phalluses in Sydney gardens, his mother whom he should have loved but didn't . . . . (p. 222)

Eddie hopes to love his mother through his mistress. His purest moments of affection for her occur when she is least sexual and most maternal. Appropriately, his urge at one such time is to nuzzle her breasts like a suckling child (p. 255).

But ultimately Marcia can be no more help than Greg, since both are surrogates. Instead of opening the past to him, they block it. The end comes when Eddie evades still another aspect of his past. A visit from the Golsons sends him into hiding, thus incurring Marcia's bewildered wrath. In revenge, she revives an interrupted affair with Don Prowse, the station-manager. When she later sees Eddie again and tells him she is pregnant by him, he can only respond with contempt and cruelty. The news inspires terror in him, the terror of assuming a role which has been so mismanaged in his own case. These feelings, added to the equivocal status of his relationship with Don, drive him from the Lushingtons' station, Bogong, and, quickly thereafter from Australia.

Don Prowse, the stereotypically masculine station-manager, has challenged Eddie's emotions from their first meeting. On Eddie's part, an uneasy attraction grows into compassion which he is afraid to express in the touch that might be misinterpreted. He is also uncertain of how to respond to Don's gruff affection. Events prove that Eddie has surprised in Don what he later decides was 'an aggressive anima walled up inside her tower of flesh' (p. 294). When that anima breaks free, Don rapes him. Eddie is humiliated, less by the act itself than his acceptance of it, a response which threatens the heterosexual self he has manufactured to match his dirty work clothes and blistered palms. When Don offers himself in apology and recompense, Eddie is further disgusted to find his initial impulse to comfort the man, an impulse he identifies as feminine, giving way to 'what was less lust than a desire for male revenge' (p. 296). His fragile sexual and emotional self now in shreds, Eddie can only indulge his urge to run, leaving Marcia to have, lose and bury his child with her other dead children, and his mother to write the letter mourning their joint bereavements.[47]

Of the novel's three parts, Part Two is the longest, perhaps because here Eddie wrestles most determinedly and protractedly with the self he is trying to realize. Realization none the less eludes him. Indicative of the status of his selfhood in this section is the fact that, of all those he meets at Bogong, he identifies only with the hare-lipped girl Helen. Their sad kinship is founded on 'signs of monstrosity or hopelessness' which each recognizes in the other (p. 267). Among the other relationships he sees, the one which seems most stable is that between the half-wit Denny and the wife he was ordered to marry to legitimize a child begotten by her father. Thinking of Denny, who cannot know or care that the child isn't his, Eddie bitterly decides, 'Happiness was perhaps the reward of those who cultivate illusion, or . . . have it thrust upon them by some tutelary being, and then are granted sufficient innocent grace to sustain it' (p. 249). Throughout Part Two, Eddie has sought to discard illusion, but has located only a frightening vacancy. In Part Three, he elects Denny's way.

When we next meet the protagonist, now whoremistress Eadith Trist, the real world has been replaced by that of 'the novelette she enjoyed living' (p. 310).[48] In other words, Eadith has accepted herself as a fiction, which, like her make-up and dress, is 'poetic as opposed to fashionable or naturalistic' (p. 310). Years have passed since Eddie left the Monaro, years to which White never alludes. It is London in the days before the Second World War, but Eadith ignores rumours of war as Eudoxia had in St Mayeul. The outside world is of little importance to her except as it supplies the audience for the baroque charade she has made of her life. Installed in rococo extravagance in a brothel which accommodates the most exotic tastes, Eadith views herself as the abbess of dedicated nuns, the director of talented actresses, or sometimes the warden of willing inmates. Images of the convent, stage and prison proliferate in this part of the novel, always suggesting a withdrawal from the world. Eadith's attempts to come to terms with self are now reserved for the half-light between false and true dawn.[49] At other times she gratefully resumes her disguise.

As she has rejected life, except in its more fantastic forms, so too has she renounced the 'trampoline of love' with its terrible risks (p. 316). When her patron, Lord Gravenor, arouses her love and returns it, she both longs for and fears the renascence he offers. She worries that Gravenor 'might have wrecked the structure of life by overstepping the limits set by fantasy' (p. 322). This concern refers not only to the heterosexual Gravenor's probable reaction to discovering her anatomical gender. Equally horrific would be the claims he might make on her for real love from a real self. Her dreams reveal a deep need to love and nurture, but even these betray her desire to impose on the beloved an imprisoning protection from the hostile world. She dreams, for example, of a horde of children seeking exodus from an airless, womblike room. In the dream, she attempts to convince them that they are safe only inside. Love for Gravenor might open some doors.

Occasionally, Eadith acknowledges the connection between love and reality with Gravenor threatens to make in her life. At one point she goes so far as to recognize that 'whatever form she took, or whatever the illusion temporarily possessing her, the reality of love, which is the core of reality itself, had eluded her and perhaps always would' (p. 336). Eadith has White's endorsement here in naming love as the 'core of reality', but she is mistaken in thinking that it has eluded her. More to the point, she has eluded both love and reality. Like Hurtle Duffield, she prefers to interpose art between herself and life's demands, and, like Elizabeth Hunter, she becomes her own most dazzling creation.

Appropriately, she casts the burlesque of her life with characters even less authentic than herself. Among them is Gravenor's sister Ursula, who was collected by her husband, much as Browning's Duke or James's Maggie Verver bought their spouses. Even the name given to Ursula's country house – 'Wardrobes' – contributes to the motif of masquerade and disguise in this part of the novel. Also in the retinue is Cecily Snape, whose past is farcical in its unlikelihood: 'One of the outwardly flawless English flowers, Cecily had been forced to leave the country for a while after an affair with an entire negro band ending in the death of a drummer and exposure of a drug ring' (p. 337).[50]

In the midst of this bizarre company, Eadith believes her own past to be safely irrecoverable until Joanie Golson intrudes again. Their meeting reverses and echoes the meeting of Joanie and Eudoxia, for her Joanie collapses and Eadith comes to the rescue. Although unaware of Eadith's identity, Joanie immediately poses the threat of the past which also terrified Eudoxia. The threat deepens a few days later when Gravenor unprecedentedly calls Eadith 'Eadie', and Australian dinner guests of Ursula's reveal that Judge Twyborn has died and his widow is in London.[51] At this announcement, the past returns with such force that Eadith is Eddie again. Although she quickly recovers her current self, Eadith begins to believe that the past is unavoidable. As she puts it, 'Eadie must recur during what remained of life' (p. 394).

In Eadith's subsequent thoughts about Eadie and on the several occasions when she watches her mother from a distance, White insistently links the older woman to the possibility of redemptive grace. Eadith observes her mother in a series of churches, sitting quietly and humbly with her prayer book. In Eadith's imagination, Eadie seems a saint, from whom her penitent child might hope for intercession (pp. 403–4). Even her mother's physical being, bowed 'under the ashes of resignation, the scars of retribution, the weight of grief', evokes the martyrs (p. 404). In one highly symbolic scene, Eadith and Eadie pass on parallel escalators, Eadie ascending and Eadith descending. Eadith does not acknowledge her mother, and the refusal takes on religious implications. White says, 'the moment of longed for, but dreaded expiation had once more been evaded, and was followed by one of passionate regret' (p. 405). Eadith is not redeemed, but is rather 'received into the lower depths' (ibid.).

Eadith's dread is unnecessary. Her mother is not the judge her father was. Widowed of his penchant for justice and judgement, she offers Eddie/Eadith uncritical acceptance and unqualified love. When she and Eadith finally do make contact, it is Eadie who initiates it. Trembling and speechless with recognition, Eadie passes Eadith a note reading, 'Are you my son Eddie?' Her response to the answer, 'No, but I am your daughter Eadith', is to say, 'I am so glad. I've always wanted a daughter' (pp. 422–3).

At this point, however, Eadith cannot yet accept her mother's offer of forgiveness. Like a character in a morality, she is buffeted between the claims of justice represented by her father and the appeals of mercy lodged by her mother. Thus she resists her mother's plea that she return with her to Australia, saying, 'I mightn't be allowed' (p. 423). She still feels like a felon under sentence.

It is Gravenor, her rejected lover, who shows her that justice may be tempered by mercy. Like all the men she has loved, Gravenor is linked with Justice Twyborn, most strikingly in a dream in which Eadith is Eddie again and Gravenor takes on the role of the father who is his judge and inadequate protector (pp. 375–6). In a further linkage, the precarious relationship between Eadith and Gravenor, built as it is on carefully nurtured illusion and mutually respected boundaries, recalls that of Eddie and Judge Twyborn. But Gravenor acts as angel of mercy in a letter which both reaffirms his love and hints that this love has survived enlightenment. He assures her

> that we might have loved each other, completely and humanly, if we had found the courage. Men and women are not the sole members of the human hierarchy to which you and I can also claim to belong.
>
> I can see your reproving face, your explosive jaw rejecting my assertion. If I can't persuade you, I shall continue to accept you in whatever form . . . you should appear. . . .
>
> 'Love' is an exhausted word, and God has been expelled by those who know better, but I offer you the one as proof that the other still exists.   (p. 426)

By granting that the human race contains more than men and women, Gravenor leaves room in reality for such androgynous creatures as Eddie/Eadith, while at the same time implying his knowledge of his/her sexual uncertainty. More importantly, he affirms love, acceptance and forgiveness, those aspects of God which Eadie has symbolized and made accessible to Eadith. Finally, the letter connects fleshly and divine love, *eros* and *agape*, in a way which recalls and glosses the strange story told to Lieutenant Twyborn by a captain in the First World War. The captain has remembered a chance sexual encounter in which he and his partner transcended orgasm to reach a moment of mystical beatitude (pp. 418–19). Gravenor's letter implies that the two kinds of love are linked on a great continuum which enables the movement from sexual to spiritual.

Apparently all these intimations of reconciliation, connection and resolution inspire Eadith to make a last attempt to renounce her 'world of fragmentation and despair' for a life more whole and consecutive (p. 420). At once, however, White calls this project into question, and its status as well as outcome are kept equivocal throughout the novel's few remaining pages.

In ill-fitting man's clothes and a haircut, but still inadvertently wearing Eadith's make-up, Eddie leaves the brothel with the enigmatic explanation that he needs to 'go in search of some occupation in keeping with the times' (p. 427). His move seems to signal that at last he is willing to confront his past, to re-enter time. Moreover, he appears intent on remaking himself from his recalcitrant fragments. He has reclaimed his original identity, while retaining remnants of the other, and heads first for Eadie's hotel, to initiate rebirth through a 'short but painful visit to his mother's womb' (p. 428).[52] But suddenly the past he seeks is irrevocably violated. The war Eadith has refused to countenance makes itself felt amidst falling bombs, and by their light Eddie watches personal and global history 'crumbling' (p. 428):

> In a moment it seemed to Eddie Twyborn as though his own share in time was snatched away, as though every house he had ever lived in was torn open, the sawdust pouring out of all the dolls in all the rooms, furniture whether honest or pretentious still shuddering from its brush with destruction, a few broken bars of a Chabrier waltz scattered from the burst piano, was it the Judge-Pantocrator looking through a gap in the star-painted ceiling, the beige thighs hooked in the swinging chandelier could only be those of that clumsy acrobat Marcia, all contained in the ruins of this great unstable temporal house, all but Eddie and Eadith, unless echoes of their voices threading pandemonium. (p. 429)

Clearly this is far from White's typical epiphany. Its cataclysm and chaos are at odds with the usual ambience of reconciliation. Still, as it blasts apart the pieces of Eddie's fragmented life, it does achieve a kind of union in inclusiveness, while also rewarding Eddie's re-entry into time by wrenching him from time into eternity.[53] We cannot be sure what implications White intends here. One thing, however, is certain. By coalescing and collapsing the historical and personal past, this 'vision', if such it is, obviates any further effort in that direction, leaving Eddie in his few remaining moments to face the other great challenge of his life, that of relationship.

The bomb has also felled a young soldier, who lies 'head on, making almost a straight line on the pavement' with Eddie's body (p. 429).[54] The two retain this alignment, the soldier 'trying to share the brim of his protective hat with one who could hardly remain a stranger', until another bomb kills them both (ibid.). White could hardly have chosen a more emphatic way to stress their relationship. Eventually they make, as it were, a single corpse. Yet the implications of this image are also equivocal, for it is the soldier, not Eddie, who offers himself. Eddie has not made the redeeming gesture of relationship. Finally, in still another perversion or revision of the Whitean illumination, Eddie experiences the sense of outward expansion only by 'flowing onward' on the 'crimson current' of his own ebbing blood (p. 430).

It might be proposed, then, that this implied resurrection makes suggestion of rebirth, a suggestion reinforced by the next sentence, in which White uses the term 'expecting' to describe Eadie Twyborn's wait for her daughter (p. 430). The description of Eddie's death is also linked to birth by echoing his earlier thought while watching his mother's age-spotted hands: 'those blotched hands must have pressed on her own belly to help expel in blood and anguish the child struggling out of it' (p. 424). Thus White does allow the hope that the phoenix Eddie always felt himself has risen from the ashes of world conflagration.[55]

It might be proposed, then, that this implied resurrection makes Eddie Twyborn 'twice born'.[56] On the other hand, Eddie may have been 'twice born' from the beginning, born with the irreducible duality of male and female identities. Under this interpretation, the fact that, when he dies, he is wearing a man's clothes and a woman's make-up would enforce our awareness of this unresolved dichotomy, as would the posture of his death which juxtaposes him with a very different other, but refuses to unite them. If these are the suggestions White intended, part of the novel's lesson would be that learned by Theodora Goodman of *The Aunt's Story*: that of the 'irreconcilable halves' which constitute being and experience (p. 280). Here, then, the image of the hermaphrodite, while continuing to suggest wholeness, would have to do so by insisting on the discrete components of that wholeness. Moreover, this wholeness may be one which Eddie can neither understand nor experience. The fact that Eddie himself is far from reconciled, even to his final, double-sexed self, is suggested by his own assessment: 'There was far too much hasty improvisation about the current version of Eddie Twyborn . . . ' (*TA*, p. 427). Improvised or not, however, the 'current version' incorporates both male and female.

Eddie may also attain new life in yet another way, intimated by the novel's coda. Here a moment of peace, a moment White later describes as one of 'grace' (*FG*, p. 257), descends as Eadie, oblivious of bombs, returns in her imagination to her Sydney garden. Envisaging a future life with her son/daughter, she celebrates the fact that her child, 'this fragment of my self which I lost is now returned where it belongs' (*TA*, p. 432). Thus, Eddie may be reconciled with both his parents: reunited with his father in his final vision, and reincorporated, almost reified, within his mother's memory. The similarities in the protagonist's three names and those of his parents hint at this ultimate unity.

White deliberately prevents our settling on any firm interpretation. Not even Ellen Roxburgh's modest and sobering realizations are granted Eddie, much less Elizabeth Hunter's exultant moment in the storm, or Hurtle Duffield's embrace of the Indigod. What Eddie comes to understand, if anything, is left wholly to the reader's conjecture and must be inferred from amidst a welter of conflicting clues.

White refuses to interpret these clues for us, and his subsequent work offers little help. While his 1982 play *Signal Driver* ends with a light which suffuses stage and audience and suggests the loving embrace of a heavenly power, the 1983 play *Netherwood* is set in a hell on earth where humans contend only 'to find out who's the bigger dill' (p. 52). If we read the plays as pursuing the direction pointed by *The Twyborn Affair*, we are still at a loss to decide whether Eddie is translated or simply extinguished. Yet the earlier play affirms the possibility of enduring love, and the later sides with the 'unorthodox' as they confront 'the sanity in insanity and the insanity in sanity'.[57] Thus the plays perhaps do comment obliquely on *The Twyborn Affair*. An enigma to himself and others, Eddie is forced to Theodora Goodman's recognition that there is little to choose between illusion and reality. White also hints that Eddie's dormant capacity for love and involvement stirs near the novel's end. In particular, the withdrawal from life with which he began Part Three gives way to an engagement so intense that, paradoxically, it kills him. We must not forget that a final attempt at rebirth sends him out on the streets to his death.

Moreover, to observe that White delivers Eddie from the world need not lead, as it has led some critics, to the conclusion that the author rejects that world of fragmentation.[58] On the contrary, the novel affirms life in all its pain and particularity, and, within it, the love which is its 'core of reality' (p. 336). Without love, the love Eddie is only beginning to locate when he dies, life remains unreal, a fiction or charade. With love, as Gravenor's letter asserts, life brims with evidence of God. For Eddie, as for Ellen Roxburgh, love is all that keeps us here.

But Eddie, of course, doesn't stay. His failure, like that of Ellen Roxburgh and Elizabeth Hunter, is one of love. He begins by failing to love himself and later withdraws his love from others. To some degree, his failures in love are inevitable. Human love will never match its transcendental model, but in *The Twyborn Affair*, as in the two previous novels, the one testifies to the other. Near the end of the work, Eadith reflects on her failures:

> Failed love in particular. Her every attempt at love had been a failure. Perhaps she was fated never to enter the lives of others, except vicariously. To enter, or to be entered: that surely was the question in most lives.   (p. 374)

The final sentence carries obvious sexual implications, and it is typical of White to undercut a solemn moment with a ribald *double-entendre*. But the sentence also has important thematic resonances, for Eddie has avoided either entering or being entered by other lives. In this sense, he has been neither homosexual nor transsexual, but asexual and, for that reason, sterile. At the novel's close, however, as he hurries to his mother, he may be starting into fruitful life in earnest.

The mother who awaits him also acknowledges the power of love and her failure to use it. Musing on 'Eddie Eadith her interchangeable failure' (p. 431), she vows hereafter to embrace her child, of whatever sex, as a part of herself. The suggestion may be that she has accepted the wholeness of androgyny as

Eddie never could. Eddie lies dead in the street, but a life has been entered after all. Thus, like so many of White's protagonists, Eddie achieves a profound, if paradoxical, success.

5 Style and Technique: the Discipline of Failure

> *... the roses sparkled drowsed brooded leaped flaunting their earthbound flesh in an honorably failed attempt to convey the ultimate.* (*ES*, p. 191)

Near the end of *Riders in the Chariot*, White describes Alf Dubbo painting his two masterpieces. Of the Christ in his *Deposition* the author says, 'Much was omitted, which, in its absence, conveyed. It could have been that the observer himself contributed the hieroglyphs of his own fears ...' (p. 502). The later *Chariot* painting is similarly unfinished and evocative:

> Where he cheated a little was over the form of the Chariot itself. Just as he had not dared completely realize the body of the Christ, here the Chariot was shyly offered. But its tentative nature became, if anything, its glory, causing it to blaze across the sky, or into the soul of the beholder. (p. 505)

In both passages, White might be indicating features of his own artistic practice. Both stress uncertainty, ambiguity and suggestive omission, as well as the need for the observer/reader to contribute his own deepest self to the project of recovering meaning. It is in the very 'soul' of the beholder, says White, that the artist's 'tentative' offering takes on its full significance. As Henry James said the writer should, White therefore 'makes the reader very much as he makes his characters' and makes him well enough that the 'reader does quite the labour'.[1]

White's particular demands upon the reader spring from a philosophical premise which aligns him most closely with writers such as Conrad and Faulkner, and philosophers such as Kierkegaard and Simone Weil.[2] The premise is a radical distrust, both of the self as perceiving instrument and of language as expressive instrument. Conrad repeatedly insisted that language can be used for unscrupulous purposes; it is the source, for example, of much of Kurtz's dark power. In White's case, an understanding of language's limits and hazards often silences him before the vastness he would voice. Like Derrida, he sees that the signifier can never be firmly tethered to the signified, that meaning slithers free of constraints, and that, consequently, language is finally unreliable.[3]

For White, as perhaps for Faulkner, the distrust which gives rise to this awareness is grounded in the acknowledgement of failure as a necessary and valuable component of the human condition. In the quest for meaning undertaken by White's character, failure both motivates continued attempts and suggests the impossibility of success.[4] Indeed, White might say of his characters, as Faulkner did of other writers, that they are to be judged 'on the basis of their splendid failure to do the impossible'.[5]

Preceding chapters have traced the theme of failure as it emerges and develops in White's fiction.[6] I have tried to show that he subjects his major characters to moral or spiritual failure for several purposes: to prepare the character for entrance into a state of awareness in which such dichotomies as failure/success can be encompassed; to provoke him into further struggle towards the goal; to admit him to a deeper understanding of the nature of human existence; and to permit him to be most fully and essentially himself while paradoxically demanding surrender of the selfhood he has worked to perfect.[7] In his treatment of different protagonists, White stresses different aspects of the larger theme. For example, Theodora Goodman fails to destroy herself and is permitted to embrace, although not to obliterate, antitheses; Hurtle Duffield is driven by his repeated failures toward continued attempts to realize the phenomenal world and to reach the unnamable Indigod; Ellen Roxburgh is initiated into awareness of human culpability for failure; and Himmelfarb becomes most Messianic when he gives up hope of redeeming others. In White's work, failure is often rewarded by increased understanding, but it is not transcended; it remains humiliation. The self finds itself both in and as failure, and such discovery is seen as imperative to its full humanity.[8] At the same time, however, attainment of the comprehensive understanding to which failure admits the protagonist represents humankind's only possible success.

What I now suggest is that White the artist subjects himself to a similar discipline of failure, and with similar results. Like his fictional constructs – Voss, Hurtle Duffield and Alf Dubbo – his fiercely individual vision seeks matching expression. Like theirs, his work is a search for self. Yet he ceaselessly reminds us and himself that his vision dims before what it is meant to convey. He also shares with Orwell the sense that individual vision is necessarily inadequate. Such an ideological framework would dictate the author's concern lest, like Hurtle, he violate life's complexity and beauty by rendering it into art, or, like Voss, betray his own humanity by manipulating it in others. Perhaps he also struggles with Himmelfarb's need to redeem or Arthur Brown's more modest longing to be his brother's keeper. In any case, while his work testifies to the means by which man approaches wholeness, love and truth, the author acknowledges that he, like his protagonists, is incapable of their perfect expression. Instead, he sets himself the task of cultivating a humbling awareness of inadequacy. As he says in 'The Prodigal Son', 'Certainly the state of simplicity and humility is the only desirable one for artist or for man. While to reach it may be impossible, to attempt to do so is imperative.'[9] Typically he condemns himself to failure even to acknowledge his own failures. A reading of *Flaws in the Glass* reveals that for White the ultimate goals, those sought through 'faith, art and love', can only be reached 'in diminished terms' (pp. 74 and 197).

The very act of writing *Flaws in the Glass* may be viewed as a deliberate exercise in self-abasement, approached through the exploration of failure. At one point in the book, White defends himself against the charge of misogyny by explaining, 'Of course my women are *flawed* because they are also human beings, as I am, which is why I'm writing this book' (p. 252). The implication is that, in part at least, he wrote to delineate his own flaws and failings. The book's title suggests an emphasis on faults; both reflection and reflected are imperfect.[10] As White says, he wanted here to 'make and mar a portrait', to create a work which, unlike Hurtle Duffield's idealized self-portrait, would expose what he finds petty and repugnant in himself (p. 134). His recounting of certain incidents, in fact, suggests that *Flaws* is an analogue of Hurtle's portrait smeared with excrement. It refutes and punishes the self it also celebrates.

Another way White has sought humility is through his characters.[11] He has said that all his characters are fashioned from himself, and has even insisted that there is more of himself in odious characters than in others, 'Because I disparage my own flaws.'[12] Thus, when Voss abdicates the throne of God for resumption of human status, when Hurtle becomes an instrument to be painted with and through, when Himmelfarb knows he cannot redeem the world's sins, when Elizabeth Hunter admits her failure to love despite the lessons of the eye of the storm, or when Eddie Twyborn despairs of locating a convincing self, it is in part their creator who is chastised.

But this, if it were all, would be too easy. To impose failure only upon alter egos would be to appropriate to himself as artist a success and complacency antithetical to his understanding. As he has thematically demonstrated the need to fail, he must also do it technically, using such tools of the trade as diction, sentence structure, tone, point of view, narrative voice, and genre conventions. I will argue here that much of what is distinctive (and often disturbing) in White's work might be explained by examining its place in a self-imposed discipline of failure.

STYLISTIC PREFERENCES

Among the most characteristic features of White's style is his preference for subjunctive, conditional, and generally conjectural constructions, preferences he shares with Faulkner and Virginia Woolf.[13] Sometimes a sense of the uncertain is attained simply by the use of 'as if', 'or else' or 'could'. Of the despicable Mrs Jolley in *Riders in the Chariot* he writes, 'she drew in her breath, as if she were restraining wind. Or else she could suddenly have been afraid' (p. 78). Both possibilities are posited; from the one she suffers a physical indignity, from the other a moral diminution. In such a construction, the author keeps himself ostensibly on the side of realism (she *looked* as if restraining wind), while gesturing toward less verifiable, but more richly suggestive, alternatives. A similar effect is achieved by the use of 'perhaps' in a passage describing a conversation between Mrs Goldbold and Himmelfarb, from the viewpoint of the watching Mrs Flack and Mrs Jolley:

It was obvious that the woman's flat, and ordinarily uncommunicative face had been opened by some experience of a private nature, or perhaps it was just the light, gilding surfaces,

> dissolving the film of discouragement and doubt which life
> leaves behind, loosening the formal braids of hair, furnishing
> an aureole, which, if not supernatural – reason would not
> submit to that – provided an agreeable background to motes
> and gnats.   (p. 236).

Here the natural effects of light are offered as the explanation
preferred by the uneasy onlookers, Mesdames Flack and Jolley.
At the same time, White mocks their dependence on reason by
mentioning the sanctifying aureole and thus pushing even the
naturalistic in the direction of the supernatural. The pivotal
'perhaps' begins as a retreat into reason and ends by opening
perception to the transcendental.

This postulating of both spiritual–psychological and physical–
naturalistic accounts of the same phenomenon holds meaning in
suspension and the reader in uncertainty while also enlarging the
field of potential significance. It is related to another favourite
Whitean tactic, the use of syllepsis. Examples are the passage
from *Happy Valley* in which Mrs Moriatry is described as 'moulten
with self-pity and sweat' (p. 124), and the implicit syllepsis of
'cats lifted the lid off all politeness' (*TM*, p. 21). Sometimes the
effect is predominantly witty, akin to that which Pope achieves
with the same device.[14] But White also uses startling yokings as
did the Metaphysical poets, to suggest an interpenetration of the
profane and the divine. In this case, the stylistic device epitomizes
what the novel's action demonstrates: that the mundane and
transcendent, or comic and tragic, like other opposites, engage
in perpetual dialectic. We remember the tangled circus and
funeral processions of *Riders in the Chariot* and the fact that
beatitude descended on Elizabeth Hunter as she strained on her
commode. White's world view is that which Leslie Fiedler ascribes
to the modern writer, for whom 'the distinction between comedy
and tragedy seems as forced and irrelevant as that between
hallucination and reality'.[15] Relevant here, too, is White's fondness for synaesthetic imagery, such as that he uses to describe Alf
Dubbo's death: 'the sharp pain poured in crimson tones into the
limited space of the room and overflowed' (*RC*, p. 505). In
White's hands, synaesthesia becomes another instrument for
undermining familiar distinctions, such as those among sensory
functions, thus establishing a disquieting sense of flux
counterpointed with a reassuring sense of comprehensiveness.[16]

A somewhat different effect is produced by other uses of conditionals. In the short story 'The Woman who Wasn't Allowed to Keep Cats', White says of a couple who have been visiting Greece, 'the call of business made it necessary for the Hajistavri to return to New York. Probably they saw the Alexious again, on the other hand there may not have been time' (*BO*, p. 268). *The Eye of the Storm* opens with these lines: 'The old woman's head was barely fretting against the pillow. She could have moaned slightly' (p. 11). A further example is found in *A Fringe of Leaves*, where White quotes Miss Scrimshaw replying to a question 'in a rush, which transposed what must have been a deep voice into a higher, unnatural key' (p. 9). In these passages, the sometimes omniscient narrator disclaims knowledge of whether the Hajistavri saw the Alexious again, whether Elizabeth Hunter actually moaned, or whether Miss Scrimshaw's voice is normally deep. These deliberate evasions serve several functions. First, they signal the resignation of the prerogatives which normally accrue to the omniscient narrator, placing White for these moments where the reader is: outside of character and action and with only humanly limited faculties for their evaluation. Secondly, and consequently, they encourage the reader to sharpen those very faculties. It is evidently going to be his job to sort out the muddle. Finally, and again as a direct result, they enlist the reader as a partner in the apprehension of meaning. He both seeks and contributes to the novel's emerging significance.

Much the same analysis might be applied to another of White's trademarks, the use of the sentence fragment, both in narration and in dialogue. A striking example of this practice is the short-story title 'The Night the Prowler'. The unfinished phrase begs for a verb, and the reader attempts to supply it. But the fragmentary title resonates with implications for the story, in which the reader's uncertainty over what the prowler did or didn't do generates suspense for some two-thirds of the narrative. The truncated phrase also suggests the horror with which polite society greets such intrusions; the whole matter is apparently too tasteless, too appalling, to go into. Ultimately, the title phrase faces the reader with the story's crux, the question of what the prowler did, not *to* but *for* his victim, and of what the experience has meant to her subsequent life. In all its implications, the title engages the reader.

White's frequent use of second-person narration may also be

viewed as a means of encouraging reader involvement, but here involvement shifts toward implication.[17] A telling instance occurs in *The Living and the Dead* in a scene between Eden Standish and her mother (White does not use quotation marks):

> You're pale darling, Mother said.
> It made you turn your face.
> I need exercise, she said. I'll have to start walking some of the way in the morning.
> She wanted to be left alone. Making events they are your very own, also the consequence, whether the bitter abstraction of your own subsequent regrets, or the even more relentless concrete kind. Because Eden Standish found that she was pregnant.
> It was one of those things that didn't, couldn't happen to yourself.... (p. 168)

Here the use of 'you' puts the reader uncomfortably in Eden's place and warns him against her delusions of impunity. Similarly, in *The Vivisector* White employs the second person to recall to the reader childhood's helpless inarticulacy. In this scene between Hurtle and Pa Duffield, the reader shares the boy's tongue-tied confusion:

> You weren't all that interested in the old brass medals from off the harness, but liked to bring out the light in them. You got pretty good at it, and Pa began to drool, suspecting that his son might, after all, have been born with a skill.
> 'Apprentice yer to some good honest tradesman', on one occasion he said. 'Learn a trade. It's all very well to read and write. But you can go too far.'
> Because you didn't know what to answer, you went away. You didn't love books all that much but wouldn't have known how to tell Pa you neither loved an 'honest trade'. You loved – what? You wouldn't have known, not to be asked. (p. 18)

The effect of these passages is very different from that achieved by Hemingway in *A Farewell to Arms*, for example, where 'you' functions largely as a substitute for the grammatically proper but stuffy 'one'. White's second-person narration seeks to include and even trap the reader.

The techniques so far discussed are used primarily to do one of two things. They either posit several layers of meaning simultaneously or compel reader participation in the making of meaning. But the most unmistakably Whitean sentence structures, those complex sentences beginning with an 'if' clause, accomplish both effects. Here, for example, is a passage describing Voss's departure on his expedition; Voss and Laura have been saying goodbye, and Voss has taken her hand: 'As soon as a decent interval had elapsed, Laura withdrew her hand. If Voss did not notice, it was because he was absorbed' (p. 115). A similar construction occurs in *A Fringe of Leaves* after a conversation between Austin Roxburgh and the steward Spurgeon.

> 'The affection of a faithful animal is most gratifying,' Mr Roxburgh conceded; he found himself stuttering for what must have been the first time, 'but–mmmorally there is no comparison with the love of a devoted woman.'
> 'Don't know about that', the steward replied. 'I weren't born into the moral classes.'
> If Mr Roxburgh did not hear, it was on account of a sense of guilt he was nursing, for the many occasions on which he had abandoned someone else to drowning by clambering aboard the raft of his own negative abstractions.   (p. 210)

Sometimes the main clause is also made conditional, as in this sentence from *The Eye of the Storm* in which Arnold Wyburd reacts to a letter Basil has sent Mrs Hunter: 'If he had been more than temporarily relieved by the evasions of the letter, he might have rejected some of her scorn' (pp. 253–4).

In every case the use of the conditional puts the reader off balance and renders meaning problematical. In the *Voss* passage, the reader wonders whether Voss did, in fact, notice Laura's withdrawn hand, and, if he didn't, whether the proposed explanation is supplied by the narrator or by Laura's injured feelings. (In this case, the effect of the conditional is complicted by uncertainty in point of view, a Whitean penchant to which I shall return.) In the passage from *A Fringe of Leaves*, one interpretative alternative is that Mr Roxburgh *does* hear, and that it is Spurgeon's remark which engenders the guilt he feels over clinging to abstractions. On the other hand, he may have chosen not to hear, but instead to luxuriate in guilt (itself an abstraction) and thus to evade the human imperative posed by the situation. Finally, his guilt may have nothing whatever to do with Spurgeon's remark and may come from his awareness of his own sententiousness. Analogous but even more complex ambiguities arise from the *Eye of the Storm* sentence. In each case, the possibilities for interpretative pluralism deny the reader closure.

Wayne Booth has supplied us with a label for this and related narrative techniques, grouping them under the rubric 'conjectural description'. Booth explains their operation in Faulkner's *Light in August*:

> [Faulkner] is always saying that nobody could tell whether it was such-and-such or so-and-so, but *both* of the alternatives he suggests convey the evaluation he intends: they establish a broad band of possibilities within which the truth must lie.[18]

Booth goes on to insist that, although use of this device makes the author appear to confine himself to what any observer might see, in reality he retains control of the reader's response by restricting the range of meaning.

White uses the technique to similar purposes. He guides interpretation by giving access to a certain spectrum of meaning. In the passage from *A Fringe of Leaves*, *all* interpretative options give us valid insight into Austin Roxburgh. Yet at the same time White fails to settle on a single meaning, fails to exercise the privileges of the omniscient narrator while continuing to reserve them. It is a stance of purposeful self-limitation from which meaning proliferates and readers are drawn into partnership. But the failed author also forces his readers to fail, and so to experience the human limitations of their own perceptive and analytic apparatus. Meaning can never be certainly fixed. It remains as fluid as the fictive world which gives rise to it.

NARRATIVE STANCE

Many of the same observations can be made about White's reticence to endorse unequivocally either his protagonists or the precepts they voice.[19] The hero and heroine of *Voss* are an excellent case in point. White spoke revealingly about this novel, as well as his generally ironic perspective, in a 1973 interview where he said,

> I am myself suspicious of the heroic. I don't think any of my novels is heroic. All are certainly ironic – the fact that one is alive at all is an irony. Voss was a monomaniac, rather than a hero, and like almost all human beings flawed and fallible.[20]

In a White novel, then, irony is an omnipresent possibility. But White employs degrees of irony, and readers who miss its subtler manifestations will be misled. In *Voss*, the ironic undercutting of the title character is unmistakable. The author repeatedly reminds us, especially at moments when Voss would prefer to feel most godlike, of his weaknesses, pettiness, selfishness and unwitting buffoonery. But the reader must also recognize that Laura receives analogous, although less caustic, treatment, especially in the beginning, where her agnosticism and arrogance are the subject of amused authorial scrutiny. Even in the novel's final scene, where she appears as a fountainhead of knowledge, strength and love, she is still a tiresome and dowdy woman who sermonizes and then wonders aloud about her lozenges.[21] The juxtaposition of Laura's spiritual beauty and scratchy throat in this passage is related to the sylleptic pattern already identified. But it serves a further function here as well. The fact that Laura is always a trifle ridiculous complicates her evaluation of Voss and his experience.[22] When she sums up Voss as a man who has struggled with his own evil and failed, but at the same time recovered full humanity, do her words have White's endorsement? The text suggests that they do. Yet the fact that the author has pro-blematized both her character and testimony keeps open the questions raised by Voss's life and death. The work ends with Laura's claim that Voss's 'legend will be written down, eventually, by those who have been troubled by it' (p. 445). This prediction places Patrick White among those troubled, and extends the invitation to the reader to work through his own uneasiness by rewriting Voss's 'legend' in his own terms.

Often the uncertainty about where White stands in relation to character or concept is a function of a rapidly shifting or ambiguous point of view.[23] The shift is usually accomplished by an unmarked slide from direct to indirect discourse. In *Voss*, again, a passage describes the explorer reading Le Mesurier's very personal prose poems:

> If he continued to glance through the notebook, and peer at
> the slabs of dark scribble, on the smudged pages, with the
> fluffy edges, he no longer did so with enthusiasm. To be
> perfectly honest, he did not wish to see, but must. The slow
> firelight was inexorable.
>   So his breath pursued him in his search through the blurred
> book.   (pp. 293–4)

Probably the narrator's point of view is in force in the first and
final sentences, although the inclusion of details about the
notebook's appearance suggests that Voss may be using close
observation to distract himself from his guilt over this invasion of
privacy, and thus posits Voss's as the working point of view. But
who is being 'perfectly honest' and to whom is the firelight
'inexorable'? Surely this is Voss, yet point of view is so slippery
here that the reader can't be sure. Moreover, Voss is plainly not
being perfectly honest, nor is the inexorability of firelight a
convincing rationale for perusing private papers. These
observations encourage the hypothesis of a controlling narrator
speaking through and thereby satirizing Voss, much as Jane
Austen does with her character Emma. The reader is left to sort
out the viewpoint confusion and attendant tonal ambiguities.
      In cases such as this, the narrator's point of view is superimposed
upon that of the character, producing a stereoscopic effect which
allows for oblique and often satiric commentary. Another example
is this sentence, which describes Voss in a moment of supreme,
but misplaced, self-confidence: 'He was laughing good-naturedly,
and looked handsome and kind in his burned skin, and besides,
he was straddling the world' (p. 47). The narrator's ironic
hyperbole, grafted to what is clearly Voss's view of himself, wryly
reflects on his self-assurance. At the same time, White's use of the
disturbing adjective 'burned', one which Voss would not have
chosen, suggests the price one may pay for hypertrophied pride.
      The quickly shifting point of view may also be used for
purposeful evasion. In *The Twyborn Affair*, for example, White
abrogates access to Eadith's thoughts at the crucial moment when
she fails to acknowledge her mother as they pass on the escalators:

> Mrs Trist did not lean over to touch. Once more her will
> had faltered, the moment had eluded her. She would never
> find out. The answers were not for her.
> She looked back at narrow shoulders in a damp black

raincoat disappearing into the upper reaches.

A person on Eadith's present level, glancing sideways as they crossed on the down and up, was fascinated by the despair of a strong, but curiously violet chin, the mouth in a soggy face sucking after life it seemed.   (p. 405)

The reader may resent being excluded from Eadith's consciousness in such a crisis. But White's momentary switch to an outsider's perspective gives us a measure of the depths of Eadith's despair which she could not provide. Particularly effective in view of her rejection of her mother is the image of a futile 'sucking after life'. The observer's viewpoint, which notices what looks like an unshaven chin, also reminds us of Eadith's anomalous existence as a woman in a man's body, a condition which is at the heart of her pain and anomie. Finally, the sudden shift in angle of vision may represent the narrator's tactful withdrawal, in recognition of the fact that Eadith cannot endure exposure at that moment. In addition to heightening the sense of realism, such a technique sets author and reader a boundary beyond which uncertainty obtains.

One more related technique deserves mention. In the fluid interweaving of mental and physical realities which characterizes novels such as *Voss* and *Riders in the Chariot*, White is not so much shifting point of view as shifting genre, but the effect on the reader is analogous. Here, for example, is a passage from *Voss* describing an oneiric vision which Laura has during her fever:

Once in the night, Laura Trevelyan, who was struggling to control the sheets, pulled herself up and forward, leaning over too far, with the natural result that she was struck in the face when the horse threw up his head. She did not think she could bear the pain. . . .

When she was more controlled, she said very quietly, 'You need not fear. I shall not fail you. Even if there are times when you wish me to, I shall not fail you.'

And again, with evident happiness: 'It is your dog. She is licking your hand. How dry your skin is, though. Oh, blessed moisture!'

Whereupon, she was moving her head against the pillow in grateful ecstasy.

Such evidence would have delighted the Palethorpes, and

mystified the Bonners, but the former were not present and
the latter were drooping and swaying in their own sleep on
their mahogany chairs.

So the party rode down the terrible basalt stairs of the
Bonners' deserted house, and onward.   (pp. 356–7)

In later novels, such passages tend to be marked as dreams or
musings; thus their ontological status is rarely in doubt. Still,
their impact is comparable. Such scenes present disquieting
conglomerates of levels of existence and consciousness which seem
fraught with significance and tease the reader towards attempts
to decipher them. In the quoted passage, the fever-ridden Laura
in her bed coincides with an imagined Laura in a desert which
is both actual and hallucinatory, present and absent, the whole
thing anchored in a real but oblivious world of Bonners,
Palethorpes and mahogany chairs. Although such moments in
the fiction never yield themselves fully and finally, they remain
provocative, not least because, within them, point of view seems
simply abandoned.

These several methods by which White varies, disrupts or
renounces point of view all function to preclude certainty,
encourage reader involvement, and set limits for the author and
the reader. Given that his goal is to face his readers with a
framework of existence staggeringly greater than themselves and
impervious to full understanding, the techniques are well suited
to his purposes. Again, they seem to arise from a deliberate
imposition of failure – the failure to be unequivocal – undertaken
as a way of reminding himself and the reader of their shared
inadequacies.

This kind of wilful self-limitation is also reflected in a development which has already been noticed: White's increasing refusal
to articulate what his questers seek and sometimes find. In the
course of his career, the vantage point from which revelation is
viewed sinks deeper and deeper into shadow. From the explicitness
of *The Tree of Man*'s garden vision, he has progressively retreated
before the ineffability of visionary experience. His latest work
even leads us to wonder if there *is* a vision for Eddie Twyborn.
In his fiction and in interviews,[24] he insists on the incompetence
of language to convey understanding, but in each succeeding
work he puts his precept further into practice. For White,
language, too, must finally fail.

IMAGERY AND STRUCTURE

In their imagery and structure, the novels also attest to their author's purposeful and fruitful failure. His imagery manifests itself in both of what Northrop Frye has called apocalyptic and demonic modes; that is, the same image, colour or pattern will carry both positive and negative suggestions.[25] The colour green is used this way in *Voss* to connote both tender spring growth and corrosive decay. Green is associated with the life which returns to the expedition in the spring, and with the life-giver Laura. But it appears in its demonic cast when the swelling corpse of Harry Robarts becomes a 'green woman' (p. 386). Similarly, the bird imagery in *The Cockatoos* comes to evoke the energy of life, whether gentle or vicious, and the colour white in the fiction accrues associations which range from purity to nullity. Since such modulations overrun categories, they imply the impossibility of polarizing good and evil, positive and negative, and suggest instead their oxymoronic apposition and occasional coincidence. Similarly, White's use of the pathetic fallacy, as, for example, in the opening pages of *The Tree of Man*, not only violates realistic conventions, but posits a world in which spirit and matter so interpenetrate as to become sometimes indistinguishable.[26] Imagery thus corroborates our sense that the world as portrayed by White is beyond his or anyone's power to analyse, catalogue, order or control.

Structurally, the novels tend towards episode and epiphany, White's preference for the latter perhaps owed to Joyce. The episodic progress of plot, interrupted by frequent and sometimes unexplained gaps in time, suggests a world in which human actions are rarely attuned to nature's rhythmic constancy. This is especially apparent in the contrast of Voss's fits and starts toward salvation with the Australian outback in its stately revolution of seasons. A similar effect is produced by setting Eddie Twyborn's frenetic and sporadic attempts at relationship against the calm subtleties of the Monaro country. In addition, White's near silence about certain phases of his characters' lives (for instance, the war experiences of Stan Parker, Hurtle Duffield and Eddie Twyborn), and his tendency to disrupt chronology (as in *Riders in the Chariot*, *The Solid Mandala* and *A Fringe of Leaves*), both support a view of human experience as discontinuous and fragmentary. The possibility of wholeness is retained, but it is often apprehended in epiphanies over which the character has little control.[27] Grace and divine design exist in White's universe, but in their very existence they mortify the reasoning human mind which seeks a logical approach to them.

Thus meaning, which is not to be apprehended through rational processes, reveals itself in other ways – not only through epiphany, but also in suggestive juxtaposition of image or event and in the symphonic intermingling of themes and motifs. Like Mr Gage, the artist of *The Tree of Man*, White sometimes fashions a continuum of imagery, from the ant on the pavement to the sun in the sky, which sets man as its middle term and suggests that all share the same vital impulse. Alternatively, actions may illuminate each other by their contiguity. For example, in *The Solid Mandala*, Mrs Feinstein tells Arthur and Waldo about visiting her European relatives:

'I don't know what Daddy would have to say to so much Jewish emotionalism. I was thankful we did not have him with us, either in Paris or Milan. Poor things, *they* are devout.' Mrs Feinstein smiled for the sick, though it could have been she enjoyed the sickness. 'Of course we did whatever was expected of us while we were there. We did not have the heart to tell them we have given up all such middle-aged ideas, to conform,' she said, 'to conform with the spirit of progress. Daddy, I am afraid, who is more forceful in his expression, would have offended.'

After that she disappeared, trailing the outdoor coat she was wearing. It was so out of place. It was also so shapeless it might have been inherited.   (p. 132)

Simply by appending the trailed, 'inherited' coat to Mrs Feinstein's smugly modern point of view, White comments ironically on her hope that the inheritance of faith may be discarded. At the same time, the repetition of the word 'conform' suggests that her modernism reflects nothing more than capitulation to a new kind of pressure.

A related technique is the evocative blending of a novel's themes and motifs in a single scene, a practice which seems to owe as much to music as to literature. Perhaps the best example comes from *The Solid Mandala*, for, in Arthur's mandalic dance, imagistic motifs associated with each major character and with several thematic concerns are counterpointed in a comprehensive pattern which centres the novel's meaning in a possible order, harmony and wholeness. Again, meaning is seen to elude logical processes and pigeonholes, but to proliferate when approached from the state of grace.

A final word should be said about structure in White's fiction. With rare exceptions such as *The Vivisector*, the novels end not with the climactic moment of revelation, but with a coda in which the quest is renewed by some heir to the protagonist's experience: Stan Parker's grandson in *The Tree of Man*, Mary de Santis in *The Eye of the Storm*, the protagonists themselves in *The Aunt's Story* and *A Fringe of Leaves*.[28] In part, this structural preference seems a way of insisting that the search is on-going, but it also keeps the novels open-ended. In this way, the reader is invited to assume the burden of evaluating what he, too, has inherited. That burden grows in the later novels. Whereas Stan Parker understood his place in the scheme of things, Eddie Twyborn may have no place at all. Whereas Stan is reconciled to the great overarching One, we can only guess whether Eddie is reconciled even to himself. Most importantly, the transcendent reality which validates Stans's vision is far clearer than that which stands behind Eddie or, for that matter, Elizabeth Hunter or Ellen Roxburgh. The later works are designedly more disturbing, more resistant to resolution.

In this way, too, we find the author forcing himself to fail and renouncing success as simplistic. In his *Strains of Discord*, Robert Adams points out that an author's opting for the unresolvedness of open form may reflect a kind of deliberate failure. He identifies two modes this process takes, both of which are applicable to White:

When the mind turns the sharp edge of its satiric disapproval against its own nature, we get an openness which in its austerity, compression, and self-limitation seems classical. Such openness seems to be the opposite, but is really the complement, of romantic openness, in which the mind strains to remain unresolved before the fullness or magnitude of an experience and will not close form because to do so implies exclusion. Both patterns involve and express a sort of humiliation of the mind, which, since it is always in art presumed a free agent, must inevitably appear to wish its own defeat, hence to be perverse. Yet it is often anguished as well, and its action involves not only a testing but ultimately a negation of individual identity . . . .[29]

Like his characters, White apprehends an order of being before which his vision is stretched to its limits, but is none the less found wanting and must finally be surrendered. The surrender is motivated in the manner Adams suggests: both by his ironic estimation of his own capacities and by the enormity of what he would impart. Open form is thus a fitting vehicle for the author's thematic and philosophical preoccupations. He also uses the form to face his readers with their own failures.[30] In place of closure, responsive readers will find their assumptions unsettled and their horizons expanded. White might well say with Gide, 'I come to disquiet.'[31]

GENRE AND TRADITION

Among the many disquieting features of White's fiction, genre must also be ranked. The question of what kind of novels he writes has troubled his critics for decades, as has the problem of placing him in a 'tradition'.

White's psychological realism and his 'carpentry' of plot have been termed Jamesian.[32] These aspects of his writing, coupled with his Dickensian galleries of supporting characters and the length and scope of his works, suggest a derivation from the nineteenth-century tradition which White has claimed and within which some critics locate him.[33] Further supporting such place-ment is his fluency both in the gentle satire of Jane Austen's novels and the more virulent variety practised by Thackeray. He also seems to have inherited George Eliot's compassion and Hardy's sober sense of the human predicament, as well as the latter's hope that 'loving-kindness', a term both he and White employ, might ameliorate it.[34] White's roots in the nineteenth century go even deeper, because he also draws on the work of European, Russian and American writers of the period. Stendhal and Flaubert are among the authors he most admires, and he traces his portrayal of extra-ordinary experiences to the influence of such writers as Dostoyevsky.[35] In the works of the French realists, he appears to have studied methods of non-judgemental and unsentimental character presentation, while the Russian works, particularly those of Dostoyevsky, showed him states of mind and modes of perception beyond the reach of strictly realistic treatment. In other affinities with earlier continental literature, the influence of German romanticism is evident in *Voss* and *The Vivisector*, although both novels question its values and premises. Finally, although White rarely mentions American writers of the past century, elements in his work which are variously called 'Romantic' and 'Gothic' have been linked to the fiction of Melville and Hawthorne. Chief among these are a kind of deliberate excess and dramatic intensity which *Voss* shares with *Moby Dick*, and a sense that White has created a world of 'romance' in which, as Hawthorne defined this genre, the 'Actual and Imaginary may meet'.[36]

What meets the 'actual' in White's world, however, is not the 'imaginary', but the supra-real, a greater reality which authorizes and validates the one we know.[37] Clearly, White cannot be said to use absurdist or surrealist techniques or to be composing the 'new novel' along French lines. His work does not radically undermine the assumptions on which the novel has traditionally rested, in the manner of a Beckett or a Robbe-Grillet. Rather, his kind of suprarealism adds supplemental dimensions to a reaffirmed real. In the last analysis, his world is less that of a Buñuel or an Ionesco than of a García Marquez, a world in which, in the midst of the mundane and credible, the transcendent unexpectedly opens. Yet to observe this affinity and to note as well White's facility with other modernist conventions is to see that, no matter how strong his links to the nineteenth century and earlier (for his novels also display the experimental eclecticism of much eighteenth-century fiction,)[38] his work finally breaches the conventions of the realistic–naturalistic tradition and demands that its genre be sought elsewhere.

For many critics, the genre of choice has been allegory. Having noticed that White's characters are often weighted with a significance incommensurate with their roles in the novel's plot, these students of his work argue that, in true allegorical fashion, characters stand for ideas or concepts beyond themselves on which the reader's attention is finally to focus.[39] In some of White's fiction, the allegorical equivalents are fairly patent.[40] The four Riders in the Chariot can be understood as embodying four facets of the whole human being: intellect (Himmelfarb), instinct (Mary Hare), emotion (Ruth Godbold) and imagination (Alf Dubbo). Even such a character as Ellen Roxburgh of *A Fringe of Leaves* quite gracefully assumes the role of every man/woman on an earthly pilgrimage. The notion is also attractive since, with a slight adjustment in perspective, the novels can be seen as allegories of psychic integration, in which characters encountered by the protagonist (or, in the case of *Riders in the Chariot*, the protagonists themselves) are aspects of a single self to be accepted and incorporated.[41] The people Theodora Goodman meets at the Hôtel du Midi, for example, can be interpreted as fragments of herself projected from a fractured consciousness. Since White has said that all his characters are fashioned from himself, his fiction could thus be understood as the allegorical record of his own quest for wholeness, moving him toward the forgiving acknowledgement of even the self's least admissible aspects. Such a quest might culminate in his 'self-portrait', *Flaws in the Glass*, where these aspects receive disproportionate emphasis.

To a certain extent, this approach to White's work is a fruitful one, but problems arise when the emphasis on allegorical significance interferes with a human response to his very human characters. By virtue of the genre's purposes, the characters of allegory tend not to be full, dense and complex beings, but mere transparent pointers to the work's field of values. We do not really tremble for the dangers faced by Spenser's Britomart, nor do we pity or mourn for Bunyan's Faithful, although the death he suffers is surely among the most hideous in literature. But White's characters *can* elicit reader sympathy and interest. Theodora Goodman may on one level be a Ulysses figure, but the reader none the less experiences her Odyssey as painful and personal. Similarly, Rhoda Courtney of *The Vivisector* is in part the hump Hurtle must hoist on his own shoulders, but she also inspires horrified pity as she stumps Sydney streets, feeding stray cats from her cart of stinking horseflesh. In a third instance, much of the impact of *The Twyborn Affair* derives from the reader's uneasy, often unwilling, recognition of himself in Eddie's piecemeal life and consciousness. White's characters are not mere symbolic ciphers, but must be granted a primary existence as full human beings, calling forth empathy and worthy of efforts to penetrate their minds and souls.[42]

Perhaps the most useful way to approach the question of genre in Patrick White's fiction is in terms suggested by Erich Auerbach. Contrasting the realism of the Christian works of late antiquity and the Middle Ages with modern realism, Auerbach offers the term 'figural' to describe the earlier mode. In figural realism, he says, an occurrence on earth signifies not only itself but at the same time another, without prejudice to the power of its concrete reality here and now. The connection between occurrences is not regarded as primarily a chronological or casual development but as a oneness within the divine plan, of which all occurrences are parts and reflections.[43]

In other words, within the conventions of figural realism, characters and events 'mean' both themselves and something else. Their reality obtains in the here and now, but is also predicated on a comprehensive plan from which everything draws significance and value.

White's fiction constantly affirms a controlling and often explicitly divine design; even Eddie Twyborn believes his various incarnations are chosen not by, but for, him, and White has expressed the same feelings about his own life and work.[44] Within this context of design and direction, the author uses figural realism precisely as Auerbach suggests: to provide a linkage between events or characters which can only be interpreted by reference to the supervening scheme. Examples are the repetitive cycles of experience undergone by Hurtle Duffield, or the way in which moments of *The Eye of the Storm* seem either to predict or recall the paradigmatic moment of beatitude. Neither of these patterns makes sense unless it is seen as mandated by or reflective of some larger design. But perhaps a more striking instance is the vision shared by the four Riders. To each, it has a deeply personal impetus and import, yet the vision is fundamentally the same for all four and originates in a transpersonal sphere. It thus connects them to its source and to each other, just as the interpretative assumptions Auerbach speaks of connect the sacrifice of Isaac to that of Christ and both to the Divine Will.

Characters may also be both intensely themselves and signposts to significance, but the fact that they serve these simultaneous functions does not preclude their growth. Though there is some critical opinion to the contrary, White's characters do change (we have only to think of the timid Mary Hare plunging into Himmelfarb's burning shack or Voss abdicating the Throne), although it must be admitted that their growth often seems a fulfilment of predetermined potential.[45] Nor does White's use of figural realism rule out engagement with meaningful, 'real world' issues. As Brian Kiernan has remarked, his fiction shows a fondness for 'parody' in the sense of 'adoption of a response to life that is a cultural *donnée*' and its critical testing against life more fully and clearsightedly conceived.[46] Kiernan cites Voss's Nietzschean drive colliding with 'bourgeois practicality', but Hurtle Duffield's Romantic conception of the artist is also subjected to ironic reassessment. Furthermore, White has often voiced his hopes that readers will recognize the relevance to their own real lives of his characters' fictional experiences. He sees himself engaged in a civilizing and humanizing mission, or, as he says in 'The Prodigal Son', the effort 'to people a barely inhabited country with a race possessed of understanding'.[47]

In Patrick White's hands, then, figural realism is a versatile instrument. It also shares with other aspects of his style and technique the capacity to jar the reader with its open-ended implications. Departures from the strictly naturalistic handling of character and plot, such as figural realism allows, have the effect of critiquing and even displacing cherished assumptions about order, form and meaning. This is, of course, precisely what White intends, but he subjects himself as well as his readers to this dislocation. In other words, genre provides him with yet another arena for failure. By stressing the point that his work refers to something beyond itself which can never be fully grasped, White assumes a position of failure *vis-à-vis* his vision. Like Auerbach's medieval writer, he can finally only mediate meaning which is beyond his comprehension.

Yet White's choice of this posture may have won him the success he bestows on his visionaries. We have seen his protagonists expand, melt and merge at the moment of consummate awareness, to the point where they might say with Whitman, 'I stretch around on the wonderful beauty.'[48] Their creator has also been enlarged. His novels of quest enlist readers as questers and offer them the experience of illumination and assent. Thus White begins to extend himself amongst them and to make the connections implicit in his work. Like his creations, he succeeds in most closely approaching his vision when he concedes and even celebrates his failure to attain it.

THE SHAPE OF FAILURE

In *Voss*, White describes Le Mesurier recording his awkward but moving prose poems:

All that this man had not lived began to be written down. His failures took shape, but in flowers, and mountains, and in words of love, which he had never before expressed, and which, for that reason, had the truth of innocence.   (p. 140)

The language of this passage stresses the humbling, cleansing and creative aspects of failure, as well as its power to motivate – to prod Le Mesurier toward what he has not yet voiced. The author continues,

When his poem was written, it was burning on the paper. At last, he had done this. But although he was the stronger for it, he put his poem away, afraid that someone might accuse him of a weakness. Often he took it out, and if some of it had died, for then, there opened out of it other avenues of light. It was always changing, as that world of appearances which had given him his poem. Yet, its structure was unchanged.
   So he was truly strong.   (p. 140)

As so often in White's work, the paradoxes accumulate: strength in weakness, constancy in change, life and light in death and darkness. The controlling paradox is the Christian mystery of finding a life by losing it, and recovering the self in self-sacrifice. It is the shape of a life infused by facilitating failure.

Christianity has importantly influenced White's thought, but it is the wider, Judeo-Christian concepts of religious quest and its necessary failure which White endorses and his fiction enacts. As Adin Steinsaltz explains it in his study of Jewish belief, the very idea of success in such a quest vitiates the desire to pursue the goal while at the same time underestimating its challenge. The Infinite, by definition, must be infinitely sought. Steinsaltz also remarks that the seeker's awareness of failure may 'stimulate his progress' by creating in him a thirst for good proportionate to the evil he once imbibed, and by fuelling his drive toward goodness with the energy formerly drained by his evil.[49] In Jungian terms, we might say that such a man had acknowledged the shadow self, and, by turning it from adversary into ally, had added its force to his own.[50] Thus failure need not debilitate, but may increase the strength and enthusiasm brought to the quest. Or, as John Fowles drily puts it in *Daniel Martin*, it may be found that 'failure is the salt of life'.[51]

Steinsaltz makes another observation pertinent to White's work:

The seeker is caught in a paradox. He is dismayed to learn that the resolution of the search for the self is not to be found in going into the self, that the centre of the soul is to be found not inside the soul but outside of it, that the centre of gravity of existence is outside of existence.[52]

White's protagonists learn precisely this lesson. The self ultimately fails to yield the significance they seek and must be surrendered.[53] The centripetal movement toward the core of self gives way to centrifugal extension. But, again paradoxically, it is only through the endeavour fully to realize the self that its imperfectibility is found and confessed. As Jung saw, man must bend all his energies toward 'individuation' while knowing it beyond his power.[54] Only thus does one produce a self worthy of surrender.

Perhaps, then, the most crucial failure in White's fiction is the failure to destroy the self. For self is finally seen as continuous with the 'MORE' it has sought.[55] A consanguinity is affirmed between temporal and eternal, finite and infinite, creation and creator.[56] Or, as Himmelfarb phrases it in Neoplatonic terms, the 'infintessimal kernels of sparks' which flicker inside human beings are seen to have their source in 'the bosom of divine fire' (*RC*, p. 155). Worship, for White, thus comes to be defined as the simultaneous awareness of insurmountable difference and ineffable oneness. The self is rediscovered and recovered in the Godhead.

This whole process of self-discovery, surrender and recovery is riddled with paradox. As Jung and Kierkegaard have remarked, paradox both describes the divine and marks man's encounter with it.[57] Kierkegaard has pointed to the paradoxical necessity of 'losing one's mind' – that is, one's rational faculties – in order to win to a condition of belief.[58] White, too, enforces this failure of human capacities, but like many such failures, it opens the way to success: the success of achieving full humanity and attaining to a vision of the circumscribing whole. Himmelfarb's 'mystery of failure' is penetrated and the paradox resolved at the instant when the limits of self dissolve in the infinite which had heretofore imposed those limits. What was constraining and enfeebling then liberates and vivifies; the fragmented self is healed into wholeness.

Much of this study has been concerned with explicating this recurring pattern and its implications for White's *oeuvre*. Beyond this, I suggest that the author's own assumption of the goading, humbling but liberating condition of failure accounts for certain features of his style and technique. White himself fails: to articulate the vision, to distinguish the sublime from the ridiculous, to honour the prerogatives of the omniscient narrator, to resolve ambiguity, to clarify point of view, fully to endorse a character or precept, to provide comfortable closure in his novels, or to write works which fit uncomplainingly into pre-established genres. In his failure, he approaches doing justice to his sense of being in the world.

This is not to argue that White is praiseworthy *because* he fails, but rather that these deliberate technical failures represent the successful incorporation of philosophical vision within fictional technique. The concept of necessary failure which permeates White's vision also shapes its thematic, structural, stylistic and generic expression, thereby providing the novels with an enigmatic unity which mirrors, although it distorts, that which obtains in the full world of being. Our glass is flawed, the glass of the novels more so; but in both cases the marred reflection gestures toward the more real and more perfect.

Failure thus becomes felicitous. White's understanding of its function is epitomized in the passage from David Malouf's *An Imaginary Life* which he chose as an epigraph for *The Twyborn Affair*: 'What else should our lives be but a series of beginnings, of painful settings out into the unknown, pushing off from the edges of consciousness into the mystery of what we have not yet become'. In 'what we have not yet become' lie the mysterious possibilities with which Patrick White sees life so richly furnished. His work confirms that the paradox of fortunate failure entails the most profound of these possibilities.

Notes

PREFACE

1. A gentleman hand on a sheep station, learning the business with a view to later running a station of his own.

2. Patrick White, 'The Prodigal Son', *Australian Letters*, 1, no. 3 (Apr 1958) 37–40; repr. in *The Vital Decade, Ten Years of Australian Art and Letters*, ed. Geoffrey Dutton and Max Harris (South Melbourne: Sun Books, 1968) p. 156.

3. Patrick White, *Flaws in the Glass: A Self-Portrait* (New York: Viking Press, 1981) p. 100.

4. For more on White's life, see his *Flaws in the Glass* and 'The Prodigal Son'; also Thelma Herring and G. A. Wilkes, 'A Conversation with Patrick White', *Southerly*, 33 (1973) 132–43; John Beston and Rose Marie Beston, 'A Brief Biography of Patrick White', *World Literature Written in English*, 12 (1973) 208–12; John Beston, 'The Family Background and Early Years of Patrick White', *Descent*, 7 (Sep 1974) 16–29; and John Beston, review of *Flaws in the Glass*, in *World Literature Written in English*, 21 (1982) 83–6.

5. John Hetherington, 'Patrick White: Life at Castle Hill', in his *Forty-Two Faces* (Melbourne: Cheshire, 1962; repr. Freeport, NY: Books for Libraries Press, 1969) p. 144.

6. *Nation*, 13 Jan 1962, p. 17.

7. Andrew Clark, 'The Private Patrick White', *New York Times Book Review*, 27 Apr 1980, p. 32.

8. Craig McGregor (ed.), *In the Making* (Melbourne: Nelson, 1969) p. 220.

9. See Leon Cantrell, 'Patrick White's First Book', *Australian Literary Studies*, 6 (1974) 434–6.

10. As Noel Macainsh reports. See 'The Poems of Patrick White', *LiNQ*, 4, nos 3–4 (1975) 18.

11. Thelma Herring, 'Odyssey of a Spinster: A Study of *The Aunt's Story*', in G. A. Wilkes (ed.), *Ten Essays on Patrick White: Selected from 'Southerly' (1964–67)* (Sydney: Angus & Robertson, 1970) p. 3.

CHAPTER ONE: AUSTRALIA: THE MYSTERY OF FAILURE

1. See G. A. Wilkes, *A Dictionary of Australian Colloquialisms* (Sydney: Sydney University Press, 1978) p. 109.

2. As Russell Ward reports. See 'The Social Fabric', in *The Pattern of Australian Culture*, ed. A. L. McLeod (Ithaca, NY: Cornell University Press, 1963) p. 109.

3. Manning Clark, *A Discovery of Australia*, 1976 Boyer Lectures (Sydney: Australian Broadcasting Commission, 1976) p. 17.

4. Ibid., p. 18. See also Manning Clark, *A Short History of Australia*, rev. edn (New York: Mentor, 1969) p. 17.

5. Clark, *Discovery*, p. 26.

6. Ibid., pp. 20 and 29.

7. Richard Campbell, 'The Character of Australian Religion', *Meanjin*, 36 (1977) 187–8. See also D. R. Burns, 'Australian Fiction versus Austrophobia', *Overland*, no. 90 (Dec 1982) 44–51; and Paul Sharrad, '*Pour mieux sauter:* Christopher Koch's Novels in Relation to White, Stow and the Quest for a Post-Colonial Fiction', *World Literature Written in English*, 23 (1984) 208–23.

8. Veronica Brady, 'The Novelist and the New World: Patrick White's *Voss*', *Texas Studies in Literature and Language*, 21 (1979) 173.

9. Geoffrey Dutton, 'Strength through Adversity', *Bulletin*, 29 Jan 1980, p. 129. For more on this theme in Australian literature, see also R. F. Brissenden, 'On the Edge of the Empire: Some Thoughts on Recent Australian Fiction', *Sewanee Review*, 87, no. 1 (Winter 1979) 147; and T. Inglis Moore, *Social Patterns in Australian Literature* (Berkeley, Calif.: University of California Press, 1971) *passim*.

10. David Martin has described this reigning critical temper as 'being dazzled by the bright, democratic foreground'. See his 'Among the Bones: What are our Novelists Looking for?', *Meanjin*, 18 (1959) 53.

11. This capsule summary of Phillips is offered by H. P. Heseltine in 'Australian Image: (1) The Literary Heritage', *Meanjin*, 21 (1962) 35; it should be noted, however, that Phillips does not entirely ignore darker themes in Australian literature. See also Brian Kiernan, *Images of Society and Nature: Seven Essays on Australian Novels* (Melbourne: Oxford University Press, 1971) ch. 7.

12. See, for example, Heseltine, 'Australian Image', *Meanjin*, 21, who traces this theme from Australia's nineteenth-century writers forward (pp. 40–6). Heseltine sees 'Australia's literary heritage as based on a unique combination of glances into the pit and the erection of safety fences to prevent any toppling in'.

13. All quotes are from White, 'The Prodigal Son', as repr. in *The Vital Decade*, pp. 156–8.

14. White, 'Flaws in the Glass: Sketches for a Self-Portrait', *Bulletin*, 29 Jan 1980, p. 151; see also *FG*, p. 70.

15. See, for example, Leonie Kramer, 'Patrick White's Götterdämmerung', *Quadrant*, 17, no. 3 (May–June 1973) 8–19; and Dorothy Green's response in her 'The Edge of Error', *Quadrant*, 17, nos 5–6 (Dec 1973) 36–47. See also Leonie Kramer, '*The Tree of Man*: An Essay in Skepticism', in W. S. Ramson (ed.), *The Australian Experience: Critical Essays on Australian Novels* (Canberra: Australian National University Press, 1974) pp. 269–83; and A. M. McCulloch, *A Tragic Vision: The Novels of Patrick White* (St Lucia: University of Queensland Press, 1983).

16. McGregor, *In the Making*, p. 218.

17. Peter Beatson, *The Eye in the Mandala: Patrick White: A Vision of Man and God* (London: Paul Elek, 1976) p. 167.

18. Herring and Wilkes, 'Conversation with White', *Southerly*, 33, pp. 136–7; and *FG*, pp. 143–5.

19. Jim Sharman, 'A Very Literary Luncheon', *National Times*, 30 June

1979, p. 27. See also Geraldine O'Brien, 'No-one Realises How Frivolous Patrick White Can Be', *Sydney Morning Herald*, 10 Dec 1983, p. 31.

20. McGregor, *In the Making*, p. 218.

21. Stephen E. Whicher (ed.), *Selections from Ralph Waldo Emerson* (Boston, Mass.: Houghton Mifflin, 1957) p. 102.

22. Michael Cotter would seem to agree. See his 'Fragmentation, Reconstitution and the Colonial Experience: The Aborigine in Patrick White's Fiction', in Chris Tiffin (ed.), *South Pacific Images* (St Lucia: South Pacific Association for Commonwealth Literature and Language Studies, 1978) p. 174.

23. Manly Johnson makes a similar point and links it to the part of the Australian self-image which grew out of Australia's experience as a penal colony. See his '*Twyborn*: The Abbess, the Bulbul, and the Bawdy House', *Modern Fiction Studies*, 27 (Spring 1981) 163.

24. Peter Beatson alludes briefly to this theme in White and locates it within a similar, albeit three-stage pattern of spiritual progress in the novels. See *The Eye in the Mandala*, p. 30. For a treatment of its specific relation to *Voss*, see Susan A. Wood, 'The Power and Failure of "Vision" in Patrick White's *Voss*', *Modern Fiction Studies*, 27 (Spring 1981) 141–58.

25. The nature of this unity and its apprehension have been the focus of much critical attention. The best and most interesting fruits of this inquiry are to be found in Patricia Morley, *The Mystery of Unity: Theme and Technique in the Novels of Patrick White* (Montreal and London: McGill–Queen's University Press, 1972); Beatson's *The Eye in the Mandala*; and William J. Scheick, 'The Gothic Grace and Rainbow Aesthetic of Patrick White's Fiction: An Introduction', *Texas Studies in Literature and Language*, 21 (1979) 131–46.

26. Herring and Wilkes, 'Conversation with White', *Southerly*, 33, pp. 138–9.

27. White, 'Prodigal Son', in *The Vital Decade*, p. 158.

28. McGregor, *In the Making*, p. 219.

29. A good idea of the nature and range of critical concerns raised in current discussions of White can be had by consulting Adrian Mitchell, 'Eventually White's Language: Words and More than Words', and John Colmer, 'Appendix: Two Critical Positions, 1', both in Ron Shepherd and Kirpal Singh (eds), *Patrick White: A Critical Symposium* (Adelaide: Centre for Research in the New Literatures in English, 1978) pp. 5–16 and 135–6. For the directions one of White's best and most conscientious critics thinks White criticism should take in future, see Alan Lawson, 'Meaning and Experience: A Review–Essay on Some Recurrent Problems in Patrick White Criticism', *Texas Studies in Literature and Language*, 21 (1979) 280–95.

30. See, for example, John McLaren, 'Patrick White's Use of Imagery', in Clement Semmler (ed.), *Twentieth Century Australian Literary Criticism* (Melbourne: Oxford University Press, 1967) pp. 269–71; Peter Shrubb, 'Chaos Accepted', *Quadrant*, 3, no. 3 (1968) 14; and R. F. Brissenden, *Patrick White*, Writers and their Work, no. 190, rev. edn (Harlow: Longmans, Green, 1969) pp. 32–4. This sort of criticism is carried to its illogical extremes by Jack Beasley in the Marxist journal *Realist Writer*, no. 9 (1962) 11–14. See also the statement by that journal's editorial board in no. 12 (1963) 3–4.

31. For example, see John Colmer, 'Duality in Patrick White', in Shepherd and Singh, *White: A Critical Symposium*, pp. 70–6.

32. As Manfred Mackenzie does; see his 'Patrick White's Later Novels: A Generic Reading', *Southern Review*, 1 (1965) 5–18.

33. Veronica Brady, 'The Novelist and the Reign of Necessity: Patrick White and Simone Weil', in Shepherd and Singh, *White: A Critical Symposium*, pp. 108–16.

34. Mackenzie himself suggests such a ground. See Manfred Mackenzie. 'Yes, Let's Return to Abyssinia', *Essays in Criticism*, 14 (1964) 435.

CHAPTER TWO: THE EARLY WORKS: ANATOMY OF FAILURE

1. There was also another, unpublished novel, written between *Happy Valley* and *The Living and the Dead*. White claims to have destroyed the manuscript before leaving the Sydney suburb of Castle Hill for his current residence in Sydney's Centennial Park. See Thelma Herring and G. A. Wilkes, 'A Conversation with Patrick White', *Southerly*, 33 (1973) 136.

2. For speculation of the significance of names in *Happy Valley*, particularly the name 'Hagan' as it appears in Germanic and Scandinavian legends and in Wagner's *Ring des Nibelungen*, see Morley, *The Mystery of Unity*, pp. 43–4; and Ingmar Björksten, *Patrick White: A General Introduction*, tr. Stanley Gerson (St Lucia: University of Queensland Press, 1976) p. 30. See also Peter Wolfe, *Laden Choirs: The Fiction of Patrick White* (Lexington: University Press of Kentucky, 1983) ch. 2, for parallels and echoes in White's treatment of the two affairs.

3. Morley, *The Mystery of Unity*, p. 46.

4. Barry Argyle, *Patrick White* (New York: Barnes & Noble, 1967) p. 13.

5. Patricia Brent, 'The Novelist Patrick White Talks to Patricia Brent. He Has Just Been Awarded the Nobel Prize for Literature', *Listener*, 25 Oct 1973, p. 545.

6. See Brian Kiernan, 'The Novelist and the Modern World', in Don Anderson and Stephen Knight (eds), *Cunning Exiles: Studies of Modern Prose Writers* (London: Angus & Robertson, 1974) p. 82.

7. Adelaide herself is something of a Gudrun, albeit a flighty and domesticated one, and, to complete the parallel, she has a husband named Gerald.

8. That there *is* an explicit and unequivocal theme or 'message' can be said of no other White novel. The fact marks one of the book's principal weaknesses.

9. See Herring, 'Odyssey of a Spinster', in Wilkes, *Ten Essays on Patrick White*, p. 6.

10. David Tacey suggests that these are mandalic symbols. See his 'Denying the Shadow as the Day Lengthens: Patrick White's *The Living and the Dead*', *Southern Review*, 11 (July 1978) 170.

11. Brissenden, *Patrick White*, p. 13.

12. See Manfred Mackenzie, 'Abyssinia Lost and Regained', *Essays in Criticism*, 13 (1963) 293; Herring, 'Odyssey of a Spinster', in Wilkes, *Ten Essays on Patrick White*, p. 14; and D. R. Burns, *The Directions of Australian Fiction, 1920–74* (North Melbourne: Cassell Australia, 1975) p. 162.

13. As White himself comes close to admitting. See *FG*, p. 63.

14. McGregor, *In the Making*, p. 219. White makes a similar remark in *FG*, p. 77.

15. An interesting exception to this trend is J. F. Burrows. See his ' "Jardin Exotique": The Central Phase of *The Aunt's Story*', in Wilkes, *Ten Essays on Patrick White*, pp. 85–108. This essay offers an illuminating study of the second section of the novel, a longstanding critical bugaboo.

16. Northrop Frye, *Fearful Symmetry: A Study of William Blake* (Princeton, NJ: Princeton University Press, 1947) pp. 212–13.

17. For speculation on *The Aunt's Story* as an allegory generally and particularly an allegory of *Rasselas*, see Mackenzie, 'Patrick White's Later Novels', *Southern Review*, 1, pp. 5–18.

18. See Frye's *Anatomy of Criticism: Four Essays* (Princeton, NJ: Princeton University Press, 1957) pp. 141–50. This point about White's use of imagery is also made by Peter Beatson in his *The Eye in the Mandala*, p. 136.

19. *The Aunt's Story* is laced with references to the *Odyssey*, and the novel's characters take on different roles at different times. Theodora, for example, is variously Nausicaä, Telemachus and Odysseus himself. For an exploration of White's use of Homeric reference, see Herring, 'Odyssey of a Spinster', in Wilkes, *Ten Essays on Patrick White*, pp. 3–20.

20. J. F. Burrows, in a perceptive study of this section of the novel, describes Theodora's interactions with the other guests at the Hôtel du Midi as having two phases: first, 'That where, in Sokolnikov's words, Theodora "creates the illusion of other people"; and [secondly,] that where, "once created, they choose their own realities"' (*AS*, p. 239). During the first phase, Theodora is 'facing her own problems in the subtly altered perspectives that these other lives afford'. In the second phase, she is very often helping others to face their problems through her perspective. See Burrows, ' "*Jardin Exotique*" ', in Wilkes, *Ten Essays on Patrick White*, pp. 89–90.

21. The whole question of Jung's influence on White is an extremely vexed one. Especially since White made explicit use of the Jungian concept of the mandala in *The Solid Mandala*, Jungian readings of most of his other novels have been offered. But, in a footnote to such a reading of *The Aunt's Story*, David Tacey admits that White did not read Jung until the early sixties. And, in a later piece for *Australian Literary Studies*, Tacey concludes that White's use of Jungian archetypes and concepts makes a better case for Jung's claims regarding the role of the unconscious in the creative process than for White's deliberate borrowing from Jung. See Tacey's 'The Secret of the Black Rose: Spiritual Alchemy in Patrick White's *The Aunt's Story*', *Adelaide ALS Working Papers*, 2, no. 2 (Mar 1977) 78; and his 'Patrick White: Misconceptions about Jung's Influence', *Australian Literary Studies*, 9 (1979) 245–6. We also have in evidence White's 1973 reply to Ingmar Björksten, when asked about Jung's influence on him: 'You are fairly right in the line you seem to be taking, but I should play down the Jung part. I have great admiration for him and his findings, but I also have a belief in a supernatural power of which I have been given inklings from time to time . . . ' (Björksten, *White: A General Introduction*, p. 24). I think it wisest to follow White's advice and 'play down the Jung part', despite his recent admission of Jung's importance to him (*FG*, p. 146).

22. Carl Jung, *Collected Works*, tr. R. F. C. Hull, Bollingen Series xx, ix.ii (New York: Pantheon Books, 1959) p. 71.

23. Acquaintances upon whom some of these characters were based are described in *FG*, pp. 76–7.

24. Burrows agrees; see ' "*Jardin Exotique*" ', in Wilkes, *Ten Essays on Patrick White*, p. 106.

25. See Herring and Wilkes, 'Conversation with White', *Southerly*, 33, p. 135.

26. Mackenzie, 'Patrick White's Later Novels', *Southern Review*, 1, p. 12.

27. Björksten, *White: A General Introduction*, p. 30.

28. See Joseph Campbell, *The Hero with a Thousand Faces*, Bollingen Series XVII, 2nd edn (Princeton, NJ: Princeton University Press, 1968) esp. pp. 73, 152–4, and 162. The hermaphrodite carries the same implications in Plato's *Symposium*. See Edith Hamilton and Huntington Cairns (eds), *The Collected Dialogues of Plato, Including the Letters*, Bollingen Series LXXI (Princeton, NJ: Princeton University Press, 1963) pp. 542–6.

29. Recently in Andrew Clark, 'The Private Patrick White', *New York Times Book Review*, 27 Apr 1980, p. 32; and *FG*, p. 145.

30. McGregor, *In the Making*, p. 220; see also *FG*, pp. 143–4.

31. See Herring and Wilkes, 'Conversation with White', *Southerly*, 33, p. 135; and *FG*, pp. 127–9.

32. White, 'Flaws in the Glass: Sketches', *Bulletin*, 29 Jan 1980, p. 151; see also *FG*, pp. 20–2.

33. 'Patrick White Interviewed by Rodney Wetherell about Art and the Novel', National Library of Australia, NLA/TRC551, cassette (n.d.); and *FG*, p. 144.

34. White, 'The Prodigal Son', in *The Vital Decade*, p. 157.

35. Herring and Wilkes, 'Conversation with White', *Southerly*, 33, pp. 136–7. See also *FG*, pp. 143–5, where White recounts in more detail his recovery of religious faith and suggests that, like many of his characters, he could find faith only when 'truly humbled'.

36. Herring and Wilkes, 'Conversation with White', *Southerly*, 33, p. 136.

37. This sentence has always recalled to me lines from the Dylan Thomas poem, 'Light Breaks Where No Sun Shines': 'Light breaks on secret lots,/On tips of thought where thoughts smell in the rain'. The implications of poet and novelist are similar, but I have no indication of any influence.

38. The incident recalls the blind man whose sight was restored when Christ anointed his eyes with clay moulded from His spittle (see John 9:1–7). If the echo is deliberate, it suggests that Stan's God is immanent in even the lowliest forms of matter. I do not wish to enter far into the continuing argument over whether that God *is* immanent, transcendent, both or neither. However, a sampling of critical opinion will suggest the terms of this debate.

G. A. Wilkes concludes that 'For all the insistence in *The Tree of Man* on immersing oneself in the ordinariness of living, the novel itself shows that fulfilment lies in liberation from that condition – lies in divinely sanctioned transcendence.' See G. A. Wilkes and I. C. Reid, *The Literatures of the British Commonwealth: Australia and New Zealand*, gen. ed. A. L. McLeod (University Park: Pennsylvania State University Press, 1970) p. 114.

Patricia Morley shifts this emphasis a bit, insisting that 'Stan's discovery of God in a gob of spittle . . . is a profoundly orthodox expression of the Christian doctrine of the divine transcendence as immanent in this created world, one which follows from belief in the Incarnation of God as man.' See *The Mystery of Unity*, p. 114.

On the other hand, A. P. Riemer decides that Stan's affirmation that God is in a gob of spittle 'is man's confirmation of his own divinity', and that Stan is thereby 'able to perceive that man must find in himself his own divinity, his own very private grandeur'. See his 'Visions of the Mandala in *The Tree of Man*', in Wilkes, *Ten Essays on Patrick White*, p. 120.

And Leonie Kramer, who has begun to say this sort of thing about all

White's novels, claims that 'Stan discovers . . . neither the immanence nor the transcendence of God, but God's irrelevance. Only after spitting out God is he able to see that "One, and no other figure, is the answer to all sums". . . . his expulsion of God at the end is a rational act, backed by his full realisation of his human powers. . . . He no longer needs supernatural support.' See Kramer's '*The Tree of Man*: An Essay in Skepticism', in Ramson, *The Australian Experience*, p. 277.

My own opinion is that Stan's spitting *out* a God who is present in a gob of spittle is deliberately contrasted with his earlier spitting *at* an absent God after discovering Amy's infidelity (*TM*, p. 345). The point seems to be that the God he had once emptied out of himself has re-entered and permeated him. God is now inside, outside and everywhere, to be found in everything. Thus I would answer Riemer and Kramer. But since White has answered them himself, stressing time and again in published interviews and statements his belief in God and the importance of that belief to his work, the whole debate seems a bit foolish.

39. Marjorie Barnard, 'The Four Novels of Patrick White', *Meanjin*, 15 (1956) 156–70.

40. Quoted in Alan Lawson, 'Unmerciful Dingoes?: The Critical Reception of Patrick White', *Meanjin*, 32 (1973) 382. The sentences to which White refers are to be found in Barnard, 'Four Novels', *Meanjin*, 15, pp. 166 and 170.

41. A number of critics have examined the novel's four-part structure, both seasonal and symphonic, and have pointed to the way in which natural disasters punctuate the seasons of the Parker's lives. See, for example, Björksten, *White: A General Introduction*, p. 47; Brissenden, *Patrick White*, pp. 21–2; Mackenzie, 'Patrick White's Later Novels', *Southern Review*, 1, pp. 14–15; and Morley, *The Mystery of Unity*, p. 99. Vincent Buckley offers an interesting variation on the prevailing view by seeing the natural disaster as initiating rather than culminating or recapitulating a phase in the Parkers' development. See his 'Patrick White and his Epic', in Grahame Johnston (ed.), *Australian Literary Criticism* (Melbourne: Oxford University Press, 1962) p. 190.

42. The flood and the man stuck in the tree may recall to the reader Tom Brangwen of D. H. Lawrence's *The Rainbow*, who is drowned in a flood and found in a hedge. In fact, much about Stan and Amy (their characters, relationship, and respective attitudes toward religion) seems reminiscent of the earlier novel's Tom and Anna Brangwen. Moreover, the language of both works is sometimes similarly biblical in phrasing and cadence. Obviously, then, Lawrence continues an influence although not so transparently as in White's first two novels. Vincent Buckley treats some facets of the influence of Lawrence and specifically *The Rainbow* on *The Tree of Man*; see 'White and his Epic', in Johnston, *Australian Literary Criticism*, pp. 187–97.

43. We may, in these instances, be penetrating Amy's mind and overhearing her own thoughts about herself. Point of view cannot be attributed with absolute certainty. Still, this is probably the narrator's view of Amy, since she would never allow herself to progress so far towards self-recognition.

44. See Ch. 2, n. 34.

45. G. A. Wilkes, 'Patrick White's *The Tree of Man*', in *Ten Essays on Patrick White*, p. 24.

46. A. D. Hope, 'The Bunyip Stages a Comeback', *Sydney Morning Herald*, 16 June 1956, p. 15.

47. See Lawson, 'Unmerciful Dingoes?', *Meanjin*, 32, p. 381.

48. As Nancy Keesing notes in her introduction to *Australian Postwar Novelists: Selected Critical Essays* (Milton, Queensland: Jacaranda Press, 1975) pp. 3–4.

CHAPTER THREE: THE MAJOR PHASE: THE MYSTERY OF FAILURE

1. White, 'Flaws in the Glass: Sketches', *Bulletin*, 29 Jan 1980, p. 152; and *FG*, p. 103.

2. For related views of the function of success and failure in this novel, see Wood, 'The Power and Failure of "Vision" in *Voss*', *Modern Fiction Studies*, 27, pp. 141–58; and Wolfe, *Laden Choirs*, pp. 112–13.

3. White encourages such a perspective on these characters in *Flaws in the Glass* by identifying 'the Brown brothers as my two halves' (p. 146) and admitting 'knowing Voss–Laura to be myself' (p. 197).

4. On this point, also see Morley, *The Mystery of Unity*, pp. 120–1.

5. How much the character of Voss owes to various historical and philosophical sources and prototypes is the subject of endless debate. White's published statements on the genesis of *Voss* and his aims in creating the character are to be found in Ian Moffitt, 'Talk with Patrick White', *New York Times Book Review*, 18 Aug 1957, p. 18; Hetherington, 'Patrick White: Life at Castle Hill', in his *Forty-Two Faces*, p. 144; in two of White's essays: 'The Prodigal Son', in *The Vital Decade*, p. 157, and 'Flaws in the Glass: Sketches', *Bulletin*, 29 Jan 1980, p. 152; and in *FG*, pp. 103–04. In addition, see White's remarks in correspondence, quoted by James McAuley in his 'The Gothic Splendours: Patrick White's *Voss*', in Wilkes, *Ten Essays on Patrick White*, p. 37.

Readers interested in similarities between the character and experience of Voss and the characters and experiences of historical Australian explorers, especially Eyre and Leichhardt, should consult J. F. Burrows, '*Voss* and the Explorers', *AUMLA*, 26 (1966) 234–40; and Don D. Walker, 'The Western Explorer as Literary Hero: Jedediah Smith and Ludwig Leichhardt', *Western Humanities Review*, 25 (1975) 243–59. Among the primary sources are Daniel Bunce, *Travels with Dr Leichhardt in Australia* (1859; repr. Melbourne: Oxford University Press, 1979); A. H. Chisholm, *Strange New World* (Sydney: Angus & Robertson, 1941); and E. M. Webster, *Whirlwind on the Plain: Ludwig Leichhardt, Friends, Foes, and History* (Melbourne: Melbourne University Press, 1980); as well as Eyre's and Leichhardt's journals. For the journals, see Ludwig Leichhardt, *Journal of an Overland Expedition in Australia from Moreton Bay to Port Essington* (London, 1847) Australiana Facsimile Editions, no. 16 (Adelaide: Libraries Board of South Australia, 1964); and Edward John Eyre, *Journals of Expeditions of Discovery into Central Australia, and Overland From Adelaide to King George's Sound*, 2 vols (London, 1845), Australiana Facsimile Editions, no. 7 (Adelaide: Libraries Board of South Australia, 1964).

Nietzsche is frequently evoked in discussions of *Voss*, despite the evidence of a 1973 letter to Ingmar Björksten, in which White writes, 'I've read very little Nietzsche – some of *Also Sprach Zarathustra* when I was at Cambridge. He doesn't appeal to me.' See Björksten's *White: A General Introduction*, p. 59. Among the recent treatments of this issue are Carlene Keig, 'Nietzsche's Influence on Australian Literature', *Adelaide ALS Working Papers*, 1, no. 2 (Oct 1975) 50–63;

Keith Garebian, 'The Desert and the Garden: The Theme of Completeness in *Voss*', *Modern Fiction Studies*, 22 (Winter 1976–7) 569; and two works by Ann McCulloch: 'Patrick White's Novels and Nietzsche', *Australian Literary Studies*, 9 (1980) 309–20; and *A Tragic Vision*. Others find that the novel owes more to Hegel and Schopenhauer. See, for example, Dorothy Green, '*Voss*: Stubborn Music', in Ramson, *The Australian Experience*, pp. 304–5; and J. Cowburn, 'The Metaphysics of *Voss*', *Twentieth Century*, 18 (Winter 1964) 352–61. Still others, such as Patricia Morley, conjecture about a debt to Kierkegaard (see *Mystery of Unity*, p. 131), while John Coates notes aspects of *Voss* which recall the thought of Jacob Boehme. See Coates's '*Voss* and Jacob Boehme: A Note on the Spirituality of Patrick White', *Australian Literary Studies*, 9 (1979) 119–22.

6. Veronica Brady, 'The Hard Enquiring Wind: A Study of Patrick White as an Australian Novelist', dissertation (University of Toronto, 1969) p. 88.

7. One critic feels that she does not escape this danger. See Peter Beatson, 'The Three Stages: Mysticism in Patrick White's *Voss*', *Southerly*, 30 (1970) 118.

8. Robert Langbaum, *The Poetry of Experience: The Dramatic Monologue in Modern Literary Tradition* (1957; repr. New York: Norton, 1963) pp. 63–4.

9. For another approach to *Voss* as allegory, see Brissenden, *Patrick White*, pp. 25–30.

10. Sometimes feminine and canine are conflated. For example, shortly after shooting the mongrel bitch ostensibly because she is of no use to the expedition, but actually as a means of punishing himself for loving her, Voss thinks of Laura's 'soft coat of love' and imagines her as 'dog-eyed love' itself (*V*, pp. 264–5).

11. For an interpretation of Judd as Judas, see Martin, 'Among the Bones', *Meanjin*, 18, p. 54. Veronica Brady, while she does not call Judd a Judas, places herself in this camp by suggesting that he is punished for his desertion of Voss with the death of his family and loss of his land. See her 'The Novelist and the New World', *Texas Studies in Literature and Language*, 21, pp. 180–1. For discussion of Judd as natural man, or for McAuley a 'Caliban', see McAuley, 'The Gothic Splendours', in Wilkes, *Ten Essays on Patrick White*, pp. 39–40; Green, '*Voss*: Stubborn Music', in Ramson, *The Australian Experience*, pp. 294–8; and Morley, *Mystery of Unity*, pp. 135–9.

Other critics, however, assign a very different role to Judd. To Geoffrey Dutton, for example, he is 'a sort of angel of judgment' sent by Sanderson to 'scourge' Voss. See his *Patrick White*, 4th edn, Australian Writers and their Work, gen. ed. Grahame Johnston (Melbourne: Oxford University Press, 1971) p. 24. And, for W. D. Ashcroft, Judd is the 'true visionary' who knows that 'transcendence is immanent in the experience of ordinary reality'. See his 'More than One Horizon', in Shepherd and Singh, *White: A Critical Symposium*, p. 128.

12. Critical opinion on Palfreyman has also varied widely. For Geoffrey Dutton, Palfreyman 'deserves' his martyrdom (see *Patrick White*, p. 26), and, for James McAuley, Palfreyman's death may allow Voss to reject Christian sacrifice as meaningless and to substitute his own concept of sacrifice (see 'The Gothic Splendours', in Wilkes, *Ten Essays on Patrick White*, p. 39). Conversely, for John Rorke, Palfreyman's death may be the very sacrifice which atones for Voss's sin in Christian terms. See his 'Patrick White and the Critics', *Southerly*, 20 (1959) 71.

13. See, for example, Hilary Heltay, 'The Novels of Patrick White', *Southerly*, 33 (1973) 95. She discusses nature in the novel as the 'objective correlative of

the landscapes of the soul'. Another writer, William Walsh, finds the implications of landscape in *Voss* to be almost Wordsworthian. See his *Patrick White: 'Voss'*, Studies in English Literature no. 62, gen. ed. David Daiches (London: Edward Arnold, 1976) p. 27. For conjecture on the handling of landscape in a projected film of *Voss*, see David Mercer, 'A Film Script of *Voss*: Interview by Rodney Wetherell', *Australian Literary Studies*, 8 (1978) 395–401.

14. Whether or not this communication is 'telepathic' and, if so, whether or not White is justified in using it are today questions of little more than historical interest. Readers wishing to pursue the matter should consult Margaret Walters, who refuses to accept the 'telepathic intimacy' of Voss and Laura – 'Patrick White', *New Left Review*, no. 18 (1963) p. 45; Peter Wolfe, who finds that such communication works against the novel's emphasis on the 'palpable, contingent world' (*Laden Choirs*, pp. 117–18); James McAuley, who defends its inclusion ('Gothic Splendours', in Wilkes, *Ten Essays on Patrick White*, p. 41); Noel Macainsh, who sees it as part of an overall structure which endorses non-conventional over conventional forms of communications – 'Voss and his Communications – A Structural Contrast', *Australian Literary Studies*, 10 (1982) 437–47; and John Rorke, who claims that Voss's and Laura's relationship and communication involve no 'mysticism' and are explicable in naturalistic terms ('Patrick White and the Critics', *Southerly*, 20, p. 72). White's own opinion on what constitutes 'dream material' is offered in a 1973 letter to Ingmar Björksten (cited in Björksten's *White: A General Introduction*, p. 3), where he claims that he is often uncertain himself whether something has actually happened or been dreamed, imagined, or remembered from one of his books.

15. Earlier in the novel, lilies have been associated with Laura and with sexual union (*V*, pp. 184–6). For more on the significance of lily imagery in the novel, see Sylvia Gzell, 'Themes and Imagery in *Voss* and *Riders in the Chariot*', in Clement Semmler (ed.), *Twentieth Century Australian Literary Criticism* (Melbourne: Oxford University Press, 1967) p. 262.

16. Brian Kiernan also suspects that Laura's humility may be inverted pride. See his *Images of Society and Nature*, p. 118.

17. Despite the fact that she does so function, White has insisted that no allusion to Petrarch was intended in Laura's name. See Herring and Wilkes, 'Conversation with White', *Southerly*, 33, p. 141.

18. White, 'The Prodigal Son', in *The Vital Decade*, p. 157.

19. Quoted in Frederick W. Dillistone, *Patrick White's 'Riders in the Chariot': Introduction and Commentary*, Religious Dimensions in Literature, gen. ed. Lee A. Belford (New York: Seabury Press, 1967) p. 11.

20. 'The Harp and the King', quoted in Wilkes and Reid, *The Literatures of the British Commonwealth: Australia and New Zealand*, p. 138.

21. See Carl Jung, *Collected Works*, tr. R. F. C. Hull, Bollingen Series XX, XI (New York: Pantheon Books, 1958) p. 190.

22. For Patricia Morley, the Riders together make up one perfect man (see *Mystery of Unity*, p. 173). Dorothy Green links the Riders to Blake's four Zoas. See her 'The Edge of Error', *Quadrant*, 17, nos 5–6, pp. 45–6. Frederick Dillistone relates the four Riders to the elements and to components of Australian society (see *White's 'Riders in the Chariot'*, pp. 12, 20); while Edgar Chapman identifies each rider not only with an element, but also a Jungian faculty, mystical tradition, and bodily sense. See his 'The Mandala Design of Patrick White's

Riders in the Chariot', *Texas Studies in Literature and Language*, 21 (1979) 188.

23. See Adolphe Franck, *The Kabbalah: The Religious Philosophy of the Hebrews* (New York: Bell, 1940) p. 117.

24. It is frequently alleged by critics that the evil which Mrs Flack and Mrs Jolley set in motion is insufficiently motivated. See, for example, J. F. Burrows, 'Archetypes and Stereotypes: *Riders in the Chariot'*, in Wilkes, *Ten Essays on Patrick White*, pp. 65–6. Others, however, have argued with John Colmer that these women's actions are credible. See his *'Riders in the Chariot'*, *Patrick White*, Studies in Australian Literature (Melbourne: Edward Arnold Australia, 1978) p. 42. A related objection is the unlikelihood of the crucifixion. As R. F. Brissenden and others have said, it is hard to believe that Blue and his mates would be either malicious or inventive enough to conceive of the mock crucifixion (see Brissenden, *Patrick White*, p. 33). But White has not committed himself to writing a naturalistic work. Moreover, he believes that such atrocities are all too likely.

25. As Brissenden believes; see *Patrick White*, pp. 32–34.

26. See White's *Reimpression de Les Prix Nobel en 1973 Biography* (The Nobel Foundation, 1974) p. 224. Also see *FG*, p. 112.

27. For more on the function of these interlocked processions, see Morley, *Mystery of Unity*, p. 181.

28. See Jim Sharman, 'A Very Literary Luncheon', *National Times*, 30 June 1979, p. 26; and Andrew Clark, 'The Private Patrick White', *New York Times Book Review*, 27 Apr 1980, p. 32.

29. Herring and Wilkes, 'Conversation with White', *Southerly*, 33, p. 138.

30. Robert M. Adams, *Strains of Discord: Studies in Literary Openness* (Ithaca, NY: Cornell University Press, 1958) pp. 80–1.

31. Whicher (ed.), *Selections from Ralph Waldo Emerson*, p. 219.

32. For more on Adam Kadmon, see Jung's *Collected Works*, xi, 55–6. This Adam Kadmon is also said to be the figure which dominates Ezekiel's chariot, one of the models for the novel's chariot visions. The Kabbalah has been regarded by some as an instrument for 'lowering the barriers' between Christianity and Judaism, one of the novel's concerns. See Franck, *The Kabbalah*, pp. 77, 90–1 and 193. For the role of the Shekinah and its associations with the feminine, see ibid., p. 103; and Adin Steinsaltz, *The Thirteen Petalled Rose*, tr. Yehuda Hanegbi (New York: Basic Books, 1980) pp. 52, 97 and 176.

Kabbalistic concepts and references, especially in regard to the novel's chariot symbolism, have been explicated by several critics. See, for example, Mackenzie, 'Abyssinia Lost and Regained', *Essays in Criticism*, 13, 296–97; Burrows, 'Archetypes and Stereotypes', in Wilkes, *Ten Essays on Patrick White*, pp. 47–71; and Colin Roderick, *'Riders in the Chariot*: An Exposition', *Southerly*, 22 (1962) 62–77.

For the sources of the passages Himmelfarb reads in mystical treatises, see Chapman, 'The Mandala Design', *Texas Studies in Literature and Language*, 21, pp. 193 and 201.

33. Peter Beatson agrees, calling Mary's project a 'heresy of reduction'. See his *The Eye in the Mandala*, p. 86.

34. Despite the similarity in their names, Ruth Godbold bears little resemblance to Professor Godbole of E. M. Forster's *Passage to India*. She has not his subtle mind nor his grasp of philosophical complexities. However, with the

other Riders, she does contribute to a world view which Godbole would endorse, the belief that good and evil are both aspects of the Lord and that the lack of clear distinctions constitutes meaning rather than blurring it.

35. Interestingly, Tom Godbold meets Ruth Joyner when he, the new iceman, delivers ice to the house where she works as a servant.

36. Miss Docker, however, differs from Ruth Godbold in that the former's 'good deeds' are motivated not by love, but by the lust for power over others. Miss Docker uses charity to bludgeon people into submission.

37. See Steinsaltz, *The Thirteen Petalled Rose*, p. 28. White's primary source for Judaism was probably Gershom Sholem, *Major Trends in Jewish Mysticism* (New York: Schocken, 1961).

38. See Franck, *The Kabbalah*, pp. 15–21 and 117. For more on White's use of the Merkabah tradition, see Mackenzie, 'Abyssinia Lost and Regained', *Essays in Criticism*, 13, pp. 296–7.

39. See Steinsaltz, *The Thirteen Petalled Rose*, pp. 17–18.

40. Of course, virtually everyone who writes on the novel has something to say about the chariot, and most are in rough agreement as to its function. A marked exception is Leonie Kramer, who suggests that the chariot vision may be a projection of the Riders' delusions. See her 'Patrick White's Götterdämmerung', *Quadrant*, 17, no. 3, p. 11; and see Dorothy Green's rebuttal in 'The Edge of Error', *Quadrant*, 17, nos 5–6, p. 44. For the relationship of chariot symbology to the novel's theme of failure, see Wolfe, *Laden Choirs*, pp. 126–7.

41. For speculation on other functions of Xanadu in the novel, particularly the motif of Xanadu as Eden, see Burrows, 'Archetypes and Stereotypes' in Wilkes, *Ten Essays on Patrick White*, pp. 60–2.

42. Jung frequently attaches these suggestions to the concepts of duality, trinity and quaternity. See, for example, his *Collected Works*, XI, 57–9, 118–28 and 187–8.

43. Manning Clark, an historian and personal friend of White's, has said that for White the most damning sin is to destroy in another the capacity to love (in conversation, Canberra, Australia, Nov. 1979).

44. White's 'Clay' shares little with Joyce's *Dubliners* story of that name except that both convey the helpless futility of the central character's life and the affinity he has with death.

45. 'Mandalas' appears as an appendix to *The Archetypes and the Collective Unconscious*, in Jung's *Collected Works*, tr. R. F. C. Hull, Bollingen Series XX, IX.i (New York: Pantheon Books, 1959) pp. 387–90. White has acknowledged being greatly influenced by Jung's *Psychology and Alchemy* when writing *The Solid Mandala* (see *FG*, p. 146).

46. For Jung's comments on this, see his *Collected Works*, IX.ii, 69–70.

47. William Walsh has discussed the novel's structure as a series of concentric circles, and Michael Cotter finds that it approximates to the mandalic symbol. See Walsh's *Patrick White's Fiction* (Totowa, NJ: Rowman & Littlefield, 1977) p. 87; and Cotter's 'The Function of Imagery in Patrick White's Novels', in Shepherd and Singh, *White: A Critical Symposium*, pp. 22–3.

48. This issue will be examined in Ch. 5.

49. White's very sensitive and successful use of indirect discourse perhaps accounts for the surprising conclusion by some critics that Waldo is a sympathetic

character, or is at least less ruthlessly exposed than Mrs Flack and Mrs Jolley. For this point of view, see, for example, Kiernan, *Images of Society and Nature*, p. 128; and Wilkes and Reid, *The Literatures of the British Commonwealth: Australia and New Zealand*, p. 118. Others, such as Thelma Herring, however, believe that Waldo is denied White's compassion. See her 'Self and Shadow: The Quest for Totality in *The Solid Mandala*', in Wilkes, *Ten Essays on Patrick White*, p. 77.

50. This remark recalls Conrad's famous statement in his Preface to *The Nigger of the 'Narcissus'*: 'My task which I am trying to achieve is by the power of the written word, to make you hear, to make you feel – it is, before all, to make you *see*'. However, Arthur's speech obviously places Conrad's project in an ironic perspective.

51. This passage appears in a footnote to Jung's *Psychology and Alchemy*, in his *Collected Works*, tr. R. F. C. Hull, Bollingen Series xx, xii (New York: Pantheon Books, 1953) p. 144. It suggests that White may have read at least some Jung before writing *Riders in the Chariot*, since the passage recalls Himmelfarb's dream of himself as Adam Kadmon carrying his bride under his left breast (see *RC*, p. 472).

52. Thelma Herring has noticed the association, evident in this passage, of Dulcie with the moon and whiteness and of Mrs Poulter with the sun and sun colours. See her 'A Note on Some Recurrent Images in *The Solid Mandala*', in Kessing, *Australian Postwar Novelists*, pp. 206–7.

53 Surely the pun on 'poltergeist' is intentional, but its implications are unclear. Perhaps the suggestion is that the spirit of the times is a mischievous and malicious sprite unrelated to the divine spirit which has presided over other ages.

54. Several other critics have also concluded that Arthur himself becomes the 'dwelling of the god' and the solid mandala. See H. G. Kippax, 'The Dwelling of the God', *Sydney Morning Herald*, 14 May 1966, p. 15; Herring, 'Self and Shadow' in Wilkes, *Ten Essays on Patrick White*, p. 81; and Morley, *Mystery of Unity*, p. 207. White himself has indicated that persons may function as 'solid mandalas' (*FG*, p. 116; see also p. 100). Ann McCulloch, on the other hand, believes that Arthur is not the bearer of Christ but 'a replacement for Christ'. See *A Tragic Vision*, pp. 32–3.

55. Manfred Mackenzie, on the other hand, contends that Arthur discovers the Grand Inquisitor in himself and suffers a crucifixion into self-consciousness. See his 'The Consciousness of "Twin Consciousness": Patrick White's *The Solid Mandala*', *Novel*, 2, no. 3 (Spring 1969) 248–51.

56. Quoted in the introduction by Harold Rosenberg to Fyodor Dostoyevsky, *The Idiot*, tr. Henry and Olga Carlisle (New York: New American Library, 1969) p. vii.

57. See Jung, *Collected Works*, ix. ii, 42–4 and 62–9.

58. See Jung, *Collected Works*, xi, 121 and 180–8.

59. McGregor, *In the Making*, p. 220.

60. Mackenzie, 'The Consciousness of "Twin Consciousness" ', *Novel*, 2, no. 3, p. 253.

61. His other likely choice would have been a musician, but, of course, the musician Kathy Volkov figures significantly in the novel. Musicians also appear in several other White novels. Alys Browne of *Happy Valley* is a pianist of sorts, and in *The Living and the Dead* Catherine Standish's last lover is a saxophonist.

The cellist Moraïtis takes a small but significant role in *The Aunt's Story*, as does Professor Topp in *Voss*. Finally, Dulcie of *The Solid Mandala*, while a somewhat indifferent musician, is an ardent music lover, as is Arthur.

62. White, 'The Prodigal Son', in *The Vital Decade*, p. 157.

63. McGregor, *In the Making*, p. 218.

64. See Herring and Wilkes, 'Conversation with White', *Southerly*, 33, pp. 138–9; and *FG*, pp. 60 and 150.

65. White has several times described his own artistic enterprise in similar terms. In a 1970 interview he says, 'I can write only the way it comes out. Or rather, it half comes out. The rest is dragged out with forceps.' See Elizabeth Riddell, 'A Morning at Mr White's', *Australian*, 1 Aug 1970, p. 15; repr. in *The Armchair Australian, 1969–70*, ed. James Hall (Sydney: Ibis, 1970) p. 105. A few years later, he told another interviewer that novels 'continue to force their way out of me'. See 'Patrick White Interviewed by Rodney Wetherell about Art and the Novel'. Finally, in *Flaws in the Glass*, he describes 'the resistant novels I had inside me' as like 'a calf twisted in a cow's womb' (p. 139).

66. Patricia Morley, 'Doppelganger's Dilemma, Artist and Man: *The Vivisector*', *Queen's Quarterly*, 78 (1971) 409. John Docker is among those who see a Lawrentian theory of imagination at work in the novel. See his 'Patrick White and Romanticism: *The Vivisector*', *Southerly*, 33 (1973) 48–9.

67. See Yeats's 'Pardon, Old Fathers', in *Responsibilities* (1914).

68. Veronica Brady, 'The Artist and the Savage God: Patrick White's *The Vivisector*', *Meanjin*, 33 (1974) 136.

69. Elizabeth Perkins, 'Sterile Critics and Fecund Artists: Old Themes Brought Up to Date', *LiNQ*, 1, no. 1 (1971) 44–5.

70. However, Robert S. Baker has shown that White's use of Romantic categories and conventions is frequently 'radically dismissive'. See 'Romantic Onanism in Patrick White's *The Vivisector*', *Texas Studies in Literature and Language*, 21 (1979) 203–25. For discussions of *The Vivisector*'s debts to Romanticism and Decadence, see Docker, 'Patrick White and Romanticism', *Southerly*, 33, pp. 44–61; John Berger, 'A View of the Artist as Lucifer', *The Times*, 22 Oct 1970, p. 8; Richard N. Coe, 'The Artist and the Grocer: Patrick White's *The Vivisector*', *Meanjin*, 29 (1970) 526–9; and Terry Smith, 'A Portrait of the Artist in Patrick White's *The Vivisector*', *Meanjin*, 31 (1972) 167–77.

71. See Morley, 'Doppelganger's Dilemma', *Queen's Quarterly*, 78, p. 407. Incidentally, this whole article traces parallels between the lives of Hurtle and Kathy Volkov on the one hand, and that of Rimbaud on the other.

72. The Hardy novel also bears comparison to *The Vivisector* in its exploration of the relationship between artistic creativity and sexuality. It is interesting to note in this regard that Hardy is mentioned in *The Vivisector* and is the only author so named (p. 158).

73. Herring and Wilkes, 'Conversation with White', *Southerly*, 33, p. 143.

74. Clark, 'The Private Patrick White', *New York Times Book Review*, 27 Apr 1980, p. 32.

75. Robert S. Baker explores White's use of this and the related broken glass imagery and sees the chandelier as a 'form whose integral unity is composed of diversity'. He observes that, through this form, unified white light is broken down into 'the *vivisected* colors of the "flickering rainbow" of the sensory world and the artist's palette'. Baker links White's intentions in using this motif to

the implications of Shelley's 'dome of many-coloured glass'. See 'Romantic Onanism', *Texas Studies in Literature and Language*, 21, pp. 209–12.

76. This whole episode is recalled by experiences White relates, largely in the 'Journeys' section of *Flaws in the Glass*. See esp. pp. 124, 157 and 180–1.

77. A further aspect of Rhoda as a mirror for Hurtle is suggested by the connection Jung draws between dwarf gods and creativity. See his *Collected Works*, xii, 149–50.

78. McCulloch agrees that Hurtle fails to love Rhoda, but links this to White's failure to write 'tragedy' in this novel. See *A Tragic Vision*, p. 93.

74. Both Robert Baker and Peter Beatson speak to this aspect of the novel's rhythm. See Baker's 'Romantic Onanism', *Texas Studies in Literature and Language*, 21, p. 215; and Beatson's *The Eye in the Mandala*, p. 19.

80. John Docker remarks that, after his first stroke, Hurtle must relearn his craft and even his language, like a child first learning to speak and act; see 'White and Romanticism', *Southerly*, 33, pp. 59–61.

81. D. R. Burns suggests that in this novel, as well as in *The Solid Mandala*, White may be using the mouldering of waste matter as a metaphor for imaginative germination. See his *The Directions of Australian Fiction, 1920–1974* (North Melbourne: Cassell Australia, 1975) p. 200.

82. Patricia Morley also believes that the novel affirms the oneness of *Dreck* and the sap of life. See *Mystery of Unity*, p. 231.

83. McCulloch sees his death at this moment as evidence that his effort is fraudulent. See *A Tragic Vision*, pp. 93–4.

84. A. P. Riemer suggests that this cryptogram also contains 'I in God'. See 'The Eye of the Needle: Patrick White's Recent Novels', *Southerly*, 34 (1974) 253–4. Another critic, Paul M. St. Pierre, discusses 'the indigo god' as implying 'the infinite within the finite'. See 'Coterminous Beginnings', in Shepherd and Singh, *White: A Critical Symposium*, pp. 105–6.

CHAPTER FOUR: THE LATER WORKS: THE STATE OF FAILURE

1. Personal communication, 27 Nov. 1979. Significantly, White ranks *The Twyborn Affair* with *The Aunt's Story* and *The Solid Mandala* as his favourites among his books. See A. Clark, 'The Private Patrick White', *New York Times Book Review*, 27 Apr 1980, p. 32; and *FG*, p. 145.

2. For White's feelings about the fall of the Whitlam Australian Labor Party government, see David Leitch, 'Patrick White: A Revealing Profile', *National Times*, 27 Mar – 1 Apr 1978, p. 32; Sharman, 'A Very Literary Luncheon', *National Times*, 30 June 1979, p. 31; and *FG*, pp. 231–2.

3. Manfred Mackenzie has argued that Elizabeth's character is in some ways a composite of aspects of Amy and Madeleine, or of the Amy–Madeleine which Amy imagines herself. See his ' "Dark Birds of Light": *The Eye of the Storm* as Swansong', *Southern Review*, 10 (1977) 278–84.

4. She also owes a good deal to White's own mother, as her husband owes much to his father. See *FG*, esp. pp. 10, 11, 15, 41–2, 48 and 149–50.

5. 'Patrick White Interviewed by Rodney Wetherell'.

6. A similar point is made both by William Walsh and Christopher Ricks. See Walsh's *Patrick White's Fiction*, p. 112; and Ricks's 'Gigantist', *New York Review of Books*, 4 Apr 1974, p. 19.

7. As did White himself as a child. See *FG*, p. 49.

8. For more on the skiapod and its significance, see Manly Johnson, 'Patrick White: The Eye of the Language', *World Literature Written in English*, 15 no. 2 (Nov 1976) 346–7.

9. 'Patrick White Interviewed by Rodney Wetherell'.

10. Susan Gingell-Beckmann discusses the number, colour, and nature of the swans, finding in this image 'a symbolic indication of the way in which opposites are reconciled in the divine'. She also considers the novel's use of the symbols of dolls, roses, water, mirrors, and the dance. See 'Seven Black Swans: The Symbolic Logic of Patrick White's *The Eye of the Storm*', *World Literature Written in English*, 21 (1982) 315–25.

11. Manfred Mackenzie elucidates this and other aspects of swan symbolism relevant to the novel. See his ' "Dark Birds of Light" ', *Southern Review*, 10, pp. 270–6. Incidentally, White claims not to have known of the swan's symbolic connection with death until after writing *The Eye of the Storm*. See Herring and Wilkes, 'Conversation with White', *Southerly*, 33, p. 140.

12. Remarking on this tendency in White, George Steiner invokes Yeats to explain, 'Love has pitched his mansion in the place of excrement, but so has spirit. It is this enigmatic intimacy and the grotesque realities it entails that fascinate White.' See 'Carnal Knowledge', *New Yorker*, 4 Mar 1974, p. 109.

13. The identification of the Hunter children with Goneril and Regan is made explicit at several points in the novel. See, for example, *ES*, P. 236.

14. On this correspondence, see also Brian Kiernan, *Patrick White*, Macmillan Commonwealth Writers Series, gen. ed. A. N. Jeffares (London: Macmillan, 1980) pp. 119–20.

15. This opinion is also advanced by Annegret Maack. See 'Shakespearean Reference as Structural Principle in Patrick White's *The Tree of Man* and *The Eye of the Storm*', *Southerly*, 38 (1978) 123–40, for more on this as well as further allusions to *Lear* in the novel. However, Ann McCulloch sees the absence of Cordelia or of a true Lear as suggesting that the novel treats 'a post-tragic world'. See *A Tragic Vision*, pp. 115–21. White's use of *Lear* in *The Eye of the Storm* has interested other critics as well. See esp. Johnson, 'White: The Eye of the Language', *World Literature Written in English*, 15, no. 2, pp. 339–43; and Patricia Clancy, 'The Actor's Dilemma: Patrick White and Henri de Montherlant', *Meanjin*, 33 (1974) 298–302.

16. See, for example, Riemer, 'The Eye of the Needle', *Southerly*, 34, p. 263; and Wolfe *Laden Choirs*, p. 180.

17. Susan Whaley notes the prevalence in this novel of imagery of food and its consumption. See 'Food for Thought in Patrick White's Fiction', *World Literature Written in English*, 22 (1983) 197–212.

18. For a discussion of White's use of *The Charterhouse of Parma* in *The Eye of the Storm*, see Manfred Mackenzie, 'Tradition and Patrick White's Individual Talent', *Texas Studies in Literature and Language*, 21 (1979) 153–60.

19. Manfred Mackenzie elaborates on these and other possible motives involved. See his ' "Dark Birds of Light" ', *Southern Review*, 10, pp. 276–8. Kenneth Burke also speaks to the relationship of parricide and suicide and the need to obliterate one's ancestry in order to achieve rebirth. Burke goes on to say that incest may also express a kind of narcissism. See *The Philosophy of Literary Form: Studies in Symbolic Action*, 3rd edn (Berkeley, Calif.: University of California Press, 1973) pp. 41–2.

20. Because the issues of kinship and connection, as well as the question of religious experience and service, are of such importance to this novel, White is able to derive multiple thematic implications from the fact that in Australia nurses are called 'sisters'.

21. Manly Johnson finds that this juxtaposition of scenes and the mention of roses in both reinforce our sense that Lotte and Mary are experiencing their own moments at the eye of the storm. See 'White: The Eye of the Language', *World Literature Written in English*, 15, no.2, p. 354.

22. See, for example, Kiernan, *Patrick White*, pp. 119–20. See also the close of *Flaws in the Glass*, where White describes his own imagined end in similar terms.

23. Björksten, *White: A General Introduction*, p. 114.

24. Incidents and circumstances which recall this story and no doubt served as its basis are recounted in *FG*, pp. 102, 110 and 123.

25. On this point, see also David Myers, *The Peacocks and the Bourgeoisie: Ironic Vision in Patrick White's Shorter Prose Fiction* (Adelaide: Adelaide University Union Press, 1978) p. 133.

26. This ambiguity has been responsible for diametrically opposed readings of the novel in light of its ending. John Colmer, for example, concludes that *A Fringe of Leaves* marks in White's work 'the first wholly satisfactory account of the reintegration of the visionary outsider into the social world with no loss of integrity, but rather a gain in love and compassion'. See his *'Riders in the Chariot'*, p. 3. See also his 'Duality in Patrick White', in Shepherd and Singh, *White: A Critical Symposium*, p. 75. On the other hand, Kirpal Singh argues that Ellen's return is a 'defeat'. See his 'Patrick White: An Outsider's View', ibid., p. 122.

27. The standard source for Mrs Fraser's story is Michael Alexander's *Mrs Fraser on the Fatal Shore* (New York: Simon & Schuster, 1971). Both Randolph Stow in 'Transfigured Histories: Recent Novels of Patrick White and Robert Drewe', *Australian Literary Studies*, 9 (1979) 32–8, and Jill Ward in 'Patrick White's *A Fringe of Leaves*: History and Fiction', *Australian Literary Studies*, 8 (1978) 402–18, discuss the relationship of Eliza Fraser's story to that of Ellen Roxburgh and speculate on why White may have used, ignored or revised certain details of the Fraser adventures. As Stow points out, White's interest in the story may have been aroused by Sidney Nolan's 1957 series of paintings on the subject, a conjecture supported by White's brief comments on the novel's genesis in *Flaws in the Glass* (p. 171). As early as 1964 White was reported to be working on the libretto of an opera based on Mrs Fraser's history. Nolan was to be the production designer for this later abandoned project. See John Small, 'Patrick White's Opera: The Advent of Peter Sculthorpe', *Bulletin*, 13 June 1964, p. 47.

28. See, for example, Herring and Wilkes, *'Conversation with White'*, *Southerly*, 33, p. 139, in which White states, 'I feel that my novels are quite old-fashioned and traditional – almost nineteenth-century.' Asked to describe the tradition in which he would place himself, he names, among others, Stendhal, Flaubert, Balzac and Dickens. In a taped interview with Rodney Wetherell, he claims again that his novels are 'basically nineteenth-century' (see 'Patrick White Interviewed by Rodney Wetherell'). Critics have also recognized affinities with nineteenth-century writers. George Steiner has found him at times 'intensely Jamesian' ('Carnal Knowledge', *New Yorker*, 4 Mar 1974, p. 111), and Peter Wolfe discusses this novel's debts to Victorian conventions (*Laden Choirs*, pp.

197–8). The question of White's affinities with nineteenth-century writers will be further addressed in Ch. 5.

29. See Manly Johnson, '*A Fringe of Leaves*: White's Genethlicon', *Texas Studies in Literature and Language*, 21 (1979) 238–9.

30. Manly Johnson briefly discusses White's use of Virgilian themes (ibid., pp. 226–8); also see Manfred Mackenzie, who describes the way Virgil is 'accommodated to the Australian environment' ('Tradition and Patrick White's Individual Talent', *Texas Studies in Literature and Language*, 21, pp. 160–66).

31. Addressing the issue of Ellen's passivity, Dorothy Green sees the novel as testing and criticizing the moral assumption 'which considers it more *human* to act than to be acted upon', but Suzanne Edgar stresses the active strength underpinning Ellen's docility. See Green's review of *A Fringe of Leaves*: 'White's Tale of Survival', *Nation Review*, 22–8 Oct 1976, p. 20; and Edgar's 'A Woman's Life and Love: A Reply to Leonie Kramer', *Quadrant*, 21, no. 10. (Oct 1977) 69–70.

32. Peter Wolfe links this green shawl to Ellen's 'repressed eroticism'. See *Laden Choirs*, pp. 204–8. Both Wolfe and John Colmer note the suggestion in the novel's title that civilization fringes the elemental, especially in Australia. See *Laden Choirs*, p. 197; and Colmer's 'Patrick White's *A Fringe of Leaves*', *Literary Half-Yearly*, 23, no. 2 (July 1982) 88–9.

33. On this, see also Johnson, '*Twyborn*: The Abbess, the Bulbul, and the Bawdy House', *Modern Fiction Studies*, 27, pp. 163–4.

34. Brian Kiernan makes a similar point and goes on to link it with the Nietzschean notion that society is based on the rationalization of cruelty (see *Patrick White*, pp. 131–3).

35. Don Anderson sees this moment as central to the novel and suggests that in her gnawing of the phallic thigh bone she may be 'metaphorically, *eating the patriarchy*' and thereby nourishing 'her essential "she-ness" '. See his 'A Severed Leg: Anthropophagy and Communion in Patrick White's Fiction', *Southerly*, 40 (1980) 399–417.

36. David Tacey speaks to related matters in his article, 'A Search for a New Ethic: Patrick White's *A Fringe of Leaves*', in Chris Tiffin (ed.), *South Pacific Images*, pp. 186–92. According to Tacey, the novel 'argues that there is no ethical or spiritual health until we become acquainted with our own darkness'. Tacey also feels that, in Jack, Ellen confronts her own evil.

37. Several critics of this novel have pointed to the imagery of birth, infancy and childhood which proliferates upon Ellen's arrival at the Oakeses' farmhouse. See, for example, Manly Johnson, 'Patrick White: *A Fringe of Leaves*', in Shepherd and Singh, *White: A Critical Symposium*, p. 91; and Edgar, 'A Woman's Life and Love', *Quadrant*, 21, no. 10, pp, 70–1.

38. Elizabeth Perkins speaks briefly to this recognition on Ellen's part. See her 'Escape with a Convict: Patrick White's *A Fringe of Leaves*', *Meanjin*, 36 (1977) 267.

39. Randolph Stow takes a very different view of the significance of garnets in the novel, finding them to be associated with moral infection (see 'Transfigured Histories', *Australian Literary Studies*, 9, p. 37).

40. It has also been suggested that the tea-spilling represents a final baptism. See Johnson, '*A Fringe of Leaves*: White's Genethlicon', *Texas Studies in Literature and Language*, 21, pp. 238–9.

41. The novel's structure has been likened to a triptych. See Jim Davidson,

'Patrick White's Latest Novel: A Rich and Enigmatic Triptych', *National Times*, 24 Nov 1979, p. 54. Noel Macainsh notes a unity in the book's structure which contrasts with the disjointed life portrayed and encourages the reader's search for meaning. See 'A Queer Unity – Patrick White's *The Twyborn Affair*', *Southerly*, 43 (1983) 153.

42. For this discussion, I shall adopt White's practice in the novel, that of using the gender of personal pronoun appropriate to the identity the protagonist has assumed at the time under consideration.

43. Leonie Kramer remarks that the novel's 'submerged subject' is that of family relationships. See her 'Pseudoxia Endemica', *Quadrant*, no. 155 (July 1980) 67.

44. A. P. Riemer shows that with the name 'Vatatzes' he might well be so connected. Riemer also discusses the significance to Greek history of the names 'Angelos', 'Eudoxia' and 'Anna' (Angelos's late wife). See his 'Eddie and the Bogomils – Some Observations on *The Twyborn Affair*', Southerly, 40 (1980) 13. John McLaren translates the name 'Eudoxia' as 'pleasant orthodoxy' but also notices the suggestion attaching to the English slang term 'doxy'. See 'Seeking the Self in an Uncertain World', *Australian Book Review*, no. 16 (Nov. 1979) 8.

45. Geoffrey Tout-Smith suggests that by seducing the reader into belief in Eudoxia, White short-circuits stock responses to the discovery of her transvestism. See 'Nightmare Uncertainties', *Overland*, no. 78 (Dec 1979) 65.

46. White's own feelings for the Monaro country are akin to Eddie's and expressed in *Flaws in the Glass* (p. 49).

47. In a macabre touch, White puts his own birthday on a child's headstone in the Lushington family graveyard.

48. Peter Wolfe speculates on the surname White gives Eddie in this incarnation, noticing its implications of *triste*, 'tryst', 'Tristan' and 'trust'. See *Laden Choirs*, pp. 223–4. Wolfe cites Rosemary Dinnage, 'Her Life as a Man', *New York Review of Books*, 17 Apr 1980, p. 25.

49. John McLaren agrees that Eadith's life as a madam 'is more an evasion than a discovery of herself'. See 'Seeking the Self', *Australian Book Review*, no. 16, p. 9; see also Andrew Motion, 'Time Trouble', *New Statesman*, 28 Sep 1979, pp. 470–1.

50. Andrew Motion finds that the inclusion of such material disrupts the novel's heretofore grave tone so badly that it is irrecoverable (ibid., pp. 470–1).

51. The scene in which these naïve Australians are induced to demonstrate the 'coo-ee' for the contemptuous British and an agonized Eadith provides a textbook example of what Australians call the 'cultural cringe'.

52. Jim Davidson also sees Eddie's life as a growth toward acceptance of his mother and his identification with her, but finds that Eadie, not Edward, is Eddie's true judge. See 'Patrick White's Latest Novel', *National Times*, 24 Nov 1979, p. 54.

53. Riemer believes that this passage represents Eddie's coming to terms with the judge and being received out of the world by him as Pantocrator (see 'Eddie and the Bogomils', *Southerly*, 40, p. 25).

54. In *Flaws in the Glass* (p. 82) White recounts a similar incident which happened to him on the 'opening night' of the bombing of London in the Second World War.

55. Critical opinion on the meaning of the novel's ending varies widely. For

example, Hena Maes-Jelinek agrees that it conveys a suggestion of rebirth, while Ann McCulloch sees Eddie as 'neither redeemed nor damned', but 'simply dead', and Peter Wolfe finds the book's resolution 'bleak, puzzling' and weak. See Maes-Jelinek's 'Altering Boundaries: The Art of Translation in *The Angel at the Gate* and *The Twyborn Affair*', *World Literature Written in English*, 23 (1984) 172; McCulloch's *A Tragic Vision*, pp. 185–6; and Wolfe's *Laden Choirs*, pp. 224–5.

56. To the speculations on the implications of Eddie's 'twice-born' status, Manning Clark adds the observation that he is a 'twicer' both in his sex life and in his search for a mode of existence unavailable to him in Australia. See 'Concerning Patrick White', *Sydney Morning Herald*, 13 Oct 1979, p. 20. S. A. Ramsey finds that, although Eddie undergoes three incarnations in the novel, he is born only twice: 'as a man and as a woman'. See '*The Twyborn Affair*: "The Beginning in an End" or "The End of a Beginning"?', *Ariel*, 11, no. 4 (1980) 88. And Manly Johnson offers the opinion that Eddie is born again in Patrick White himself, whose 'real life, after 1940, is an extrapolition [*sic*] of Eddie's fictional life which ended in 1940'. See '*Twyborn*: The Abbess, the Bulbul, and the Bawdy House', *Modern Fiction Studies*, 27, p. 160.

57. O'Brien, 'No-one Realises how Frivolous Patrick White Can Be', *Sydney Morning Herald*, 10 Dec 1983, p. 31.

58. A. P. Riemer, for example, finds the whole novel informed by a Manichean disgust for the world and the flesh (see his 'Eddie and the Bogomils', *Southerly*, 40, pp. 12–29). Similarly, Benjamin De Mott claims that the novel scorns human attachment, and Jean Bedford decides that Eddie comes to believe he 'will never find the truth in human relationships'. See De Mott's 'The Perils of Protean Man', *New York Times Book Review*, 27 Apr 1980, p. 3; and Bedford's 'Drawn Subtly inside a Transexual's Experience', *National Times*, 24 Nov 1979, p. 55. On the other hand, several readers have argued for the novel's emphasis on compassion. See Manning Clark, 'Concerning Patrick White', *Sydney Morning Herald*, 13 Oct 1979, p. 20; and G. A. Wilkes, 'White Has Not Yet Begun to Write', *Weekend Australian Magazine*, 10–11 Nov 1979, p. 12. McCulloch holds a related but different view. She sees the novel as concerned with the life of this world and as embodying White's post-modernist tragic vision. See *A Tragic Vision*, ch. 5.

CHAPTER FIVE: STYLE AND TECHNIQUE: THE DISCIPLINE OF FAILURE

1. Henry James, 'The Novels of George Eliot', *Atlantic Monthly*, Oct 1866, p. 485; repr. in James E. Miller, Jr (ed.), *Theory of Fiction: Henry James*, (Lincoln, Nebr.: University of Nebraska Press, 1972) p. 321.

2. For the relationship of White's work to Weil's thought, see Veronica Brady, 'The Novelist and the Reign of Necessity: Patrick White and Simone Weil', in Shepherd and Singh, *White: A Critical Symposium*, pp. 108–16.

3. Ann McCulloch discusses White's failure to find words to convey his vision, but argues that this gives way in *The Twyborn Affair* to the creation of authentic post-modernist tragedy. See *A Tragic Vision*, esp. chs 1 and 5.

4. White's understanding of the necessity of failure is in many ways akin to Faulkner's as elucidated in Walter Slatoff's *Quest for Failure: A Study of William Faulkner* (Ithaca, NY: Cornell University Press, 1960). The two writers share

especially the sense that failure acts as an impetus toward further struggle and that language will always be inadequate to vision.

5. This statement is taken from a 1955 interview quoted by Slatoff (ibid., pp. 145–6). White has admitted reading and admiring Faulkner. See Ashley Owen, ' "Old Age I am Afraid of, but Not Death": Patrick White's Story', *Australian Financial Review*, 11 July 1972, p. 3.

6. Several other writers have also recognized this theme in White's work and have treated it briefly. See, for example, Beatson, *The Eye in the Mandala*, pp. 30–39; Björksten, *White: A General Introduction*, p. 34; Colmer, *'Riders in the Chariot', p. 1; and Morley, The Mystery of Unity*, pp. 238–40. Peter Wolfe calls White's characters 'saints of failure'. See *Laden Choirs*, p. 231.

7. The importance to White's work of struggle and the dialectic of struggle and surrender is noted by several critics, among them Kiernan, *Images of Society and Nature*, pp. 138 and 146; Johnson, 'Patrick White: *A Fringe of Leaves*', in Shepherd and Singh, *White: A Critical Symposium*, p. 88; and McCulloch, *A Tragic Vision, passim*.

8. As David Myers has pointed out, both White and Kafka employ this theme to suggest failure's inevitability. He discusses this and other similarities between the two writers in *The Peacocks and the Bourgeoisie*, pp. 160–9.

9. White, 'The Prodigal Son', in *The Vital Decade*, pp. 157–8. In a later interview, however, White admits that total humility would preclude positive action. See Sharman, 'A Very Literary Luncheon', *National Times*, 30 June 1979, p. 31.

10. As Humphrey Carpenter also notices. See his 'Patrick White Explains Himself', review of *Flaws in the Glass*, in the *New York Times Book Review*, 7 Feb 1982, p. 9.

11. See also Nadine Gordimer, who in 'Mysterious Incest', review of *Flaws in the Glass*, in *New York Review of Books*, 15 Apr 1982, p. 14, notes that White is 'hard on himself, in [his characters]'.

12. He makes the first claim in Owen, 'Old Age I am Afraid of', *Australian Financial Review*, 11 July 1972, p. 3; McGregor, *In the Making*, p. 220; Herring and Wilkes, 'Conversation with White', *Southerly*, 33, p. 139; Sharman, 'A Very Literary Luncheon', *National Times*, 30 June 1979, p. 27; White, 'Flaws in the Glass: Sketches', *Bulletin*, 29 Jan 1980, p. 149; and *FG*, p. 20. The second claim is made in Sharman, 'A Very Literary Luncheon', *National Times*, 30 June 1979, p. 31.

13. Slatoff notes that Faulkner also uses this posture to keep meaning open. See *Quest for Failure*, pp. 143–4. Erich Auerbach has pointed to Virginia Woolf's adoption of a similar stance 'by representing herself to be someone who doubts, wonders, hesitates, as though the truth about her characters were not better known to her than it is to the reader'. Auerbach shows that Woolf uses this technique to question the nature of objective reality. White, on the other hand, is more interested in the technique's implications for the narrator. For Auerbach's remarks, see *Mimesis: The Representation of Reality in Western Literature*, tr. Willard R. Trask (1946; repr. Princeton, NJ: Princeton University Press, 1968) p. 535.

14. I do not intend to deal more than peripherally here with White's wit or comic sense, although these are areas which deserve exploration. A brief catalogue and discussion of the varieties of wit to be found in White's work is offered by Ian Reid, 'Review Article: Distractions and Definitions, Studying Commonwealth Literature', *Southern Review*, 4 (1971) 318–20. Geoffrey Dutton

also acknowledges White's talent for comedy. See his *Patrick White*, 4th edn, pp. 22–3.

15. Leslie Fiedler, 'No! In Thunder', repr. in William Stafford (ed.), *Twentieth Century American Writing* (New York: Odyssey Press, 1965) p. 562.

16. Alan Lawson also discusses White's use of syllepsis and synaesthesia, seeing them as 'ways of expressing a desire to bring together, to combine the opposites, to transcend the distinctions'. See 'Meaning and Experience: A Review–Essay on Some Recurrent Problems in Patrick White Criticism', *Texas Studies in Literature and Language*, 21 (1979) 291.

17. Carl Harrison-Ford remarks that White uses second person narration to 'badger the reader's involvement toward complicity'. See 'Shorter White', *Australian*, 22 June 1974, p. 24.

18. Wayne Booth, *The Rhetoric of Fiction* (Chicago: University of Chicago Press, 1961) p, 184. Alan Lawson also cites Booth's term as applicable to aspects of White's style. See his 'Meaning and Experience: Review–Essay', *Texas Studies in Literature and Language*, 21, p. 287. See also Harry Heseltine, 'Patrick White's Style', *Quadrant*, 7, no. 3 (1963) 73–4, for a brief discussion of White's use of the conditional.

19. David Myers discusses this aspect of White's style as it operates in his short fiction; see *The Peacocks and the Bourgeoisie*, pp. 17–18.

20. Herring and Wilkes, 'Conversation with White', *Southerly*, 33, pp. 137–8.

21. Peter Beatson remarks that the ironic perspective White takes on his characters often reflects his awareness of the 'pathetic incongruity' between the inner being and its outer manifestations; see *The Eye in the Mandala*, p. 87.

22. Brian Kiernan argues that Laura's is merely one of several possible evaluations of Voss's experience offered in the novel. See his *Images of Society and Nature*, pp. 116ff.

23. Ron Shepherd relates such uncertainties in White's fiction to Indian philosophy. See 'An Indian Story: 'The Twitching Colonel'' ', in Shepherd and Singh, *White: A Critical Symposium*, pp. 28–33.

24. See, for example, Herring and Wilkes, 'Conversation with White', *Southerly*, 33, pp. 138–9.

25. For more on this matter, see Sylvia Gzell, 'Themes and Imagery in *Voss* and *Riders in the Chariot*', *Australian Literary Studies*, 1 (1964) 180–95; and Beatson, *The Eye in the Mandala*, p. 136. The terms 'demonic' and 'apocalyptic' as applied to imagery are explained in Frye's *Anatomy of Criticism*, pp. 131–50.

26. As Harry Heseltine has remarked (see 'Patrick White's Style', *Quadrant*, 7, no. 3, pp. 72–73). William J. Scheick also speaks to White's use of the pathetic fallacy. See 'The Gothic Grace and Rainbow Aesthetic of Patrick White's Fiction', *Texas Studies in Literature and Language*, 21 (1979) 140.

27. Scheick remarks that White's prose induces in the reader 'fleeting and revelatory experiences similar to those undergone by White's characters' (ibid., p. 144). See also David Myers, who discusses the function of epiphany in White's shorter fiction (*The Peacocks and the Bourgeoisie*, esp. pp. 3, 54 and 176).

28. Brian Kiernan also notices this pattern. See his *Patrick White*, p. 139.

29. Adams, *Strains of Discord*, p. 180.

30. The effects of open form upon the reader are discussed both by Adams and by Walter Slatoff. See Adams, *Strains of Discord*, esp. pp. 32–3 and 49; and Slatoff's *With Respect to Readers: Dimensions of Literary Response* (Ithaca, NY: Cornell University Press, 1970) esp. pp. 14, 129 and 148. Slatoff remarks that

'Little of our critical work contemplates the extent to which much of our greatest literature involves a disordering as well as an ordering of experience and the extent to which the life and power and even form of a work may come from that disordering or from the very struggle or even failure of the artist to provide order' (p. 14).

31. Quoted in Adams, *Strains of Discord*, p. 214.

32. George Steiner, 'Carnal Knowledge', *New Yorker*, 4 Mar 1974, p. 111.

31. For White's comments, see Herring and Wilkes, 'Conversation with White', *Southerly*, 33, p. 139; 'Patrick White Interviewed by Rodney Wetherell'; and *FG*, p. 96. For a discussion of nineteenth-century aspects of White's fiction, see Zulfikar Ghose, 'The One Comprehensive Vision', *Texas Studies in Literature and Language*, 21 (1979) 262.

34. In White's work, this term appears most conspicuously in *Riders in the Chariot* and *A Fringe of Leaves* (see, for example, *RC*, p. 311, and *FL*, p. 376). For Hardy's use of the term, see esp. *Jude the Obscure*, where 'loving-kindness' remains one of the few values affirmed in a world where others prove bankrupt.

35. Again, see Herring and Wilkes, 'Conversation with White', *Southerly*, 33, p. 139; also McGregor, *In the Making*, p. 221; Ingmar Björksten, 'A Day with Patrick White', tr. John Stanley Martin, *Nation Review*, 21–7 June 1974, p. 1179; and Sharman, 'A Very Literary Luncheon', *National Times*, 30 June 1979, p. 27.

36. For the Melville linkage, see Dutton, *Patrick White*, 4th edn, p. 28. The comparison with Hawthorne is made by R. P. Laidlaw in 'The Complexity of *Voss*', *Southern Review*, 4 (1970) 3. Hawthorne's description of romance is from the 'Custom House' section of *The Scarlet Letter*.

37. Peter Wolfe calls White a 'super-realist' (*Laden Choirs*, p. 22).

38. White also mentions eighteenth-century authors as among his favourites, particularly Fielding and Smollett. See Andrew Clark, 'The Private Patrick White', *New York Times Book Review*, 27 Apr 1980, p. 33; and Björksten, 'A Day with Patrick White', *Nation Review*, 21–7 June 1974, p. 1179.

39. For examples of this position, see Beatson, *The Eye in the Mandala*, p. 91; Björksten, *White: A General Introduction*, pp. 65 and 121; Mackenzie, 'Yes, Let's Return to Abyssinia', *Essays in Criticism*, 14, pp. 433–5; and Colmer, *'Riders in the Chariot'*, p. 2. In a related formulation, David Martin sees the novels as parables ('Among the Bones', *Meanjin*, 18, p. 52), while Robert McDougall covers all the bases, by labelling White 'an intensely realistic allegorist and mystic' – *Australia Felix: Joseph Furphy and Patrick White*, Commonwealth Literary Fund Lecture (Canberra: Australian National University Press, 1966) p. 13. The most thorough discussion of White as an allegorist that I am aware of is Manfred Mackenzie's 'Patrick White's Later Novels', *Southern Review*, 1, pp. 5–18.

40. For some, all *too* patent. See, for example, John Colmer, 'Duality in Patrick White', in Shepherd and Singh, *White: A Critical Symposium*, pp. 70–71.

41. This is the tack taken by Peter Beatson and John Colmer. See Beatson, *The Eye in the Mandala*, p. 91; and Colmer's *'Riders in the Chariot'*, p. 2. See also in this context Adrian Mitchell, 'Eventually, White's Language: Words and More than Words', in Shepherd and Singh, *White: A Critical Symposium*, p. 8.

42. Manfred Mackenzie has stressed the need to see White's characters as functioning on at least these two levels. See his 'Yes, Let's Return to Abyssinia', *Essays in Criticism*, 14, p. 435; and 'Patrick White's Later Novels', *Southern Review*, 1, pp. 5–18.

43. Auerbach, *Mimesis*, see pp. 73–6 and 554–5.

44. See, for example, his essay 'Flaws in the Glass: Sketches', p. 149, where White says his work is 'chosen' for him, and his book *Flaws in the Glass*, where he extends this awareness of guidance or compulsion to apply to his whole life (p. 215).

45. Kirpal Singh speaks to a related point, claiming that White has an Aristotelian concept of character as vehicle, fulfilling a tragic destiny. See 'Patrick White: An Outsider's View', in Shepherd and Singh, *White: A Critical Symposium*, pp. 120–1.

46. Kiernan, *Images of Society and Nature*, p. 97.

47. White, 'The Prodigal Son', in *The Vital Decade*, p. 158. For more about White's hopes for his impact on Australians, see Ian Moffitt, 'Australian Myths Debunked', *Sunday Mirror* (Sydney), 3 Dec 1961, p. 19; White, *Reimpression de Les Prix Nobel en 1973 Biography*, p. 224; Sharman, 'A Very Literary Luncheon', *National Times*, 30 June 1979, p. 26; and Patrick White, 'It seems as though life itself now depends on sport with a Prime Minister who materialises miraculously as a cheer-leader at every sporting event', *Sydney Morning Herald*, 26 Jan 1984, overpage of Australia Day supplement.

48. In *Aspects of the Novel* (New York: Harcourt, Brace, 1927) E. M. Forster speaks of the way Dostoyevsky's characters 'expand' toward infinity, and finds the creation of such characters the sign of the writer as prophet. In his emphasis on the everyday reality of the fiction interpenetrating the ineffable, he might have been speaking of White, who could also be seen as 'prophetic' in Forster's terms (see pp. 132–4). The Whitman quote comes from *Song of Myself*, Deathbed ed, 1.810.

49. Steinsaltz, *The Thirteen Petalled Rose*, pp. 131–6.

50. See Jung, *Collected Works*, ix.ii, 42–4; xii, 152; and xi, 196–8.

51. John Fowles, *Daniel Martin* (1977; repr. New York: Signet, New American Library, 1978) p. 366.

52. Steinsaltz, *The Thirteen Petalled Rose*, pp. 145–6.

53. As Veronica Brady has observed, in White's world 'The order of the universe is not ultimately intelligible, but demands the submission of intelligence and will.' See 'The Novelist and the New World', *Texas Studies in Literature and Language*, 21, p. 174.

54. See P. V. Martin, *Experiment in Depth: A Study of the Work of Jung, Eliot, and Toynbee* (1955; repr. Boston, Mass.: Routledge & Kegan Paul, 1976) pp. 164ff.

55. William James's term, the 'MORE', is taken from *Varieties of Religious Experience*, quoted in Martin's *Experiment in Depth*, pp. 131–2; see also pp. 178–9.

56. Robert S. Baker agrees, describing this discovery of relationship between the self and the transcendent by saying that White's characters 'conclude their dark and vagrant theodicies with a gesture of obedience towards an incomprehensible power that, paradoxically, seems born of their own deepest possibilities and energies'. See his 'Romantic Onanism', *Texas Studies in Literature and Language*, 21, p. 203.

57. See Jung's *Collected Works*, ix.ii, 69–70.

58. Søren Kierkegaard, *Fear and Trembling [and] The Sickness Unto Death*, tr. Walter Lowrie (1941; repr. Garden City, NY: Doubleday, 1954) p. 171.

Bibliography

In the hopes that this bibliography will be of service to other students of Patrick White's work, I have included works consulted, as well as those cited.

PRIMARY SOURCES (ARRANGED CHRONOLOGICALLY)

White, P., *Thirteen Poems*, Fisher Library, University of Sydney, RB 1630.19 (1930?).
——, *The Ploughman and Other Poems* (Sydney: Beacon Press, 1935).
——, 'The Twitching Colonel', *London Mercury*, 35, no. 210 (Apr 1937) 602–9.
——, 'The House behind the Barricades', *New Verse*, 30 (Summer 1938) 9.
——, *Happy Valley* (1939; repr. New York: Viking Press, 1940).
——, 'Cocotte', *Horizon*, 1 (May 1940) 364–6.
——, *The Living and the Dead* (New York: Viking Press, 1941).
——, 'White, Patrick', in *Twentieth Century Authors*, ed. Stanley J. Kunitz and Howard Haycroft (New York: Wilson, 1942) pp. 1509–10.
——, 'After Alep', in *Bugle Blast: An Anthology from the Services*, 3rd ser., ed. Jack Aistrop and Reginald Moore (London: Allen & Unwin, 1945) pp. 147–55.
——, *The Aunt's Story* (1948; repr. New York: Avon, 1975).
——, *The Tree of Man* (1955; repr. New York: Avon, 1975).
——, 'White, Patrick', in *Twentieth Century Authors*, 1st suppl., ed. Stanley J. Kunitz and Vinetta Colby (New York: Wilson, 1955) p. 1074.
——, *Voss* (1957; repr. New York: Avon, 1975).
——, 'The Prodigal Son', *Australian Letters*, 1, no. 3 (Apr 1958) 37–40; repr. in *The Vital Decade, Ten Years of Australian Art and Letters*, ed. Geoffrey Dutton and Max Harris (South Melbourne: Sun Books, 1968) pp. 156–8.
——, *Riders in the Chariot* (1961; repr. New York: Avon, 1975).
——, letter, *Nation*, 13 Jan 1962, p. 17.
——, 'About the Play', Australian Elizabethan Theatre Trust Programme for *The Ham Funeral*, Sydney, July 1962.
——, 'Gerry Lewers has Left Us', *Sydney Morning Herald*, 18 Aug 1962, p. 12.
——, *The Burnt Ones* (1964; repr. Harmondsworth: Penguin, 1968).
——, letter, *Bulletin*, 27 June 1964, p. 3.
——, *Four Plays* (1965; repr. South Melbourne: Sun Books, 1967).
——, letter, *Bulletin*, 22 Jan 1966, p. 26.
——, *The Solid Mandala* (1966; repr. New York: Avon, 1975).

—— ,letter, *Australian Book Review*, 6, no. 8 (June 1967) 132.

—— ,letter, *Sydney Morning Herald*, 13 Dec 1967, p. 2.

—— ,letter, *Nation*, 11 May 1968, p. 15.

—— , *The Vivisector* (1970; repr. New York: Avon, 1975).

—— ,*et al.*, letter, *Australian*, 16 Sep 1970, p. 14.

—— ,letter to John Beston, 9 July 1972, John Beston Letters, National Library of Australia, Canberra, NLA/MS 4629.

—— ,letter to John Beston, 17 Sep 1972, John Beston Letters, National Library of Australia, Canberra, NLA/MS 4629.

—— ,letter, *Sydney Morning Herald*, 7 Nov 1972, p. 6.

—— ,*et al.*, letter, *Sydney Morning Herald*, 23 Nov 1972, p. 8.

—— ,'Centennial Park Rally, June 18, 1972: Grass-Roots Conservation', *Wildlife and the Environment*, 9, no. 4 (Dec 1972) 116.

—— , *The Eye of the Storm* (1973; repr. New York: Avon, 1975).

—— ,letter, *Sydney Morning Herald*, 5 Nov 1973, p. 6.

—— ,letter, *Australian*, 26 Dec 1973, p. 6.

—— , *The Cockatoos* (1974; repr. New York: Viking Press, 1975).

—— ,*Reimpression de Les Prix Nobel en 1973 Biography* (The Nobel Foundation, 1974).

—— ,'Patrick White's Tribute to the Whitlam Government', *Meanjin*, 33 (1974) 220–1.

—— ,*et al.*, letter, *Canberra Times*, 5 July 1974, p. 8.

—— ,letter, *Australian*, 20 Oct 1974, p. 8.

—— ,'The Perils of Art in Sydney Town', *Sydney Morning Herald*, 2 Nov 1974, p. 16.

—— ,letter, *Australian*, 28 May 1975, p. 8.

—— ,*A Fringe of Leaves* (1976; repr. New York: Viking Press 1977).

—— , *The Night the Prowler* (Harmondsworth: Penguin, 1976).

—— ,'Fête Galante', *Meanjin*, 36 (1977) 3–24.

—— ,*et al.*, 'Looking for Johannes Donald Bjelke-Dunstan', *Bulletin*, 27 Aug 1977, p. 60.

—— ,*Big Toys* (Sydney: Currency Press, 1978).

—— ,*et al.*, letter, *Canberra Times*, 16 July 1978, p. 2.

—— , *The Twyborn Affair* (London: Jonathan Cape, 1979).

—— ,'Books I Read in 1978', *National Times*, 6 Jan 1979, p. 41.

—— ,*et al.*, 'November 11: Four Years Later', *National Times*, 17 Nov 1979, p. 12.

—— ,'Flaws in the Glass: Sketches for a Self-Portrait', *Bulletin*, 29 Jan 1980, pp. 146–54.

—— ,'Patrick White Speaks on Factual Writing and Fiction', text of address given for the National Book Council Awards, 1980; repr. in *Australian Literary Studies*, 10 (1981) 99–101.

—— ,*Flaws in the Glass: A Self-Portrait* (New York: Viking Press, 1981).

—— ,*Signal Driver: A Morality Play for the Times*, Currency Plays, gen. ed. Katharine Brisbane (Sydney: Currency Press, 1983).

—— ,*Netherwood*, Current Theatre Series (Sydney: Currency Press, 1983).

—— ,'It seems as though life itself now depends on sport with a Prime Minister who materialises miraculously as a cheer-leader at every sporting event', *Sydney Morning Herald*, 26 Jan 1984, overpage of four-page Australia Day Supplement.

SECONDARY SOURCES (ARRANGED ALPHABETICALLY)

Books

Abrams, M. H., *Natural Supernaturalism: Tradition and Revolution in Romantic Literature* (New York: Norton, 1971).

Adams, R., *Strains of Discord: Studies in Literary Openness* (Ithaca, NY: Cornell University Press, 1958).

Alexander, M., *Mrs Fraser on the Fatal Shore* (New York: Simon & Schuster, 1971).

Anderson, D., and Knight, S. (eds), *Cunning Exiles: Studies of Modern Prose Writers* (London: Angus & Robertson, 1974).

Argyle, B., *Patrick White*, Writers and Critics, ed. A. Norman Jeffares and R. L. C. Lorimer (New York: Barnes & Noble, 1967).

Auerbach, E., *Mimesis: The Representation of Reality in Western Literature*, tr. W. R. Trask (1946; repr. Princeton, NJ: Princeton University Press, 1968).

Beatson, P., *The Eye in the Mandala: Patrick White: A Vision of Man and God* (London: Paul Elek, 1976).

Björksten, I., *Patrick White: A General Introduction*, tr. S. Gerson (St. Lucia: University of Queensland Press, 1976).

Booth, W. C. *The Rhetoric of Fiction* (Chicago: University of Chicago Press, 1961).

Brissenden, R. F., *Patrtick White*, Writers and their Work, no. 190, rev. edn (Harlow: Longmans, Green, 1969).

Bunce, D., *Travels with Dr. Leichhardt in Australia* (1859; repr. Melbourne: Oxford University Press, 1979).

Burke, K., *The Philosophy of Literary Form: Studies in Symbolic Action*, 3rd edn (Berkeley, Calif.: University of California Press, 1973).

Burns, D. R., *The Directions of Australian Fiction, 1920–74* (North Melbourne: Cassell Australia, 1975).

Campbell, J., *The Hero with a Thousand Faces*, Bollingen Series XVII, 2nd edn (Princeton, NJ: Princeton University Press, 1968).

Cantrell, L. (ed.), *Bards, Bohemians and Bookmen: Essays in Australian Literature* (St. Lucia: University of Queenland Press, 1976).

Chisholm, A. H., *Strange New World* (Sydney: Angus & Robertson, 1941).

Clark, M., *A Discovery of Australia*, 1976 Boyer Lectures (Sydney: Australian Broadcasting Commission, 1976).

—— , *A Short History of Australia*, rev. edn (New York: Mentor, 1969).

Colmer, J., *Patrick White*, Contemporary Writers, gen. eds M. Bradbury and C. Bigsby (London and New York: Methuen, 1984).

——,'Riders in the Chariot', *Patrick White*, Studies in Australian Literature (Melbourne: Edward Arnold Australia, 1978).

Dillistone, F. W., *Patrick White's 'Riders in the Chariot': Introduction and Commentary*, Religious Dimensions in Literature, gen. ed. L. A. Belford (New York: Seabury Press, 1967).

Docker, J., *Australian Cultural Elites: Intellectual Traditions in Sydney and Melbourne* (Sydney: Angus & Robertson, 1974).

Dostoyevsky, F., *The Idiot*, tr. H. and O. Carlisle, intro. H. Rosenberg (New York: New American Library, 1969).

—— ,*The Possessed*, tr. C. Garnett (New York: Dell, 1961).

Dutton, G. (ed.), *The Literature of Australia*, rev. edn (Harmondsworth: Penguin, 1976).

—— ,*Patrick White*, 2nd edn, Australian Writers and their Work, gen. ed. G. Dutton (Melbourne: Lansdowne Press, 1962).

—— ,*Patrick White*, 4th edn, Australian Writers and their Work, gen. ed. G. Johnston (Melbourne: Oxford University Press, 1971).

—— ,and Harris, M. (eds), *The Vital Decade, Ten Years of Australian Art and Letters* (South Melbourne: Sun Books, 1968).

Dyce, J. R., *Patrick White as Playwright* (St. Lucia: University of Queensland Press, 1974).

Eyre, E. J., *Journals of Expeditions of Discovery into Central Australia, and Overland from Adelaide to King George's Sound*, 2 vols (1845), Australiana Facsimile Editions, no. 7 (Adelaide: Libraries Board of South Australia, 1964).

Forster, E. M., *Aspects of the Novel* (New York: Harcourt, Brace, 1927).

Fowles, J., *Daniel Martin* (1977; repr. New York: New American Library, 1978).

Franck, A., *The Kabbalah: The Religious Philosophy of the Hebrews* (New York: Bell, 1940).

Frye, N., *Anatomy of Criticism: Four Essays* (Princeton, NJ: Princeton University Press, 1957).

—— ,*Fearful Symmetry: A Study of William Blake* (Princeton, NJ: Princeton University Press, 1947).

Gathorne-Hardy, G. M., *A Short History of International Affairs, 1920–1939*, 4th edn (London: Oxford University Press, 1950).

Gleeson, J., *Modern Painters, 1931–1970*, Australian Painting Studio Series, gen. ed. J. Henshaw (Dee Why West: Lansdowne Press, 1971).

Hamilton, E. and Cairns, H. (eds), *The Collected Dialogues* of Plato, *Including the Letters*, Bollingen Series LXXI (Princeton, NJ: Princeton University Press, 1963).

Hamilton, K. G. (ed.), *Studies in the Recent Australian Novel*, Australian Studies Centre (St Lucia: University of Queensland Press, 1978).

Heseltine, H. P. (ed.), *The Penguin Book of Australian Verse* (Harmondsworth: Penguin, 1972).

Hetherington, J., *Forty-Two Faces* (Melbourne: Cheshire, 1962; repr. Freeport, NY: Books for Libraries Press, 1969).

Johnston, G. (ed.), *Australian Literary Criticism* (Melbourne: Oxford University Press, 1962).

Jung, C., *Collected Works*, tr. R. F. C. Hull, Bollingen Series XX (New York: Pantheon Books) IX.i (1959), IX.ii (1959), XI (1958) and XII (1953).

Kennedy, B., *Cities of the World: Sydney* (London: J. M. Dent, 1970).

Keesing, N. (ed.), *Australian Postwar Novelists: Selected Critical Essays* (Milton, Queensland: Jacaranda Press, 1975).

Kierkegaard, S., *Fear and Trembling [and] The Sickness Unto Death*, tr. W. Lowrie (1941; repr. Garden City, NY: Doubleday, 1954).

Kiernan, B., *Images of Society and Nature: Seven Essays on Australian Novels* (Melbourne: Oxford University Press, 1971).

—— ,*Patrick White*, Macmillan Commonwealth Writers Series, gen. ed. A. N. Jeffares (London: Macmillan, 1980).

Langbaum, R., *The Poetry of Experience: The Dramatic Monologue in Modern Literary Tradition* (1957; repr. New York: Norton, 1963).

Leavis, F. R., *The Great Tradition* (1948; repr. New York: New York University Press, 1973).

Leichhardt, L., *Journal of an Overland Expedition in Australia from Moreton Bay to Port Essington* (1847), Australiana Facsimile Editions, no. 16 (Adelaide: Libraries Board of South Australia, 1964).

Martin, P. W., *Experiment in Depth: A Study of the Work of Jung, Eliot, and Toynbee* (1955; repr. Boston, Mass.: Routledge & Kegan Paul, 1976).

McCulloch, A. M., *A Tragic Vision: The Novels of Patrick White* (St Lucia: University of Queenland Pres, 1983).

McDougall, R., *Australia Felix: Joseph Furphy and Patrick White*, Commonwealth Literary Fund Lecture (Canberra: Australian National University Press, 1966).

McGregor, C. (ed.), *In the Making* (Melbourne: Nelson, 1969).

McLeod, A. L. (ed.), *The Pattern of Australian Culture*, Ithaca, NY: Cornell University Press, 1963).

Miller, J. E., Jr (ed.), *Theory of Fiction: Henry James* (Lincoln, Nebr.: University of Nebraska Press, 1972).

Moore, T. I., *Social Patterns in Australian Literature*, (Berkeley, Calif.: University of California Press, 1971).

Morley, P. A., *The Mystery of Unity: Theme and Technique in the Novels of Patrick White* (Montreal and London: McGill–Queen's University Press, 1972).

Myers, D., *The Peacocks and the Bourgeoisie: Ironic Vision in Patrick White's Shorter Prose Fiction*, (Adelaide: Adelaide University Union Press, 1978).

Phillips, A. A., *The Australian Tradition*, 2nd edn (Melbourne: Longman Cheshire, 1980).

Ramson, W. S. (ed.), *The Australian Experience: Critical Essays on Australian Novels* (Canberra: Australian National University Press, 1974).

Roberts, A., and Mountford, C. P., *The Dreamtime: Australian Aboriginal Myths* (Adelaide: Rigby, 1965).

Robinson, R., *Aboriginal Myths and Legends* (South Melbourne: Sun Books, 1966).

Scholem, G. G., *Major Trends in Jewish Mysticism* (New York: Schocken, 1961).

Semmler, C. (ed.), *Twentieth Century Australian Literary Criticism* (Melbourne: Oxford University Press, 1967).

—— ,and Whitelock, D. (eds), *Literary Australia* (Melbourne: Cheshire, 1966).

Shepherd, R., and Singh, K. (eds), *Patrick White: A Critical Symposium* (Adelaide: Centre for Research in the New Literatures in English, 1978).

Slatoff, W. J., *Quest for Failure: A Study of William Faulkner* (Ithaca, NY: Cornell University Press, 1960).

—— ,*With Respect to Readers: Dimensions of Literary Response* (Ithaca, NY: Cornell University Press, 1970).

Stafford, W. T. (ed.), *Twentieth Century American Writing* (New York: Odyssey Press, 1965).

Steinsaltz, A., *The Thirteen Petalled Rose*, tr. Y. Hanegbi (New York: Basic Books, 1980).

Summers, A., *Damned Whores and God's Police: The Colonization of Women in Australia* (Harmondsworth: Penguin, 1975).

Tiffin, C. (ed.), *South Pacific Images* (St Lucia, Queensland: South Pacific Association for Commonwealth Literature and Language Studies, 1978).

Walsh, W., *Patrick White: 'Voss'*, Studies in English Literature, no. 62, gen. ed. D. Daiches (London: Edward Arnold, 1976).
—— ,*Patrick White's Fiction* (Totowa, NJ: Rowman & Littlefield, 1977).
Wannan, B., *Legendary Australians* (Adelaide: Rigby, 1974).
Wilkes, G. A., *A Dictionary of Australian Colloquialisms* (Sydney: Sydney University Press, 1978).
—— (ed.), *Ten Essays on Patrick White: Selected from 'Southerly' (1964–67)* (Sydney: Angus & Robertson, 1970).
—— ,and Reid, I. C., *The Literatures of the British Commonwealth: Australia and New Zealand*, gen. ed. A. L. McLeod (University Park: Pennsylvania State University Press, 1970).
Wolfe, P., *Laden Choirs: The Fiction of Patrick White* (Lexington: University Press of Kentucky, 1983).

Letters, articles, recordings, theses and personal interviews
Akerholt, M., 'Story Into Play: The Two Versions of Patrick White's *A Cheery Soul*', *Southerly*, 40 (1980) 460–72.
Anderson, D., 'A Severed Leg: Anthropophagy and Communion in Patrick White's Fiction', *Southerly*, 40 (1980) 399–417.
'Australia Abhorrent to Writer', *Canberra Times*, 7 Mar 1978, p. 7.
Baker, R. S., 'Romantic Onanism in Patrick White's *The Vivisector*', *Texas Studies in Literature and Language*, 21 (1979) 203–25.
Barbour, J., 'Cheery Souls and Lost Souls: The Outsiders in Patrick White's Plays'. *Southerly*, 42 (1982) 137–48.
Barnard, M., 'The Four Novels of Patrick White', *Meanjin*, 15 (1956) 156–70.
—— ,'Theodora Again', *Southerly*, 20 (1959) 51–5.
Beasley, J., 'The Great Hatred: Patrick White as Novelist'. *Realist Writer*, no. 9 (1962) 11–14.
Beatson, P., 'The Three Stages: Mysticism in Patrick White's *Voss*'. *Southerly*, 30 (1970) 111–21.
Bedford, J., 'Drawn Subtly inside a Transexual's Experience', review of *The Twyborn Affair*, in the *National Times*, 24 Nov 1979, p. 55.
Berger, J., 'A View of the Artist as Lucifer', review of *The Vivisector*, in *The Times*, 22 Oct 1970, p. 8.
Beston, J. B., 'Dreams and Visions in *The Tree of Man*', *Australian Literary Studies*, 6 (1973) 152–66.
—— ,'The Family Background and Early Years of Patrick White', *Descent*, 7 (Sep 1974) 16–29.
—— ,review of *Flaws in the Glass: A Self-Portrait*, in *World Literature Written in English*, 21 (1982) 83–6.
—— ,'White: A Seal on Greatness', *Sydney Morning Herald*, 20 Oct 1973, p. 6.
—— ,and R. M. Beston, 'A Brief Biography of Patrick White', *World Literature Written in English*, 12 (1973) 208–12.
Björksten, I., 'A Day with Patrick White', tr. J. S. Martin, *Nation Review*, 21–7 June 1974, p. 1179.
Blythe, R., ' "We Torment Each Other Round the World and Back" ', review of *Flaws in the Glass: A Self-Portrait*, in the *Listener*, 10 Dec 1981, pp. 722–3.
Bradley, D., 'Australia through the Looking-Glass: Patrick White's Latest Novel', review of *Riders in the Chariot*, in *Overland*, no. 23 (Apr 1962) 41–5.

Brady, V., 'The Artist and the Savage God: Patrick White's *The Vivisector*', *Meanjin*, 33 (1974) 136–45.

——, ' "Down at the Dump" and Lacan's Mirror Stage', *Australian Literary Studies*, 11 (1983) 233–7.

——, '*A Fringe of Leaves*: Civilization by the Skin of our Teeth', *Southerly*, 37 (1977) 123–40.

——, 'The Hard Enquiring Wind: A Study of Patrick White as an Australian Novelist', dissertation (University of Toronto, 1969).

——, 'The Novelist and the New World: Patrick White's *Voss*', *Texas Studies in Literature and Language*, 21 (1979) 169–85.

——, ' "A Single Bone-Clean Button": The Achievement of Patrick White', *Literary Criterion*, 15, nos 3–4 (1980) 35–47.

——, 'Why Myth Matters', *Westerly*, no. 2 (June 1973) 59–63.

Brand, M., 'Another Look at Patrick White', *Realist Writer*, no. 12 (1963) 21–2.

Brent, P., 'The Novelist Patrick White Talks to Patricia Brent. He Has Just Been Awarded the Nobel Prize for Literature', *Listener*, 25 Oct 1973, p. 545.

Brisbane, K., '*Big Toys*: Patrick White's Power without Glory', review of *Big Toys*, in the *National Times*, 1–6 Aug 1977, p. 26.

Brissenden, R. F., 'Inferno in the Greenbelt: Patrick White's Wasteland', review of *The Burnt Ones*, in the *Australian*, 28 Nov 1964, p. 12.

——, 'On the Edge of the Empire: Some Thoughts on Recent Australian Fiction', *Sewanee Review*, 87, no. 1 (Winter 1979) 142–57.

——, personal interview, 6 Nov 1979.

——, 'The Plays of Patrick White', *Meanjin*, 23 (1964) 243–56.

——, 'Some Recent Australian Plays', *Texas Quarterly*, 5, no. 2 (Summer 1962) 185–92.

Broadbent, D., 'Mud in your Eye from Author White', *Age*, 7 Mar 1978, p. 3.

Burns, D. R., 'Australian Fiction versus Austrophobia', *Overland*, no. 90 (Dec 1982) 44–51.

Burrows, J. F., 'Patrick White's Four Plays', *Australian Literary Studies*, 2 (1966) 155–70.

——, reviews of *Studies in the Recent Australian Novel*, ed. K. G. Hamilton, of *Patrick White: A Critical Symposium*, ed., R. Shepherd and K. Singh, and of D. Meyers, *The Peacocks and the Bourgeoisie: Ironic Vision in Patrick White's Shorter Prose Fiction*, in *Australian Literary Studies*, 9 (1979) 407–10.

——, '*Voss* and the Explorers', *AUMLA*, 26 (1966) 234–40.

Campbell, R., 'The Character of Australian Religion', *Meanjin*, 36 (1977) 178–88.

——, 'For and against *Voss*', review of *Voss*, in the *Daily Telegraph* (Sydney), 26 July 1958, p. 14.

Cantrell, L., 'Patrick White's First Book', *Australian Literary Studies*, 6 (1974) 434–6.

Carpenter, H., 'Patrick White Explains Himself', review of *Flaws in the Glass: A Self-Portrait*, in the *New York Times Book Review*, 7 Feb 1982, pp. 9 and 41.

Carroll, D., 'Stage Convention in the Plays of Patrick White', *Modern Drama*, 19, no. 1 (Mar 1976) 11–24.

Chapman, E. L., 'The Mandala Design of Patrick White's *Riders in the Chariot*', *Texas Studies in Literature and Language*, 21 (1979) 186–202.

Chellappan, K., 'Self, Space, and Art in a Few Novels of Patrick White', *Literary Half-Yearly*, 24, no. 1 (Jan 1983) 24–34.

Clancy, P., 'The Actor's Dilemma: Patrick White and Henri de Montherlant', *Meanjin*, 33 (1974) 298–302.

Clark, A., 'Portrait of a Powerful Australian Woman', *Bulletin*, 24 Apr 1979, pp. 55–63.

—— , 'The Private Patrick White', *New York Times Book Review*, 27 Apr 1980, pp. 32–3.

Clark, M., 'Concerning Patrick White', review of *The Twyborn Affair*, in the *Sydney Morning Herald*, 13 Oct 1979, p. 20.

—— , personal interview, 6 Nov 1979.

—— , 'Shaking off the Philistines', *Bulletin*, 29 Jan 1980, pp. 114–24.

Clarke, D., 'The Image of Australian Man', *Australian Quarterly*, 37, no. 2 (June 1965) 67–78.

Coates, J., '*Voss* and Jacob Boehme: A Note on the Spirituality of Patrick White', *Australian Literary Studies*, 9 (1979) 119–22.

Coe, R. N., 'The Artist and the Grocer: Patrick White's *The Vivisector*', *Meanjin*, 29 (1970) 526–9.

Colmer, J., 'Patrick White's *A Fringe of Leaves*', *Literary Half-Yearly*, 23, no. 2 (July 1982) 85–100.

'Column 8', *Sydney Morning Herald*, 11 Apr 1975, p. 1.

Conway, R., 'White Sees Pains in the Glass', Rev. of *Flaws in the Glass: A Self-Portrait*, in the *Australian Weekend Magazine*, 24–5 Oct 1981, p. 8.

Cook, R., review of *Four Plays*, in *Harper's Magazine*, Sep 1966, p. 114.

Cope, J. F., 'Mr Patrick White', Australian House of Representatives, *Debates*, 29 Nov 1973, p. 4081.

Core, G., 'Forging a Country of the Imagination', review of *The Twyborn Affair*, in *Wall Street Journal*, 18 June 1980, p. 22.

—— , 'Patrick White and the Commonwealth Imagination', review of W. Walsh, *Patrick White's Fiction*, in the *Sewanee Review*, 87, no. 1 (Winter 1979) ii–vi.

—— , 'A Terrible Majesty: The Novels of Patrick White', *Hollins Critic*, 11, no. 1 (Feb 1974) 1–16.

Covell, R., 'Patrick White's Plays', *Quadrant*, 8, no. 1 (Apr–May 1964) 7–12.

Cowburn, J., 'The Metaphysics of *Voss*', *Twentieth Century*, 18 (Winter 1964) 352–61.

'Crash Course', *Bulletin*, 15 Aug 1970, p. 13.

Crowcroft, J., 'Patrick White: A Reply to Dorothy Green', *Overland*, no. 59 (Spring 1974) 48–53.

Davidson, J., 'Patrick White's Latest Novel: A Rich and Enigmatic Triptych', review of *The Twyborn Affair*, in the *National Times*, 24 Nov 1979, p. 54.

Deiley, R., 'Patrick White: A Shy Genius', *Daily Telegraph* (Sydney), 20 Oct 1973, p. 19.

DeMott, B., 'The Perils of Protean Man', review of *The Twyborn Affair*, in the *New York Times Book Review*, 27 Apr 1980, p. 3.

Docker, J. '*The Cockatoos*: Patrick White's Short Stories Set Society against the Silent ' "Natural" Man', review of *The Cockatoos*, in the *National Times*, 4–9 Nov 1974, p. 22.

—— , 'Patrick White and Romanticism: *The Vivisector*', *Southerly*, 33 (1973) 44–61.

Drewe, R., 'The Confessions of Patrick White in a Searing Autobiography', review of *Flaws in the Glass: A Self Portrait*, in the *Bulletin*, 20 Oct 1981, pp. 26–30.

Drysdale, R., letter to John Beston, 3 Oct 1972, John Beston Letters, National Library of Australia, Canberra, NLA/MS 4629.

DuBose, M., 'Opening Choice an Act of Faith', review of *The Night the Prowler*, in the *Sydney Morning Herald*, 5 June 1978, p. 7.

Dutton, G., 'Strength through Adversity', *Bulletin*, 29 Jan 1980, pp. 124–32.

Edgar, S., 'A Woman's Life and Love: A Reply to Leonie Kramer', *Quadrant*, 21, no. 10 (Oct 1977) 69–72.

'Eight Head Australian Order', *Sydney Morning Herald*, 14 June 1975, p. 1.

Ellis, B., 'The Great Annual . . .', review of *The Night the Prowler*, in the *Nation Review*, 22–8 June 1978, p. 17.

Emeljanow, V., 'Too Long and Obsessive,' review of *A Cheery Soul*, in the *National Times*, 3 Feb 1979, p. 42.

Fitzgerald, R. D., letter to John Beston, n.d., John Beston Letters, National Library of Australia, Canberra, NLA/MS 4629.

Flantz, R., 'To Live and to Create', *Overland*, no. 35 (Nov 1966) pp. 53–4.

Frykberg, J., 'Patrick White Sees "Sinister Overtones" ', *Sydney Morning Herald*, 29 Nov 1975, p. 1.

Garebian, K., 'The Desert and the Garden: The Theme of Completeness in *Voss*', *Modern Fiction Studies*, 22 (Winter 1976–7) 557–69.

Ghose, Z., 'The One Comprehensive Vision', *Texas Studies in Literature and Language*, 21 (1979) 260–79.

Gilbert, M., 'Stan Parker's Apocalypse: A Study in White.' *Adelaide ALS Working Papers*, 1, no. 2 (Oct 1975) 42–9.

Gilbert, S. M., 'Costumes of the Mind: Transvestism as Metaphor in Modern Literature', *Critical Inquiry*, 7 (1980) 391–417.

Gingell-Beckmann, S., 'Seven Black Swans: The Symbolic Logic of Patrick White's *The Eye of the Storm*', *World Literature Written in English*, 21 (1982) 315–25.

Gordimer, N., 'Mysterious Incest', review of *Flaws in the Glass: A Self-Portrait* in the *New York Review of Books*, 15 Apr 1982, pp. 14–15.

'Govt Puts up $350,000 for Film of Patrick White Story', *Sydney Morning Herald*, 7 July 1977, p. 1.

Grattan, C. H., 'One-Way Journey into a "World of Desert and Dreams" ', review of *Voss*, in the *New York Times Book Review*, 18 Aug 1957, p. 4.

Green, D., 'The Edge of Error', *Quadrant*, 17, nos 5–6 (Dec 1973) 36–47.

—— ,'Patrick White's Nobel Prize', *Overland*, no. 57 (Summer 1974) pp. 23–5.

—— ,'White's Tale of Survival', review of *A Fringe of Leaves*, in the *Nation Review*, 22–8 Oct 1976, p. 20.

Hadcraft, C., 'The Theme of Revelation in Patrick White's Novels', *Southerly*, 37 (1977) 34–46.

Harris, M., 'Patrick White's Chariot', review of *Riders in the Chariot*, in the *Nation*, 21 Oct 1961, pp. 21–2.

—— ,'The Public Severity and Private Sincerity of Patrick White', *Australian*, 5 Apr 1969, p. 10.

—— ,'Recent Publishing and the Australian Identity', *Hemisphere*, 10, no. 2 (Feb 1966) 2–6.

Harrison-Ford, C., 'Dying in Jewels', review of *The Eye of the Storm*, in the *Australian*, 29 Sep 1973. p. 18.

—— ,'Shorter White', review of *The Cockatoos*, in the *Australian*, 22 June 1974, p. 24.

Harrower, E., personal interview, 27 Nov 1979.

Hastings, P., 'The Writing Business: William Collins and Patrick White', *Observer*, 21 Mar 1959, pp. 175–6.

Hazzard, S., 'Letter from Australia', *Nation Review*, 5–11 May 1977, pp. 692–4.

—— ,'Problems Facing Contemporary Novelists', *Australian Literary Studies*, 9 (1979) 179–81.

Heltay, H., 'The Novels of Patrick White', tr. J. B. Beston, *Southerly*, 33 (1973) 92–104.

Herbert, X., letter to John Beston, 10 Sep 1972, John Beston Letters, National Library of Australia, Canberra, NLA/MS 4629.

Hergenhan , L. T., 'Convict Legends, Australian Legends: Price Warung and the Palmers', *Australian Literary Studies*, 9 (1979) 337–45.

Herring, T., and Wilkes, G. A. 'A Conversation with Patrick White', *Southerly*, 33 (1973) 132–43.

Heseltine, H. P., 'Australian Image: (1) The Literary Heritage', *Meanjin*, 21 (1962) 35–49.

—— ,'Patrick White's Style', *Quadrant*, 7, no. 3 (1963) 61–74.

—— ,personal interview, 16 Nov 1979.

—— ,'Writer and Reader: *The Burnt Ones*', review of *The Burnt Ones*, in *Southerly*, 25 (1965) 69–71.

Hope, A. D., 'The Bunyip Stages a Comeback', review of *The Tree of Man*, in the *Sydney Morning Herald*, 16 June 1956, p. 15.

Houbein, L., 'A Case for the Inclusion of *Happy Valley* in the Canon of Patrick White's Novels', *Adelaide ALS Working Papers*, 1, no. 1 (June 1975) 5–10.

Howard, M., 'What it was Like', review of *Flaws in the Glass: A Self-Portrait*, and S. T. Warner, *Scenes of Childhood*, in *Atlantic*, Mar 1982, pp. 83–4.

Hutton, G., 'A Poet at Loose on Cow Cockies', review of *The Tree of Man*, in the *Age*, 12 May 1956, p. 17.

Johnson, M., '*A Fringe of Leaves*: White's Genethlicon', *Texas Studies in Literature and Language*, 21 (1979) 226–39.

—— ,'Patrick White: The Eye of the Language', *World Literature Written in English*, 15 (1976) 339–58.

—— ,'*Twyborn*: The Abbess, the Bulbul, and the Bawdy House', *Modern Fiction Studies*, 27 (Spring 1981) 159–68.

Keig, C., 'Nietzsche's Influence on Australian Literature', *Adelaide ALS Working Papers*, 1, no. 2 (Oct 1975) 50–63.

Kelly, F., 'The External Triangle Goes into the Uranium Debate and Explodes', review of *Big Toys*, in the *Australian Weekend Magazine*, 30–1 July 1977, p. 9.

Kepert, L. V., 'New Fiction', review of *The Aunt's Story*, in the *Sydney Morning Herald*, 7 Aug 1948, p. 6.

Kiernan, B., personal interview, 25 Oct 1979.

—— ,'Treble Exposure', *Southerly*, 42 (1982) 165–73.

—— ,'White's Latest Vision', review of *The Vivisector*, in the *Australian*, 17 Oct 1970, p. 22.

Kippax, H. G., 'The Dwelling of the God', review of *The Solid Mandala*, in the *Sydney Morning Herald*, 14 May 1966, p. 15.

Kramer, L., 'On the Edge of Despair', review of *The Cockatoos*, in the *Sydney Morning Herald*, 22 June 1974, p. 13.

—— ,'Patrick White: "The Unplayed" ', *Quadrant*, 18, no. 1 (Jan–Feb 1974) 65–6.

—— ,'Patrick White's Götterdämmerung', *Quadrant*, 17, no. 3 (May–June 1973) 8–19.

—— ,personal interview, 17 Oct 1979.

—— ,'Pseudoxia Endemica', review of *The Twyborn Affair*, in *Quadrant*, no. 155 (July 1980) 66–7.

—— ,'A Woman's Life and Love', *Quadrant*, 20, no. 11 (Nov 1976) 62–3.

Laidlaw, R. P., 'The Complexity of *Voss*', *Southern Review*, 4 (1970) 3–14.

Lawson, A., 'Meaning and Experience: A Review–Essay on Some Recurrent Problems in Patrick White Criticism', *Texas Studies in Literature and Language*, 21 (1979) 280-95.

—— ,personal interview, 15 Nov 1979.

—— ,'Unmerciful Dingoes?: The Critical Reception of Patrick White', *Meanjin*, 32 (1973) 379–92.

—— ,'White for White's Sake: Studies of Patrick White's Novels', *Meanjin*, 32 (1973) 343–9.

Leitch, D., 'Patrick White: A Revealing Profile', *National Times*, 27 Mar–1 Apr 1978, pp. 30–5.

Lindsay, J., 'The Alienated Australian Intellectual', *Meanjin*, 22 (1963) 48–59.

Loder, E., '*The Ham Funeral*: Its Place in the Development of Patrick White', *Southerly*, 23 (1963) 78–91.

Maack, A., 'Shakespearean Reference as Structural Principle in Patrick White's *The Tree of Man* and *The Eye of the Storm*', *Southerly*, 38 (1978) 123–40.

Macainsh, N., 'Patrick White – Fragments of a Swedish Correspondence' *LiNQ*, 4, nos 1–2 (1975) 7–12.

—— ,'Patrick White – A Note on the Pheonix', *LiNQ*, 5, no. 1 (1976) 15–19.

—— ,'The Poems of Patrick White,' *LiNQ*, 4, nos 3–4 (1975) 18–22.

—— ,'A Queer Unity – Patrick White's *The Twyborn Affair*,' *Southerly*, 43 (1983) 143–54.

—— ,'Voss and his Communications -- A Structural Contrast', *Australian Literary Studies*, 10 (1982) 437–47.

Macartney, K., 'Patrick White's Four Plays', *Meanjin*, 24 (1965) 528–30.

Mackenzie, M., 'Abyssinia Lost and Regained', *Essays in Criticism*, 13 (1963) 292–300.

—— ,'The Consciousness of "Twin Consciousness": Patrick White's *The Solid Mandala*', *Novel*, 2, no. 3 (Spring 1969) 241–54.

—— ,' "Dark Birds of Light": *The Eye of the Storm* as Swansong', *Southern Review*, 10 (1977) 270–84.

—— ,'Patrick White's Later Novels: A Generic Reading', *Southern Review*, 1 (1965) 5–18.

—— ,personal interview, 23 Oct 1979.

—— ,'Tradition and Patrick White's Individual Talent', *Texas Studies in Literature and Language*, 21 (1979) 147–68.

—— ,'Yes, Let's Return to Abyssinia', *Essays in Criticism*, 14 (1964) 433–5.

Maes-Jelinek, H., 'Altering Boundaries: The Art of Translation in *The Angel at the Gate* and *The Twyborn Affair*', *World Literature Written in English*, 23 (1984) 165–74.

Mann, E., 'A Suspenseful Saga from Australia's Finest', review of *A Fringe of Leaves*, in the *Greensboro News* (NC), 17 Apr 1977, Mitchell Library, Sydney, ML Document 2793.

Martin, D., 'Among the Bones: What are our Novelists Looking for?', *Meanjin*, 18 (1959) 52–8.

Mathews, C. R., and Whitlam, E. G., 'Mr Patrick White: Suggested Recognition by Parliament', Australian House of Representatives, *Debates*, 7 Nov 1973, p. 2882.

McCarthy, C., 'White Won't Pick up his Nobel Book Prize', *Daily Telegraph* (Sydney), 20 Oct 1973, p. 5.

McCulloch, A., 'Patrick White's Novels and Nietzsche', *Australian Literary Studies*, 9 (1980) 309–20.

McIntosh, P., 'Journey Back to Reality', *Age*, 24 Sep 1977, p. 22.

McLaren, J., 'The Critical Point', reviews of B. Kiernan, *Criticism*, of A. D. Hope, *Native Companions: A Collection of Essays and Comments on Australian Literature*, of D. Green, *Ulysses Bound: Henry Handel Richardson and her Fiction*, of P. Morley, *The Mystery of Unity: Theme and Technique in the Novels of Patrick White*, of B. Matthews, *The Receding Wave: Henry Lawson's Prose*, and of *The Australian Experience: Critical Essays on Australian Novelists*, ed. W. S. Ramson, in *Overland*, no. 61 (Winter 1975) 56–8.

—— ,'Seeking the Self in an Uncertain World', review of *The Twyborn Affair*, in the *Australian Book Review*, no. 16 (Nov 1979) 8–9.

Meaney, N., 'Exploring Leichhardt', reviews of E. M. Webster, *Whirlwind on the Plain: Ludwig Leichhardt, Friends, Foes, and History*, and of G. Connell, *The Mystery of Ludwig Leichhardt*, in *Quadrant*, no. 155 (July 1980) 69–70.

Mercer, D., 'A Film Script of *Voss*: Interview by Rodney Wetherell', *Australian Literary Studies*, 8 (1978) 395–401.

—— ,'Writing the Screenplay for the Film of *Voss*', writer's programme, Australian Broadcasting Company, 23 Apr 1978, University of Queensland, St Lucia, AV Collection, PR 8000.W7/1978/no. 35.

Michelmore, P., ' "One of the Most Gifted of Living Novelists is an Australian Little Regarded in his own Country . . . " ', review of *The Vivisector*, in the Sydney Morning Herald, 22 Aug 1970, p. 11.

Mitchell, A., personal interview, 17 and 24 Oct 1979.

Moffitt, I., 'Australian Myths Debunked', *Sunday Mirror* (Sydney), 3 Dec 1961, p. 19.

—— ,'Talk with Patrick White', *New York Times Book Review*, 18 Aug 1957, p. 18.

Morley, P. A., 'Doppelganger's Dilemma, Artist and Man: *The Vivisector*', *Queen's Quarterly*, 78 (1971) 407–20.

—— ,'Patrick White's *A Fringe of Leaves*: Journey to Tintagel', *World Literature Written in English*, 21 (1982) 303–15.

Motion, A., 'Time Trouble', reviews of *The Twyborn Affair*, of S. O'Faolain, *And Again?* and of Q. Crisp, *Chog*, in the *New Statesman*, 28 Sep 1979, pp. 470–1.

Naipaul, V. S., 'Australia Deserta', review of *The Burnt Ones*, in the *Spectator*, 16 Oct 1964, p. 513.

'National Notebook: Dobell's Week', *Bulletin*, 12 May 1962, p. 4.

'National Notebook: New Works', *Bulletin*, 11 July 1964, p. 9.

Nelson, T. G. A., 'Prosperpina and Pluto, Ariadne and Bacchus: Myth in Patrick White's "Dead Roses" ', *Australian Literary Studies*, 10 (1981) 111–14.

'New Novels', review of *Happy Valley*, in the *Sydney Morning Herald*, 1 Apr 1939, p. 20.

'New Novels: An Australian Sophisticate', review of *The Living and the Dead*, in the *Sydney Morning Herald*, 27 Sep 1941, p. 10.

'No Knights for Patrick White', *Sydney Morning Herald*, 23 June 1976, p. 24.

'Nobel Prize Man to Support Whitlam', *Sydney Morning Herald*, 10 May 1974, p. 2.

'Nobel Winner Gives $80,000 Prize to Aid Fellow Writers', *Australian*, 27 Oct 1973, p. 3.

O'Brien, D., 'Suddenly . . . an Australian Film Industry?', *Bulletin*, 1 Aug 1970, pp. 35–8.

O'Brien, G., 'No-one Realises How Frivolous Patrick White Can Be', *Sydney Morning Herald*, 10 Dec 1983, p. 31.

O'Grady, S., 'Diamonds and Furs are Diane's Big Toys', *Weekend Australian Magazine*, 20–1 Oct 1979, p. 10.

Oakley, B., 'White on Green', *Quadrant*, no. 150 (Jan–Feb 1980) 68–9.

Owen, A., ' "Old Age I am Afraid of, but Not Death": Patrick White's Story', *Australian Financial Review*, 11 July 1972, pp. 2–3.

'Patrick White Boosts Labor at Rally', *Age*, 29 Nov 1975, p. 5.

'The Patrick White Controversy', *Realist Writer*, no. 12 (1963) 3–4.

'Patrick White Defends *Portnoy* as "Classic" ', *Australian*, 28 Oct 1970, p. 3.

'Patrick White Film Opens Tonight', *Sydney Morning Herald*, 2 June 1978, p. 4.

'Patrick White Interviewed by Rodney Wetherell about Art and the Novel', National Library of Australia, Canberra, NLA/TRC 551, cassette (n.d.).

'Patrick White Names the Men who Matter', *Australian*, 26 Jan 1974, p. 1.

'Patrick White Refuses his Soup', review of *The Living and the Dead*, in the *Bulletin*, 22 Oct 1941, p. 2.

'Patrick White Reported to Have Quit Order', *Sydney Morning Herald*, 21 June 1976, p. 1.

'Patrick White versus "Great God Sport" ', *Sydney Morning Herald*, 18 Mar 1972, p. 1.

'Patrick White Wants to Honour Three "Mavericks" ', *Sydney Morning Herald*, 26 Jan 1974, p. 1.

'Patrick White Warns of Slide Back to Apathy under Libs', *Australian*, 29 Nov 1975, p. 5.

'Patrick White's Nightmare', review of *Voss*, in the *Observer*, 22 Feb 1958, pp. 19–20.

'People', Bulletin, 27 Oct 1973, p. 28.

Perkins, E., 'Escape with a Convict: Patrick White's *A Fringe of Leaves*, review of *A Fringe of Leaves*, in *Meanjin*, 36 (1977) 265–9.

—— ,'Right Conditions to Grow?', review of *The Eye of the Storm*, in *LiNQ*, 3, no. 1 (1974) 23–6.

—— ,'Sterile Critics and Fecund Artists: Old Themes Brought Up to Date', review of *The Vivisector*, in *LiNQ*, 1, no. 1 (1971) 43–6.

'Personal Item', *Bulletin*, 9 Dec 1959, p. 16.

Pierce, P., 'How Australia's Literary History Might Be Written', *Australian Literary Studies*, 11 (1983) 67–79.

Porter, H., letter to John Beston, 11 Sep 1972, John Beston Letters, National Library of Australia, Canberra, NLA/MS 4629.

—— ,'Patrick White', in *Contemporary Novelists*, ed. J. Vinson (London: St James Press, 1972) pp. 1345–8.

'Portnoy Complaints', *Bulletin*, 12 Sep 1970, pp. 27–8.

Prerauer, M., 'The Wit and Wisdom of Patrick White', *Sunday Telegraph* (Sydney), 12 Aug 1973, pp. 23 and 47.

Prescott, P., 'Self-Abuse', review of *Flaws in the Glass: A Self-Portrait*, in *Newsweek*, 1 Mar 1982, pp. 71–2.

Pringle, J., 'Survival Trail Leads to Discovery', Rev. of *A Fringe of Leaves*, in the *Sydney Morning Herald*, 25 Sep 1976, p. 15.

Ramsey, S. A., '*The Twyborn Affair*: "The Beginning in an End" or "the End of a Beginning"?', *Ariel*, 11, no. 4 (1980) 87–95.

'Reflections', review of *Flaws in the Glass: A Self-Portrait*, in the *Economist*, 31 Oct 1981, p. 101.

Reid, I., 'Review Article: Distractions and Definitions, Studying Commonwealth Literature', *Southern Review*, 4 (1971) 316–26.

Ricks, C., 'Gigantist', review of *The Eye of the Storm*, in the *New York Review of Books*, 4 Apr 1974, pp. 19–20.

Riddell, E., 'A Morning at Mr White's', *Australian*, 1 Aug 1970, p. 15; repr. in *The Armchair Australian, 1969–70*, ed. James Hall (Sydney: Ibis, 1970) pp. 102–6.

——,'A Quiet Man Finds a Big Prize Was a Door Knock at Night', *Australian*, 20 Oct 1973, p. 3.

——,'The Whites: Patrick, Pastoralists and Polo Ponies', *Bulletin*, 8 Jan 1980, pp. 44–50.

Riemer, A. P., 'Eddie and the Bogomils – Some Observations on *The Twyborn Affair*', *Southerly*, 40 (1980) 12–29.

——,'The Eye of the Needle: Patrick White's Recent Novels', *Southerly*, 34 (1974) 248–66.

——,'Landscape with Figures – Images of Australia in Patrick White's Fiction', *Southerly*, 42 (1982) 20–38.

Roderick, C., '*Riders in the Chariot*: An Exposition', *Southerly*, 22 (1962) 62–77.

Rohde, H., reviews of *The Tree of Man*, *Voss* and *Riders in the Chariot*, tr. N. Macainsh, in *LiNQ*, 3, nos. 3–4 (1974) 34–6.

Rorke, J., 'Patrick White and the Critics', *Southerly*, 20 (1959) 66–74.

Rosenthal, T. G., 'Ironic Musings in Moronic Suburbia', review of *The Solid Mandala*, in the *Australian*, 2 Apr 1966. p. 10.

Ross, R., 'The Ultimate Expatriation: A Look at Patrick White's *The Twyborn Affair*', paper presented at Modern Language Association Convention, New York, Dec 1981.

Rowbotham, D., 'The Black in White', review of *Flaws in the Glass: A Self-Portrait*, in the *Courier-Mail Saturday Magazine* (Brisbane), 24 Oct 1981, p. 5.

——,'Profile of a Great Man's Privacy', *Courier-Mail* (Brisbane), 30 Mar 1970, p. 2.

Scheick, W. J., 'The Gothic Grace and Rainbow Aesthetic of Patrick White's Fiction: An Introduction', *Texas Studies in Literature and Language*, 21 (1979) 131–46.

Seymour, A., letter to John Beston, 20 Sep 1972, John Beston Letters, National Library of Australia, Canberra, NLA/MS 4629.

Sharman, J., 'A Very Literary Luncheon', *National Times*, 30 June 1979, pp. 26–7 and 30–1.

Sharrad, P., '*Pour mieux sauter*: Christopher Koch's Novels in Relation to White,

Stow and the Quest for a Post-Colonial Fiction', *World Literature Written in English*, 23 (1984) 208–23.

Shepherd, R., 'CRNLE Patrick White Seminar', *SPAN* (newsletter of the South Pacific Association for Commonwealth Literature and Language Studies), no. 6 (Apr 1978) 9–14.

Shrubb, P., 'Patrick White: Chaos Accepted', *Quadrant*, 3, no. 3 (1968) 7–19.

Sides, A., 'Patrick White's New Plays', *Overland*, no. 30 (Sep 1964) 46–8.

Singh, K., 'The Fiend of Motion: Theodora Goodman in Patrick White's *The Aunt's Story*', *Quadrant*, 19, no. 9 (Dec 1975) 90–2.

Slessor, K., 'Patrick White's Triumph: Novelist and his Tree', review of *The Tree of Man*, in the *Sun* (Sydney), 5 Aug 1956, p. 41.

Small, J., 'Patrick White's Opera: The Advent of Peter Sculthorpe', *Bulletin*, 13 June 1964, p. 47.

Smith, M., 'Patrick White in Perspective', *Social Alternatives*, 3, no. 1. (Oct 1982) 68–70.

Smith, T., 'A Portrait of the Artist in Patrick White's *The Vivisector*', *Meanjin*, 31 (1972) 167–77.

Souter, G., 'White in the Literaries', *Sydney Morning Herald*, 12 Jan 1974, p. 15.

Steiner, G., 'Carnal Knowledge', review of *The Eye of the Storm*, in the *New Yorker*, 4 Mar 1974, pp. 109–13.

Stewart, D., 'The Big Boss Voss', review of *Voss*, in the *Bulletin*, 5 Mar 1958, pp. 2 and 58.

—— ,'*The Tree of Man*', review of *The Tree of Man*, in the *Bulletin*, 18 July 1956, pp. 2 and 35.

Stow, R., review of *A Fringe of Leaves*, in *The Times Literary Supplement*, 10 Sep 1976, p. 1097; repr. in the *National Times*, 11–16 Oct 1976, p. 25.

—— ,'Transfigured Histories: Recent Novels of Patrick White and Robert Drewe', *Australian Literary Studies*, 9 (1979) 26–38.

Sykes, J., '*Voss* has Problems for Film-Maker: Top Director Visits Patrick White', *Sydney Morning Herald*, 14 Feb 1974, p. 3.

Tacey, D., 'Denying the Shadow as the Day Lengthens: Patrick White's *The Living and the Dead*', *Southern Review*, 11 (1978) 165–79.

—— ,'Patrick White: Misconceptions about Jung's Influence', *Australian Literary Studies*, 9 (1979) 245–6.

—— ,'The Secret of the Black Rose: Spiritual Alchemy in Patrick White's *The Aunt's Story*', *Adelaide ALS Working Papers*, 2, no. 2 (Mar 1977) 36–78.

Taylor, A., 'White's Short Stories', *Overland*, no. 31 (Autumn 1965) 17–19.

Tennant, K., 'Death Scene of Queen Lear', review of *The Eye of the Storm*, in the *Sydney Morning Herald*, 6 Oct 1973, p. 22.

—— ,'Poetic Symbolism in Novel by Patrick White', review of *Voss*, in the *Sydney Morning Herald*, 8 Feb 1958, p. 12.

—— ,'The Quiet Man who Won the Nobel Prize', *Australian Women's Weekly*, 7 Nov 1973, p. 8.

—— ,'Writes in Stained Glass', *Sydney Morning Herald*, 22 Sep 1956, p. 10.

'They Want a Centennial Park . . . Not a Car Park!', *Sydney Morning Herald*, 19 June 1972, p. 2.

'Thirty-Nine Sign Publicly to Defy National Service Act', *Sydney Morning Herald*, 10 Dec 1969, p. 9.

Thomas D., 'Patrick White's Gift Show', *Sydney Morning Herald*, 12 Dec 1974, p. 7.

Tout-Smith, G., 'Nightmare Uncertainties', review of *The Twyborn Affair*, in *Overland*, no. 78. (Dec 1979) 65–7.

Tucker, A., *et al.*, 'The Legend and the Loneliness: A Discussion of the Australian Myth', *Overland*, no. 23 (Apr 1962) 33–8.

Turner, G., 'A Hurtle Duffield Retrospective', *Overland*, nos 50–1 (Autumn 1972) 93–5.

———,'Looking at a Portrait: An Approach to *Flaws in the Glass*', *Overland*, no. 87 (1982) 20–7.

Walker, D. O., 'The Western Explorer as Literary Hero: Jedediah Smith and Ludwig Leichhardt', *Western Humanities Review*, 25 (1975) 243–59.

Wallace-Crabbe, C., 'Crucifixion at Sarsaparilla', review of *Riders in the Chariot*, in the *Bulletin*, 25 Nov 1961, pp. 35–6.

Walsh, W., 'Centres of the Self', review of *The Twyborn Affair*, in *The Times Literary Supplement*, 30 Nov 1979, p. 77.

———,'Fiction as Metaphor: The Novels of Patrick White', *Sewanee Review*, 82, no. 2 (1974) 197–211.

———,'White and the Violence of Being', review of *The Cockatoos*, in the *Sewanee Review*, 83, no. 3 (1975) lxxii–lxxvi.

Walters, M., 'Patrick White', *New Left Review*, no. 18 (1963) 37-50.

Ward, J., 'Parick White's *A Fringe of Leaves*: History and Fiction', *Australian Literary Studies*, 8 (1978) 402–18.

Warren, T. L., 'Patrick White: The Early Novels', *Modern Fiction Studies*, 27 (Spring 1981) 121–39.

Whaley, S., 'Food for Thought in Patrick White's Fiction', *World Literature Written in English*, 22 (1983) 197–212.

'White Award Goes to Poet', *Sydney Morning Herald*, 17 Nov 1978, p. 3.

'White Award Honors Qld Poet', *Sydney Morning Herald*, 22 Nov 1976, p. 2.

'White Prize for Christina Stead', *Sydney Morning Herald*, 14 Nov 1974, p. 13.

'Whitlam and the Stars Draw 11,000 to Opera House Rally', *Sydney Morning Herald*, 11 May 1974, pp. 1–2.

Whitman, R. F., 'The Dream Plays of Patrick White', *Texas Studies in Literature and Language*, 21 (1979) 240–59.

Wilding, M., 'Short Story Chronicle', *Meanjin*, 30 (1971) 255–67.

Wilkes, G. A., 'An Approach to Patrick White's *The Solid Mandala*', *Southerly*, 29 (1969) 97–110.

———,personal interview, 22 Oct 1979.

———,'Understanding Patrick White', *Sydney Morning Herald*, 11 June 1974, p. 12.

———,'White Has Not Yet Begun to Write', review of *The Twyborn Affair*, in the *Weekend Australian Magazine*, 10–11 Nov 1979, p. 12.

Wolf, V., 'A Note on the Reception of Patrick White's Novels in German Speaking Countries (1957–1979)', *Australian Literary Studies*, 11 (1983) 108–19.

Wolfe, P., 'Patrick *Who?* From *Where?*' review of *The Eye of the Storm*, in *New Republic*, 5 and 12 Jan 1974, pp. 17–18.

Wood, P., 'Moral Complexity in Patrick White's Novels', *Meanjin*, 21 (1962) 21–8.

Wood, S. A., 'The Power and Failure of "Vision" in Patrick White's *Voss*', *Modern Fiction Studies*, 27 (Spring 1981) 141–58.

Wyatt, L., 'Heroine Followed along on Voyage of Discovery', review of *A Fringe of Leaves*, in the *London Free Press*, 12 Mar 1977. Mitchell Library, Sydney, ML Document 2793.

Wylie, A. D., 'New Australian Verse', *Bulletin*, 10 July 1935, p. 4.

BIBLIOGRAPHIES

'Annual Bibliography of Studies in Australian Literature', *Australian Literary Studies*, 6 (1974) 288ff.; 7 (1975) 72ff.; 7 (1976) 294ff.; 8 (1977) 64ff.; 8 (1978) 317ff.; 9 (1979) 77ff.; 9 (1980) 346ff.; 10 (1981) 79ff.; 10 (1982) 358ff.; 11 (1983) 80ff.

Lawson, A., *Patrick White*, Australian Bibliographies, gen. ed. G. Johnston (Melbourne: Oxford University Press, 1974).

Lock, F., and Lawson, A., *Australian Literature: A Reference Guide*, 2nd edn, Australian Bibliographies, gen. ed. G. Johnston (Melbourne: Oxford University Press, 1980).

Scheick, W. J., 'A Bibliography of Writings about Patrick White, 1972–78', *Texas Studies in Literature and Language*, 21 (1979) 296–303.

The Fryer Library, University of Queensland, St Lucia, Queensland, maintains complete and up-to-date files of bibliographical entries for the study of Australian literature.

Index